SIENNE VEGA

This is a work of fiction. Names, characters, places, and incidents either are the product of the author's imagination or are used fictitiously. Any resemblance to actual persons, living or dead, events, or locales is entirely coincidental.

Copyright © 2024 Sienne Vega

All rights reserved. No part of this book may be reproduced or used in any manner without written permission of the copyright owner except for the use of quotations in a book review. For more information, visit: www.siennevega.com.

Cover Design by Maldo Designs

First paperback edition October 2024

BLURB

It was supposed to be a harmless crush.
At least… it started out that way.

Professor Adler was known to be cold and uncompromising.
Most students dreaded his class for this reason.

As for me, I hoped to impress him.
Make him notice me.
Be his favorite.

Then, one night, things go too far.
And we find ourselves dabbling in what's forbidden.

But there's a side to him I never imagined possible.
Dark truths that never should've seen the light of day.

Secrets so wicked, they were better taken to the grave…

Tell me every terrible thing you did, and let me love you anyway.
-Sade Andria Zabala

CONTENT WARNING

PLEASE READ THIS!

I want to be clear about what you're getting yourself into reading this book. This is a dark taboo age gap romance between a professor and his student. If a large gap in age bothers you at all, then please note this is NOT the book for you.

The same goes for power dynamics between a professor and a student. Professor Adler is not only twice Miss Oliver's age in this story, he is her *professor*. If this is an ick for you, I totally understand, but please seek a different book to read.

I want to be clear that this story is **FICTION**. I do not at all condone any of the events in this book as they apply to real life.

The relationship between Professor Adler and Nyssa Oliver is inappropriate and taboo. It can be interpreted as toxic and unhealthy. These characters are extremely flawed and imperfect. **Both the MMC and FMC do very bad things.** I understand not everyone likes to read about characters like these, so I only ask that you please decide for yourselves if this is a dealbreaker for you, and if you do proceed, read responsibly.

Below is a detailed list of some of the sensitive content that will be included:

- Gore and violence
- Serial killer storyline
- Stalking
- Age Gap between MMC and FMC
- Attempted sexual assault
- Dubious sexual consent
- BDSM and explicit sexual content, including impact play, bondage, anal, role play, double penetration
- Animal abuse
- Mentions of pedophilia
- Mentions of bullying/hazing
- Alcoholism
- Substance abuse
- Usage of homophobic slur
- Mentions of racism and misogyny
- Fat shaming
- Slut shaming
- Potentially some other content that could be upsetting, so please do read responsibly!

This book is **absolutely not** suitable for readers under the age of 18.

Now that all the warning and lecturing is out of the way, I really hope you're somewhere comfy with some snacks and drinks. This is a long, twisted, taboo journey you're about to go on with Professor Adler and Miss Oliver!

Sienne

PROLOGUE - THERON
THE PERFECT GIRL - MAREUX

NOVEMBER 2004

I WAS TWENTY-TWO THE DAY I MET HER.

Golden brown leaves blew across the campus lawn, the wind whistling as ominous storm clouds migrated in. Occasional specks of drizzle fell, cold drops dotting bare skin, 'til finally the floodgates opened and the deluge of rain pelted down.

The few people still traveling between classes picked up the pace. Girls shrieked, hurriedly covering their stylized hair with whatever they held in their possession—scarves, books, bags, anything so as not to ruin their decidedly casual beachy waves.

I shook my head and returned my gaze to the heavy book resting in my lap—*Tort Law and Social Morality*. I was eight pages into a ninety-seven page reading assignment.

...it was going to be a long night.

But while the others fled from the downpour, I basked in it. I sat parked on the ledge of a large, glassless lancet window and enjoyed the tinkling soundtrack of raindrops falling.

These kinds of days were my favorite. The kind of afternoons where autumn sunlight was chased away by angry, dark clouds and the landscape morphed into a Claude Monet painting. *Etretat in the Rain* or *Morning on the Seine*. Maybe even *Cliffs at Pourville*.

Lightning flashed across the murky gray sky, promptly followed by a sharp whip of thunder. I looked up as the sound echoed for what must've been miles, just in time to spot the latest traveler in my vicinity.

Her.

Glancing once, then twice, torts and social morality immediately slipped to an afterthought. I found myself tracking her every harried move across the lawn. A secret spectator as she juggled an armful of books and once-springy curls lay flat and drenched around her face.

What was she thinking?

No jacket. Leather boots with a heel that stuck in the sodden grass. Books that looked like they might weigh more than she did.

She staggered through the courtyard, almost slipping in a puddle. But where she saved herself, her stack of books wasn't so lucky—they flew out of her arms and landed with a *splat* in the muddy water. She hung her head in frustration, then stooped low to pick them up.

I grabbed the book on top first. Her eyes flicked to my face in startled surprise. We both slowly rose to full height, shielded by the large umbrella I was holding onto. I glanced down at the book and read the title aloud.

"*Inside the Criminal Mind.*"

She bared her teeth in a wince, round nose scrunching up. "And now it's soaked cover to cover."

"You kidding? Hang this baby out to dry on a warm afternoon and it'll be good as new... err, well, with some wrinkled pages. But still very much legible."

"Which is all that matters in law school." She gave a small wry laugh.

"Let me guess. Professor Vise?"

"The one and only... otherwise known as Professor Hardass," she answered, holding out her hand. I forked over the soggy law book, then bent to scoop up the rest for her. She mouthed a 'thank you' as I did, opening her arms as if to accept them.

Instead I held them to my chest with one arm, gripping my large black canopy of an umbrella with the other.

"How about I walk you? You're drenched, and I need the exercise."

Uncertainty flickered in her carob-colored gaze, though she eventually obliged with a nod.

"Yeah, okay, alright. Thanks."

We started off slow across the sopping grass, producing squish noises with the soles of our shoes. Mother Nature continued pelting us with her fiercest, fattest drops of rain yet, though neither of us seemed to notice.

We were much more focused on the stranger we were walking beside.

"I'm Theron, by the way. Theron Adler."

A smile just as hesitant as her head nod inched onto her lips. "Josalyn Webber. First year or second?"

"Second. Thankfully. But you're first, right?"

"How did you know?"

"Wild guess. You still have hope shining in your eyes. Second years usually have dead stares. Case in point, myself."

Her once-small smile grew, joined by an amused hum from her throat. "I guess I have a lot to look forward to."

"There's a reason I was sitting out in the rain. After a few manic episodes, you learn to embrace the chaos."

"Is it terrible that that sounds amazing right now?" she asked, shaking wet curls out of her face. She turned to me as we finally reached the dry safety of the exterior hallway.

I did the same, reacting off her, shifting to face her. It was my first real chance for close study and I more than took advantage—the second in between that seemed like a blink-and-miss-it moment but it was really an eternity of drinking her in.

Her dark curls shone, dripping wet. Her cheeks rounded and her full lips parted to reveal a beautiful smile. Even standing where I was, I could smell the scent of fresh rain on her skin. A scent I already appreciated, making my pulse elevate. My heart beat faster.

Josalyn Webber was as perfect up close as she was far away...

"Well, I guess we part ways," she said after a pause. "I can take my books now. Promise I usually carry them better than what you just saw."

"Oh. Right. Here."

We came together in an awkward dance of exchanging an armful of books. She stepped back once she had the heap secure in her arms and shot me her brightest smile yet.

"See you around, Theron."

I watched her go, tracking her every step like I had across the sodden courtyard. "Yeah, see you..."

Soon she disappeared entirely out of view. She was headed home to her apartment, in the building a few streets away from campus where most law students attending Castlebury University chose to live. She would go home and spend the next two to three hours studying.

Because that's what she always did on Tuesday evenings after class.

I knew all too well.

Josalyn Webber didn't realize it, but today wasn't the first time I had seen her.

And it certainly wouldn't be the last.

1

NYSSA

GHOST IN THE MACHINE - SZA
FEATURING PHOEBE BRIDGERS

TWENTY YEARS LATER...

If there's one lesson I've learned in my brief twenty-two years on this earth, it's that nothing tastes sweeter than revenge. Some feel an eye for an eye leaves the whole world blind. Others believe the best revenge is moving on and living well.

I'm not one of those people.

Moving on is not an option until I've evened the score.

For Mom. For myself. In the interest of karmic justice.

Only *then* will I live well.

It's the promise I've made to myself. It's why I'm doing what I'm doing...

"Does this dress make you want to fuck me?" Heather Driscoll asks, interrupting my thoughts. Her long golden hair sways with every subtle move of hers as she models in front of the floor length mirror in my bedroom. She strikes a pose, hand on her hip in the short little Saint Laurent number she's wearing. "You know, if you were a guy. Would you want to fuck me?"

I quirk a brow from where I stand by the easel propped up next to the window. "Is that the dress for the funeral?"

"It's all black, isn't it?"

"Your *dad's* funeral..." I add.

Heather rakes fingers through her golden strands, pausing to think. "I'll wear tights. Black ones. And this—isn't it so chic? Fits my aesthetic perfectly."

She's popped on a tiny fastener hat complete with beaded lace dramatically covering the left side of her face.

I take one look at her pursing her lips in the mirror, admiring her various angles, and I remember how I've never wished for Heather Driscoll's downfall more.

And I've known her almost her entire life.

Even if she hasn't known me...

"You don't belong here. Your daddy's dead and your mommy's broke," the younger Heather sneered, her hair golden in the sunlight. "Go away, loser! Nobody wants you around."

The group of kids hovering behind her laughed.

They laughed while I blinked to tears in my eyes...

I blink again and the past fades out for the present.

Heather hasn't noticed I've half tuned out of the conversation. She's still admiring herself in the mirror.

"Your aesthetic," I repeat slowly, swallowing down cruel nostalgia. I go back to playing pretend. "Which would be what? Funeralcore? You might start a trend on TikTok."

She laughs airily. "I just might, Nyssie. Everything I do, everyone else does. Especially Katie."

"She's your best friend. She looks up to you."

"Please," she scoffs. "More like she thinks kissing my ass keeps her safe. I know how many noses she's had. Now she's addicted to filler. You wouldn't understand. You're still new to town."

I understand better than you realize...

I pretend I'm refocusing my attention on the sketch I'm working on. It's in the beginning stages, a couple quickly drawn outlines of songbirds and blooming flowers.

"Katie's not like the rest of us. She's not very cute. Can you believe how much weight she's gained? No wonder she's so desperate. Anyway, you'll help me with the eulogy, won't you?"

"I barely knew Mr. Driscoll, Heather."

"But you're good at these kinds of things. You've written speeches before. Everyone loved that valedictorian speech."

"I don't think it would be a good idea."

"I hated him," she blurts out. Her bird-like features sharpen and her voice fills with raw contempt. Gone is the dreamy tone she's known for. "I *still* hate him. But I'll love him a lot more buried in the ground. Sooo much more with his money deposited in my bank account."

"According to the police, he was murdered."

She sniffs. "What does that have to do with what I said?"

"Don't you want to find out who did it?" I ask. "There's a rumor the murderer could be the Valentine Killer. The card that was left at the scene resembles the ones left all those years ago—"

"I couldn't care less," she says. "It doesn't matter to me if some Valentine guy took him out or if his heart did. He's gone. Which means so is his control over everything. If only the person could come back and finish off my hag of a stepmother."

While Heather's shrill voice fills with glee, I shake my head to myself.

It figures Heather would be more concerned with the potential inheritance she'll receive in the wake of her oil tycoon father's death. He was found poisoned in his office barely two weeks ago, slumped over his desk with the heart-shaped card.

Speculation had broken out in the media and throughout our wealthy enclave known as Castlebury that the murder was eerily similar to the Valentine Killer, some serial killer from two decades ago.

But none of that matters to Heather Driscoll. She loathed her father and sees the funeral as a celebration of his murder.

"Okay, this is it," she says. "This is the look. What do you think, Nyssie? Isn't it per—AHHH!"

Her scream comes seemingly out of nowhere, her arms flailing in the air as she almost tips over.

It's not until I catch sight of orange fur whizzing by that I realize what's scared her.

Peaches scurries across my room at blurring speed, slowing down only once she's at my feet. I smile and crouch low to scoop her up in my arms.

"It's just Peaches," I say, scratching the cat under her chin. "She's harmless."

Heather sniffles. "We have different definitions of harmless, Nyssie. She came out of nowhere. No wonder I don't do pets."

"They don't seem fond of you either."

"Probably because I'd Cruella De Vil them," she says with a laugh. "Only kidding! I know you love your little orange fur ball. Anyway, I should get going. I'm meeting up with someone special."

"And who would that be?"

"Some secrets aren't meant for repeating, Nyssie. Not even to you. So is that a yes on the eulogy?"

Peaches settles into the crook of my arm as I stroke her spine. "I'll proofread what you come up with. That's all."

"I knew I could count on you. You're the best. Way better than Katie. See you tomorrow for orientation?"

Heather Driscoll hardly waits for my answer as she promptly collects her purse and the shopping bags she's brought with her to my apartment and then shows herself out. As she strides through the door, I catch snippets of the phone call she's making, likely to the special someone she mentioned.

Already moving on from her impromptu visit to my apartment.

It's a relief more than anything.

I prefer a warning when I'm going to have to deal with her.

And *most* people in Castlebury.

I'm not even a fan of the idea that I'll be attending Kane Driscoll's funeral. The wealthy oil tycoon had reeked of cigars and had a penchant for pinching the asses of his female staff; he'd been sued for sexual harassment too many times to count.

But the rest of the Driscoll family's hardly better. The rest of the community in Castlebury isn't winning any Good Samaritan awards anytime soon either.

Mom hates that I've chosen to return to her alma mater.

I transferred my junior year at Roseburg so I could go to Castlebury University and finish my undergrad in Art History. She was even more upset when she learned I'd stay at Castlebury U for law school.

I went through with it anyway.

Where better to excel academically than at the same university that had destroyed my family's life two decades before?

"Don't worry, Peaches," I whisper to the ginger cat. "You won't have to deal with Driscoll much longer. We'll get the last laugh."

She purrs softly as if understanding what I've said. I set her loose to answer my iPhone. Without glancing at the screen, I'm aware of who it is.

"You can still change your mind," Mom says as her version of hello. "Say the word, Nys, and I'll be there to pick you up."

I give a laugh as if she's told a joke. "How many times do I have to tell you? I'll be fine."

"Baby girl, you don't know these people. You don't know what you're dealing with. I *do*."

"I can handle them. I've been doing it for two years."

Mom blows out a frustrated breath. "The longer you're there, the easier it'll be for them to realize who you are."

"You're kidding, right? These people are so self-obsessed, they wouldn't notice Jack the Ripper in front of their faces."

"Promise me you'll be careful."

After assuaging Mom's fears for the fiftieth time since summer began, we hang up. I pocket my phone and almost return to my sketch of songbirds and blooming flowers.

Instead, I step to the huge window next to the easel and peer out at the well-to-do town of Castlebury. Though my apartment's one of the farther ones from campus, I can still spot the historic Ivy League college from my bedroom window.

Its skyscraping clock tower rises high among the

surrounding buildings and tree line. The hands on the clock tick away, counting down the minutes until my first day as a law student at Castlebury U.

Mom was worried for good reason. Twenty years ago, her life was destroyed on that same campus. Families like the Driscolls, Fairchilds, Rothenbergs, and Wickers were responsible.

But though Mom might think it's too risky, I'm willing to walk the same halls. I'm willing to do what I need to in order to ensure the right people are held accountable. At last, we'll have our revenge.

Revenge that will taste so sweet, it'll all be worth it...

I'm late. *Extremely* late. So late, I'm tripping down the hallway of my apartment, shrugging on a cardigan blouse. I make it to the door while fastening the last button.

The alarm on my phone failed me again. You'd think I'd learn by now to have a backup in the event the clock app on my phone's hell bent on sabotaging me; you'd *think* I'd learn to wake up extra early the morning of my first day at law school.

I just had to stay up late working on my sculpture for the art festival.

I throw a quick glance at the antique gold-framed mirror hanging on the wall that I bought for five bucks at a thrift store and then rush out the door.

The university's a twenty minute walk on a morning where slow strolls through town can be afforded.

On a morning where I'm already running ten minutes late, a rideshare is my best option.

Five minutes later, I'm leaping from the backseat of the Honda Civic that picked me up.

Castlebury University spreads out before me, so massive it's almost its own town altogether.

Younger than Harvard but older than Princeton, the esteemed university is one of the country's biggest Ivy League juggernauts. Known for its top tier academics and impressive alumni, the university shows off its Gothic collegiate architecture at every turn.

Limestone buildings cover the campus, a dense pine forest serving as the backdrop.

I sprint past these buildings on my way to orientation, crunching over the golden foliage September has brought with it.

I finally make it to Harper Hall, named after the university's founder. Dashing up the stack of stone steps, I'm panting by the time I'm reaching for the brass door handles.

The entrance hall splinters off into three separate narrower halls, three separate parts of the building. I skip past the sign posted at the front that lists the locations of the different orientations being hosted in this building.

There's no time when I already know.

I've memorized every detail outlined in the welcome email we were sent.

I turn right down the hall, rounding a corner without slowing down.

Someone else happens to be coming the opposite way around the same corner. Our bodies collide straight on, knocking what little wind I have left out of me. The books I'm carrying slip out of my arms, tumbling to the ground, and the coffee the man's clutching flips out of his grasp.

It crashes to the floor, but not before splashing all over the front of his tweed blazer.

Horror cinches my insides, making me choke out a gasp.

For a beat afterward, the two of us stand still and gape at the mess in silence. My jaw's dropped open while his has clamped shut tight, like he's holding in his outrage.

It's not until the shock washes away that I reach for my bookbag, fumble for a moist towelette, and begin dabbing at him.

It's not until I've stepped so close I can pick up his woodsy, spiced scent that I realize what I'm doing.

And who I've run into.

The Professor Theron Adler.

I freeze, blinking dumbly up at him, the towelette in my hand still pressing into the tweed fabric of his blazer.

Professor Theron Adler is known for his strict and uncompromising standards. He's one of the professors in the law school—on the entire campus—most students dread. Considered a subject matter expert on criminal law, he was once a practicing defense attorney who won numerous high profile cases.

Somehow, he's even *more* intimidating in person.

More attractive.

He's tall, with the natural build of a runner. Thin but toned in all the right places, his shoulders wide but his waist trim. The tweed blazer fits him to a T, clearly professionally tailored that way. The once white button-up shirt he's wearing underneath—now stained with coffee—has developed a sheer quality to its fabric.

See-through enough that I can tell he's sporting some seriously drool worthy abs.

I blink several times, forcing my gaze back up to his

face, only for mine to warm. He's scowling at me, the square black frames of his eyeglasses knocked slightly askew. But they could never block the dark mystery that is his eyes.

Darker than my own. A mahogany brown that's almost obsidian. That holds a permanent shine in them and mirrors my mortified reflection back at me.

The rest of his face is like a composite of all the features women tend to like—a strong jaw that's hardly disguised by fast-growing stubble and an aquiline nose that complements his wide cheekbones.

His hair's floppy and slightly unruly, straight but with subtle silver hairs threaded through the naturally dark strands.

He's so handsome, it almost makes up for his brutal personality.

As if sensing my thoughts, he clears his throat and raises both of his thick brows.

The hoarse sound zaps me out of my trance-like state. I drop my hand from dabbing coffee off him.

"I... I'm so... sorry," I stammer out lamely.

His jaw clenches tighter. "What's your name?"

"Oliver. Nyssa Oliver. I'm... I was... the year one law orientation..."

Oh god. Nys, could you sound like a bigger dumbass?! UGH!

I can't tell what he's thinking except to conclude it can't be anything good. A flicker of something—distaste, dislike, general judgment—passes in his dark gaze as he spends a couple seconds surveying me. He takes a step back and gestures to the mess on the floor.

My books scattered everywhere *and* the puddle of coffee.

"Clean this right now," he snaps. "Then hurry up to the orientation. You're late."

Before I can even utter the word *yes*, Professor Adler's walking around me, brushing past to continue on his way.

I sigh and kneel to pick up my things. Dread pits in my stomach. I've not only made the worst first impression imaginable; I've just put a huge target on my back.

And made my crim law professor hate me.

2

THERON

TOO SWEET - HOZIER

Five a.m. sharp.

The birds haven't even started twittering yet when my alarm blares. I turn it off with a swat of my hand and then reach blindly for my glasses.

Eyesight restored, I'm up to start my day.

It begins the same as always. Ten minutes in the shower. Five minutes in front of the sink trimming my facial hair and brushing my teeth. A quick change into some gym shorts, and then it's off to the kitchen to get the coffee started and take out Atticus.

He wags his fluffy tail as he dashes out the kitchen door to go do his business.

The rest of the neighborhood is dead silent, a neat row of equally perfect family homes that scream Americana. Part of the charm of living in a suburb outside of Castlebury.

Many years ago, I bought this house with the intention of starting a family.

Many years ago, I was hopeful, if not bordering on delusional.

These days, spying the manicured lawns and painted shutters fills me with nothing more than hot irritation.

Atticus races back into the kitchen just as my coffee machine stops tinkling. He's ready to chow down on his breakfast while I'm more preoccupied with grabbing the newspaper off the front step.

Some would say it's archaic that I still have the daily paper delivered.

This isn't the twentieth century anymore. In today's era of instant gratification, I could have the news at my fingertips. A quick internet search away.

Most people are too self-involved to truly appreciate the printed word. They're addicted to their electronic devices like junkies hooked on crack cocaine. I see it day in, day out on campus.

Students glued to the glowing screens in their hands, pupils dilated.

I prefer tradition. The silken feel of the freshly printed paper and the potent smell of the black ink. The crinkling sound you make when you turn to the next page in between sips of hot coffee. Quality writing instead of mind-numbing internet jargon.

I've never seen an article in the *Castlebury Tribune* reference anyone's 'rizz' nor do I give a damn to learn what the latest 'bop' is.

But before I can turn back inside my house to indulge in my morning ritual, I stop short. My gaze lands on my BMW XI parked in the driveway and the giant scratch mark keyed into the side.

Veronica.

I go from priding myself for not touching my phone in over twelve hours to desperately fumbling for it, fuming enough to shake. My breaths come out of me in ragged puffs as I dial her number by memory.

Once, she'd been saved as a contact. My *most frequent* contact.

That was before we started hating each other…

She answers with a sleepy yawn. "Hello?"

"My BMW," I snarl. "It's been keyed!"

She yawns again. "Theron?"

"You know who it is!"

"Why're you calling so early? It's barely even—"

"Answer me!" I bellow. "Did you key my car?"

"I've been sleeping."

"It's a simple yes or no question. Just when I think you couldn't stoop any lower."

Her drowsy tone disappears. Scorn takes its place. "I've stooped low? You're one to talk."

"I never keyed your car!"

"So what? You wasted how many years of my life?"

"I wasn't aware that's a crime!"

"You make yourself a victim every time," she says. "I don't think I've ever met another person with zero self-awareness like you. Ever think this is karma paying you back?"

"Veronica, if I find out you keyed my fucking car—"

"Goodbye, Theron. Don't call me again. We're done, remember? Your words."

The line goes dead.

When I try to redial her number, I'm sent straight to voicemail. My knuckles whiten from how tightly I'm gripping the phone, waiting for the beep.

"You fucking bitch," I rage the second the recording starts. "You really think you'll get away with this? You think I'm not about to hold you accountable? Just wait and see."

The recording cuts me off before I can finish the rest of my rant.

I howl in anger and hurl my phone across the room. Not the most rational decision considering it smashes into the antique brass scales of justice perched on my wall shelf. An heirloom that's been in my family for decades. The scales tumble to the ground with a violent clang.

My rage only intensifies. I release a second howl like some feral beast.

A rarity for me. But the explosion is warranted.

Veronica knows exactly what she's doing.

She knows I'll never go to the police. She's aware this will have to be handled between the two of us.

That's exactly what she wants.

Instead of a clean, amicable break up, she wants to prolong the toxicity.

I force calming breaths through my lungs and remind myself I won't give it to her.

Her passion and unpredictability are what kept me coming back for more in the past. From the time we were in college, we were back and forth, on again and then off again.

We'd even gotten *engaged*.

I collect my phone off the floor and call the only real friend I have—my sister, Theo.

The one person I can trust in this world.

Theo is the type of loyal that would have her showing up at three a.m. to bury a body. No questions asked.

"Calling me before business hours? You must be in trouble, bro."

I grit my teeth. "Veronica keyed my car."

"*Again*? Didn't she key your last car? The Mercedes?"

"That was the broken window in the living room. But she swears to this day it wasn't her."

"Mhm," Theo hums from her end of the line. "And I'm Mother Theresa."

"Not exactly helping."

"What do you want me to say, asshole?" she snipes with a laugh. "You have just about the worst taste in women? Didn't I warn you about her a gazillion times already?"

This is true.

...but far from what I want to hear.

"Why do I even call you?" I ask, voicing my rhetorical question aloud. I've walked down the stairs to slide on my running shoes so I can begin my morning workout. "You're supposed to be on my side."

"I *am* on your side. It's not my fault you're attracted to crazy like most men."

"And you're not crazy?"

"But I'm a lesbian. So I'm kinda off the table for your entire gender. Anyway, I've got to go. As you know, it's the first day of the semester, which means I've got plenty of college kids nagging my ass about their housing problems."

"I'm still astonished they've entrusted you with an entire building."

"Whatever, asshole. Dad's rec certainly helped get me in good with the building owner, the father of that nutty ex of yours. But let me know if Fatal Attraction comes around again. You know I'd love to smack a bitch. Even if I lose my job."

Theo hangs up like only she can, without a real goodbye, cracking a crude joke.

It's enough to set me straight. Remind me that Veronica isn't worth the trouble.

Her tantrums are just that. A hissy fit worthy of a toddler.

On that note, I finish my morning ritual, ready to start the new school year.

"She gives good dome, bro," guffaws Lucas Cummings, his freckled face lit up. "She came over after that pool party Driscoll threw. Took me fifteen minutes to get her to suck my dick."

His grin spreads as he recounts the crass story in line for a coffee at the student union. He doesn't care that he's loud and others overhear. As he and his friend Samson Wicker take up more space than they should, he feels invincible. They twirl their rugby ball and wear their letterman jackets and stand wide and immovably, blocking passage for others.

Including myself.

"Doesn't surprise me," Wicker replies, laughing too. "The chubby ones are always easy."

"Dude, that's your sister!"

"So what? Doesn't mean she's not a slut. Katie's always been a doormat. I don't care if you mess with her."

"What about you and Oliver?" he asks. "She cave yet?"

"Working on it. Any day now."

"Don't bother with the prissy bitches. Once you turn them out, it's boring."

I clear my throat, forcing their attention. They both glance over their shoulders, surprised anyone in the student union has the audacity to interrupt them.

I remain nonplussed.

Stoic and unreadable.

Though on the inside, irritation simmers to a boil.

I've had my fill of listening to idiotic jock banter about which college girls they have and have not screwed.

"Gentleman," I say in a tone that's calm yet underscored by authority. "How about you step aside if you're more preoccupied with your very colorful conversation than ordering a coffee? Some of us would like to carry on with our mornings."

Cummings's brow furrows in primitive anger until Wicker slaps a meaty hand to his shoulder, recognizing who I am at a glance. The blond does the opposite of his slow-witted friend—he cracks a smile at me and then steps aside.

"Yeah... of course, Professor. Right on."

I pass through them sensing the opposite energies. Cummings's offense and Wicker's oaf-like sense of humor.

But neither matter.

I wasn't concerned with stupid meathead types like them many years ago when I attended this same college.

I'm certainly not today as a professor.

The barista hands me my coffee looking grateful I've broken up the mini frat party. Though something tells me the second I'm out of earshot, two douchebags as big as Samson Wicker and Lucas Cummings will pick up right where they left off.

Armed with my peppermint mocha, I head toward Harper Hall for the year one law orientation. I'm mere footsteps outside the hall when Dean Rothenberg appears in his latest tailored suit jacket and pocket watch combo.

The gold chain practically glints in the pale autumn sunlight as he grins broadly at me, and a gust of wind blows through his thinning, peppered hair. He drips arrogance with every step he takes; he's from such an affluent family that his position as dean is more for optics than anything. Handed down to him from his father, the dean before him.

He holds out his hand for me to shake. "Theron, how was your summer?"

"Uneventful," I answer, begrudgingly accepting his handshake. "I did manage to get plenty of reading done."

He chuckles, the lone fastened button on his jacket straining against the paunch of his belly. "That's about what I'd expect of you. It must run in the family. I vacationed on Montbec Island for the summer. Notice the tan?"

"Yes," I grit out. "You are redder than usual."

"You're always welcome to join," he says, ignoring my slight. "Me and the other bachelors on the trip met some very attractive—very *young*, might I add—women at the beach. We had the time of our lives. Maybe next year you'll live a little. Get out more and have an eventful summer."

He strolls off whistling a tune.

I'm fuming on the inside for the third time today and it's not even ten a.m. yet. I'm not normally a hot-tempered man—and find those who are reductive—but today's an exception.

After checking the time, I don't bother heading to my office. Orientation for the first years starts in twenty minutes.

"Theron, there you are. Since you're already up, will you make sure no one else is lost in the hall?" calls our faculty head, Pamela Williamson, the second I walk into the room where the orientation is being held. She's up at the front of the room barking orders at the other professors that'll be briefing the group.

The rows of chairs have slowly filled up as our year ones trickle in uncertainly and then nab a seat. A deep breath leaves me as I don't bother challenging her. The more time I spend out of the room, the better.

Orientation has never been a part of the semester that I've enjoyed.

Williamson insists all the year one professors attend to put faces to the names and to ease the students' anxiety about their upcoming classes. I sip from my peppermint mocha heading out into the hall, glancing around for any stragglers.

It's as I turn the corner that I collide with one of them.

She's bustling down the hall, clutching her books and leather bag, hardly paying mind to where she's going. The books she's carrying fly out of her arms. My cup of coffee tumbles out of my hand and splashes along the front of my tweed jacket.

The drink's still warm, quickly staining.

A second passes where she freezes and her eyes double in size. I've gone still too, for different reasons.

The same pulse of anger I've felt all morning long returns in yet another scowl.

If there was one word to describe her, it would be mortified. Her lips have parted, drawing attention to how glossy and plump they are. She has a beauty mark on the apple of her cheek and long lashes that frame brown eyes that change shades in the light—with the sun pouring in through the arched windows, they've turned almost gold.

Her hair's full and curly, neatly smoothed back into a thick ponytail. The rosy strip of fabric matches the cropped cardigan she wears. As she quickly digs around for a towelette in her bookbag, the hem of her cardigan rises and reveals a sliver of bare skin.

An inch of her flat, taut stomach exposed.

It draws attention to how the pleated skirt she wears sits enticingly at her rounded hips.

She's not very tall. More than a head shorter, as she comes to her senses and then steps back from me.

It seems to occur to her that she shouldn't be standing so close, rubbing coffee off a professor the way she is.

"I... I'm so... sorry," she stammers out.

My jaw clenches tighter. "What's your name?"

"Oliver. Nyssa Oliver. I'm... I was... the year one law student orientation..."

If possible, I regard her more harshly. No forgiveness can be found in my expression. Just irritation and judgment.

She should've been paying attention to where she was going. She should've been on time instead of rushing in last minute.

"Clean this right now," I snap. "Then hurry up to the orientation. You're late."

I don't wait for a response before stalking off. I've had enough of today, and Nyssa Oliver just so happens to be the breaking point.

3
THERON
DARK RED - STEVE LACEY

Twenty sets of slow-blinking eyes stare at me, about as witless and empty-headed as cows put out to pasture. Their hands itch to reach for their phones. Their thoughts already a mile away from where we are in my classroom. Nothing to offer the world but memes and redundant catchphrases about pop culture.

I stick both hands in the pockets of my trousers and scowl back at them. "Welcome to Criminal Law One. I am your professor, Theron Adler. You will refer to me as Professor Adler. *Just* Professor Adler. Inside *and* outside of the classroom. Over the next five months, you will be gaining a foundational understanding of criminal law. You will be required to provide intelligent and thoughtful insight to theories and case studies that are examined.

"If you fail to be a productive, contributive member of this ongoing discussion, I will gladly fail you. If you are caught plagiarizing or cheating in any capacity—to include the use of artificial intelligence—I will gladly fail you," I continue, peering at each face in the room. Two to three seconds on each student before I move on to intimidate the next. "If you do not participate in the required reading or assignments that will be given, I will gladly fail you. If you do not prove to think on the critical level which is needed at this point in your graduate education, guess what?"

The class murmurs along, "I will gladly fail you."

A rare grin slashes onto my face. I push my glasses back up the bridge of my nose. "You catch on fast. Let's hope that's a good sign. I am not an easy professor. I am not a kind one. I am certainly not the *cool* one you'll want to friend on Facebook or whatever asinine social media platform you use these days. I am simply here to evaluate your understanding of criminal law. Who can tell me the difference between criminal and civil law?"

The girl with vomit green hair and a nose ring sitting in the front row raises a hesitant hand. "It's, um, isn't civil between two people off the street?"

"I don't know, Miss Fochte. You tell me. Is it?" I ask in return. When she blinks at me a couple more times like a deer in headlights, I look around at the rest of the class. "Someone else. Someone with *confidence*."

"It's all part of the system. Criminal is, like, what kind of harm is done to society," says a blonde from the back row. I recognize her at once—another trust fund baby being funneled through Castlebury. Heather Driscoll twirls a lock of strawberry blonde hair around her finger like she's wholly unconcerned by what I think of her. She's more preoccupied with her spa appointment that comes after.

"Is that the best you can do?" I say. "At the graduate level? Really? So my already low expectations will be sinking even lower?"

Heather Driscoll openly rolls her eyes. But the girl seated next to her does the opposite—she raises her hand in the air with a confidence vomit-green-haired girl hadn't and with a politeness that's not in Heather's vocabulary.

I recognized her from the moment she set foot inside the classroom this morning.

Nyssa Oliver.

She's on Heather's left as though part of the posse, which includes the other two seated directly in front of them, Katelyn Wicker and Macey Eurwen. She's patient and attentive in a way they're not, sitting up with shoulders poised and deep-set brown eyes brightened by curiosity.

The next heartbeat in my chest skips.

A second-long malfunction that leaves me stuck.

Then the second ends and the thump returns.

I blink out of the momentary glitch and rasp out her name. "Yes, Miss Oliver?"

"Criminal law is a body of law defining offenses against society at large. It takes into consideration the harm committed and how these offenses are investigated, charged, tried, and sentenced in a court of law," she explains succinctly. "Some examples would be murder or assault. In the past, it was often called penal law."

My eyes narrow behind the lens of my glasses. "I see someone knows the basics. Not all hope is lost. But can you tell me the two fundamental elements of crime?"

She doesn't pause before answering. "*Mens rea*, which is Latin for guilty mind. The other would be *Actus reus*. Latin for action. As in the physical action a crime involves."

Every other student in the room bounces their attention between us. One glance at Miss Oliver and then a glance back at me once she replies. Their two dozen gazes fall on me in interest for what I'll have to say to her answer.

I let the moment linger on longer than I probably should.

The two of us are locked into a stare that every other student sits on the outside of.

They're spectators as I stand mildly surprised at how accurate and succinct she's been. Finally, I accept that she's risen to the challenge—and she knows she has.

A small little smirk has bloomed onto Nyssa Oliver's face. It's subtle and slow, curling her bottom lip and lighting up her eyes.

Confidence that's not easily shaken.

The awareness that she's correct. The hint of teasing that she is.

No one else in the room catches it. No one else in the room is privy, despite being present.

Clearing my throat, I force myself to cut the moment short. I gesture to the blackboard. "Reading. Open your textbooks to page four-hundred and sixty-two. You have fifteen minutes to read the chapter, absorb the material, and tell me the significance of crime classification."

It's an emergency escape hatch.

A distraction for myself as they practically groan and begin flipping to the assigned reading page. I turn my back on the class and go to my desk feeling like I've just had warm coffee spilled all over me a second time.

For the second time by Miss Oliver and Miss Oliver alone.

My afternoon is devoted to grading the essay question I gave today's class after their required reading. I'd spent my lunch hour on the phone with the surveillance company that's installing a camera system on my property.

Should Veronica ever have the guts to return, I'll have everything on camera.

Tangible proof she keyed my car.

For the next hour, I'm engrossed in grading the essay questions. It comes as no surprise that most of the papers sound like they've been written by some AI generator. When I encounter the sixth paper that sounds like a regurgitation from ChatGPT, I sigh and drop my pen.

Castlebury University is allegedly a prestigious institution of higher learning, yet the students that come through are routinely below standard. If they're not glued to their personal devices, they're lazing around smoking weed and sleeping in 'til noon.

A sullen expression bleeds onto my face at the bitter thoughts.

Was I ever this unintellectual? Was I ever lacking so much depth?

Sure, I had my moments, as many young adults do. I dabbled in my share of frat parties and keggers. Occasionally, I skipped class and cut corners on coursework.

But I was never this useless. This content with being mediocre. Less than mediocre... painfully below standard.

I mark down the next essay question with an aggressive swipe of my pen. The red ink is inexorably satisfying on the page.

Jason Hendricks will learn the hard way his staying up late gaming then nodding off during class will not pay off. He'll be one of many failures.

I come to the next student's paper, reading the name scrawled up top in neat, swoopy letters:

Nyssa Oliver

Ah, yes.

The girl that met my challenge today in class. The girl who spilled coffee on me yesterday. I have plenty of red ink for her...

"Ahem. Professor?"

I look up, almost feral from excitement, a wavy lock of hair falling over my brow, and find myself staring across the desk at the girl.

None other than Nyssa Oliver herself, like she's materialized out of thin air.

She's unassuming compared to earlier, where she'd challenged me and *smirked*.

Right now, she's all cropped cashmere sweater and headful of curls, clutching what looks like a large coffee from the student union. The lighting in the room emphasizes the exact cinnamon shade of her wide, deep-set eyes.

Eyes that couldn't be more earnest if they tried.

A sliver of guilt stabs at me until I clear my throat and sift fingers through my hair, trying to appear more dignified and professional. She must've wandered into my classroom at the height of my irritation, as I slashed away at the papers.

"Miss Oliver," I say, forcing an even tone, "to what do I owe a visit after classroom hours?"

"I wanted to apologize for yesterday. You know, what happened with the coffee."

"Oh." I blink a couple times, unsure how else to respond. "You already apologized when it happened."

"I know. They say not to cry over spilled milk—or in this case, coffee—but I wanted to make it up to you. So, here. A large peppermint mocha with almond milk. I asked the barista at the student union what you typically ordered, and luckily she knew."

Nyssa sets the large paperboard cup down next to my stack of bleeding papers. The subtle quirk of her brows hint at her shock to see so much red.

For a moment that easily lasts five, maybe six, seconds, neither of us say a word. As the pause grows, Nyssa seems to second-guess her gesture. She frowns, then takes a step back, her slender fingers finding the strap of her leather bookbag.

"Sorry," she says. "This was dumb of me, right? And I interrupted your work. Why would you need me to replace the coffee? I didn't mean to make things awkward—"

"No," I answer hastily, "it's alright. Err... thank you. It's a, err, nice gesture. It is appreciated."

"It is?"

"Now I have no excuse to penalize you when I grade your paper."

Surprise flits across her features, her brows rising higher, her lips parting just slightly. She's regretting her decision to come by.

This olive branch that she's extended me.

I take pity on the girl. Even after the flub from yesterday and the challenge from earlier today.

Peering at her over the rim of my glasses, a vague grin quirking at the corners of my mouth, I say, "That was a joke, Miss Oliver. I'm usually not very good at making them, but most students take pity on me and laugh anyway."

That earns a smile out of her—a big, relieved one that lights up her face. It's the kind of smile the men her age would probably work desperately for. The kind of smile that comes alive before your eyes. That blooms like a flower would in spring.

And this hypothetical man expressing interest in her

would feel his temperature rise and his nerves grow. He'd likely realize he was somehow even more hopelessly into her.

He would be coming under her spell, unable to help himself. He couldn't do a damn thing, nor would he want to...

"Um, Professor?"

"Hmmm, yes?" I snap out of my rambling thoughts.

Nyssa's puzzled, blinking at me. "I asked if you were interested in attending the downtown art festival this Sunday? All the school faculty is invited."

"Right," I murmur, suddenly mindful of how warm it is in the room. Of the funny knot in my stomach. "I don't attend those types of gatherings. My time is my time."

"Oh," she says, then nibbles at her bottom lip almost to the point of distraction. She hesitates a second longer, hugging her book to her chest, and then digs around in her bag for something. A flyer that she slides onto my desk. "Well, just in case you change your mind. Here's one of the flyers we've been putting up around campus. Over fifty students will be showcasing their work. Um, including me. But I understand if you can't make it."

I glance at the flyer that's covered in flowery graphic art design worthy of Canva and produce a hum from my throat.

The door on the opposite side of the room suddenly opens.

Both of us look up like we're in the middle of committing a heinous crime.

The big, meaty oaf I recognize as Samson Wicker stands in the doorway. He's clutching that damn rugby ball and wearing the letterman jacket he's so proud of.

"Hey, babe, there you are. Looked everywhere for you. Thought you wanted to meet up after class?"

Nyssa seems caught between finishing our exchange and addressing Wicker. Her gaze pans from me to the large oaf, her face alight with surprise before she decides.

"Enjoy the coffee, Professor," she murmurs. "Hope to see you at the art festival."

Then she's hitching her bookbag higher onto her shoulder and rushing toward the door. Wicker grins proudly when she meets him where he is and he gets to curl a possessive arm around her waist.

Never mind that twenty-four hours ago he was loudly boasting in the student union about bedding her...

I watch unblinkingly, wordlessly, almost fixed into a trance.

I'm staring so long that the door thuds shut. So long that I don't realize my red pen has veered off the page... and begun to mark up the wooden surface of my desk.

Damn it.

I toss my pen away and clench the art flyer Miss Oliver has left behind. Taking aim to hurl it at my trashcan, I have a last second change of heart. The crumpled piece of paper gets straightened out as best as it can, then goes in my satchel.

Maybe...

4
NYSSA
DEMI GOD - KIMBRA FEATURING SAHTYRE

"Nyssa darling, lovely you're here," slurs Mrs. Driscoll. The recently widowed woman totters over in heels she's unsteady on, clutching a wine glass that's been refilled many times. She presses her warm cheek against mine in a kiss hello. "It means so much you could be here for the funeral."

I return her slurred greeting with a polite smile. "Thank you, Mrs. Driscoll… and may I offer my sincerest condolences. Mr. Driscoll was a treasure to the community. He will be missed."

…by no one.

"You are sooo sweet. I'm always telling Heather, why can't she be more like you?"

"Heather's great on her own," I lie, my smile frozen on my face. "But I haven't been able to find her."

Mrs. Driscoll scoffs, the red wine sloshing precariously inside her glass. "Who knows with that girl? She could be off screwing the help for all I know."

"I'm sure I'll find her," I say, keeping my tone neutral. "She's probably speaking to some of the other guests."

"Mhm, I'm sure. Don't forget, dinner is at five." The widowed matriarch looks wholly unconvinced as she gives me her best bleary-eyed, tipsy smile and then sashays away.

I watch her go, amazed by how the lush can make her wine glass as fashionable as the designer black dress she wears.

Others have noticed she's had a few too many, though no one dares say anything. They're here for the social cred they'll earn by being invited to such a private family affair by *the* Holly Driscoll.

Thanks to her husband's death, she's now the wealthiest person in the community. Which means it's social suicide to admit she may have a drinking problem.

Not that it's anything new. Mom's told me all about how Holly Driscoll—maiden name Bunton—was big on the party scene during her Castlebury University days.

The degree was just for show. Holly partied while students like my parents worked hard, and when she graduated, she went on to marry a man a few decades her senior in Kane Driscoll.

I've always preferred older men myself, but *usually* men who aren't knocking on death's door.

"Babe, there you are," Samson says. He appears at my side, planting a wet kiss on my cheek. "You're like a ninja sometimes."

"A ninja?" I raise a brow, thrown by the comparison.

"Yeah. Appearing and disappearing. You were beside me at the funeral. Then I looked over and you were gone."

"Ladies room," I answer, picking up a glass of sparkling water. "I couldn't find you when I came back."

Samson's suspicion fades thanks to his short attention span. He's noticed we're alone at the refreshment's table and decided it's the perfect opportunity to make a move. His heavy hand creeps onto my hip, squeezing the flesh like he wishes my dress would disappear into nothing.

"How about we head back to my place? Nobody'll notice."

I break his hold by taking a wide step to my left. "Please tell me you're kidding. This is Heather's dad's funeral."

"So what?"

"She's my friend."

"She hated the guy," he grunts. "Everybody hated the guy. Even my dad only golfed with him 'cuz he had to. They were both on the board for the school and—"

"Shhh," I hush, glancing around. "The answer's no, Samson. I won't go back to your place to fuck you."

A glower spreads on his ruddy face. "There's always an excuse with you."

"Maybe if you were around more and not always at rugby practice, we could spend time together."

"Or maybe there's nothing I can do to satisfy you."

Before I can even think up a rebuttal, he's gone, shouldering his way through the parlor. I roll my eyes and cuss him out under my breath.

Typical Samson Wicker.

He's more petulant child than grown, college-aged man. Spoiled rotten by his old money family, he's never been told *no*.

...until he started dating me and realized I wasn't going to buckle under his pressure. Samson views me as a conquest while I view him as a means to an end to achieve my goal. He won't be satisfied 'til he gets inside my pants, while I'm more concerned with using our relationship to access the right circles.

But the funniest thing about him is that he's like everyone else in this narcissistic community. Oblivious to the fact that I'm not the new face he thinks I am. I've simply returned after fifteen years, fully realized as a young adult woman. He has no idea I'm the little girl he tormented so many years ago.

"Nobody likes you or your crappy family!" Samson cackled. "Why won't you go away?"

I slid out from my desk and rushed toward the classroom door. The rest of the kids were watching in interest, several guffawing along.

When I passed by Samson's desk, he stuck his foot out. I came crashing down hard on my stomach, my chin colliding with the tiled floor and my breath leaving my body. The pain that throbbed through me was so intense, I could barely scramble to my feet to make it the rest of the way to the door.

Ms. Zhang, the second grade teacher, shook her head at me, pity in her eyes, though she never made any attempt to help me.

She made no attempt to stop them...

The chorus of their laughter fades out for the background chatter buzzing in the parlor.

To this day, Samson's touch makes me sick to my stomach. He thinks I'm being a frigid bitch when really, I'm repulsed by him and everything he represents.

I'm only able to tolerate him because of the finish line that waits for me. The day I finally get the revenge I've worked so hard toward...

"Nyssa," chuckles his balder, fatter, penguin-shaped father, Mr. Jackson Wicker. He grabs onto me much like his son had, wrapping an arm around my shoulders to squeeze me against his side. "I saw my boy charging off. Have a fight, did you?"

"Mr. Wicker, hello. I didn't see you coming up."

"Say the word and I'll knock some sense into that son of mine. He's been in a mood since he flunked senior year and is having to repeat his classes. He better be treating you right... or you should find a real man who will." He winks not-so-subtly at me, allowing his hand to drift from my shoulder, lower down my back.

"Right," I say, so stiff under his touch my revulsion should be obvious. I scan the room in desperate search of someone, *anyone* to escape to.

Instead, all I see are vapid faces mingling with others equally as narcissistic and vapid.

All wealth and prestige and zero substance.

Mr. Wicker's hand is dangerously close to my ass when a savior finally arrives. Among the sea of funeral attendees, Professor Adler appears. He's wandered into the parlor with his glasses and permanent scowl fixed onto his face, his floppy, ruffled dark hair charmingly imperfect. He's in a suit and tie, though he couldn't look less enthused to be here.

He's searching the room much like I am—for an escape hatch.

"Excuse me, Mr. Wicker," I say graciously, "I see my professor and need to ask him a question about class."

Mr. Wicker parts his lips like he's about to object, though I'm gone quick enough that he doesn't get a chance. I weave in between Dean Rothenberg laughing with Veronica Fairchild and cross to the other side of the room.

Professor Adler's at the french doors, peering out the glass cutouts to the terrace. I give a soft clear of my throat, slowly approaching at his side.

"Hello, Professor," I say, hoping my sudden nerves don't

give me away. "I didn't realize you were attending the Driscoll funeral."

He glances over like he doesn't recognize me at first, so entrenched in his head, then he nods. "This was a one-time favor to my father. He couldn't make it today, so that unfortunately means I'm the Adler representation."

"Your family has quite the history at the school." When his thick brow lifts slightly, I quickly add, "From what I've read. I've read your bio. All of my professors' bios. I... I remember from yours, you graduated from Castlebury U yourself. Top of the class. But you weren't the only one— it's your family's alma mater going back over a century."

I'm rambling by the time I trail off, realizing how silly and overeager I must sound. My heart is pitter-pattering inside my chest as I cast him an unreturned smile and clutch my glass of sparkling water like it's a lifeline.

Damn it, Nys. Chill.

But my scolding's countered by my more understanding, sympathetic half.

It's not my fault he's so... so him. I can't help that I admire him!

A moment of uncertain silence passes between us where I'd rather sink through the floor than risk rambling on any further, and Professor Adler's gaze hasn't left me. His eyes, dark and fathomless, feel like hot coals on my skin.

I force a shuddery breath through my lungs, then say, "If I'm interrupting you—"

"You really read your professors' biographies?" he interrupts sharply, almost *accusatorially*. "It sounds like you have mine memorized."

Face warm, I rub my neck with my free hand and give half a shrug. "I... erm, I like to be prepared."

"I see." He sticks both hands in the pockets of his suit pants and returns his attention to the glass cutouts in the french doors. "But, yes, you're correct, Miss Oliver. Every Adler in my family has gone to Castlebury. It's something of a tradition. And your family?"

"Oh... it's not," I stammer. "I'm the first of my family."

"That would explain why you're so sharp."

"I'm not sure I... I don't understand."

The edges of his mouth quirk, framed by the stubble on his jaw. I can't help thinking about how sexy he'd look with a full grin on his face. Something tells me they're extremely rare.

"Look around you, Miss Oliver," he says. "You're surrounded by legacy families and trust fund babies. People who have never truly worked to earn a thing they have in their lives. Everything has been handed to them. That includes their Ivy League education."

"But what about—"

"That includes myself," he interrupts. "My family is no better. I'm no better. The difference is, I'm *aware* of my privilege. Honestly speaking, it's probably why I can't stand being in rooms like these. Why I can't stand people like these. So I do everything within my power to stay the hell away from them." He turns to me, his body angled partially for another studious look at me. "I suggest you do the same."

I'm thrown by the candor for a couple seconds to come. Both impressed and charmed while confused and surprised he's proven what I've sensed from the moment I read his biography.

Just his biography and no one else's. Despite what I told him.

He's not like the rest.

Professor Theron Thurman Adler is different from

everyone else in the room. He's the only other person besides myself who holds this distinction.

I smirk, my eagerness melting away as I hit a new comfort level. "I wouldn't be here if it weren't for the quality education, Professor. But you're probably right—I *did* escape to you after my boyfriend's father almost copped a feel."

He goes from directing his attention onto me to cutting a glance over his shoulder. Presumably to pick out the man I'm talking about in the room. His head shifts back toward the french doors, though his jaw's noticeably tighter.

"You'll find nothing's off limits, Miss Oliver. Not in this world," he says, his voice thicker. "My advice? Avoid him if you can but make sure to go for the knee-to-the-groin move if you have to. It's an oldie but goodie."

It's the end of our little moment as he grips the door handles and pushes open the French doors, stepping out onto the terrace.

I'm still warm seconds after he's left my side. Sips from my sparkling water don't help. Neither does taking in a couple fresh breaths.

Professor Adler simply has a visceral effect on me.

Around him, I'm no better than a silly schoolgirl with a crush.

Eventually, I make my way from the parlor, preparing to leave the funeral service altogether since I can't find Heather anywhere and no one else has seen her either. I set down my empty glass once filled with sparkling water on a credenza table and start down the entrance hall.

"Nyssa... hic... Nyssa... that you, darling?"

I place the slurred words immediately.

Mrs. Driscoll's calling out to me from the ajar door that's a guest bathroom. Any fuzzy feelings about Professor

Adler fade away for the determination I have any other time. This could be a moment used to my advantage...

"Yes, Mrs. Driscoll?" I poke my head through the door.

She's collapsed on the floor with a wine bottle, her dress ridden up. The toilet's filled with red-tinted bile that emits a foul sour stench in the small room.

"I... don't..." she slurs from the floor. "The wine... might've had..."

She can't even complete a sentence.

Holly Driscoll is a pathetic lush who can't even speak or stand. I'd feel sorry for her if she weren't everything wrong with this community personified. If she hadn't stabbed Mom in the back so many years ago...

"Mrs. Driscoll, you need help," I say, stepping into the room. I snap shut the door for discretion and kneel at her side. "How about we get you some water and take you upstairs?"

"My... my... hic... the others..."

"They won't have to know. No one will."

The first thing I do when I make it home is kick off my heels and hug and snuggle Peaches. My ginger girl purrs softly from within my arms and paws gently at my cheek in her own version of stroking my face.

The second thing I do when I make it home is dig out my Composition Notebook from under the mattress of my bed and turn to the correct page. My pen drifts down the lined page filled with a dozen plus names listed, then I cross off the latest update.

Kane Driscoll (struck through)
Holly Banton Driscoll (struck through)
Heather Driscoll

Right below her husband but right above her stepdaughter, Heather.

The progress fills me with satisfaction. Their community is imploding with barely a nudge from me. They're destroying themselves and barely even recognize that they are.

Mom calls as if sensing the update. "Baby girl, how'd it go?"

"Surprisingly better than I thought."

"Love to hear it. Anything new?"

I'm pressing the phone into my ear as I wander into my kitchen in only my bra and panties. "You were right about Holly Driscoll. She's a mess."

"Always has been. Always will be."

"Something tells me she'll be getting the help she needs."

Mom laughs as if I've told a joke. "Sometimes I forget you're my daughter. You might just be pettier than me."

"It's not like it isn't deserved."

"But you know what's most important, baby girl. Your safety."

"And justice," I say. "Making sure everyone who did you wrong gets a little karma. I've been doing some of my own research on them too. The school library has come in handy. You know it would be even easier if you told me more about my dad. I've been trying to find him in the archives—"

"Baby girl, I've told you everything there is to know. He lost his life because of these people. I was expelled from the school because I dared to be a young woman who got pregnant. Don't go around campus asking too many questions. They'll figure out who you really are. That's the last thing we need. This is why I worry about you."

I spend the next few minutes reassuring Mom I have a handle on everything and then move onto my sculptures in my living room.

Tomorrow's the art festival, and I'll be showcasing some of my work.

I invited Professor Adler.

My belly flutters with nerves remembering how he'd glanced down at the flyer. Curiosity had flickered in and out of his hard expression.

I wasn't imagining things. He was intrigued.

Throwing myself down on my quilted sofa and grabbing a throw pillow, I listen to Mom tell me about everything going on where she lives in Roseburg.

But really, I'm distracted with thoughts of Professor Adler.

And hope that he'll show up to see me.

5
THERON
DISTRACTION - MONTELL FISH

"It's not that bad," are the first words out of Theo's mouth. She's turned up on my doorstep like she so often does—in her uniform of athleisure wear, a slouchy beanie to cover her bedhead hair and the largest size of coffee the local Java King offers. She slurps down some of the coffee as she pays another glance over her shoulder at the damage. "You're such a drama queen, Theron."

"And you're such a slob. Ever heard of pants? *Real* pants?"

"The kind with no stretch? That shame me every time I gain a pound? I don't need that kind of negativity in my life. So sue me."

"I would, but all I'd win in the judgment would be poorly knitted slouchy hats and your Java King stamp card."

"Hey, I'm two more stamps away from a free sixteen ounce," she says, shouldering past me in the doorway. She shrugs off her windbreaker jacket and kicks off her scuffed-up sneakers.

I'm like a vacuum, picking up the discarded items in her wake.

Theo and I have always been polar opposites. She's a people-loving, thrill-seeking cat lady who survives off iced coffee and takeout, while I'm the rigid, sullen, borderline hermit older brother who would be perfectly satisfied if I never had to interact with the general public again.

"Well?" she prompts once she reaches my immaculate kitchen. Theo, being Theo, scans the gleaming, crumb-less space and shakes her head almost as if in disappointment.

I fold her jacket over the top of a barstool and rush to set down a coaster for her melting iced coffee. "Well... what?"

"Well, what did you do about it?"

"One day, Theo, you'll learn to speak in full, coherent sentences."

"Don't be a dick!" she snaps, chucking her fuzzy rabbit foot keyring at me.

The severed floof ball of a foot smacks into my chest before dropping to the ground and rolling under the barstool. I raise both brows at her to her eye roll.

"You know what I mean—what are you going to do about batshit fucking cray cray Alex Forest keying up your car?" she asks. "Are you taking that lying down?"

"Alex Forest? The lady from *Fatal Attraction*?"

"Theron, this is serious. It starts with keying cars. Then it's fifty gazillion texts and voice messages. Then, next thing you know, you're returning home to Atty's severed head."

"A bit of a stretch, don't you think?"

"You say that now. But a girl crazy enough to key the shit out of your car is crazy enough to chop your dog's head off."

"Five minutes ago you said it wasn't that bad... remember?"

"Sarcasm, bro. Language of the millennial. Remember?"

"Veronica's harmless."

"And that's why she keyed your car," Theo says. "The bitch knows she can get away with it. You want me to confront her?"

"Stay away from the situation. The absolute last thing I need is for my *kid sister* to fight my battles."

"Say the word and I will. Anyway, why aren't you dressed? Have you forgotten what today is?"

"Today is Sunday, Theo. Which means I'll be doing my grocery shopping, laundry, and other chores about the house. I'll cook dinner and then settle in the den by six with a good book."

"Sounds thrilling. Sometimes I forget you're forty-two, not eighty-two," she says dryly.

"Forty-one. I won't be forty-two until October thirty-first."

"Otherwise known as Halloween. But you won't actually spend the day pretending you're eighty, bro. Because you already promised to come with me to the art festival!"

"When was this?"

"Weeks ago. Remember... Atty was sick and you needed me to run home to take him to the vet 'cuz you were stuck in a meeting?"

The disgruntled glare I shoot her makes her laugh. "The last time I accompanied you to one of your things, you met up with some greasy-haired stoner named Doobie. *Unironically.*"

Theo places her hands on her wide hips, never mirroring our stern and authoritative mother more than in this moment. It tracks, considering they're both wavy-haired brunettes with smattered freckles. The difference being, Theo goes out of her way to be the antithesis to everything Mom stands for...

"Theron Thurman Adler, put some damn clothes on—ones with no stretch—and grab the keys to your fucked up, keyed BMW. We're swinging by the art festival."

"Is this the part where I say, 'yes mother'?"

"This is the part where you live a little. For once. Don't you have students that'll be there?"

"All the more reason not to go."

Theo narrows her eyes, her chin setting.

I sigh, throwing in the proverbial towel. If I go along with Theo's idea, I can bide my time for the inevitable moment something new and shiny steals her attention. Then she'll wander off, and I can get the hell out of dodge and go do things I really should be doing on a Sunday.

Boring things. Mundane things.

Things like carefully selecting produce at the grocery store and settling down with a new book and some brandy.

It's as I head upstairs to change that I come across the crumpled note from the other day in class. It had been tucked under the flyer Nyssa Oliver had given me. I hadn't even read it until after she left the room with her oafish boyfriend.

It had earned the slightest tremor of amusement inside me.

Now, as I come across the note, I'm drawn to the delicate loops and svelte lines of her penmanship. Picking up the piece of vellum stock paper, I unfurl it 'til I'm able to reread the note in its entirety:

A wise man once said you only get one chance at making a first impression. That wise man never heard of bribing someone with their favorite caffeinated beverage. Hope this makes up for it. :)

Miss Oliver

My lips twitch in much the same manner as the other day when she'd delivered the peppermint mocha to my classroom.

...and just like the other day, I can't bring myself to discard the crumpled note. Instead I set it back down, completely unfurled, on top of my dresser drawers, and then move onto changing into real clothes.

Something without stretch.

Twenty-six minutes, forty-eight seconds into the art festival, Theo does what Theo does best. She spots an old friend from her Castlebury U days and chases them down like a dog fetching its newest toy.

"Emma!" she yells. "Emma... it's me, Theo!"

Without the slightest second thought, she's off. Theo shoulders her way through the crowd of curious passersby, on a spontaneous quest to find the girl named Emma. I hang back, both hands tucked into the pockets of my pants, and watch my baby sister disappear like some magic trick.

After thirty-eight years of sharing the earth with her, it's no surprise at all.

Theodora Adler was always one of the more popular girls at school. Around the neighborhood. *In our family*.

Then there was her dark, scowling, brooding older

brother that kept his nose in a book and couldn't make pleasant conversation if his life depended on it.

I'd taken pride in that fact. I still do, so many years later.

Which is why, as I set off at a casual stroll down the center lane of the crowded art festival, I'm fine being alone.

Others browse on the arm of their partner or in the middle of animated chatter with their closest friend. Families wander by pushing strollers where drowsy toddlers nod off.

Everyone everywhere needs someone.

But not me.

Because I'm a proud lone wolf who gave up on the concept of real love many years ago.

That's what my family never understood. The students at school and colleagues at work. *Veronica*.

She thought it was personal that I was distant and aloof. In reality, she simply didn't understand the inner workings of the man she claimed she loved enough to marry. Breaking things off with her is the smartest decision I've made in years.

A quality paint job can always fix the scratch marks on my BMW XI. A small price to pay to be rid of Veronica's curse for good.

My parents weren't happy about the breakup—they hoped our relationship would finally lead to giving them grandchildren—but I couldn't care less. They can make as many snide comments as they want.

Veronica and I are over for good.

The autumnal wind blows through the art festival in a cool wave. Leaves scatter across the ground, crunching under many pairs of wandering feet. If not for the baseball cap I've put on, my hair would look as much of a tousled mess as the people around me.

But while festival goers seem indifferent to the blustery weather, the artists who have put their work on display guard their pieces with their lives.

As I pass through, quietly observing as much as I'm judging, a painter rushes to keep her watercolor canvas from flying off its easel. Never mind that her work is unremarkable—her brush strokes are amateur and uneven and fruit bowls are always derivative. Poor girl, she loses the battle against the wind as her uninspired fruit bowl crashes to the ground and the canvas bends in half, smeared by mud.

The next section of artists happens to be my least favorite type of art that exists: pop art.

I walk through the lazy displays of technicolor vectors and feel like I'd rather gouge my eyes out than look at anymore.

How long is socially acceptable to hang around before leaving the person you came with? Should I even care when Theo's probably forgotten all about me?

I *was* her ride, but she's always been a people person. Maybe this Emma she wanted to talk with so badly can give her a ride home.

I'm on the verge of about-facing in the direction of my car when I hear my name in the distance.

"Professor Adler?!"

Nyssa's stretching her arm in the air, on tiptoe in an attempt to stand out among the crowd. Little does she realize she already does—while half of them match Theo's uniform of endlessly stretchy athleisure wear, the other half look like burnouts who got dressed in the dark, donning wrinkled flannel and ripped jeans.

I'd expect nothing more out of college students and the adults willing to attend the art festival they've put on.

And then there's Nyssa.

She's put-together like she's been put-together the other handful of times I've seen her. A beret sits atop the springy curls which frame her face, and her eyes light up as she sees I've noticed her. She's in a simple black and mauve dress with buttons and tiny flowers that's loose enough to be casual yet still somehow hints at her curves underneath.

As I make it closer, I realize the tiny flowers are dahlias.

Perfect for autumn. Perfect for the feminine and polished look she has while still being uniquely *her*.

Seconds pass and I'm still lost in thought, digesting every observable detail about her. The bright smile she's given me begins to dim, and she slowly lowers her arm as if realizing her mistake.

Her message.

Her chance at a second first impression.

The hope's fading. Something indescribable clicks inside of me and I take a couple steps forward, closer toward her booth.

"Miss Oliver," I say, nodding. "I'd say I'm surprised to see you here, but you *are* the one who mentioned the festival to me."

"And you've decided to come check out the art." She clears her throat, likely sensing the eager lilt to her voice. She tries again in a slightly lower register. "I mean, if that's why you're here. We *did* set up in the middle of downtown."

My shoulders lift in a shrug, hands still deep in my pockets, using the opportunity for a glance around the festival. "I'm not sure if I'd call it my decision. More so one that was made for me. I'm accompanying someone who really wanted to attend."

"Dragged here by a friend. That seems to happen a lot here."

"Not a friend."

"Girlfriend? Sorry, is it strange that I said that? It's none of my business."

"Also not a girlfriend," I cut in quickly. I've become acutely aware of every move I make. How I've drifted closer and closer to her booth with every word exchanged. "My sister. She's around here somewhere."

"That's... strangely endearing." Nyssa's smile returns in its bright, perfect-toothed glory, even lighting her eyes a golden brown. Then she seems to realize what I have, that we've gotten sidetracked, and she flinches, gesturing to the sculpture on her right. "What do you think? It's one of the pieces I've showcased for the festival."

My brows draw together. I take yet another step closer. "You did this?"

"Painstakingly," she answers with a soft laugh. "It took me three weeks, two days, and one sleepless night, but I finished in time. I call it *Touch of a Lover*."

I'm caught in a situation I rarely find myself in—without a single word readily available. I've bridged the rest of the gap between Nyssa's booth and where I had stood, coming within a few inches for an up-close study.

The sculpture's well done.

That much is immediately clear. The expertise is everywhere, from the smooth, polished finish to the delicate lines of its very design.

Two human hands curled toward each other. One slender and smaller. The other larger and almost overpowering. Each with their own human sensibilities caught in clay form. Eyeing the rounded knuckles in the larger hand juxtaposed against the sharper, oval-shaped nails on the smaller hand, it's hard not to be impressed.

I marvel how Nyssa took the time to etch so many

details right down to the uniquely human lines on the inside of their palms.

But while the hands curl toward each other, fingers close to grazing, there's a distinct coldness to the sculpture. Some sort of distance she's communicating here, like two lovers yearning for closeness while being denied.

The elusiveness that sometimes comes with being so hopelessly in love...

I come to my senses with a hard blink against a sharp gust of wind, checking out of my rambling thoughts. Checking back into the moment where I find Nyssa watching me, wearing an expression that can only be described as uncertain.

She bites her bottom lip as if preparing for my brutal critique. As a student in my class, she'd know better than most that it's what I'm capable of.

"It's good," I say finally. "It's actually... very impressive."

"You think so?! I wasn't sure if it was too on-the-nose."

"Not at all."

"It's supposed to portray the duality of love," she explains. "Physical touch but also... the emotional aspect of what it means to be touched by a lover."

"And sometimes how that love can be so close but so far," I finish for her.

She nods. "Physically. Emotionally."

"It's great work. I'm sure most experts would agree. Though, admittedly, I'm no expert myself."

"It means a lot anyway. But you seem to know about sculpture. I wouldn't have pegged you as an art enthusiast."

"There's a joke there somewhere. What field do people who failed out of art school pursue?"

"Law," she laughs.

"Would that be the case for you?"

She shakes her head so that her tight curls bounce. "Oh... no. Art school was never even an option."

"You would be good enough. *More* than good enough."

"Babe!" calls Samson Wicker suddenly. The brawny blond lumbers through the crowd with his heavy footsteps and letterman jacket like we're not in the middle of a conversation.

As he shoulders his way into the small space Nyssa and I have created for ourselves, her smile loses its luster. It becomes more pained than anything.

"Samson," she sputters. "What are you doing here?"

"Being a good boyfriend like you complained about. You know you're always nagging me... saying I don't show up to your stuff," he says gruffly. "When do you go on break from this thing anyway? Let's go do something fun."

"You're kidding, right? I can't leave my art booth unmanned."

"So, uh, have this guy watch it. You can do that, right, Professor?" The oaf acknowledges me for the first time, flashing a toothy grin.

Tension screws shut my jaw. Normally, I'm able to censor emotion from bleeding into my expression. Now is not one of those times—my glare darkens as it zeros in on Samson Wicker and Samson Wicker alone.

Hot irritation rises from the inside. Boiling and white hot.

It must come across clear as day, because even an idiot like him catches on.

His grin falters and he turns to Nyssa instead. "I'm sure you can get somebody else. I saw Macey around here somewhere. Or Katie..."

"I'm not leaving my booth," she snaps, folding her arms. "So if you really do want to spend time with me, you'll have to stay here with me. You know, like a good, supportive boyfriend would."

He blows out a sigh, his sour expression lacking subtlety. "Fifteen, twenty minutes tops, babe. That's the best I can do. I've got practice later."

It takes me several more seconds to talk myself down from the ledge. The heat that has spread fast like a raging fire recedes, cooling off for the usual withdrawn, aloof mask I wear. I clear my throat to force their attention while ignoring the oaf and focusing on Nyssa.

"I should get going. Enjoy the rest of your afternoon, Miss Oliver."

Nyssa frowns like she wishes to protest, though she remains silent.

It would be useless for me to try to make sense of Nyssa's reaction as I turn and walk off. Yet I do so anyway, as I cross through the crowded festival and make my way to my car. For a minute or two to come, I sit behind the wheel and mull over the look she'd given me. The kind of look that said she wished I could stay. She wanted our conversation to continue.

Before doucheface interrupted.

How could that oaf be her boyfriend when she could barely stand his presence?

The negative energy seemed mutual; he could hardly stand being around her either. Had he even paid any mind to the sculpture she had on display? Did he take time to notice her artwork? Did he even give any thought to the meaning behind it?

Of course not. Oafs like Wicker rarely do. It's part of what makes them douches.

I've long wondered why women like Nyssa put up with men like Samson Wicker. Knocking on forty-two's door, I'm no closer to understanding than when I was twenty-two. It must be some type of allure. Some draw to bad boys, as cliché as it sounds.

On that note, I shove aside any more thoughts on the matter, turning on my BMW with a press of a button. Finally, a chance to do what I really want on a Sunday...

"You left me!" Theo cries out five hours later. "How could you just leave without saying anything?"

I raise both brows at her as she pulls open the passenger's side door and slides in. "Did you forget you wandered off without a word? Emma, Emma, over here!"

"I haven't seen her in three years. Can you believe she got divorced and moved back to Castlebury to start over? She's working admin at the police station and told me she's into men... *and* women nowadays."

"How fascinating," I say sarcastically. "But I had no intention of spending my entire Sunday at some university art festival."

Theo sighs, clicking on her seatbelt. "You're insufferable. Why do I put up with you again?"

"It probably has something to do with that pesky blood relation."

"Oh. Right. That. Are we sure we're related? Maybe I got switched at birth."

"Wishful thinking on your part," I say, turning the wheel to pull away from the curb. "Whatever helps you sleep at night."

Theo launches into how she's spent her afternoon, telling me all about catching up with her college friend Emma. I'm only halfway listening as I drive us back to my house where her apple-green Volkswagen Beetle's parked.

Apparently, she spent the entire time wandering the art festival with Emma. They dined on finger foods available from the vendors present at the event and drank copious amounts of iced coffee. They had originally been making plans to attend a show at a local dive bar but decided against it due to the stormy weather.

Fat raindrops speckle the windshield as I brake for a red light. The breezy, sunlit autumn weather from earlier in the day has long since faded. Thick clouds and chilling winds have taken its place, with streetlights popping on and most people rushing home.

The red light turns green. My foot presses down on the gas as we pass another block, and then a woman walking fast down the street captures my attention. She's immediately familiar with her button-up dress and springy curls.

Nyssa Oliver, walking home in the rain. I almost slam on the brakes.

Almost hook a U-turn in the middle of the road.

As my BMW drifts further down the road, my eyes flick to the rearview mirror and I watch her slip out of sight.

A sensation like sinking stones hits my stomach. I check the rearview several more times on the drive home as if expecting Nyssa to suddenly reappear.

But she never does. She's miles behind, at the mercy of the impending rainstorm.

"Thanks for being a decent brother and coming back to pick me up. I know how inconvenient it was for you to stop in the middle of your evening reading," Theo says. She's unclicked her seatbelt and begun gathering the knick-knacks she bought at the festival.

I blink and realize I've pulled into my driveway. I drove

the rest of the way home without even recognizing that I had.

"Did I have any choice?" I ask, my words coming slower than usual. "You would've called Mom and tattled on me if I hadn't."

Theo whacks me one last time with the paper bag she's clutching and then wishes me good night. I stay behind the wheel as she slips behind hers, twisting on her headlights and carefully backing out of the driveway.

She waves goodbye yet again before she finally drives off. I give a nod, counting the seconds until she's rounded the street corner.

White noise roars in my ears. My heart beats faster, my pulse elevating. I'm not sure what comes over me other than to describe it as the rush spontaneity brings. In a rare turn of events, I make a snap decision. I go against habit and shift gears into reverse.

Backing out of my driveway, I turn in the same direction I've come from—the same route that'll take me back to the art festival, and hopefully, the street where I'd seen Nyssa Oliver walking home in the rain...

6

THERON

NEW PERSON, SAME OLD MISTAKES - TAME IMPALA

WHAT'S DRIZZLE WHEN I START MY DRIVE BACK TOWARD THE ART festival quickly spirals into cold, wet bullets pelting down. The windshield wipers blur across my windshield as they attempt to keep up with the downpour.

Streetlights blot into fuzzy dots, and the glass fogs up from the cold air. I lean closer to the steering wheel, squinting at the road ahead.

Evergreen Road turns into Manchester turns into Castlebury Drive.

The occasional straggler car passes me by on the opposite side of the road, high beams bright enough to blind.

I keep squinting. Keep searching.

Scanning the sidewalks for the slightest sign of Nyssa. Where could she be? Did she make it home that fast?

It couldn't have been more than five, ten minutes since I drove by with Theo. Unless someone else spotted her and gave her a ride.

Someone she knew. Someone who would ensure she made it safely home.

Not someone with nefarious intentions. Not someone of the psychotic-serial-killer-picking-up-a-vulnerable-young-woman-on-the-side-of-the-road variety... *right*?

A thousand possibilities unravel inside my overanalytical mind. Dozens of potential scenarios of what could've happened and where Nyssa could've gone. After Kane Driscoll's recent death, some in town are worked up into a frenzy at the rumor the long elusive Valentine Killer has returned. He's slowly about to start picking people off like he'd done twenty years ago.

What if he'll target vulnerable young college students next? Someone like Nyssa?

And then there's the most sensible thought of all—the possibility she's already warm, cozy, and dry at her apartment.

I shake off the rampant thoughts spiraling beyond my control, my grip tightening on the wheel as I come to my senses.

This is ridiculous. Not just ridiculous.

This is stupid.

I drove all the way home and then proceeded to drive back toward the festival in the pouring rain to look for a student. All because I happened to see her walking home in stormy weather. What business of mine is it if she was?

Scoffing at how irrational I've behaved, I flick on my turn signal to make a U-turn. In the second before I do, Nyssa materializes out of the sheets of rain. She's half a block up, the umbrella she's walking with flapping inside out due to the hostile winds.

As I initially thought, she hasn't made much traction in the few minutes since I drove by. My pulse picks up, returning to the same level it had reached once I'd made the spontaneous decision to come back for her. I switch off my turn signal and push down on the gas to drive by.

The abrasive honk of a horn sounds from the lane to the right of me. The truck it belongs to comes barreling down the road, whizzing by me, halting on a dime as it pulls over against the sidewalk where she's walking.

She spins around in surprise, and I duck behind the steering wheel as if expecting to be seen.

But really, she's turned toward the gas-guzzling pickup truck that's just stopped at her side. Her startled expression melts away as the driver's door springs open and out hops Wicker.

Otherwise known as doucheface in my head.

Of course.

He jogs over in his letterman jacket like he's a superhero swooping in to save the day. Never mind the downpour and the way it soaks him as he steps onto the sidewalk and they come face to face. He takes her umbrella from her to hold it higher over the both of them and their lips move, exchanging words I can't make out.

It would be convenient to be a skilled lipreader right about now...

I squint, my windshield wipers still whooshing back and forth across the glass view I'm afforded. You'd think I hadn't stopped in the middle of the road the frivolous way I'm idling, staring at them from half a block down.

If anyone else were out in this weather, they'd care.

Whatever Wicker says to Nyssa cancels out his doucheness from earlier in the day. A small smile breaks onto her face as she tosses her arms around his neck and he lifts her off her feet.

By the time he sets her down, his meaty hand has drifted lower, sweeping down her spine toward her backside. He's so tempted, it couldn't be more obvious—he wants to go for a grab.

A real handful.

He doesn't do it, possibly because he knows she'd slap his hand away. But his temptation is palpable enough that I deem it provocation.

His desire to is problematic enough.

Mr. Doucheface has college date rape written all over him. The fact that rumors have swirled around him and his jock friends for a while now only strengthens my suspicions. Does Nyssa know what she's doing being involved with him?

He opens the passenger's side door for her to climb in. Once she's crawled inside, he slams it shut and trots back toward the driver's side. His obscenely large pickup lurches forward with rubber squealing against the slippery asphalt.

I stay put, still half a block down, stopped in the middle of the street like an imbecile. I'm not sure why other than it's my brain's way of processing what I've just witnessed.

A bright, promising student and gifted artist like Nyssa Oliver shouldn't be anywhere near the meathead oaf she's attached herself to. If they're truly together, why would he let her walk halfway home in the rain? Shouldn't he have picked her up from the get-go, once the festival was over?

I'm no award-winning-quality boyfriend by any stretch of the imagination—and I'm sure Veronica has a long list of complaints—but I'd never let my girlfriend walk home alone so late in the evening.

Much less in the rain.

My fingers drum against the steering wheel, on the cusp of another turning point. Another pivotal fork in the metaphorical road. The *literal* road ahead of me.

Both options come into focus amid the blurry, rain-drop-speckled car windows. The taillights of Wicker's pickup truck shrink farther down the road. Behind me is the path home.

Atticus is probably waiting by the door with his favorite tennis ball, tail wagging nonstop.

The book I started is still sitting on the seat of my armchair by the window where I left it. Theo had called me complaining about leaving her. I had leaped up to grab the keys.

It's dark out and the rain won't be stopping anytime soon. Any other Sunday evening I'd be content at home with my books, my dog, my solitude. I detested the times Veronica would try to drag me out to some concert or social event. She complained I was about as interesting as a senior citizen in a retirement home.

But as Wicker's truck slips out of view, I decide for the second time tonight to go against my usual routine.

My foot presses down on the gas. My BMW jolts forward in Nyssa and the meathead's wake.

The moment warps like it had earlier, where I'd made a snap decision to swing out of my driveway and seek Nyssa out on the rain-soaked streets. Pulse beating in my ears, I'd searched the streets with eagle eyes.

Now, I'm speeding like a madman. I'm gripping the wheel and rushing through a light that blinks from yellow to red. I'm at one end of the next block while Wicker is at the other. So long as I keep him within my sight, it's good.

I'll know where he's headed.

Where is he taking you, Miss Oliver? Is he driving you home? Or... somewhere else?

A wise philosopher once said curiosity is the lust of the mind. There is no harm so long as its pursuit serves some benefit.

I rationalize that there is.

Sure, there's a chance following your student and her boyfriend late on a rainy evening wasn't what Thomas Hobbes had in mind, but I prefer to think liberties are allowed.

All I need to do is make sure he drops her off at home, safe and sound. No frat boy antics. No douchebag tricks. Nothing harmful or dangerous in any way.

Then I'll head home.

Since when do you care about what your students do in their off time?

My inner critic hisses at me like I'm a petulant child. Rightfully so, all things considered.

"Since I heard him laughing about bedding her. Since I witnessed what that meathead is like and how he treats her," I answer myself aloud. "I might be hands off with my students, but I'm still a professor. I have a code of ethics to abide by. A moral obligation if I believe something's amiss. Something nefarious might happen. And I do—he has permanent doucheface!"

I end my tangent with a triumphant nod of my head, as though I've perfectly illustrated my point.

My secret pursuit carries on for another handful of miles. As a row of apartment buildings emerge, the pickup truck slows down and pulls over. Both Nyssa and the jock step out, with him glancing at the street.

I recognize the building at once. It's the same apartment building Theo manages for the university.

Nyssa lives here.

"Shit," I mutter under my breath, ducking behind the steering wheel. I've pulled over too, keeping distance for plausible deniability should I be spotted.

Nyssa grabs the front of his letterman jacket and lays a

goodbye kiss on his lips. This time he takes the risk—his catcher's mitt of a hand gropes her ass. He squeezes a handful, then gives her a spank, as if he's pulled off the most romantic play since Casanova.

My face tightens in a scowl. It's no surprise he'd go for the cheap, easy cop-a-feel route. Doesn't Nyssa realize how degrading it is?

Her reaction is too obscure to tell. She dashes up the front path that leads toward her apartment building, disappearing inside.

Wicker hardly waits before he's revving his engine and barreling off somewhere else. A keg party, perhaps? Some juvenile fraternity hazing? A night of vegging out to sports like the meathead jock he is?

None of them seem particularly farfetched.

But I'm past the point of caring once he's gone. I'm more preoccupied by the sudden realization that I'm sitting outside Nyssa Oliver's apartment. I know where she lives.

Even which window is hers.

On the fourth floor, the far left window lights up and she briefly appears in full view before she draws the curtains closed, shutting me out.

I sit for a while, torn on what to do next. While the private lives of my students are none of my business, Nyssa clearly doesn't grasp who Samson Wicker truly is. She doesn't understand the trouble he'll bring her or how risky it is for her to date him.

You don't see it yet, Miss Oliver. But you will. I'll make sure of it.

7
NYSSA
TEACHER'S PET - MELANIE MARTINEZ

Widowed Holly Driscoll Found Dead Hours After Husband's Funeral Service

I'M STARING AT THE NEWS ALERT AS IT COMES UP ON MY PHONE screen when Katelyn Wicker and Macey Eurwen call out to me. We agreed to meet outside the student union to grab coffees before crim law. I look up to find both girls hurrying toward me with a scandalized look of disbelief on their faces.

Katelyn, the shorter, thicker one of the two, resembles her twin brother, Samson, to the point sometimes I feel like she's him with a brunette wig plopped onto her head. Breathless and flushed, she says, "Nyssie, did you hear the news? It's everywhere."

"About Heather's stepmom? Yeah, I did."

"They're speculating it could be Valentine again. He poisoned her just like he did Mr. Driscoll," Macey says, tutting her tongue. She's taller and willowier than both of us, an occasional model that shows up in print ads. "Ugh, how humiliating! The supposed Queen of Castlebury lying in a pool of her own vomit."

I stand by as the other two trade gossip between themselves. They wouldn't be the only ones. As we wait outside the student union, I catch snippets of the same conversation happening between other students.

A group of girls who look young enough to be undergrad freshmen walk out of the student union talking feverishly about the article in the *Tribune* and whether or not Holly Driscoll died of alcohol poisoning or if the Valentine Killer really did do her in. Two more guys pass by talking about the time they got as black-out drunk as Holly was that afternoon, and ended up streaking around campus.

Macey was right. Holly Driscoll's death will be the scandal of Castlebury for some time to come. Just like her husband's death has been.

Katie's in the middle of telling us about how it was rumored that Holly and Heather were in the beginning stages of a nasty battle over Kane Driscoll's fortune. Neither woman could stand each other and saw the other as competition for the late Driscoll's riches.

She and Macey are so engrossed in the speculation, they hardly notice Heather approaching.

"Weird timing, she happens to die too. But everyone at the funeral has said she was belligerently drunk," Katie says with rounded eyes. "I guess this means Heather will get the entire fortune—Heather! Um, hi. I didn't see you…"

Heather takes a look at the three of us and the guilt we undoubtedly have on our faces. Hers is paler than usual, her spray tan nonexistent. "Let me guess why you're suddenly silent. You were talking about me, like the rest of the world is."

"Oh, no... we weren't Heather!"

"Definitely not!"

"Shut up," Heather snaps at Katie and Macey. "I heard you. I've heard it everywhere for the last forty-eight hours. All thanks to that hag of a stepmother of mine."

The three of us remain silent. The other two are uncertain while I'm secretly entertained.

"We're, um, sorry for your loss," Katie says.

"It's no loss of mine. She did this on purpose, like she always does. She's screwed up the entire will and testament proceedings. But I shouldn't be surprised. She was a selfish old hag for a reason." Heather turns her head toward the mousy brunette. "You should be more relieved than anyone, Katie. No one's talking about you blowing Lucas Cummings at my end of summer pool party after he was nice to you for five minutes."

Macey's jaw drops open. Mine almost does too.

Katie's chin quivers as she holds in emotion. "You don't have to be cruel, Heather."

"Who's been cruel? I'm being honest. Just like you spreading news about my stepmom. Besides, it's not exactly a secret you'll sleep with anyone who's nice to you, Katie. We call that common knowledge."

Katie rushes off while me and Macey hang back in shock. Heather holds her head up high, her usual confidence returning as she struts past us into the student union.

Half an hour later, the four of us are seated in Professor Adler's class with tension thick in the air. Katie's refused to utter a peep to anyone while Heather texts away on her phone with unapologetic defiance. Macey's flirting with one of the guys in our class.

And then there's me—my attention set on the front of the room where Professor Adler's waiting for the clock to strike ten.

As entertaining as our catty frenemy group is, I'm much more interested in today's crim law lesson.

The class begins and Professor Adler commands the room.

Dark, brooding, endlessly sarcastic, he holds my attention every second I'm near him. He grills the class during his lecture with such intensity, it feels like my heart's about to bust out of my chest.

The other students exchange ominous looks when he starts scribbling on the antique blackboard at the front of the lecture hall. His writing's abysmal. Chicken scratch is more legible. But that's the point—keeping us on our toes. On edge.

Making sure we're paying attention every second we're in his class.

I thrust my arm in the air when he asks questions. I meet his gaze bravely when he peers around almost disdainfully at the rows of seats. Deep down I'm hoping, *praying* he'll call on me.

I've been waiting days for it to happen.

For the words, "Yes, Miss Oliver?" to leave his lips as he finally turns his attention to me.

But it never happens. Come the end of class, he hasn't looked in my direction once. All around me the other students collect their things and trickle out of the room. I've stayed put, my book still splayed open.

I'm not sure what I'm doing.

Only that it feels like something I have to do. I have to

stay behind and talk to him. Gain his attention and make sure I'm not going crazy.

I thought... after the funeral, after the art festival, after my token of good will with the coffee and note, I had hoped...

The last person wanders out, the door thudding shut behind him. Drawing courage into my lungs with a deep breath, I rise out of my chair and start toward his desk at the front of the room. Each step feels dangerous, like I'm walking a plank to shark-infested waters. I'm on my way to my death.

And I very well could be—what if I've completely misread the situation? What if I thought we'd made amends when really he's still pissed I spilled coffee on him? Do I really want to incur the wrath of my criminal law professor?

I come up on his desk, yet still he doesn't notice me. He doesn't look up, so focused on collecting his things for his leather satchel that I'm a non-factor. I give a small cough.

He jerks his head up like it's a total surprise to find someone's in front of him. His brow furrows, the rest of his features no less clenched from his natural scowl. A scowl that should be off-putting, yet pairs perfectly with his wavy dark hair and stubbled jaw. His glasses only add to his intensity, making him both studious and forbidding as his deep brown eyes meet my own.

My belly flips, my mind wiping blank. "Um... I was just... I mean I had a... a question."

A flicker of something I can't place passes in his gaze. "Yes, Miss Oliver?"

There. It. Is.

Three simple words I've been craving all week long. Spoken in his smooth, professional-yet-throaty baritone.

I lose the air in my lungs. When I try to inhale some more, it feels like I've been rendered permanently breathless. It's the giddy sense of excitement that fizzes inside me. The awareness that I and I alone have his full attention in this moment.

"I... I guess it's more of a statement than a question," I stammer seconds later. He folds his hands on his desk and peers up at me with a new level of interest. As if he's searching my expression for context clues.

But I'm more distracted by his hands. Clean, well taken care of hands. Large hands with prominent veins that protrude on the back as he clasps both together. Strong and sturdy. Perfect for holding the heavy books I'm sure he keeps his nose in.

...perfect for holding, grabbing other things...

What has gotten into me? Why do I suddenly feel like a silly schoolgirl with a crush?

I lick my lips and force my dry voice box to work. "You stated that economic causation does not negate malum in se criminality."

"Yes... and?"

"I... I disagree," I say, feeling both lightheaded and exhilarated under his microscope. "Research has shown that crime is closely linked to economic factors like work and education. If the opportunity gain outweighs the adverse conditions the individual is in, then some would argue it's warranted."

"That's a mighty wordy way to say you think it's fine to steal sometimes," he quips.

Ouch.

I press on anyway. "The same research says deterrence is the best solution to these economic factors—"

"I don't remember that particular aspect being part of

today's discussion, Miss Oliver," he interrupts, canting his head slightly to the side. "The discussion was regarding malum in se. Acts morally wrong, therefore they are universally frowned upon by society and considered inherently criminal. Theft is widely recognized as one of these. Regardless of the reasoning."

"But think of a starving mother and her child—"

"That was not part of the discussion." He snaps shut his satchel and then pops to his feet so fast, so aggressively, I take my own step back. He's no longer hiding behind a veil of curiosity and study. That's vanished for open irritation. The same he'd had the morning I spilled coffee on him. "Next time you get the urge to add your two cents, you might want to make sure it was asked for in the first place. Perhaps stop trying so damn hard to be the smartest student in the room. It won't do you any favors."

He strides past me in a blur that's as dismissive as it is humiliating. My skin prickles in the aftermath, the warmth like a horrible sunburn. I can do nothing but suffer in the wave of humiliation that passes. The sinking knowledge I've made a total fool of myself.

Here I was, trying to impress him, and he couldn't care less. He was *annoyed* by it.

My hands come up to my face as I shudder out a breath and chastise myself for being so dumb.

Did I think I'd be his favorite student? Did I think he'd give praise for my opinion?

I drag my feet every step out of the classroom, dreading the fact that I have another class after lunch, which means I can't run home to wallow in private. I'm stepping out of the door when I almost collide with someone else approaching.

"Oh," says Dean Rothenberg, tugging on the lapel of his business jacket. He peers down his skinny, crooked nose at me. "You're coming out of Professor Adler's class. I trust he's inside?"

"He's not, Dean. You just missed him."

"I see. You look familiar. First year law student? Your family's alma mater, I take it?" He peers at me up and down as if trying to think of the few prestigious Black families at Castlebury that he knows of.

Little does he realize, I'm fully aware of who *he* is, and how his father, the former dean of the school, played a role in ruining Mom's life...

My pulse picks up again, giving a slow shake of my head. "Not exactly. I'm hoping to be the first in my family to graduate law school at Castlebury."

"Ah, excellent. Well... carry on. If you see Professor Adler before I do, please let him know I was looking for him."

Dean Rothenberg spares me no other attention as he's off down the hall in the direction he's come from. I wait 'til I'm sure he's out of earshot, then mumble under my breath.

"I would if Professor Adler didn't hate me."

My third week of law school is *marginally* less disastrous than the first two weeks. I'm on time for every class, well-read and well-prepared. I strike a balance between participating in the class discussions and not being a complete know-it-all like I usually would be.

The workload is doable so long as you stay on top of the reading and anticipate what could be coming next.

Where Professor Griner from torts is fascinating with his anecdotes about his days as a personal injury lawyer, Professor Burrows is like a cyborg. It wouldn't at all be surprising to learn he has the entirety of the United States Constitution memorized letter for letter.

But by the end of week three, there's only one professor that I still find myself drawn to.

Despite the fact that Professor Adler ignores my existence, I couldn't be more attuned to his. He's cold and withering in his demeanor. Dismissive in every way, yet when he glares around the room, I can't help raising my hand anyway. I can't help hoping today is the day he calls on me.

I can impress him like I have in the past.

Sometimes, I even sense he's *tempted* to glance in my direction. He's restraining himself, holding back from interacting with me in any way. His jaw clenches as he avoids me at all costs.

It begins to feel like some unspoken game between us—my eager attempts to catch his attention during class and his stoic, restrained efforts to refuse me.

I see him elsewhere on campus. In the corridors and inside the student union when I'm grabbing coffee.

There's no stone in the Gothic centuries-old architecture that doesn't make me think of him.

At lunch, I enter the library to spot him browsing legal books. His face is set in deep concentration, his dark hair so rumpled, a strand hangs loose against his brow. His hand extends toward the bookshelf and I watch as he carefully selects a book, taking it into his wide palm and long fingers.

I'm there to peruse the newspaper archives from 2004—research on my late father and what exactly happened at Castlebury U two decades ago—but, suddenly, I'm hot and flushed. I'm distracted by Professor Adler as he strides by me with the same cold confidence he always possesses.

A little over an hour later, the door to my apartment's flinging open as I rush inside and toss my bookbag aside. I usually spend Thursday afternoons studying and catching up on coursework, but I couldn't stand another second on campus. I shimmy out of my jeans and rush toward my bedroom.

Peaches joins my side with loud meows that go ignored for now.

"Sorry, Peaches. Give me a moment, okay?"

I need release.

Flopping onto my bed, I grab my vibrator from the drawer of my nightstand table. The room fills with its loud buzzing as the toy vibrates against my clit and my eyes roll shut.

Fantasy takes over.

I'm imagining Professor Adler's hands everywhere. I'm picturing how firm they'd feel gripping my hips and sliding over my thighs.

A moan leaves me as pleasure tingles in my pussy and I writhe on my bed. He's kissing me, his lips warm on my naked skin. He confesses how he's found me irresistible and couldn't stop thinking about me.

I can practically hear his voice in my ear, smooth and taut like fine leather.

He settles between my thighs and pulls out his engorged, veiny dick and...

My orgasm crashes over me. I seize up with my head tipped back and the vibrator buzzing away.

For several seconds, I'm high. I'm far from coherent as pleasure quakes through me and I almost *see* him watching.

I almost see him in this room with me.

My eyes snap shut again and I ride out the rest of my orgasm 'til I'm laying still in satisfaction. Clicking off the vibrator, I let out a sigh. Peaches leaps onto the bed to join me at my side like she didn't just witness her mother getting off to a silly fantasy.

I stroke her spine and laugh to myself. "I had to get that out of my system, Peaches. He's been in my head all day."

...except as a small laugh leaves me and I get up off the bed, a part of me lingers in the fantasy. A part of me wonders what if?

Some day.

8

THERON
WHO IS SHE? - I MONSTER

I saw everything.

Nyssa Oliver writhed on her bed, beautifully naked from the waist down, as she pressed a neon pink vibrator to her clit.

She had no clue she wasn't alone. At one point, it even seemed she glanced right in my direction. Her closet door was cracked open, my eye pressed against the crevice to watch the erotic show firsthand.

It wasn't a situation I planned.

I wasn't even supposed to be *inside* Nyssa Oliver's apartment. As I approached her door with the key in hand, I swore this would be the only time I allowed myself a peek.

It started the evening of the art festival—Nyssa Oliver lived in the same apartment building Theo managed. I sat behind the wheel of my BMW in the pouring rain and witnessed her bid goodbye to her doucheface boyfriend.

The same oaf who usually had date rape allegations swirling around him and his jock pals.

I couldn't let it carry on. I had to find a way to infiltrate her life and steer her away from him. Sabotage Samson Wicker in any way I could. Ensure he brought her no harm.

In doing so, I also had to put up a solid front. For all intents and purposes, in public I had to show an icy indifference to Nyssa whenever around her.

Arm up in class?

I called on anyone else. Even Justin Hendricks with the sleep lines on his face.

Passing each other in the corridor?

I looked straight ahead as if she were invisible.

And when she finally pressed me on it, I scolded her. I made her feel as small and ridiculous as I possibly could to throw her off my trail.

The same trail that had me compulsively thinking about her, formulating a plan for how to watch over her while also sabotaging Wicker.

That had me memorizing her entire 1L schedule to the letter. Constitutional law Monday, Wednesday, Friday mornings. Tort on Tuesday and Wednesday afternoons. Civil procedure in the afternoon on Monday and Fridays. Thursday's her light day with only legal writing.

And then there was me—criminal law three days a week, late mornings after she's done with constitutional law.

On her free day, Thursday, she still hung around campus. Usually, at the library on the west side of campus, a large table greedily reserved for herself as she spread out her books and then pored over them, doing the required reading. Other times, she combed the library newspaper archives in search of what, I'm still not sure.

I know these things because I was also often at the library.

...by chance.

A funny coincidence.

Between classes, I stopped by the student union for a coffee before strolling over to the library to browse the vast selection.

It was impossible to miss her as I did.

Nyssa stands out among the twenty thousand students on campus.

In class, it was even more glaring—among her peers, she sat with refined posture, eyes sharp and focused, following my every word. I started learning her tells, picking up on the cues she gave that provide insight as to what she was thinking.

An uncertain bite of the lip. Knitted brows. Her fingers drumming against the desktop in silent debate on whether or not she should raise her hand. The parting glance over the shoulder as class ended and she followed the others out the room.

Nyssa Oliver is like a book to be read and studied. Analyzed and interpreted. I certainly made a habit of it as days went by.

Though I did my best to ignore the new bane of my existence in public, there were brief moments where I slipped. My gaze almost drifted toward her in class before I caught myself with a clench of my jaw. As soon as she turned to walk out of the room, I was watching her go.

It was impossible to completely ignore her when she was in my orbit.

Heather Driscoll was thought to be the center of the universe in the traditional sense—her Barbie doll looks and style, the smug demeanor and prestigious family name all worked in her favor—but there's no question it was Nyssa who was *really* the scene stealer.

Her calm confidence, effortless intelligence and natural

beauty outshone the spray tan and designer threads. The reputable family name only worked so much magic. It certainly didn't distract from the fact that Nyssa and her vapid best frenemy belong to two separate categories.

Nyssa Oliver was—*is*—the rare pearl you find amid a beach of empty seashells.

So when she forgot to log off the library computer and I'm lurking in the background, I couldn't resist the opportunity that arose. I gave it a beat or two, ensuring she was gone, before I casually strolled over and sat down at the computer desk.

That easily, I had access to her login information, including her iCloud.

An overreach? Perhaps.

Necessary? Absolutely.

A British philosopher by the name of Edmund Burke once said the only thing necessary for evil to triumph is when good men stand by and do nothing.

This was what had to be done. This was what I had to do in order to make sure Nyssa went unharmed and evil wouldn't prevail. Some would claim it's character assassination to categorize Wicker as evil, but given everything I know, I'd say it's perfectly justified.

I logged onto her iCloud and skimmed through many of her files. I grew curious and found her social media accounts.

It was a deep rabbit hole to fall down. So deep, at home I hardly noticed Atticus whining for his morning kibble.

It was Saturday and I had gotten so distracted, I forgot to refill his bowl.

"Alright, alright, Atty. Here you go."

I set the bowl down for him and then returned to my investigation.

My heart leaped inside my chest when I came across her Instagram profile.

She was beaming at the camera, mouth open in a laugh, brown skin luminescent under the shimmering sunshine. The photo had to be from summer break.

There was sand in the background and ocean waves crashing against the shoreline.

Was she on vacation?

Bikini top. Giant sunglasses. Her usual curls were gone for twisty braids that accentuated her face.

The same heart-pounding thrill that had pushed me to drive in the rain to look for her returned in spades.

Over eight hundred posts. Five thousand followers. A witty blurb for her bio that read, 'Living life on the sunny side up', punctuated by a sun and paintbrush emoji.

Her entire life was captured in photographic form.

My biggest peek into her world yet.

Parties. Birthday dinners. Outfits of the day. Vacations to Montbec Island and Las Vegas. Throwback photos of her freshman year at a different college. Photos of her artwork that she proudly—and somewhat shyly, in some cases—posted.

I scrolled down to the beach photo that's her profile picture, enlarging it on my screen. It was one of an entire collection. A slight grin twitched at the corner of my mouth as I swiped through the photos.

She built a sandcastle. She wore a ridiculously huge, floppy sun hat that blew away in the wind and the photographer of the photo snapped her chasing after it. At some point, she gave up, collapsed in the wet sand, her head thrown back in wild laughter.

Then I made the mistake of swiping to the very last

photo, where I discovered who must've taken all the other pictures.

It was a two-person selfie of her and Wicker. He had pointed the camera toward himself as she squeezed in from the side to kiss him on the cheek.

An irrational hatred unlike anything I've ever felt flooded me. It came on strong, cascading over me like a tsunami wave that washed out all reasonable thought.

By the time ten p.m. hit, I had practically pored over every photo on her account. I had read entire comment sections and gone to posts where she had been tagged on.

It eventually led me to Wicker's profile, where my worst nightmare had been confirmed.

He had photos of her on his profile.

I was no expert on the etiquette of college-aged people and social media, but posting photos of each other felt... serious.

It felt like ownership. Some form of claiming.

And then my descent grew even worse. The rabbit hole continued until I was on Lucas Cumming's Instagram and I read an exchange between him and Wicker in the comment section for a throwback post about last Halloween.

Some massive costume party the fraternity threw that I vaguely recall hearing about due to the police being called. Rumors about drugs, brawls, alcohol poisoning, and date rape spread like wildfire about the occasion. Dean Rothenberg fought like hell to contain the flames.

good times!!! Can't wait to do it again

> this year. dates already set. u coming or u taken? 😏

> taken n still coming! me n ms priss will be there

> nice!! i'll have the goodies ready to go. we about to throw down!

My stomach muscles clenched. My eyes narrowed rereading the message three, four more times. Eventually, I screenshotted it, saving the image to my camera roll.

Goodies. *What* goodies?

Is that code for drugs? Alcohol? Some other dangerous element?

...and did Nyssa know her boyfriend was calling her *ms priss*?

My runaway thoughts were so loud, I couldn't quiet them enough to go to sleep. After flicking off the lights, I laid awake in the dark, staring up at the ceiling, considering the million different possibilities.

I had never been more certain than in that moment.

Nyssa had no clue what kind of fire she was playing with dating Wicker. She clearly didn't grasp how much trouble he could bring her.

Don't worry, Miss Oliver. If you can't see the trouble he is, I'll show you myself.

"You never show up here," Theo laughed. "I think I've been managing these apartments for, what, two or three years? You've turned up exactly once. That time I accidentally had your laptop."

I raised both brows at her. "Accidentally? What you call an accident, I call theft, sister."

"Theft? Okay, drama queen."

"That's usually what it's called when someone takes something without permission."

"Whatever. Still weird you've come by to see me at work."

...what you call weird, I call opportunity.

I set down the large cinnamon dolce latte I had grabbed her from Java King. "Consider it returning the favor. You bring me coffee quite often. Now I'm bringing you some."

Theo plopped down behind her desk in her cramped little office where the heater blasted lukewarm air and she had a view of the freeway from the window. She snatched the cup and took a long sip, then almost spit it out.

"They made this all wrong! Where's the cinnamon and whipped cream? Lucky I have some in my mini fridge."

Theo grabbed the latte and turned her back to fuss with fixing her drink.

I had drifted over toward the corkboard on the wall where the spare sets of keys hung for every apartment in the building.

Once she was making throaty sounds of satisfaction at the extra whip and cinnamon she'd added, I was ready to go.

"See you later," she said, scooping up her phone to

scroll through. "I've got a Zoom meeting in ten. The damn board of trustees want info about the building conditions."

"Sounds very important."

I walked out of Theo's office confident she hadn't noticed the missing key and I'd have plenty of time to explore.

Nyssa was still at the school. I was sure of it. On Thursdays, she didn't usually come back to her apartment until three or four in the afternoon.

Less than five minutes later, I was outside apartment 412, *Nyssa's* apartment. The key slid right into the keyhole and untwisted the lock. The door swung open like I'd been granted special entry to a secret world most had no idea about.

The only time I'd let myself do this—*explore Nyssa Oliver's private sanctuary*.

I gently shut the door behind me and surveyed the cozy six hundred square foot space. The walls were painted a soft lavender and the plank flooring beneath my feet was various shades of muted gray.

On my right was a row of coat hooks with some of Nyssa's jackets and woolly scarves slung over the brass curvatures. On the left, hung a gold-gilded mirror that looked older than Nyssa was.

Vintage.

That seemed to be a running theme as I explored the apartment. Her kitchen was small, clean, and boxed in with a vase of assorted fresh flowers resting on the front counter.

A few more footsteps, and I was already in the living room space, flooded by natural light from the large bay window at the back wall.

"*Meow.*"

I glanced down to find a curious little orange cat

peering up at me. Her feline way of asking "who the hell are you?"

I almost grinned, crouching low to reach out a hand and let her smell me. I'd never been a cat person, but Nyssa Oliver's cat was no regular cat—just like she was no regular student of mine. As inappropriate as it was that I was in her apartment, I knew with absolute certainty this was different.

This was an exception.

"Hello," I said to the ginger. "And what's your name?"

She gave a shrill hiss, then dashed off before the palm of my hand could even brush her spine.

I stood up straight again. "That's alright. Cats aren't as trusting as dogs. I get it. I wouldn't be either if I were you."

I moved deeper into the living room and admired how Nyssa had managed to keep her space tasteful but filled it with character and personality. A quilted leather sofa with curled armrests sat against the wall and a little coffee table stood a few feet in front of it, covered with various items like candles, a TV remote, more flowers.

The corner closest to the window served as Nyssa's makeshift art studio—shelves bore past sculptures she'd created and a large easel was propped up in direct sunlight along with a stool and pottery wheel she used to mold clay.

I was fascinated by her art. I stepped closer like I had at the festival and admired the expert sculpting of each piece.

My head filled with imaginings of Nyssa perched on her stool, wearing nothing but a shirt of mine, her hands steeped in clay, as morning light haloed her. She'd look up and smile at me. I'd approach with two mugs of coffee and deliver hers with a kiss...

The image faded before my eyes and left an ache of longing in its wake.

Not entirely unfamiliar—I had once bought my home with the same type of vivid hopes. I'd look at the backyard and picture *her* pushing our child on a swing or relaxing on a lounge chair with a good book.

None of those things ever came close to coming true.

I moved onto Nyssa's bedroom, where a bed with wrought-iron bars was pushed against the wall and covered in a variety of different sized and shaped throw pillows. Her bedding was plain and off-white, but the rest of the room popped with color, from the artwork she'd hung on the walls to the melted candles and flowers spread throughout.

I smiled at the bookcase near the window that was crammed with well-loved books, spines cracked and worn. A few I owned in my collection, like *The Alchemist*.

Her cat whined from the other side of the room as though irritated I was still here.

"I'll be gone soon, alright?" I asked, halfway amused by the feline's impatience.

I'm ashamed to admit I opened drawers. I checked cabinets. I uncapped her shampoo and conditioner and inhaled the scents she used in her hair.

What was supposed to be a quick exploration of her place to gather intel on her relationship turned into a lengthy, overindulgent visit where I let myself become even more obsessed.

Leave now.
You said you would be quick.
This is not quick.

My thoughts pushed back at every turn, reminding me of my original intention. But I pressed on anyway, operating on a fanatical beat that had me blocking out these thoughts. At least for the moment.

I was browsing Nyssa's underwear drawer when her ginger feline made her loudest objection yet. She hissed and then leaped toward me as if to pounce. Her paw slapped and swatted at my loafers and produced a laugh out of me.

"Alright, alright, you don't want me here," I said, clutching a soft cotton pair of Nyssa's panties.

I was growing hard just from holding them. Imagining the fabric clinging to her *pussy*.

I stomped that thought out immediately, scolding myself for how inappropriate and unprofessional it was.

...isn't everything you're doing right now inappropriate and unprofessional?

Scowling at myself, I shoved the panties back in the drawer. Nyssa's cat was right.

It was time to go. Before I spiraled any more out of control.

"Next time, I'll bring you tuna," I promised the cat, then ran a hand through my hair.

Next time? There won't be a next time!

...right?

I was halfway down the hall, caught up in an argument with myself, when the lock in the front door jiggled.

My heart dropped into the pit of my stomach. I stopped dead in my tracks at the horrifying realization.

Nyssa was home!

"Shit," I muttered under my breath. My head snapped left, then right, as I desperately scanned the area for a place to hide.

The front door was flying open as I was slipping behind a different door.

Nyssa's closet.

Her cat still wasn't satisfied, meowing even louder to alert her.

"No," I whispered, cracking the closet door open. "Bad kitty. Shhh. Don't—*damn it!*"

The ginger cat fled from her bedroom to greet her at the other side of the apartment. I waited with a coursing pulse, holding my breath for the moment I'd be caught. Nyssa would wonder why her cat was behaving so erratically and she'd inevitably make her way into her bedroom.

How could she possibly come home and not eventually check the closet? Particularly if she begins to suspect someone was here while she was gone.

Genius, Theron. Simply fucking genius.
You just had to sneak into the girl's apartment.
So smart, you're as dumb as Wicker sometimes.

I gritted my teeth and listened for every sound playing out from the other side of the apartment.

"Sorry, Peaches. Give me a moment, okay?"

Nyssa's rushed movements grew closer and closer. She was in a hurry. Her bedroom door was shoved open and she scurried into the room already pantsless.

Interest immediately piqued, I cocked my brow higher and pressed my eye to the crack in the closet door.

She collapsed onto her bed and dug a vibrator out of her nightstand drawer.

The moment went from doom and panic, where I was convinced I was caught, to erotic and shocking.

Everything felt surreal.

Nyssa Oliver laid back against her pillows and propped her thighs open just wide enough to fit her vibrator. The room filled with the fast buzz of the toy as it stimulated her clit and she moaned along.

Her eyes rolled shut. She quaked and ground her hips against the little hot pink toy. Lost to the intense feelings taking over her, she was tuned out of the present.

It was all fantasy.

I husked out a deep breath watching her and prayed it wasn't loud enough for her to pick up. As she lay pleasuring herself on the bed, I was erect and ravenous behind the closet door. Blood had rushed to my cock, pushing against the constraints of my pants.

Her body was perfection.

Lush curves wrapped in smooth brown skin. Ample breasts jutted out as she arched her back and her blouse rode up enough to expose her flat stomach. Her thighs, the thickest part of her, were spread wide open. Though I couldn't *directly* see her pussy, I could see how her hand pressed the vibrator to the intimate area, riding the waves that crashed over her.

The fluid way her body moved was a form of art in itself. She writhed in bed, uninhibited and free, in the throes of pleasure I desperately wanted to give her myself.

"Fuck yes, Miss Oliver… touch that little pussy. Soon it'll be me," I panted quietly. I rubbed my groin area so hard I had to clench down on my jaw to keep from coming.

For a wild moment, I was certain she heard me—her eyes popped open and she looked *right at* the closet door.

But then her orgasm struck at that exact moment, and all rationale was lost. Her head fell back against the pillows and she gave a throaty cry.

She was a masterpiece as she came undone.

I reached the same peak as she did. As she orgasmed in bed, I reached my fill inside my pants.

For a few seconds, we were lost together but separately at the same time, overwhelmed by the orgasms that seized us.

Nyssa stroked her orange cat and said, "I had to get that out of my system, Peaches. He's been in my head all day."

...he who? Samson Wicker? Or someone else?

I'm so distracted by the mysterious man she's referenced that I forget to be concerned she could still open the closet and discover me.

Luckily, she gets up out of bed, grabs the pair of jeans she'd shimmied off in the doorway, and then tells her cat she'll be back. She has a few more errands she needs to run.

Peaches purrs as if in objection—probably still aware *I'm* here—but Nyssa simply grabs her bag and walks out.

Relief sweeps through me listening to the door thud shut.

Time to make my escape.

No less than ten minutes later, I'm able to slip out of Nyssa Oliver's apartment building, sight unseen. I get inside my car and look up at the far left window that's hers.

A window I've stared at more times than appropriate in recent weeks.

"Why were you watching me, Theron?" Josalyn asked, pushing past me. "I know it was you. I saw you on the street corner."

"Jos, that's not what was happening."

"It was exactly what was happening!" she snapped. "You think I don't know what you've been doing?"

"I could say the same to you! I'm just trying to look out for you."

She scoffed, her full mouth twisted into a dismissive smirk. "You really think I need you to? You have to stop."

You have to stop.

"I have to stop..." I mutter under my breath, almost catatonic. Then my fingers clench tighter on the steering wheel. At my side, my phone buzzes with an alert for Nyssa's iCloud. She's received a text from Wicker. My glare darkens as the beat of my pulse pounds harder. "*After* I get rid of him."

9
NYSSA
OLDER - ISABEL LAROSA

SAMSON WICKER IS GOOD AT SEVERAL THINGS. FOOTBALL. LIFTING furniture. Changing spare tires. Blabbing on and on about his brand new Ford F-150 truck. But kissing is far from one of those things.

I'm reminded of this sad reality as his teeth gnash against mine and slobber wets my lips. I draw back to end our kiss, but he pulls me more tightly against him. His hand's heavy on my back, holding me where I am as his tongue launches its latest assault.

He groans lashing it against mine. He leans his weight into me, rearranging us on his sofa 'til I'm under him. His barreled chest heaves with his deepened breaths. His excitement becomes more than palpable.

It's a hard bulge prodding at me.

I finally succeed in ripping my mouth away from his. "Samson, we're supposed to be studying."

"Mhmmm, babe. Later," he mumbles. No less discouraged, he pivots to kissing my jaw and throat. Kisses that are just as sloppy and wet as his others.

I sigh, rolling my eyes. I'm stuck listening to the

guttural sounds Samson makes and the music and screams coming from down the hall of his apartment. Unlike me, he lives a block outside of campus, right in the heart of the city, which means there's never a moment of peace and quiet.

Bars and lounges are only a short walk away. Parties run almost nightly. It's considered prime real estate if you're into Castlebury's nightlife and social scene.

All things I couldn't be less interested in.

I would've never set foot inside Samson Wicker's apartment in the first place had I not agreed to tutor him.

A few months of rocky dating later, I'm trapped on his sofa as he knocks our books aside and makes his latest attempt to get in my pants.

"Samson," I growl. My hands grip his shoulders to push him off. "I'm serious. If we're not studying, then I'm leaving."

"Don't be a mood killer. Just have some fun."

His mouth covers mine again in his sloppiest kiss yet. It *literally* feels like he's trying to swallow my face.

I've kissed my share of frogs in my short twenty-two years, but no frog has been as slimy and off-putting as Samson. If it didn't serve me to date him, posing a means to an end, I would've dumped him a long, long time ago.

I never would've dated him in the first place.

Samson groans, pushing his slippery tongue back into my mouth. His hand creeps between us, hardly subtle as he wedges it down the front of my jeans.

It's the final straw. I jerk against him and snap into defense mode. He might weigh twice as much as I do, but I took women's self-defense during undergrad.

"I said get off, Samson!" My knee slams into his gut, making him choke on his next breath.

Before he can do anything more than sputter and cough, I'm rolling out from under him.

"What the fuck, Nyssa?!" he wheezes out. His face, neck, and ears all redden as he shoots a glare at me. "Really? Kneeing me in the gut like I'm a fucking intruder?"

"I told you I'm here to study."

"And I'm your boyfriend! You forget about that?"

"What does that have to do with—"

"I've got a severe fucking case of blue balls, Nyssa!" he barks over me. If his squat face was red before, it's blazing scarlet now. He throws his arms up in frustration as he gets off the couch and crosses the space to the kitchen.

I spin around to track him with my gaze. "I told you when we started dating, I move at a slow pace."

"Slow pace or like a fucking turtle? It's been *four* months."

"Three and a half. And if it's a problem, then we can see other people." I follow him into the kitchen area as his phone pings, and he quickly snatches it to respond to whatever slew of texts he's received. "Samson? Who are you texting all the time? Are you going to answer me or is this more silent treatment?" I prompt when he says nothing, more preoccupied texting. Shaking my head, I shoot straight for my things on the dining room table. "This is so dumb. I'm out of here."

He slams down his phone on the kitchen counter. "Do what you want. That's what you always do."

"What's that supposed to mean?"

"It means it's always all about you, Nyssa. Whatever the fuck *you* want. Dating you's like dating some fucking tiger that's about to claw the shit outta me." He pops open the fridge to grab a beer, then leaves me alone in the kitchen area. He's returned to the couch, where he plops down, guzzling down half the can. "I thought I could deal with it. But you're not hard to get. You're *impossible* to get."

It takes me several seconds to join him back in the other room. When I do, I've finished packing my things, my leather bookbag slung over my shoulder.

"You're right," I say. "I *am* impossible... to someone low effort. I'm sorry I don't want to fuck on your couch that smells like farts and weed, Samson."

"I told you I'd light some candles. Get some roses and shit—"

"Are you taking me home?" I interrupt, folding my arms. "You said you'd drive me."

"Figure it out yourself. I've got plans. Which reminds me. Where's my phone?"

He gets up, clutching his beer can, and returns to the kitchen, presumably for another text. I've drifted toward the door, shaking my head in disbelief.

It shouldn't really be a surprise Samson would be a big enough asshole to make me find my own way home. It wouldn't be the first time. But it damn sure is the last.

"Nyssa!" he calls as I'm halfway out the door. "Did you see where I put my phone?"

"Find it yourself," I snap spitefully.

They're my parting words as I slam his door shut. I'm several steps down the hall when I hear his rumbling voice calling me out of my name. Words like "selfish bitch" would sting a lot more if I hadn't heard much worse throughout my life.

I ride the elevator down to the first floor of his apartment building and stop altogether in the vestibule to order an Uber.

I've had no luck securing a ride home otherwise.

I've texted Macey but she's out of town for the weekend

on a family trip. Katelyn's on a date with her latest dating app hook up. And Heather... Heather's most discreet of all.

"You and Samson broke up?" she says, lukewarm interest in her voice. "Nyssie, that's awful."

"Do you think you can swing by and pick me up?"

...you do live only a couple blocks away...

"Oh... um, not really," Heather answers. "Sorry, babes. You know I don't do short-notice obligations. But call me tomorrow. We'll go for mani-pedis."

I huff out a sigh when the Uber app informs me my driver's waiting two blocks down. I fire off a message to let him know he has the wrong address.

> No street parking. Ive been fined before. You'll have to walk to me.

> I'll be right outside... you won't need to park.

> The street's one way... I'd have to circle around half the neighborhood to make it back. U meet me where I am...

"You've got to be fucking kidding me," I mutter under my breath.

The request is so irritating, for a second I'm even

considering making up with Samson. Just to get a ride home. *Then* I'd break up with him all over again.

But my pride's too precious for me to stoop that low. Samson was a dick for the last time. I'll simply have to figure out other ways to ingratiate myself in the same circles. I've already found other ins that have served me well. I wouldn't be invited to mani-pedis tomorrow with the school's most popular girl if I hadn't.

Coat buttoned up and scarf snug around my throat, I brave the chilly October night. The air is crisp and cool, the lampposts like miniature spotlights every few feet down the sidewalk. Across the street, a group of college students erupt in wild cheers as they hang around outside a sports bar.

For all I know, Samson might be joining them soon. He failed his last year of undergrad for a reason.

I hover on the sidewalk unable to shake the odd feeling I'm not alone. I'm being watched even if I can't tell by who. Phone in the palm of my hand, I study the blinking green dot that's my Uber car. He better not leave. If he does, I swear I'll...

Before I can even complete the vengeful thought, I realize I really am being followed. A navy blue SUV coasts alongside me from the street, slowed down to my walking pace. I glance over as alarm rings through me, and for the second time tonight, I'm scanning my head for everything I learned in women's self-defense.

But then I make out the person behind the wheel and I can't hide the surprise that drops my mouth open.

"Professor Adler?!"

He presses the palm of his hand on the steering wheel, the horn giving a weak bleat in answer. "Miss Oliver, do you need a ride home?"

"I... I... what are you doing here?" I've taken several steps toward him until I'm on the edge of the sidewalk and he's idled in the middle of the one-way street.

"I was working late at the school, grading some papers. I was just on my way home when I saw you walking down the street."

My head tilts to the side. "But wouldn't it be easier to take Manchester home? Do you always take a side street like Monarch?"

His expression's difficult to read in the second it takes him to answer. Shadows veil half of his face, the other half all angles emphasizing his strong profile. "I cut through Monarch because I sometimes stop at the Vietnamese spot at the end of the block. They have the best pho in the city."

"Oh," I murmur, hovering uncertainly. My phone dings with an impatient message from my Uber driver.

"But," Professor Adler continues, "if you don't want, or need, a ride home, then I will be on my way. Have a good evening, Miss Oliver."

In the split second it takes me to make my decision, I'm caught between two very different choices. A hostile Uber driver that's already copped an attitude with me for making him wait and my criminal law professor who I've tried so hard to impress only to wind up with a bruised ego.

He hates me. Why would I accept a ride from him?

I nibble on my bottom lip at the question. It's promptly followed by a counterargument from my other half.

Professor Adler might hate you, but so does this Uber driver. And he's charging you three bucks per mile...

"Wait," I blurt out. "I... I do need a ride. If you don't mind. I live on the other side of the city."

"That should be fine. Get in."

His tone's matter of fact, lacking any hint of emotion at all.

He's doing me a favor. He's resigned himself into doing so not because he wants to, but because he feels obligated.

I let out a sigh as I shuffle over to the passenger side of his car and slide in. It's no surprise the interior is immaculate—the seats look and feel like new, no signs of wear or tear at all. No crumbs or dirt to be found anywhere, not even on the car mat beneath my leather booties.

Professor Adler waits in patient silence for me to click my seatbelt and settle my bookbag on my lap before he changes gear into drive.

Monarch Street slips into the background. Samson's apartment disappears from view.

We ride in silence, listening to the quiet, subtle sounds his BMW makes. It's fitting that Professor Adler wouldn't listen to music when he drives. He seems much more like the podcast or NPR type.

I fold my hands in my lap as if on my best behavior and busy myself by staring out the car window.

"I'll need your address," he says as we brake for our first streetlight.

"Oh. Right. I live near Elm and Horton. It's the apartment complex near the—"

"I know where that is," he says. Then, as if sensing he needs to clarify, he adds, "There's a great Indian restaurant across the street."

"Saffron."

"That's the one."

"Are you... uh, are you a big foodie?"

"Excuse me?"

"You mentioned the Vietnamese restaurant earlier. Now, Saffron..."

"Right," he says, his attention on the road ahead. The light's turned green again. "I suppose I am. I tend to lean toward Asian cuisine. South and East. I appreciate the flavor palette."

"What's your favorite?"

He throws a glance over at me, his eyes darker than usual. My belly flutters in reminder that I'm not supposed to be doing what I do—acting like a social butterfly that's trying to win him over with great conversation.

Those kinds of things don't matter to Professor Adler. He'd probably prefer if I didn't talk at all.

"Sorry, you don't have to answer if you don't want—"

"I appreciate Thai more than others. I suppose that would be my favorite," he interrupts after some thought. Then he directs another brief glance at me. "And yours?"

My brows quirk, startled that he's bothering to ask. "Oh, mine. I've been really into charcuterie boards lately. But if we're talking Asian cuisine, probably Thai as well. Or Japanese. I'm a sucker for sushi."

"Quality sushi can be difficult to find. Unfortunately, Castlebury lacks in that regard."

"Right, I've had better..."

We drift off into more uncertain silence. I return my focus to the car window, then resort to pulling out my phone to check on notifications I really don't care about. Things like looking at any likes and follows on my social media accounts. Answering a panicked text from Katelyn as she messages in the middle of her date. Deleting spam emails.

Anything to distract from the fact that I'm trapped in an SUV with a professor who I admire but who can't stand me.

Maybe I should've gone with the Uber after all...

"So," he says as we brake for yet another light, "what were you up to tonight, Miss Oliver?"

"Hmmm?"

"You asked why I was driving down Monarch. I'm asking the same. It's a side street of college apartments and some bars. What brought you there?"

"I was, uh… Samson and I were supposed to be studying. He lives in one of those apartments."

"I see."

"He was supposed to give me a ride home."

"Supposed to," he repeats in a tone that rings with some semblance of judgment. "I've noticed you keep using that phrase. I'm guessing no studying was actually accomplished?"

My cheeks warm from more than the heat blowing out of the dashboard's vents. It's from the awkward realization I'm about to discuss my boyfriend troubles with my professor. The same professor who made me feel smaller than small more often than not.

The same professor who I fantasized about recently when I masturbated.

"We didn't get much studying done," I answer. "Samson had… he had other ideas."

There's a pulse of inexplicable tension that follows. First felt in the clinch of the air, then witnessed by my own two eyes as I cut a sidelong glance and notice the subtle tick of his jaw. The way his knuckles bunch, clenched against the steering wheel.

As if I couldn't be more confused. Did I say too much? Am I bothering him with my frivolous problems?

"Never mind. Forget I said anything."

"I asked. You answered. No need for anything to be forgotten. I didn't answer because I was thinking about past experience," he explains, hanging a right at the next intersection. "It sounds like college-aged guys haven't changed much since I was one myself."

"That wouldn't at all surprise me. Samson's... Samson. He's the opposite of his sister. He wants what he wants and he goes for it. But he also throws a tantrum when he doesn't get it."

"I'm sure you'd prefer advice from someone other than your criminal law professor—and, frankly, I'm not sure how appropriate it is that I am about to give it—but if he's having a difficult time accepting your boundaries, then it sounds like he is not worth your time."

I smirk without thinking. "Professor, are you seriously telling me to dump my boyfriend right now?"

"I didn't... I mean, I was simply saying—"

"Because you're late," I finish with a soft laugh. "Pretty sure we're done after tonight."

He releases a breath that's hard to miss. "Well, that sounds like a smart decision on your part."

"Thanks. And thanks for the ride. You didn't have to."

"I realize I didn't. However, I would say I owe you an apology. Something somewhat rare coming from me," he says and I laugh again. "I've perhaps been too harsh on you. Harsher than I would be on other students."

"Can I ask why you never call on me? Is it something I've said? Done?"

He spends another block of our drive in thought to the point I almost give up on receiving an answer. We've slowed down as we join a short line of other cars held up by a red light. It's enough of an excuse for him to glance at me in the deep shadows of the car.

"You are a very gifted student," he says plainly. "Perhaps the smartest in any of my classes. It's impossible not to be impressed with you. But if I let you answer every question, what would the others learn? I might have overcorrected."

I'm speechless as the car rolls into motion again. My heart thumps faster in my chest, an immediate longing inside me to squeal in excitement. The professor I've tried to impress the most has taken notice. He's just as impressed as I hoped he'd be.

The validation has me biting back a smile.

We finally arrive outside my apartment complex where most of the windows are either dark or blacked out by drawn curtains.

"Here we are," he says.

"You didn't have to. I owe you another coffee."

"Think nothing of it, Miss Oliver. Go on. Head up. I'll wait."

The same belly flip from earlier makes itself known. I can't help drawing an instant comparison between this moment and all the previous times Samson's dropped me off, speeding away before I've barely made it down the sidewalk.

"Thanks," I murmur, grabbing my bookbag. My other hand goes for my seatbelt, fumbling with the buckle.

Professor Adler notices, his eyes widening behind the lenses of his black-framed glasses. "It jams sometimes. Here, let me help you."

He leans closer, his proximity like an invisible cloak thrown over me. He doesn't just come closer, he encroaches. He *invades*.

His arms extend over my lap and his woody scent, reminiscent of pages in a lengthy book, inundates my senses. His fingers, so long and sturdy and perfect, enclose on the seat buckle, applying some muscle I don't have.

I'm left sitting still, holding my breath, processing the fact that he's so close.

Too close.

His hand brushes mine. Heat shoots through me at the barest contact. Our eyes catch on each other's face. For an uncertain second, we blink at each other in the tight, confined space of his car, and it feels like my heart's about to bust out of my chest.

Then it's over. The moment ends. He lets go as the seatbelt unclicks and he recedes back onto the driver's side.

"You better go," he says, a rough edge to his voice that's new. "Good night, Miss. Oliver."

The next minute or so passes as a blur. I'm sure I mumble *goodnight* before I scramble out of his car and make my way up to my apartment. It seems the next time I'm blinking, my bookbag's crashing down on my coffee table and I'm kicking off my ankle booties.

I peel off my coat and scarf still reeling from the night I've had. I can't begin putting into words how I feel about Professor Adler's car ride home. Just that I'm more lost than ever how to take him. How to interpret him, and that bothers me.

...even if I still crave his approval.

I dig my books out of my bookbag along with my phone. The last thing I pull out is the second phone I've tucked inside. The larger, wider one with a scarlet red case in the same shade as the school's color. The right size for someone with thicker fingers like Samson.

His phone pings in my hand as another batch of texts light up his screen, confirming exactly what I suspected...

10

THERON

DEVIL'S ADVOCATE - THE NEIGHBOURHOOD

"Wouldn't it be easier to take Manchester home? Do you always take a side street like Monarch?" Nyssa Oliver had asked as I turned up out of nowhere to give her a ride home.

It was a fair question.

The kind of immediate curiosity a bright, gifted young woman like Nyssa Oliver would have.

I should've been better prepared. Sharper on my feet if I were going to pull off what I did. Luckily, the shadows of the car disguised my silent panic. They gave me the cover I needed to make up something on the spot.

Why was I on Monarch Street? How likely is it that I just happened upon Nyssa?

Not likely at all.

The unvarnished truth was that I had spent the evening watching her. Earlier in the day, Nyssa had been uncharacteristically distracted—she checked her phone *three* separate times during my class.

It was Samson Wicker texting her about his course load.

The oaf needed help with his classes again and we were barely a month and a half into the fall semester.

Nyssa agreed, accepting his invitation to come over.

All exchanges I read for myself. All messages I saw from her iCloud account.

I tracked her every move from the AirTag I had slipped into her bookbag when inside her apartment and listened to the exchange from the mic I had also planted.

So, as Nyssa went to meet her slow-witted meathead boyfriend, I was already aware. I was lurking in the neighborhood, prepared to step in if I needed to.

If he got out of line.

He almost did. She practically had to knee him in the groin just to get him off her. He refused to give her a ride home, a recurring theme that came up again after the art festival fiasco.

Nyssa was shocked that I showed up to save the day—or *night*, more accurately speaking—but it wasn't as though she didn't secretly welcome the rescue.

Days go by on the calendar, and I'm not the only one doing the seeking.

Class ends and most students pack up and vacate the scene as promptly as possible. Her friend Heather Driscoll, who should probably be grieving the recent death of her parents, leaves with Macey Eurwen at her side, talking about the shopping they'll do that afternoon.

And then there's Nyssa Oliver, who lingers at her desk, her eyes curious and gleaming, framed by long, natural lashes. Every movement of hers is slow and measured, like she's biding her time, waiting out the moment.

I shuffle papers and pack my things, pretending not to notice from the front of the room.

It's a charming little game we play. The uncertainty that

hangs between us is almost addictive. It's an exhilarating rush where we put feelers out and wait for the other's response.

Nyssa craves approval; she wants to know she has mine.

Little does she know, she already has it. She won it a long time ago. But more than that—she's earned my fascination.

Infatuation.

She clears her throat and then takes the chance.

"Err, Professor," she says cautiously, "I was wondering if we could have a word."

"Yes, Miss Oliver?"

"I had some thoughts about our discussion during class."

Of course, you did. You think much more dimensionally than the rest of the class.

On the outside, I remain nonplussed. Staring her down as she approaches, I say, "Such as?"

"It's regarding what you said about the death penalty," she says. "You stated that it typically provides justice and closure to the families of the victims."

I arch a judgmental brow at her. "Is that something you disagree with?"

"Sure, in some circumstances, but we can't overlook other elements. There's the fact that the legal system is steeped in biases. If you're rich, you can afford better representation than someone poor relying on public defenders—"

"I assure you, as a former defense attorney myself, it is substantially easier to get someone off a murder or manslaughter charge than it is to get them convicted. The bar for conviction is extremely high. There is a reason conviction rates typically pale in comparison to the number of arrests made. The number of cases that make it to trial. The same goes for rape and sexual assault."

"But what about the few who do slip through the cracks?" she presses determinedly, even taking a step toward me. "One in eight people sentenced to death row are later found innocent, Professor. That's not even touching on the racial disparities that exist in our legal system. People of color—Black people—are more likely to be prosecuted for capital murder than White people, especially if the victim in the case is White themselves."

I fold my arms and lean against my desk, half genuinely interested in what she has to say, and half attracted to how passionate she becomes.

I'm not sure I've ever been this turned on by legal arguments before.

"Valid," I admit. "Then what is the solution, Miss Oliver? Are you suggesting we eliminate the death penalty altogether? What about the families of victims from heinous crimes? Let's say, an obvious example in our own community, the Valentine Killer? Are you suggesting if he is really back—if he has truly returned—that should he or she be caught, they should not face the death penalty?"

Her brows knit closer, her internal conflict passing over her face. "Well... for someone who committed really heinous crimes... I'm not sure..."

"Part of critiquing legal theory, Miss Oliver, includes an understanding that the system will never be perfect. No legal system in the world is or ever can be. But typically, we strive for what best serves society. How familiar are you with ethical philosophy?" I ask. "I would argue much of our justice system is a utilitarianism approach, meaning what benefits the greater good prevails. Some innocents may slip through the cracks, but what is the relative cost to allowing a much larger number of not-so-good people to go unpunished?"

"People deserve to suffer for what they've done," she says with immediate conviction, making me tilt my head to the side. "If they've wronged others, then they do deserve to suffer."

"Interesting take considering the argument you just made against the death penalty."

"I'm against innocents being punished. I have no concern for bad people."

"How would you suggest delineating between the two?"

"We can start by working toward consistency. Equal treatment and punishment under the law."

"Noble concept. Agreed. Tell me some of your ideas."

An hour passes before we notice the time and our discussion comes to an end. Nyssa has another class coming up and I have grading to do.

"I can't remember the last time I lost track of time like this," she says bashfully. "I'm running late. This campus is massive and takes you ten minutes to get anywhere."

"It was designed that way. Castlebury was built centuries ago," I say with a wondrous glance at the chain-link chandelier that hangs from the ceiling. "Back when it was fashionable to have bookcases that led to other rooms and hidden dwellings underground. Many still exist today..."

"It sounds like you're very familiar with them."

"I've been here for quite a long time. You should hurry. You don't want to miss your class."

"Maybe we can pick up where we left off next time." She casts me a reluctant smile before we part ways.

I watch her go equally as reluctant, almost wishing she could stay longer.

The fact that we remained so engaged we exchanged ideas and discussed legal theory for an hour does nothing to quell my obsession. It merely fuels it further.

Nyssa challenged my positions and put me on the defensive. All things I welcomed as I countered what she said and left her to consider my perspectives in the same way.

It's the first of many after-class discussions like this.

In the coming days, Nyssa makes a habit of remaining behind after the rest of the class clears out. She always approaches my desk in the same hesitant manner, clutching her books, wearing such an inquisitive look on her beautiful face that I'm powerless to turn her away.

How can I when she's begun to take up more and more space in my head?

In the coming nights, I make habits of my own.

As Nyssa dozes peacefully, out cold after hours of late-night studying, I creep closer to her bed and gently lay a blanket over her. Her books are splayed out around her. Peaches has found her spot closer to Nyssa's head, nestled between some throw pillows.

The room's dark enough that I slink back into the shadows.

She stirs minutes later as if suddenly remembering she had been in the middle of reading. She sits up and rubs at her eyes before snapping shut the books and twisting off the reading lamp by her bed.

I stay still, hidden by the window drapes, as she wanders the dark space confidently, having memorized the placement of every stick of furniture. She's awake but not entirely so by how she shuffles into the bathroom to pee and quickly wrap up her hair.

She returns to dig out a pair of pajamas from a drawer in her dresser.

I resist the urge to make myself obvious as she changes mere feet away from me.

The skirt she'd worn today and fallen asleep in slides to the ground. She steps out of it and slips on a pair of pajama pants. The same happens with the sweater she's had on. It crumples to the ground as she stands so close by, completely topless.

Hot arousal rushes me and I become a little light-headed. I blink through it, standing firm as I drink in the beautifully erotic sight.

The situation might be mundane—Nyssa Oliver changing before bedtime—but I've begun to find everything she does fascinating in some way.

Her body would fit mine so perfectly. Her supple curves flush against my straight, lean frame. I would worship her ample, teardrop-shaped breasts and rounded hips. I'd appreciate her in ways an oaf like Samson Wicker never could...

I'm practically erect in my pants as Nyssa tugs her pajama top over her head.

She sets aside the legal books she's been reading and crawls into bed next to her ginger cat. Peaches seems to be much more situationally aware than her mother; her bright green eyes blink over at the window as if she's aware I'm in the room with them.

Luckily, we've become friends.

The purr she makes has Nyssa giving off a small sleepy laugh. The last dim light in the room, the lamp on the other bedside table, gets turned off and total darkness follows.

I wait another twenty minutes, until I'm sure Nyssa's deeply asleep, before I finally leave her bedroom.

The key to her apartment, along with my other methods of tracking her, have made it incredibly easy to do what I'm doing.

Arrive minutes before she does and then spend the evening watching her.

Even on nights I'm not inside her apartment doing it, I'm miles away doing so from her iCloud and AirTag and the camera I've installed.

All things I rationalized as being for her benefit. For her safety and well-being considering her douchebag boyfriend couldn't be trusted.

But things, if I'm being honest, I've done for my pleasure.

To feed this... *infatuation* that's quickly growing.

By the next faculty meeting, I launch my next endeavor I've aptly titled: Ruin Samson Wicker's Life.

"Most of you are aware of what we will be discussing," says Pamela Williamson, our faculty head. She peers around the room with a grim tightness about her face. "We received screenshots of messages between two students about their plans for this Halloween party. These students have been identified as Samson Wicker and Lucas Cummings. Neither one has been notified their private messages have been anonymously sent to faculty."

"I would think they deserve to know," pipes up Professor Burrows. "Their speech is their own. It is a violation of their First Amendment rights—"

"We are aware of what rights the students do and don't have, Professor Burrows. However, that goes out the window the minute we have reason to believe they are participating in illegal and illicit activities. Drug use is one of those activities."

"My boys don't do dope," pipes up Coach Shanks, folding his veiny arms. "They know better than that. They're aware they're off the team if they pop positive."

"We would like to think they are. But if these messages are true, we must act."

Another professor by the name of Percy Barker raises his hand. "Could they be fake messages?"

"That's possible too. But we've had the campus cyber officer look at them, and at this time, he doesn't believe they are."

I hide my smirk behind the peppermint mocha I've snagged at the student union. It's not uncommon that I remain on the sidelines as other faculty members debate the importance of staff potlucks and other mundane things.

But it's never been more entertaining to listen to them squawk at each other.

Particularly since it's a mess of my own creation.

I screenshotted the messages Wicker and Cummings exchanged. *I* sent the anonymous email to the faculty distro.

As Coach Shanks practiced with the rugby team on the field last Wednesday, it was me who casually strolled into the male locker room and planted the drug evidence in the side pouches of their gym bags.

It was me who snuck a few milligrams into the protein shakes I found in their lockers.

A party drug called Euphoria crushed into powder substance and stored in little plastic baggies.

I didn't typically have Euphoria on hand—or any drug beyond over-the-counter medication—but there was one thing being the older brother of a recreational user like

Theo had taught me. It was that it was shockingly easy to get your hands on drugs off the street if you knew where to look.

One quick deal under the veil of secrecy, and I was in possession of what I needed to sabotage Samson Wicker.

"We'll have to drug test the team," Pamela Williamson says, sighing. "That's the only way we find out for certain. We'll do the whole team just to be sure. Shanks, you'll have to inform them at practice later today."

The roided-out coach scoffs. "If they pop negative, you're going to have egg on your face, Pam. And potentially a lawsuit on your hands."

"We'll worry about that after the drug test. And after we search their lockers."

I walk out of the meeting practically with a pep in my step... or as much pep as someone as brooding and disgruntled as me can possibly have.

The October afternoon has turned gray and rainy, but while students prop open their umbrellas and scurry across campus, I'm taking my time. I stroll through with my peppermint mocha and grin noticing Samson Wicker and his oafish group of jock pals camped out at the student union.

He has no clue what's coming his way.

I pull out my phone and check the latest on Nyssa's iCloud. She's posted a cryptic message on her Instagram.

All things happen for a reason.

Complete with a vase of flowers haloed by natural sunlight pouring in through a window. It's a beautiful photo only an artistic mind like hers would think to capture. But she has no clue how true her blurb really is. How it so aptly fits her situation and the ways in which I'm helping her.

If only you knew all the things I'm doing for you.
Someday... you will.
Someday... you'll thank me.

I carry on toward my BMW in the parking lot.

It's been two days since I last stopped by Nyssa's apartment. I'm a man looking to sate my appetite.

One quick visit can't hurt. One fleeting moment to explore her private space again, taking in the scents, sights, and other sensory details.

According to the AirTag, Nyssa's out shopping with the likes of Heather Driscoll for the afternoon.

Peaches slinks around my ankle when I enter. I scratch behind her pointed ears just where she likes and pull out the salmon flavored cat treat I've brought her.

Yet another way I'm bettering Nyssa's life—I'm pampering her precious kitty without her even knowing I'm doing so.

Over the next hour, I study the latest developments on Nyssa's sculptures. She's started on yet another new piece, this one another recreation of the human form.

It's a female torso that has the delicate and svelte curve only someone as talented as Nyssa could pull off. But for all its beauty, there's a morbid element too.

While the right side of the torso is smooth and whole, the left side has a hole carved out as if depicting a wound of some kind.

A gaping hole where the heart should be.

My head slants to the side as I study the piece and imagine the meaning.

At the turn of the hour, I decide I've been greedy enough and should get going if I'm to avoid her. According to her AirTag, she and Heather have left the downtown area where their favorite boutiques are located.

On my way out, I notice a collection of old school newspapers dating back twenty years. I stop in my tracks and pick up the top paper to read the headline. Predictably, it's about Valentine.

Assistant Dean Roger Fairchild Found Slain in His Office

"Hmmm," I say aloud to no one, "why would you have these, Miss Oliver? Doing some research on Valentine, are you? Is that why you've been at the library so often?"

I make it out of her apartment and stride toward my car once I'm on the ground floor. Mere footsteps away, a familiar voice calls out to me.

Not Nyssa. Not even Theo.

"Theron, surprised to see you here," says Veronica. "Visiting a student?"

Tension cinches my spine, making me stop mid stride. I cast her a cold look. "My sister. She does manage the building. I could ask you the same question, Veronica. Make a habit of hanging around college apartments?"

The woman I'd once been foolishly engaged to sniffles as she crosses her arms, her dark locks framing her pale face. "Have you forgotten my family owns this building? I can come by any time I want."

"But you can't come by my home any time you want. If I ever catch you near me again—or my BMW that you keyed—you'll regret it."

Her eyes narrow. "You are unbelievable."

"No, Veronica, the only unbelievable thing is that I was ever fooled by you. That won't happen again."

I turn my back on her and finish my walk down the front path. The alarm on my BMW beeps as I approach the door and get in.

Veronica watches me in bitter silence for so long, I assume she's going to let me go with no more protests. It's as the engine starts that she calls out her own version of a farewell.

"Ever think it's not me, Theron?" she says. "Ever think the problem is you?"

I slam my foot on the gas and drive off, leaving her in the past where she belongs.

11

NYSSA

FIRE OF LOVE - JESSE JO STARK

"You look sexy as fuck," Macey says when she sees me in my costume. She's seated on my bed, already wearing hers. Slutty police officer complete with thigh high boots and a garter belt. Her shiny patent leather police cap leans lopsided on her head, though she doesn't seem to care. She's nibbling on a piece of licorice as I stroll out of the closet and twirl around for her full assessment. "I didn't think you had it in you, Oliver."

"Had what in me?" I ask, stepping toward my floor length mirror.

"The whole slutty Halloween costume thing. It seems so… beneath you."

That's because it is.

…but I also know the rules of the game.

I uncap the top of my lip gloss, carefully applying a shiny coat to my lips. "It's Halloween, Macey. You're overthinking things. Everyone dresses like this for Halloween."

"Since when are you everyone?"

"You're one to talk, Miss Supermodel."

She laughs, her string of licorice dangling from between

her teeth. "Really? Because supermodels are known to be classy."

"Are you saying I'm classy?" I smirk at her from over the tip of my shoulder.

"I'm saying..." she pauses to choose her words carefully. "Don't take this the wrong way, Nyssie. But I'm saying you've got a stick up your ass sometimes. Even by Heather's standards. And she's Queen Stick Up The Ass. Maybe that's why you're best friends."

Are we?

"Heather's best friend is Katelyn. Haven't they known each other the longest?"

Macey snorts again as if I've told a joke, then lays back on my bed to busy herself with her phone.

"What's up between them anyway?" I ask. "Heather's been icing out Katie."

"Damned if I know. I've got my own shit going on. You know my pill-popping mother's threatening to divorce my father? Like she's going anywhere. He'll just cut off the credit cards."

As is so often the case in this world, around these people, I pretend I'm listening. Really, I'm studying my outfit and making sure my hair and makeup are on point.

I'm thinking about what's to come tonight at this party.

It's the annual Halloween party the fraternity throws at their house. Every year they do, some kind of scandal emerges. An almost fatal case of alcohol poisoning or a drug overdose. Some poor girl making date rape allegations. Some younger fraternity brother coming forward about extreme hazing and violence.

This is my third year at Castlebury, yet it's the first year I'll be attending. I wouldn't if I didn't think I could work the situation to my advantage.

Make my next strategic move.

I screw back on the cap to my lip gloss and take one last look at myself.

Macey's right—I've gone the thotty route. My legs look long and shapely, my plaid mini skirt several inches shorter than I like. The same can be said for the tight button-up shirt I'm wearing that emphasizes my bust and the suspenders that only draw attention to the area. I've got a pair of what the costume store called 'nerdy' glasses on and platform Maryjane heels that give me five extra inches.

I make for a convincing naughty schoolgirl.

There's a honk outside my apartment's bedroom window. Macey scrambles over first.

"It's Claude! Ready?"

"Ready," I answer, nodding. Though my insides churn like I'm onboard a ship at sea.

I follow Macey downstairs. Along the way, she turns back toward me to check if I'm really okay.

"You know Claude's cool with Lucas, right?"

"Why would I care?"

"Lucas and Samson are practically brothers."

I shrug, pretending I'm distracted by my reflection in the elevator's chrome finish. Macey gets the hint and drops the subject altogether.

Claude greets both of us with a mellow, raspy toned, "What's up?"

Mom messages me as I'm buckling my seatbelt in the back row of his Jeep Wrangler. She means well, but sometimes I have to remind her I'm fine on my own. I don't need her worrying about me.

> I'll call you tomorrow.

For a second I even consider turning off my phone, or at least my geotag location, then I decide against it.

I've thought about tonight from every possible angle. Now's not the time to start throwing myself off.

Claude blasts his headache-inducing party jams playlist off Spotify that he seems so proud of, grinning broadly at us as we fly down the city streets. By Macey's non-reaction, she's used to his manic driving.

Me, not so much.

I grip the overhead handle and remind myself to order an Uber on my way home later tonight.

Assuming everything goes according to plan.

We arrive outside the frat house with screeching brakes, drawing jeers from the guys gathered on the front lawn.

Great. A whole audience to watch us.

I blow out a breath and open the back door. Macey's doing the same from the front of the Jeep. She immediately links arms with me as if in solidarity. Two girls arriving on the scene in scantily clad skirts to the shiny-eyed leers from the frat brothers nearby.

We're not the only ones. Another group of giggly girls in barely there costumes teeter down the sidewalk in sky-high heels, also with arms linked.

As we head toward the open doorway of the large red brick house, we're granted a preview of the crowds donning their own costumes from pirates to zombies and devils.

But one thing there's no shortage of is the skintight ensembles almost all the girls are wearing.

I blend in perfectly—and maybe that's what also makes me stick out like a sore thumb.

My hands itch to pull my skirt further down my thighs and anxiety expands in my chest like a balloon the deeper into the crowd we make it.

But I never slip up. I keep my mask on, smiling and nodding my head to the music thumping from the stereos.

We push our way through the entrance hall. Macey's scanning the area for anyone we know. Katelyn sees us first and beelines over, her face sparkling from the shimmery makeup she's put on. She's done her best to look as mermaid-esque as possible in a seashell bralette and a sequined skirt that hugs her wider hips.

"Macey, you came!" She gives Macey a quick hug before turning to me. "Nyssie, I didn't know you were coming out tonight. You usually never come to stuff like this."

"I dragged her out," Macey laughs, linking our arms again.

"Does, um, Heather know you're here?"

I act as if I'm more interested in the music and party scene around us, barely looking in Katelyn's direction as I wave distantly at someone else I know.

"Does it matter if I am?"

"Yes... no... I mean... excuse me."

She bustles off as quickly as she's approached us, swallowed up by the others. I finally turn to Macey.

"What was that about?"

Macey's hardly noticed. "I couldn't tell you. You know how Katie gets."

But I'm already aware of why Katelyn reacted the way she did. It's the sole reason I decided to come out tonight when I'd rather be home. I'd prefer to be spending Halloween night in the warm comfort of my apartment, working on my next art project and watching movies. An evening that would be much more enjoyable than freezing my ass off in this skimpy schoolgirl outfit.

"Let's dance," Macey calls out.

The thumping music has only grown louder in the last fifteen minutes since we arrived. She tugs on my arm 'til I'm staggering alongside her toward the massive horde gathered in the living room of the fraternity house.

It's full of Castlebury students dancing and grinding, even making out with whatever person they've latched onto. I'm surrounded by sweaty writhing bodies on either side, practically shoved by the crowd if I don't move along with them.

Macey joins in, shaking her hips and screaming when the next song that comes on happens to be one of her favorites.

Halfway through, we're both grabbed by frat brothers looking to dance. Macey goes along with it while I shrug out of the arm that's been slung over my shoulder.

"No thanks," I say, offering a consolatory smile.

He simply rolls his eyes and moves onto the next tipsy college girl willing to entertain him.

I'm able to slip away through a crack in the crowd, grateful for the opening as I make my escape into another hall. The earthy musk of marijuana tickles my nose, a light haze of smoke lingering in the cramped space, but I plunge on 'til I'm able to make it far enough away that the party feels like an afterthought.

Only thirty minutes and I already feel like I'm drowning.

It's just another reminder why I've never been big on the college party scene.

I've always felt... out of place. Too cognizant of what

goes on, like I'm witnessing people who aren't my peers but people I know better than.

Maybe I do.

Maybe I am the old soul Heather and Macey always jokingly say I am. I'm the one who's here from the past to hold them accountable. I'm the one who's going to make them pay for what they've done to me.

Us.

I set off through the noisy, humid frat house, on a mission. My vision tunnels 'til the finish line is all I see. Everything else in the vicinity becomes a blurred non-factor.

None of it matters so long as I haven't held them accountable.

A shot of adrenaline flows through me as I stop by a drunken Lucas Cummings on the foot of the stairs. He's swaying in place, clutching a red plastic cup, barely able to keep his hazy eyes open. He clearly gave up on his costume a long time ago, his ghost face mask shoved up over his head of unruly curls.

"Have you seen Samson?"

"Hey, Nyssa," he slurs. "Wazzup?"

"Samson? Where is he?"

"Up... bur-burrpp..." he belches, reeking of beer and weed, then tries again. "Upstairs."

I don't bother with a *thank you*, rushing past him on my way up the stairs. Lucas shouts more garbled words after me. None of which I bother trying to decipher.

The second floor landing is more chaotic than the first. People in all sorts of costumes press themselves against the wall in the middle of heavy groping and making out, like they have no concept of privacy, or simply don't care for any.

Others loiter in the space, chatting, smoking, even on the verge of a fistfight as two guys shove at each other.

I start twisting doorknobs, one door after the other in a long line that stretches on down the hall. Some are locked while others open to reveal more partying, more indiscretions going on. In the bathroom, a girl I recognize as Hannah Fochte kneels before a toilet puking her guts out. A threesome's happening in the bedroom on the left.

I keep going until I come up on the last door and push it open to find exactly what I'm looking for.

Heather and Samson jump apart as soon as the door flings open and they realize they're no longer alone. Samson scrubs a hand over his face, squinting in the same kind of inebriated confusion as Lucas. Heather shrieks and turns away to fix the top portion of her sparkly dress.

She's dressed up as Barbie.

Something that makes me laugh in the moment. The dark sound comes out of me with a shake of my head and curl of my lip.

"Just as I thought," I say. "So how long has this been going on? How long have you been fucking my best friend, Samson? How long have you been fucking him, Heather? Did you really think I wouldn't put two and two together? All the texting you've been doing? All the times you said you were meeting someone special? The secrecy and weird behavior?"

Heather's strawberry blonde locks hang more disheveled than usual. She swats hair out of her face as she says, "Nyssie, you've got no idea what you're—"

"Shut up," I snap. "I don't want to hear shit from you. Either of you. It's all over. For real this time."

"Nyssie!"

"Hang on!"

I rush out of the room as abruptly as I arrived. Their voices fade among the dozens of others, drowned out by the laughter, chatter, and most of all, the blaring music. I've never regretted a pair of heels more as I strut down the hall and then the stairs.

"Nyssa, slow the fuck down!"

I speed up, zigzagging down the obstacle course of a hallway that's the ground floor. Vaguely, I'm aware it's Samson coming up behind me.

Not that it matters—I don't want to hear anything he has to say. Tonight was simply about exposing him and Heather for what they are. The same selfish, cruel, fucked up people they've always been.

It runs in their families.

Now, I get the chance to use their betrayals to my advantage in my own special way.

I make it outside in a cool rush of air and several catcalls from fraternity guys still hanging out on the lawn. I have no idea where I'm headed except anywhere but here. Anywhere but the frat house that reeks of booze, vibrates with music deafening enough to give you a headache, and full of some of the most treacherous people I've ever met in my life.

"Nyssa, where do you think you're going?!"

"Stay away from me, Samson!" I yell from over my shoulder, crossing the barren street. Trees and bushes make up the opposite side, eventually leading into the largest courtyard of the university. Otherwise known as the quickest way to escape the fraternity.

If only Samson took a hint and gave up.

As I cross the street, he jogs after me, more determined than ever. It takes him seconds to reach me as I navigate the grassy terrain in my heels. His sausage-like fingers clench shut on my upper arm, spinning me to face him.

"Samson, what the fuck!?"

"I'm talking to you!"

"I don't want to talk to you!" I shout, my voice louder than his. "All I wanted was proof. I wanted to know for sure what I thought was going on was going on. I know that now. So get the hell away from me."

"Not 'til I've... hic... 'til I've said what I want..." he rumbles between drunken hiccups. His grip tightens on my arm and he bows closer, his breath hot and putrid. "You walked out on me... 'member that?"

"Cut the shit! You've been messing around since *before* we broke up!"

"Yeah? So what? You didn't put out!"

"Don't touch me!" I scream, squirming in his hold to free myself.

"Look... things've been rough. Heather's been there."

"And I haven't?"

"You know... hic... they're kicking me off the team? Some drug test... hic... bullshit. You even care?"

I wrench my arm from him and start walking, trying to change course from the pine trees nearby. "If you expect me to forgive you for cheating because you failed a drug test, you're an even bigger ass than I thought you were."

"Don't walk away from me!"

"We're done, Samson! What else is there to say?"

"I'm not done!" He seizes hold of me again, his grip viselike and inescapable. "You gonna finally... hic... put out? I never... hic... got to fuck you."

"Samson, fucking let go of me! You're drunk!"

"How's that fair?" he slurs, wrapping his arms around me until I'm locked in a bearhug.

Immediately, I go into defense mode, stamping on his foot and kneeing him in the groin. Both hits land, earning deep, infuriated groans of pain out of him.

But he doesn't let me go—he grips me tighter as I struggle harder. We tip over, falling into a grassy ditch under one of the many trees.

It's the first time real panic infects my lungs. My brain. My entire being as I scream into the night and punch and kick at any part of him I can. The odds are stacked against me as soon as we're on the ground, the moment feeling insurmountable.

My wrists are no match for his large, sweaty hands as he pins me down and climbs on top of me.

"SAMSON, STOP!" I cry out as if it'll make any difference at all.

He doesn't care. He's grinning crudely as he wedges a knee between my thighs to part them, my plaid skirt having ridden up.

"One... hic... one fuck for the road," he slurs, then laughs. "You know you owe me."

He sits up on his knees long enough for his free hand to fumble with the zipper of his jeans.

I'm still writhing in a wave of panic when it happens.

Samson's unfastened his jeans and pulled his dick out. His grin widens, and he moves to lean back over me.

Someone comes up from behind before he ever gets the chance. They're clutching a giant rock they must've picked up off the ground.

A giant rock they use to bash Samson over the head hard enough there's a *crack* sound, and then another and another. His skull splitting open.

Samson loses consciousness at once, collapsing half on top of me.

Shock freezes me to the bone. I'm left paralyzed and speechless, heart beating faster than it ever has before, as I blink up into the deep shadows of the grassy area.

Familiar eyes stare down at me—dark and forbidden like a mystery that'll never be solved. Eyes that belong to none other than Professor Adler, the rock-turned-attempted-murder-weapon dripping blood as it hangs at his side.

12

THERON

CHERRY WAVES - DEFTONES

"Just once it would be cool if you weren't such a grumpy dick."

Theo's lectures always strike a balance between being stern like our mother and crass like some filthy-mouthed biker in a grungy bar. She adds a dirty look in my direction as she buckles herself into my BMW.

I insisted on driving despite the fact that it's my birthday. I needed my emergency means of escape if necessary.

"It's not some punishment, you know," she says when I answer her with stubborn silence. "It's supposed to be a joyous occasion."

"I don't celebrate my birthday. How many times do I have to tell the both of you?"

"Dad thought it would be a good idea."

"Dad also thought it would be a great idea to fuck his personal assistant. How'd that turn out for him?"

"You heard him and Mom. They have an arrangement."

"Which would explain why our mother has been overseas on a sabbatical for ten months."

"Don't expect me to explain the ins and outs of their

fucked up marriage. They've been together for a million years. They still love each other in their own way."

Theo's comment isn't worth dignifying with an answer.

She can make up as many mind-bending excuses to pacify her turmoil about our parents as she wants, but I prefer to be more grounded in reality—they're married in legal status only and have no real affection for each other.

Love has been absent from our family for as long as I can remember. I was six wondering why my parents never hugged or kissed like the parents on television. I was eight when I accidentally stumbled upon Dad and the nanny in his private library. By age ten, I stopped cooperating with the farce of a family photo we took every Christmas.

At thirteen, as I went through the ringer known as puberty, I realized I never wanted to be anything like them. Successful but miserable. Married but alone. Living a lifetime of what ifs and maybes. Sneaking around in the dark because the light meant exposure.

I wanted no part of it.

I was young, naive, hopeful in my own way, noticing the opposite sex for the first real time. Their delicate beauty as they matured alongside me captivated me. It fascinated me as I fell in love—or so I thought—with the pretty girl nice enough to smile at me.

Then it was the bookish girl who asked me about the book I was reading.

In high school, I thought of my first girlfriend as the sun that lit up my sky. I wrote her poems and gave her flowers. I would've given her the world and more if she'd only loved me back. *If* she'd only loved me the same...

It was an emerging pattern that played out in disastrous fashion the older I became. The more times I had my heart broken, crushed, stomped on, the more desperately I clung to the idea I could have what I yearned for most.

Love.

The kind of love that eluded Mom and Dad.

The one thing in their perfect, sanitized, overachieving lives that they'd never been able to accomplish—true, genuine, boundless love.

Love that ran so deep, so integrally, there was no functioning without it. It was a kind of love that you'd sacrifice anything for.

There was no earthly limit to the things you'd do in order to protect it...

My version of love is nothing like the flimsy, cardboard cutout version that's my parents' marriage.

"Since when do you cuss?" Theo asks suddenly, pulling me from my thoughts. We've merged into traffic as we drive out of the city to the fancy restaurant where we'll have dinner. "And you say I'm the filthy-mouthed biker."

I sigh, fixated on the road ahead. "You are. But so am I. Now sit tight. The sooner we make it to this place, the sooner I get to fucking leave."

Theo laughs, though she yelps as I slam on the gas and floor it. We arrive to Le Canard no more than fifteen minutes later. Dad is predictably already seated and waiting on us, his square glasses perched midway down his aquiline nose. His thin mouth is downturned like it always is, as though he's pre-disappointed about what's to come.

Neither of us have lived up to his lofty expectations—he wanted more than an apartment manager for a daughter and a law school professor for a son. Add on the fact that Theo's a lesbian and neither of us have children, and his disappointment is the palpable fourth dinner guest at the table.

"Sorry we're late, daddy," Theo says, flashing a sweet smile like she's still thirteen. She kisses him on the cheek before claiming the seat on his right.

"It's alright, Theo. I've come to expect it," he replies dryly.

I skip the hello altogether, taking the farthest seat with the kind of silent, cordial nod I give coworkers.

Dad fixes his unyielding stare on me, peering across the table as if studying a complicated math equation.

If there's one thing the brilliant and renowned district judge Thurman Adler loves, it's a problem he believes he can solve.

Somehow, he's never managed to fix me in his image.

He married young and remained married no matter how unhappy. I'm officially forty-two with no marriage to my name, no matter how unhappy, because I refuse to settle for anything less than a love worth dying for.

We're polar opposites, and I couldn't prefer it more.

"Happy birthday, Theron," he says finally, his tone lukewarm. "I'm glad you made time in your busy schedule for your sister and I."

"I would appreciate the occasion more if I celebrated birthdays," I answer. I'm just as deadpan. Equally as unimpressed and bored.

Truthfully, my mind is on one thing only on a night like tonight.

Tonight may be my birthday, but more importantly, it's Halloween—and Nyssa Oliver has plans.

So far, I've resisted checking my phone, where I've been logging into her iCloud to spy on her. I vowed I'd do what I haven't often managed to do in recent times; I'd go the rest of the night without checking on her once.

But as Dad makes forced conversation about the menu

at Le Canard and halfheartedly asks Theo about her job managing the college apartments, I give in. My resolve vanishes in a desperate intake of air and I slip my phone out of my pocket, glancing down at it from under the table.

She's tagged her location as the university campus, which means she's gone through with it. She's attending the much-talked-about costume party at the frat house. I'll never understand why she would want to sully herself at such a place, where drunk losers congregate and trouble always breaks out.

Doesn't she understand she's better than that? She's better than *them*.

Whatever the reason she wanted to attend, it's not lost on me who else will be there. My plans to frame Samson Wicker have been a success so far. He's facing removal from the team, but I won't stop there. I want him expelled.

Far away from Nyssa for the rest of his life.

The problem is, my endeavor does nothing to stop him tonight. What if Nyssa's turning up to the party *for* him?

My hand curls into a fist on the dinner table and I'm clenching my jaw. The same hot pulse of anger returns, ever intensifying the deeper down the obsessive hole I seem to fall.

If he so much as breathes in her direction...

Theo notices first. "What's that look for?"

I twitch out of my rage-induced trance, blinking to find two sets of eyes on me. Theo's curiosity and our father's shrewd analyzation. He's doing what he always does, crunching numbers, figuring out probabilities, drawing conclusions.

"There was no look," I mutter, unfurling my dinner napkin. "When will we order?"

"We're waiting on someone," Dad says. His pale eyes

light up for the first time since we've arrived. "Ah, there she is. Right on time, as asked."

I glance over my shoulder to follow where his gaze has landed.

My stomach drops as if bottomless. There's no end in sight as dread fills the void. Instant, cold, paralyzing dread that has me gaping at the woman approaching our table.

Veronica pastes a bright smile onto her angular face. "Evening, everyone." Then she cuts me a special look, her smile widening. "Happy Birthday, Theron."

It's a rarity that I'm ever speechless beyond my control.

This is one of those rare moments.

I can only stare back as she takes the final empty chair at the four-person candlelit table. Theo's jaw has dropped open, her eyes bulging. But Dad couldn't be more pleased, welcoming Veronica with kind words and a mention about the wine selection.

"How's your father doing, Veronica?" he asks. "I was reading an article about him in the paper. Is it true he's considering a career in politics?"

"My father has always dreamed big," she answers primly. "It seems natural after his successful reign in banking. Which reminds me, Theron, he's been asking about you. Maybe the three of you can go golfing again sometime."

Suddenly, it all makes sense. The special birthday dinner at Le Canard. His and my mother's recent comments about my breakup with Veronica. The surprise guest.

This is about his quest to fix me. Remake me in his image.

I need the right woman on my arm from the right family. A family as rich and prestigious as the Fairchilds, who own half of Castlebury.

It wouldn't be the first time he's done this. Veronica and I first got involved because our families pushed for us to date.

I let it happen then, but how can I possibly let it happen again?

My shock takes so long to wear off that I miss half of the conversation happening around me. Theo's launched into scolding Dad for inviting her.

"How could you? You said it would just be us!"

"I don't recall those words coming out of my mouth, Theodora."

"This bitch keyed Theron's car!"

"I would rather be a bitch than a butch," Veronica snaps back, color spreading across her cheeks.

"This butch will kick your ass if you're not careful."

"Theodora," Dad hisses. "Language."

I finally regain enough sense to check back into the moment. I rise to my feet, tossing my cloth dinner napkin on the table, the pulse of anger beating thicker and hotter off me than ever before.

My usual mild-mannered demeanor is nowhere to be found.

Dad realizes this a split second too late, his eyes flickering with unease.

"This is the last time I participate in your schemes. Both of you," I say in a mix of calm rage. "If you ever come near me again, I will do something to make you regret it. I will make things very insufferable and painful for you. Stay away from me. Stay away from my life."

I stride toward the exit with only Theo bothering to follow. Wise on their part.

I'm vibrating from the inside as I enter the blustery

night. I've contained the rage as long as I can manage and now it's busting at the seams.

"Theron," Theo pants. "What're you—"

"I'm leaving. Enjoy the rest of your dinner."

"The dinner? Your dinner! It's *your* birthday!"

"Which is why I get to leave any time I want. Have a good evening, sister. Feel free to bitch slap Veronica. She deserves it after calling you what she did."

I leave Theo staring in shock after me, sliding behind the wheel of my BMW XI.

In no time, I'm speeding on the freeway with only one destination in mind.

Nyssa's still on campus. She's at the frat house... doing who knows what.

And with who.

Samson.

I'm drunk on rage and jealousy by the time I've parked in the faculty lot and am getting out of my car. Both toxic emotions surge through me, rampant and unfettered 'til I'm blinded by them. I'm a new man altogether as I cross the courtyard, headed straight for the frat house.

What I'm about to do—how reckless I'm about to be—I'm not sure.

It wouldn't be the first time I've lost my temper. But it would be the first time I've done so publicly.

I've ripped off my mild-mannered, mysterious, intellectual mask to reveal the true obsessive living underneath.

The man who would rip his beating heart out of his chest for the woman he loves and present it to her as a gift. The man would torch the world 'til it burned down just for her if she asked. The man who comes across her in a grassy ditch, about to be attacked by the same guy I've decided to destroy, and grabs the heaviest rock on the ground.

The man who rushes up from behind and bashes in the guy's skull.

The man who is me.

I slam the boulder into the back of Samson Wicker's head as if it's of no consequence I could be murdering him in cold blood. It means nothing so long as I've rescued Nyssa. So long as it means she'll be mine.

Some would find it sickening, but I find it freeing—the big reveal where my growing infatuation unleashes itself in the form of the bloodiest, goriest romantic gesture imaginable.

Insane? Yes. Sick? Also yes.

Do I regret a thing? Never in a million years.

My hand's shaking, the rock smeared in blood that's splattered from cracking Samson's head open. He's flopped down into the grass, unconscious though twitching. Nyssa gapes up at me as if she's never seen me before.

As if she's seeing me—really, truly seeing me—for the first time.

I toss the rock into a distant bush and offer my hand to help her up.

"Professor," she murmurs, swallowing hard. "Professor."

It's all she can say. All she can do but blink and stare some more.

"Shhh. We have to get the hell out of here."

We run, fleeing into the night, far across the courtyard as if being chased. I drag Nyssa along with me as she struggles in the heels and skimpy outfit she's wearing. By the time we stop, we're gasping for air, stumbling through the door of my office.

I turn toward her, a lock of my wavy hair curled against

my brow, vaguely aware of how crazed I must look. The truth staring her in the face.

For a moment filled only by the small gap between us and the air we suck into our lungs, Nyssa doesn't move. She eyes me as though I'm a feral creature she's unsure how to handle. No doubt debating if she should run or hide or scream for help.

Instead, as the moment ends and a new one begins, she rushes toward me, throwing her arms around my neck for a searing kiss on the lips.

13
THERON
HUSH - THE MARIAS

I wake the next morning wondering if it was all just a dream.

The bright autumn light floods the bedroom. Atticus dozes in his orthopedic dog bed, curled into a fluffy donut.

The rest of the neighborhood is no different. A hush has long since fallen over the tree-lined avenue of family homes and luxury sedans.

If I didn't know any better, I'd swear I'm the only man alive on the whole block.

I lay in bed, staring up at the high vaulted ceiling, and I listen to the thumping heartbeat in my chest.

The same question turns over and over again inside my head.

Was last night real? Did it really happen?

It almost feels like there's a schism taking form. Two versions of myself that are in direct conflict with each other. The sane, rational Theron Adler who is a criminal law professor at Castlebury University, who spends his evenings reading legal journals for fun, and who otherwise avoids the public at all costs.

And the feral, easily angered, slowly spiraling Adler who can't be reasoned with. He's the one who has been leaking into my real life. Some subconscious alter ego that's slipped into the driver's seat to do the most insane, risky things.

Did I really do it? Did I really beat Samson Wicker over the head with a rock?

The ceiling above me fades out for the wooded terrain that's on campus. I'd sprinted 'til my lungs ached and burned in search of her.

Nyssa was wandering off.

She had left the frat house and was headed deep into the dense pine trees.

At night.

Halloween night.

The desperation had consumed me. Toxic emotions had driven me.

Rage and jealousy coalesced into a blinding spell that washed over me as I scoured the campus. The ceiling becomes a movie screen for the memory to play on. My frantic form projects onto the blank canvas that's the ceiling, and I watch myself dash across the dark, grassy landscape. Leaves and gravel crunch beneath my feet as I come across what I've been searching for.

Nyssa splayed on the ground. Samson Wicker on top of her.

"SAMSON, STOP!" she cried out, squirming against him.

But he didn't stop. He laughed and held her down. One of his hands to both of her wrists, and he wedged a knee between her thighs. The perfect opportunity for him to use his free hand to cop a feel.

"One... hic... one fuck for the road," he slurred. "You know you owe me."

Adrenaline rushed me. Heat erupted over my skin.

The dark scene before me blurred.

Everything except for what was about to happen on the ground—Nyssa pinned under Samson Wicker as he went to unzip his pants.

I'm not a violent man. I'm a civilized man.

I use my words. Not my fists.

Yet the vastness of the world narrowed down to that singular moment.

And in that singular moment, I lost my grip on sanity. My fingers slid over the largest rock within reach and I brought it crashing down over his skull.

Instant satisfaction filled me. So I did it again. I struck him a second time and then a third.

Samson Wicker's skull cracked open and his body slumped half on top of Nyssa.

The tunneled vision faded for a sick, twisted reality.

Nyssa gaping up at me, eyes wide in shock. Samson collapsed in the grass, blood seeping from where I'd bashed his head in.

I clench shut my eyes to avoid the projection on the ceiling, yet the images still exist.

They're too fresh in my mind, playing out like in real time.

We fled.

We galloped in the night among the deep, sweeping shadows and distant party music.

It was as though we believed if we ran fast enough, we could escape the dark truth. We could pretend what just happened never did.

There was only one place on campus where we could go—my office.

Air eluded us as we gasped for breath and turned to face each other. In the dim light of my office, I felt grotesque, like some violent beast that had spiraled out of control.

Nyssa's eyes were still wide, blinking at me with thick lashes. Her full, wine-tinged lips formed the tiniest O shape.

She was as speechless as I was.

I expected her to scream. For her to hurl cruel words at me about what a monster I'd been.

These seemed to be thoughts flitting through her head too.

Things she considered before she settled on what to do—rushing toward me for a frantic kiss.

Her arms wound around my neck, and suddenly, I was inundated with every small detail about Nyssa Oliver.

Her intoxicating scent.

Some kind of musk that was as sweet and warm as vanilla but with a woodsy hint like fresh soil. Imagery of soft cashmere and strolls in the forest immediately came to mind.

The sound of her breathing.

Small, gentle intakes of air that made my own heart stammer.

And then there was the feel of her body pressed up against mine.

God, was it like fucking *heaven*.

Her nails sunk into my forearms as she rose en pointe and her supple breasts brushed against my harder, flatter chest.

I quickly curled an arm around her to hold her in place, keeping her firmly where she was.

Her soft lips tortured mine. Her mouth opened and her tongue slipped out. The little pink ribbon swiped at my bottom lip, tracing the outline.

She was teasing me, tasting me, imploring me to do the same to her.

Heat erupted from deep inside my chest. It blazed through me, traveling the length of my body until I felt like I was on fire. I was aroused, growing erect as I released a growl.

It vibrated from my throat, a hungry and impatient sound. My hand framed her face and I seized control. I kissed her harder.

I kissed her to devour her.

Our tongues twisted. Our bodies tugged and twined around each other.

We stood propped up against my desk, kissing furiously in the warm glow of my office light.

Nyssa pulsed with seduction. Her every move ensnared me. The rake of her nails against my skin. Her pouty mouth falling open for a moan. The way it became a game of cat and mouse, where she pulled away slightly, then made me chase her for another kiss.

Another lash of her tongue as I gripped her tightly and crushed my lips to hers.

It was only our first kiss and already I couldn't get enough.

She was everything off limits and forbidden.

Everything I wasn't supposed to have.

And it only made her taste sweeter.

We unraveled against my desk. Her head tipped back and my mouth found her throat. I peppered wet, hot kisses along the slender arc, inhaling her scent, hard as steel in my pants. She clutched at my arms and shoulders like she could barely contain herself.

My mouth slid down her throat until I was sucking on the space where her neck and shoulder met.

Soft, broken moans fell from her lips and became my favorite sound. Her whole body shuddered from pleasure. Her smaller hand grabbed mine—the one that wasn't loosely collared at the base of her throat—and she brought it between her thighs.

An immediate groan sputtered out of me at the silken feel of such forbidden flesh. The heat that greeted me the closer I inched toward her most intimate area.

Her pussy.

I salivated at the mere thought, sucking greedily at her throat, kissing any patch of skin I could. My hand continued, slipping closer until I was cupping her pussy through the cotton fabric of her panties, and she was shuddering all over again.

"More, Professor," she panted, nails scratching up my forearms.

I returned to her mouth to silence her.

A harsh kiss that was almost like a punishment. A twisted reprimand coming from her teacher.

So naughty. So wrong. Yet it felt so fucking good in the moment.

We shared in a groan as we traded hot kisses, and my hand slipped inside her panties. She widened her thighs to welcome me.

I was hard enough to come beforehand. When the pads of my fingers slid over the soft, slick folds of her pussy, it took everything I had to hold off.

Every ounce of control inside my body bore down on me and urged restraint.

I poured the unfettered temptation into our kisses, biting her lip and stroking her tongue with mine. All while my hand was busy inside her panties. I was rubbing her clit in slow, torturous circles and making her squirm.

"Professor," she murmured as if it were the only word she remembered.

"Shhhh," I silenced. Then I kissed her again. "You speak when you're told, Miss Oliver. Right now, all you're to do is come. Come on my damn fingers."

We were lost to the moment, lost to the desires which ruled us.

It didn't matter how wrong it was. It didn't matter that, come the light of day, we'd be riddled with regrets.

All that mattered was that right then, in that moment, it felt good.

"So good," I groaned against her lips. "You're so wet. Soaked through. Who gave you permission?"

I had slipped two fingers inside her. I was sliding them in and out of her. She was writhing and panting for air, her brown skin warm to the touch. Her once pinned back curls were no longer held down. Instead they were framing her face.

I played with her pussy, learning every tweak and graze that brought her to the edge.

Drawing back, I watched the pleasure flicker across her gorgeous face.

It was just as pleasurable for me—the soft, soaked texture of her pussy made me think about what she would feel like encasing my dick.

Another layer of torture that made me want to come.

Our kisses turned chaotic while we raced toward an ending. She thrust her hips back and forth and my fingers pumped in and out. We developed a rhythm that was faster, more aggressive by the second. The harder I rubbed her clit, the deeper my fingers curled, the more impatiently she rocked her hips toward me.

The desk legs scraped against the floor. The mug holding my pens slid to the edge, then tipped over altogether and smashed into a dozen broken pieces of ceramic. We held onto each other as we kissed and I finger-fucked her to orgasm.

The pleasure we had been working toward exploded for the both of us.

She came on my fingers, nice and slick, her pussy quivering. I gathered the pearly essence between the pads of my fingers, then slipped them past her lips so she could taste herself. I made her suckle, holding my dark, heated gaze before I dipped them into my own mouth and savored the forbidden sweetness.

It was at that exact moment the spell dissolved.

The lust-driven trance was broken, and we came to our senses. I'd come in my pants during the heat of the moment, and she was in equal disarray. We spent the next tense few minutes straightening our clothes and avoiding eye contact.

I offered to drive her home…

The memory ends just as quickly as our passion-fueled encounter had.

I'm left still in bed, listening to the loud silence of my neighborhood.

For the rest of the day I'm on pins and needles. I'm unable to stop thinking about last night. My usual Saturday routine doesn't suffice. The errands feel pointless. The books I've planned to read fail to hold my attention.

I take Atticus for a walk around the block and find my pulse beating fast. Urges fill me to the brim. It's the compulsion to pull out my phone and check Nyssa's cloud. Obsessively watch over her social media for a clue of what she's up to today. Drive by her apartment to see her... even if she doesn't see me.

"No," I whisper sternly to myself. "You'll see her Monday."

On Sunday, I exhaust myself working out. Burning pent up energy. Keeping my body moving so that my mind can't wander to her. I run eight miles on the trails winding around the pine forest and then another two when I take Atticus for his daily walk.

By the time my head hits the pillow Sunday night, I'm depleted. I'm quick to fall asleep, aware that in exactly ten hours, Nyssa Oliver will walk through the doors of my classroom.

At ten a.m. sharp, I'm seated behind my desk, waiting. Other students mill inside clutching their books and bags and caffeinated beverages. I couldn't care less, hardly paying them any mind.

The moment Nyssa strolls into the cavernous room, my skin's heating up. My gaze is locked on her, tracking her every step toward her desk. She spares me no glance, taking her seat beside Heather Driscoll like this is any other class.

Not the class of the professor she was kissing forty-eight hours ago.

The two girls avoid each other too—Heather stares anywhere but at Nyssa, and she does the same.

I can barely hold my composure enough to start the lesson. Jason Hendricks has to clear his throat and ask if class will be beginning before I come to my senses.

"Yes," I say, almost dazed. "Today we will be picking up where we left off. We will be discussing more about the model penal code."

For the duration of the class, I'm waiting on Nyssa to raise her hand. Every time I ask a question, I pause long enough for her to do so, even as other students raise theirs. She never takes me up on the offer. For the first time since the semester began, she doesn't participate at all in class.

The room begins to empty once time is up and everyone gathers their things. Heather Driscoll flips her hair over her shoulder and struts out of the room as if she's important enough to draw attention.

But I'm much more fixated on Miss Oliver.

I appear at her desk as the last student wanders out of the classroom. My arms are folded behind my back and my expression is tight but controlled. "I expected you to participate today during the discussion."

She barely glances up at me. Sliding her books into her leather bag, she busies herself with fastening it shut. "Oh, I wasn't feeling like it today."

"Something wrong?" I ask.

"No," she answers vaguely, "just wasn't in the mood."

I pause, letting the seconds tick by. I cast a cautious glance over my shoulder to ensure we're truly alone. "Would you like to go for coffee? Somewhere not in town."

Her eyes flick back up to me, brows knitting. "Coffee? Why would we go for coffee?"

The hackles on the back of my neck rise. "Why would we?" I repeat slowly. "Because... because Friday."

"I was at the frat party," she recites tonelessly. She rises from the small L-shaped desk, sliding her bookbag over her shoulder. "I don't know what you're talking about, Professor."

A short laugh slips out of me. "Really, Miss Oliver? We were in my off—"

"I have to go," she says. "Enjoy the rest of your day, Professor."

I stand back, flabbergasted as she rushes past me, straight for the door.

What the hell was that? Is she really pretending like Friday never happened?

Bitterness pools inside me as its own brand of venom.

My top lip curls in a snarl. "Miss Oliver, you know better than that. If I have to remind you, I will gladly do so."

It's nine p.m. on Tuesday night, and I'm waiting for Nyssa inside her apartment. I've chosen the living room drapes for now, in hopes she won't need to pry them open so late into the night. But I'm more concerned with the fact that she's not home yet.

Her classes ended this afternoon. Any known social engagements hours ago.

She was having dinner with a friend from the art group she's a part of and then she was supposed to make her way home.

I grit my teeth and check my phone. She's gradually migrating across town, though she spent far longer downtown than I anticipated. Was she meeting someone else? Someone I wasn't aware of?

My mind fills with the thousand different possibilities. A girl like Nyssa Oliver has limitless options. She's beautiful, smart, popular, and well-entrenched among the elite circles in Castlebury. Though it seems like she and Driscoll are having a rough patch, she's close enough to others to manage just fine.

I'm still obsessing over this mystery meeting when the

lock clicks in her door and the doorknob twists. A second later, the front door falls open and Nyssa wanders inside, already tugging off her scarf and coat. She barely remembers to lock the door again before she's padding down the hall sighing and stretching her arms in the air.

I peek out slightly from behind the window drapes, otherwise so still and silent I might as well be a statue.

My ears pick up every sound in the modest-sized college apartment. The trickling sound of water drifts over from the bathroom and the thud of opening and shutting cabinets follows. She's pulling out the items for her nighttime routine.

It's not until I'm certain she's in the shower that I step out from behind the thick window drapes. My steps are ghost-like, very light and soundless. I slowly drift toward the scent that permeates the air—her sweet, woodsy musk that makes me hard upon inhaling.

Nyssa indulges in her hot shower.

I'm lurking in the distance, out of sight but still able to steal a peek.

She stands under the heated spray of water like it's the best feeling in the world. It's certainly one of the best sights. The water cascades over her naked body, thick droplets splashing along the curve of her pert breasts and down the valley of her flat stomach.

I lick my lips and feel the arousal pulsing in my veins.

The moment couldn't be more forbidden, yet I could never bring myself to turn away.

Now that I've had a taste of Nyssa Oliver, I can't possibly give her up.

I must have her.

She takes her time lathering up her loofah and basking

in the clouds of steam. Once she's in long enough for her fingertips to prune, she reaches for a bath towel.

I retreat back into the hall, biding my time, using my senses. The second she comes too close, I draw back and slip into the nearest hiding spot.

She emerges from the bathroom still wrapped in her towel, her skin glistening from the buttery body lotion she's applied.

I'm watching in secret fascination as the towel falls and she replaces it with a large T-shirt. Her ginger cat meows and scampers over to join her on the bed.

"Peaches." She smiles, scooping the cat up into her lap. "How was your day, my sweet girl?"

I hold my breath, hoping the feline won't somehow lead her to me.

In order to avoid any issues like before, every time I visit I've brought her a can of sardines. My peace offering that she seemed to accept.

Nyssa spends a few minutes checking her phone, then it's lights out. She reaches over and twists off the antique glass lamp that sits on her bedside table.

Darkness blooms. Shadows provide cover.

The tension gathered in my shoulders lessens. I step out from where I'd hidden in the hall closet and creep to the edges of her bedroom door. She's left it partially ajar. My hand wraps around the handle and I ease it open so slowly, a minute passes before I'm done.

Stepping toward the foot of her bed, I make out the silhouette of her in the dark.

Nyssa's a stomach sleeper—she lays flat on her stomach, cheek pressed into her pillow, arms curled underneath. Peaches sleeps dutifully by her head. The duo breathes gently in the night's silence.

Sounds I find strangely soothing.

Nyssa thought she could pretend Halloween night never happened.

But she's unaware how deep my preoccupation with her goes. I didn't turn up by accident to rescue her from Samson Wicker.

I was tracking her every move that night.

Just like I'm listening to her every breath tonight.

Carefully, I inch closer until I'm at the side of her bed. My hand extends to gently stroke her cheek. The touch is featherlight. Barely a graze.

I'm not sure what I can do to make Nyssa Oliver understand there's a genuine connection between us.

I'm not even sure how we can possibly have anything meaningful given she's my student and I'm her professor.

But none of that truly matters. All that matters is that Miss Oliver is mine and mine alone…

Nyssa hardly spares time to dawdle in the morning. Her alarm goes off and she's leaping out of bed in a flurry of movement. She buzzes from her closet to the bathroom in the middle of dressing for the day.

Shimmying into a pair of distressed denim, she tugs on a fuzzy sweater and then rushes into the kitchen. Peaches meows her dissatisfaction as her owner has little time to spend petting and feeding her.

"I promise I'll be home earlier tonight, baby girl," Nyssa says. "I've got class. Water and food bowls refilled. Behave yourself!"

A smirk creeps onto my face from where I'm stationed

behind the same window drapes I first hid behind last night.

It's charming that Nyssa has entire conversations with her cat. I often do the same with Atticus.

The door thuds shut, and she's gone.

Minutes pass before I reveal myself, ensuring she's truly not returning.

Peaches spots me at once. The orange cat trots over to me as if we're now friends.

Pride swells inside my chest. I crouch low and stroke her along her spine.

"Good girl, Peaches," I say. "You didn't tell your mother about me. Next time, I'll bring you *two* cans of sardines."

She purrs her approval.

Nyssa's not the only one running late this morning.

As I finally leave her apartment, there's forty-two minutes until my first class of the day begins. I rush to my BMW several blocks down, trying my damnedest to ignore my phone when it rings. Dean Rothenberg flashes onto the screen.

I clench my jaw and begrudgingly answer. "Yes?"

"Theron," he says, "I'm glad I was able to reach you."

"Is there some reason you'd think you wouldn't be able to?"

"Well... it's just you're usually at the school by now."

"I'm missing your point, August."

"You've heard about what happened on Halloween, haven't you?" he asks, his tone grimmer than usual. "You know, the student that was attacked?"

"Right. I did hear something about that..."

"Samson Wicker. He was bludgeoned over the head. He barely survived, but he's awake now."

Tension fills me like lead, my body stiff. "Does he remember what happened?"

"Unfortunately, not yet. So far, no witnesses either."

Excellent.

"It's terrible what happened," I say. "But I'm not sure why you've called me, August."

"I've been spreading word to most of the faculty. We're trying to get ahead of the story before the media publishes it and it hits the public."

"What exactly are you talking about?"

Dean Rothenberg sighs. "The perpetrator. We think it was another attempt by him, except he failed to finish the job. The Valentine Killer—he's officially back."

14

NYSSA

MY KINK IS KARMA - CHAPPELL ROAN

Samson doesn't regain consciousness for three and a half days. I'm en route to tort when I receive a call from Katelyn telling me he's awake.

"He's in bad shape, Nyssie," she sobs. "Oh gosh, why does this happen to good people?"

I bite my tongue before pointing out that Samson Wicker is anything but good. While he was technically 'attacked' and put into a short-term coma, he was far from innocent. If Professor Adler hadn't shown up out of nowhere, he would've forced me to have sex with him.

He would've *raped* me...

All because I refused to accept his cheating ways. Because I called him out on sleeping with my best frenemy.

That's beside the fact that Samson Wicker is an all-around terrible human being. He's as insufferable as the rest of the vultures in Castlebury.

The past overtakes the present as I ditch tort and catch a rideshare to the hospital.

It was Samson Wicker who stepped forward to deal the final blow—his arms thrust out to give me a rough shove into the dirt.

I tumbled to the ground, mud splattering onto the second-hand dress I had thought was so pretty when I put it on that morning...

On Friday night, for a second time in my life, Samson had knocked me to the dirt. He sought to hurt me...

Professor Adler might not understand what he did showing up when he did, but he was interjecting himself in decades-old trauma. He was rescuing me in that moment from my tormentor.

As far as I'm concerned, Samson's concussion and cracked open skull aren't enough karma for what he's done. He deserves to go down in a fiery blaze like the rest of them.

I'll do everything within my power to ensure he does.

I show up to his hospital room to find Katie and Macey coming out. Macey has an arm tossed around Katie's shoulders as she quakes from her sobs.

"Nyssie," Macey says the second she spots me. "We were wondering when you'd come by. Samson's asking for you."

I barely conceal the incredulous quirk of my brow. "He is, is he?"

"Katie, why don't you go clean up your face in the bathroom? I'll come find you."

The mousy brunette nods between choked sobs and dabbing at her eyes with the tissues she's clutching. She plods off down the corridor, the sniffling sound she makes following her every step of the way.

Macey waits 'til she's sure Katie's gone before she speaks. "I get you and Samson are having issues right now."

"Issues?" I interrupt despite myself. "You mean like him cheating on me?"

"You know how Heather is. She sleeps around. Stealing men is her thing."

"Macey, a man can't be stolen unless he *wants* to be," I snap. "Samson made his choice. He stuck his dick in Heather—and probably other girls—and a concussion doesn't change that."

She folds her arms, her expression puckered. "All I'm saying is, people make mistakes."

"They do. I don't hate Samson."

Lies.

"But that doesn't mean I have to accept his cheating."

Nice save.

"I'm here, right?" I ask, tone blunt and unapologetic. "I care about his well-being."

...and we're back to lying.

"I want to make sure he's okay," I say. "I want to speak to him too."

Macey sighs, still with a dissatisfied bend to her mouth, but she nods. "Maybe you guys can talk it out. Come to a new understanding."

It takes a great amount of restraint to keep from rolling my eyes. I let Macey pass me by with a mention that she's going to find Katie, then I venture into Samson's room.

A calmness washes over me. More than the usual kind of calm that leaves you feeling peaceful and devoid of stressors.

It's a calm that's commanding—if such a thing exists—a calm that's born from the knowledge I'm in control the moment I walk into the room and find that we're alone.

Samson's propped up by a stack of pillows, haloed by the natural light from the hospital window. He's got IVs stuck into his arms and a thick bandage wrapped around his head. The TV's on, but it might as well be off for how much he's paying attention to it.

I come up on the side of his bed. Sensing my presence, his bleary eyes drift over to me.

"Nyssa..." he mumbles. He sounds like he has cotton in his mouth. "Hey... you came..."

"Did you think I wouldn't?"

"Nyssa..." he swallows audibly. "I didn't... mean to..."

"To what, Samson?" I ask. "Cheat on me? With my best friend, by the way."

He shakes his head, his lids hanging lower as if the medication's taking over.

I take no pity on him. I'm not here for mercy. I'm here to make one thing and one thing only clear.

"You're sorry," I say. "Is that what you expect me to believe?"

"I was drinking..."

"And you attacked me. You pushed me into the dirt. You held me down and *laughed*. One fuck for the road, right? I owe you, right?"

His nostrils flare, his usually ruddy skin blanching. He has no words. No real defense. But awareness lives in his bleary gaze.

He knows exactly what he did.

Even if he doesn't know who did what to him...

"Let's get one thing straight, Samson," I say, cutting a cautious glance over my shoulder. We're as alone as ever.

The room's quiet except for the occasional beep from the machines he's hooked up to.

"If you ever tell anyone about who attacked you, I tell everyone about who attacked me." I tug at the neckline of my sweater to reveal a vicious scratch mark along my collarbone. A memento from that night. "We'll see whose story is better."

The lump in his throat bobs. The rest of his face pulls

tight. He's trying to scowl, but the medication's fucked him up so bad, his reaction's are off. Instead, he winds up with a wincing expression, deep blinks, and a downturned mouth.

I smirk down at him. "In case it wasn't already clear, we're over. For your own good, stay away from me."

Samson mumbles in protest, his attempt to get me to stay.

But I'm already striding out the door. I meant it when I said I'm done with him. At least in the capacity I've been using him for—our short-lived relationship is over.

I've got what I wanted, and it's time to move onto the next stage of my plan.

When I return to my apartment a couple hours later, Heather's parked outside along the curb. Her chauffeur jumps out of the car to rush over and open the rear door. She steps out in dramatic fashion, giant sunglasses disguising her blue eyes and her long strawberry blonde hair swinging.

I keep walking like I haven't noticed either of them.

"Nyssie! Can I come in? I've been waiting almost an hour."

"Why is that any of my concern?"

I've shoved at the revolving glass door and entered the vestibule of my apartment building. I'm halfway toward the elevator by the time she's caught up.

"Can't you hear me out, Nyssie? I promise I can explain."

"Who says I want to hear that explanation?"

"Please," she gulps down air. As the elevator door slides

open, she rushes in after me. "Don't throw away three years of friendship!"

On the outside, I'm stone-like. I'm stoic and impenetrable to Heather's begging. Meanwhile, on the inside, I'm delighting in the fact that Heather Driscoll is practically *groveling*.

Exactly what I anticipated.

She's chasing me like a sad puppy, pleading to be my friend.

Funny how the tables turn...

The elevator dings reaching the fourth floor. I'm first out with Heather on my heels.

"Five minutes, Nyssie. That's all."

I sigh as I dig inside my bookbag for my keys. "Five minutes. Make it good."

Coming up on my door, I spot the broken potted plant next to my welcome mat and slow to a halt.

It was perfectly intact when I left this morning. Who would've broken it?

There's a crack right down the side as if it's been kicked.

Heather stops at my side. "Cute plant. Who broke the pot?"

"I'm... not sure."

"It's okay, Nyssie. If you forgive me, I'll buy you a new one!"

Peaches pounces at the two of us from the second we finally walk through the door. I'm unfazed while Heather shrieks and almost kicks her foot at the ginger cat. She catches herself right before she does, spying the look of warning I give her then pasting on a fake smile.

"Awww, sweet..." she says. "Peaches... she missed you... she's cute... very cute."

"What do you want, Heather?"

"Samson tricked me. I never would've slept with him. I was mourning my father and... and he took advantage."

"Your father? You mean the one you told me you hated?"

"Grief is complicated, Nyssie. You know that."

I toss my bookbag down on my quilted sofa and kick off my ankle boots. "When was the first time?"

She sniffles. "A few days after my dad passed away. I was feeling sorry for myself and he took advantage, Nyssie. I swear he did."

"The afternoon you came over to try on your funeral outfit. The person you were meeting with. Was it him?"

"He said you'd never find out."

"But Katie knew, didn't she? That's why you've been pissed at her."

Heather pouts, folding her arms. "She wanted to tell you. As if she doesn't sleep with whatever guy that'll have her."

"And the times after?" I ask, turning around for a look at her. "All the texting you've been doing?"

"It got out of control," she says, her chin quivering. Tears gloss her eyes. A decent performance all things considered. Maybe Heather should've pursued theater instead of law. "He was always complimenting me. Telling me how gorgeous I was."

"It sounds like he knew the things to say to stroke your ego."

"Yes, exactly! You get it, Nyssie."

"I may get it, Heather, but that doesn't mean I'll look past it."

Peaches purrs in interruption, leaping up to the armrest of my sofa. I sit down with my hand extending to scratch her behind her little pointy ears. Peering across the room at a teary-eyed, rosy-cheeked Heather, I offer what I have all afternoon.

Cold indifference.

Secret joy.

For every sniffle of Heather's, I remember how I'd cried too, all those years ago. I'd cried and Heather laughed.

Her stepmother laughed too when she stabbed my mother in the back.

It was hilarious to Holly Driscoll how she ruined my mother's life.

"Heather, I don't know what else to tell you," I say, stroking Peaches to more purrs. "You betrayed me. Both of you. It's going to take me time. If I can ever forgive you."

She shudders out a disappointed breath, then reluctantly nods. Wiping at her eyes and running mascara, she says, "I don't normally do this, Nyssie. Like, ever. But I... I might need your help."

"Oh? With what?" I ask.

But I already know.

More petty joy courses through me waiting to hear the words.

"There's some complications with my father's will," she says, looking on the verge of tears all over again. "My hag of a stepmother screwed me over dying. Her team of lawyers won't represent me now that she's gone. They're insisting I get my own. Now the rest of the family's contesting my father's will. They want everything he had! But what about me? I was his daughter! I might wind up with nothing, Nyssie. I was wondering if..."

"Yes?"

"You're so good at these things. You're already top of our class. A-and you said you come from a family of lawyers."

Silence stretches on between us. Moments of agony for Heather. Moments of glee for me.

I sit calmly stroking Peaches, pretending like I'm conflicted. "I'll think about it."

"Oh, Nyssie. You really are the best. I'd owe you everything."

Heather's still blubbering when she finally leaves. I make sure to shut and lock the door after her.

It feels like an immediate load off.

I hadn't expected to deal with Samson *and* Heather in the same day. I definitely hadn't meant to skip classes.

A slow breath rolls out of me as I run my hand over my curls and then wander over to the stack of newspapers I've collected from the library archives. Each copy from twenty years ago when I was just a toddler but Castlebury was deep in Valentine hysteria. Even sifting through the first few on top of the pile, I'm met with jarring headlines like:

Tragedy Strikes: August Rothenberg Sr., Beloved Dean of Castlebury University, Found Dead

Interview with Amelia Vise, Widow of Valentine Victim Anton Vise: How She and their 3-year-old Daughter Rosalyn will Seek Justice

Another Student Dead: Eric Fochte, 23, the Latest Victim of Valentine. Will the Police Finally Catch the Killer?

. . .

But none about my father, Edward Oliver, who Mom has always claimed was killed by Valentine at the peak of his murder spree. I haven't been able to find him in the student records at all, except for an Edward Oliver that was blond, blue-eyed, and had a smattering of freckles. A guy I *doubt* was the Edward she's speaking about.

There's still so much left to uncover. So much for me to do in order to make up for what happened in the past.

Samson's been dealt with. If he knows what's good for him, he'll drop the situation.

Heather's on the hook. She's as desperate and remorseful as I hoped she'd be.

I smile to myself, then glance over to the stack of law books on my spindly-legged coffee table. My mind immediately goes to Professor Adler.

He's the last current situation to deal with.

Yesterday was a cop out.

I sat in his class and did my damnedest to wear a poker face. I used all my energy just to pretend like I wasn't thinking about Halloween night and how it made me feel.

The moment was so complex, I didn't know where to begin.

I still don't...

It began as an assault by my ex-boyfriend, then morphed into a rescue by my crim law professor. The same professor I've spent the last couple weeks hoping to impress. The same man whose brooding glare makes my belly flip.

He'd looked so... feral and unevolved as he stood over Samson with the rock dripping of his blood. So different from his usual composed and civilized manner, it was an instant turn-on. I found myself breathless with want.

Endless desire for him.

I hadn't been able to contain myself the second we were secluded inside his office.

I went for it, seeking out his mouth.

Every time I close my eyes, I relive the passion. It flows through my body and ends as a throb in my pussy.

The guys my age hardly ever draw anything real out of me—it's all lukewarm affection. Take it or leave it sex that's forgettable and underwhelming.

But things couldn't be more different with Professor Adler. He was a composed, cold man with a secret primitive, bestial side buried deep. It reared its ferocious head in the blink of an eye as he came upon Samson pinning me down and he acted off these baser instincts.

And then when I kissed him, he gave in entirely. His stony mask fell away for the wild, passionate man underneath.

He had wanted me so badly I could feel it. His arousal rolled off him, a visceral feeling in the air.

I shudder just thinking about it, trying to block out the memory.

We can't. I can't.

He's my professor. I'm his student.

I have things to do—a goal in mind that I've worked toward for years. I came to Castlebury ready to burn it all down. Ready to destroy everyone in this community.

I can't let myself become distracted, no matter how unbelievably good Professor Adler's kiss may be.

Breathing through the temptation, I throw myself into my artwork. I promise myself that I'll keep a clear head and my hands clean. The professor might seek me out again like he did Monday after class, but I'll simply have to rebuff him.

Pretend it never happened.

"Because it's dangerous," I whisper. "*He's* dangerous."

As the hushed words leave my lips, intuition flutters on the inside.

It tells me I'm right. That maybe I'm so right, I haven't even begun to understand just how much yet...

15
THERON
LOVE ME - EX HABIT

A HUNDRED AND SIXTY-EIGHT HOURS. SEVEN DAYS, SEVEN NIGHTS since I last felt Nyssa Oliver's lips on mine. One full, torturous week.

Once Friday rolls around and my alarm goes off at five a.m. sharp, I'm a man being driven mad.

Even Atticus's sunny personality can't lighten my mood. The golden retriever bounces off the walls as I lead him down to the kitchen, where he dashes through the door, into the backyard.

I nudge my glasses further up the bridge of my nose, my expression sullen as I reach for my phone. In the past I prided myself on reaching for my phone as little as possible. Unless it was absolutely necessary, it remained untouched and ignored.

Veronica used to say it was strange. An older millennial such as myself so adverse to technology, when in many ways, it had been *my* generation who had pioneered things like smart devices and social media.

For Nyssa, I've made exceptions.

I can't stay away from my phone when it's my biggest link *to* her.

It's how I've tracked her. It's the method I've used to spy on her whereabouts and stalk her activity. As she seemingly ices me out, what else am I supposed to do?

I log onto her cloud expecting no real update since last night.

She'd come home early, ordered delivery, and spent hours pouring over her latest sculpture—a clay recreation of blooming flowers. It was simplistic in theory but incredibly detailed down to every unique petal she molded. I wondered if she's starting early for the next art festival...

Sighing when I discover I'm right about no real updates, I set down my phone. She can't possibly plan to ignore me the rest of the semester. She can't possibly think she'll be able to pretend what happened between us never did.

Later that morning, it's apparent that's exactly her plan.

For the third time this week, Nyssa sits mute in my class. She avoids my gaze at every turn. Her head bows as if she's more enthralled by the text in the book than my live instruction.

I grit my teeth as the clock strikes half past eleven and everyone in the class begins packing up.

"Miss Oliver," I say loudly, uncaring who hears. "I'd like a word. Please stay behind."

Most students pay little mind, simply happy the class is over. They carry on with their things, filing out of the room. Only Heather Driscoll lingers a second longer than she should, casting a curious glance between Nyssa and myself.

The door clicks shut behind her.

Nyssa's remained in her seat. For the first time this morning, she's chanced a look at me. Her deep-set eyes are a boundless mystery. They reveal next to nothing as I stride toward her, my loafers thudding against the wooden flooring.

I stop directly in front of her desk, peering down at her, a scowl fixed onto my face.

The tension feels suffocating. It expands between us like a third presence in the room, highlighting the unresolved conflict between us.

She's studying me like I'm studying her.

Trying to solve the puzzle of my mind while I attempt to do the same.

Her slender throat works in a slow swallow, and then she says, "I have other classes this morning. I have to go—"

"You'll go nowhere," I hiss. "Not until we have an understanding, Miss Oliver. Which is that you're to participate in my class. You're to answer my questions. You're to make eye contact. You're to be engaged the entire time. I want your full, undivided attention at all times."

Her brows knit. "That's not fair—"

"Who said anything about fair?" I crack half of a grin, my pulse beating faster. "If you insist on doing your best to ignore me—on pretending that night never happened—then my hand is forced. I'll have your attention any way I can. Including right now. After class."

"I'm leaving."

"Sit!" I snap. As she half rises out of her chair, my hand shoots out and grabs her throat.

We both freeze, breathing heavily, eyes hooked on each other.

I can feel her pulse thrumming against my fingers. Her warm flesh against my hand as I hold her by the throat and we admire each other so close, I could crush my lips to hers.

She's tempted by the idea.

Instinct tells me this.

Her little pink tongue—the same one that had played with mine only a week ago—pokes out to wet her lips.

Her eyes glimmer. Dark but bright all at once as she challenges me much in the same way she had on the first day of class. No one else may get it, but I do. I can see the awareness in her gaze, dripping from her, as she understands me like I do her.

We get there's something here.

Something forbidden and wrong but addictive and unpredictable; something we're both struggling to resist.

She swallows, throat muscles flexing against my hand. "Professor, I'm leaving. Let go of me."

I blink and suddenly come to my senses. The feral drum that had beat inside me so intensely only a second ago feels worlds away. It was an entirely different man altogether. My hand drops from her throat and I take a step back.

She hoists her bookbag onto her shoulder, then quickly arrows toward the door.

It snaps shut and sends a shockwave reverberating through me.

Confusion over what the hell I was about to do. How could I lose control so easily? So thoroughly?

I wrench off my glasses and scrub a sobering hand over my face.

In need of a dose of reality, I call the only person who will give me a proverbial bitch slap.

Theo hears my ragged breathing and grows worried. "Theron, what the hell?"

"I need you to talk sense into me."

"About...?"

I let my breathing answer for me. More ragged intakes, even rougher exhales.

She knows me well enough to understand. "Theron, for

fuck's sake, whoever she is, she's not worth it! And if it's Veronica again—I swear to god, I'm going to kick your ass! Let the chick go!"

"It's not about Veronica," I spit.

"Is this why you rushed off last Friday night? Jesus fucking Christ, Theron, what are you getting mixed up in? You heard, Dad—he's not bailing you out this time!"

"Will you calm down?" I say, scowling. "I called you to talk sense into me. Not nag me like Mom."

"It's deserved! I don't know what girl's got in your head again, but walk away."

"I have to go now."

I cut her off in the middle of her next sentence with my mind made up. Her lecturing words have done nothing but flip the script and make me realize I was right before. Classes for the day are over and it's time I stop depriving myself of what I want.

It's time I make Miss Oliver understand.

The day's breezy, brisk autumn weather vanishes by late afternoon. Thick clouds emerge, heavy with raindrops, casting a dull gray filter over Castlebury.

Campus thins out the way it always does when gloomy weather's imminent.

I stride toward my BMW with my leather satchel swathed diagonally over my shoulder. Glasses perched on my face, I'm as calm and composed as ever. I've reached a new sense of clarity, sliding behind the wheel and checking my phone.

Miss Oliver is downtown. She's in the middle of another solo outing, running errands and making stops of interest. A habit of hers I've realized she takes part in to decompress.

I cut through side streets until I'm parking in a lot designated for visitors in the downtown district. Because the long strip of boutiques, cafés, lounges, galleries, and other establishments are so nestled together, there's little room for street parking.

It's part of Castlebury's charm—a small, lush town brimming with tasteful cobblestone and gas lamps.

Nyssa's exiting an art supply shop when I come up on the street corner. I pull on the baseball cap I've brought with me and keep a distance, immersing myself among other people on the street to blend in. She wanders out of the store clutching a tiny bag.

When out alone, her expression's naturally curious, naturally thoughtful. It's as though she's admiring every sensory detail around her, from the leaded glass on a shop window to the brown leaves flurrying at her feet.

As it starts drizzling, she digs into her bookbag and pulls out a striped umbrella that looks decades old. Likely another find from the thrift store.

It happens to be her next stop, half a block down.

I'm her secret chaperone, approaching the shop once she's disappeared inside. I stand in the glazed front window and make out the shape of her as she browses the racks.

Never before have I been so captivated. So damn beholden to the obsession that's bloomed quickly over the matter of a few weeks.

This kind of longing goes beyond comprehension. Past reason and logic.

It runs deep.

All the way down to my fucking marrow.

Yet, if asked to explain, I'm not sure I could even put it into words. The only possible explanation I could begin to offer is that Nyssa Oliver is unlike any other person walking this earth—and I don't mean that in a cheesy, eye-roll-worthy reductive way, like some platitude written on the inside of a birthday card.

I mean, at her core, she's like a rare pearl that's so special, it's a wonder it even exists.

She's beautiful, made up of soft curves and springy curls.

But it's her mind that's the treasure. Even as she browses, it's hard at work, processing a thousand thoughts a minute.

She's a mystery I'm desperate to solve. I hope someday to understand.

And for her to understand me—for her to get why I'm doing what I am.

I can't walk away. I can't let go of whatever this is...

The clerk at the counter greets her and the two exchange pleasantries before she makes a small purchase. A trinket of a necklace that she stores in the same bag she'd picked up at the art supply shop.

The drizzle's hardened into rainfall by the time she's exited.

Where I once stood near the door, I've retreated. I'm a few more buildings down, peering carefully through the sheets of rain to figure out her next stop. She holds her umbrella in one hand and her shopping bag in the other and starts the opposite way down the street.

I'm left to wonder where we're going.

Is she meeting up with someone? Is she walking home? Why would she in the rain?

Two long, slick streets later, I stop short in stunned

satisfaction at where she's led us. On a late rainy afternoon, the few visitors of the Castlebury Metropolitan Museum of Art are on their way out.

Yet Nyssa is the opposite. She's on her way in.

I am too, trailing after her with a chest full of heart palpitations. Anticipation reaches a fever pitch. I'm under her spell and I can't fucking help it.

The museum's normally lit by the bright light of the day.

In the midst of dreary weather, it's darker, moodier than usual. The long halls stretch on endlessly, the walls lined with some of the most beautiful art pieces in the world.

Nyssa wanders among them, always headed deeper into the bowels of the museum. Every so often, she pauses long enough to admire a piece that catches her eye. The infamous Fall of Man painting depicting Adam and Eve or the Angel with a Crown statue many love.

After she's moved on, I'm replacing her at the artwork. My eyes rove over the masterful craftsmanship of each piece, sensing it's what she appreciated most. Then I'm carrying on in her wake, keeping to the shadows.

The museum empties to the point it seems we're the last two. The cavernous space seemingly echoes with her footfalls. The breaths she draws.

It'll be closing soon.

I'll leave when she leaves.

Curiosity swims in my stomach as I drift after her and wonder which piece of artwork she's seeking out.

A few seconds later, I have my answer. But only after another discovery—Nyssa knows she's not alone.

As she enters the next hall, she casts the briefest glance over her shoulder.

Her shining dark eyes greet mine.

Then she continues, picking up her pace, venturing farther into the underbelly of the museum.

My pulse explodes. I break out into a fast stride to catch up with her. Desperation reawakens like it had a week ago, where I'd sought her out and scoured the entire campus.

Nyssa stops before a marble statue that demands reverence.

Undine Rising from the Waters is showcased in its own room, surrounded by emerald-papered walls and a generous skylight.

I come up behind her, my gaze lifting to admire the work of art. Far from the first time I've visited the museum to view the piece, there's something more special about it now.

Witnessing it alongside Nyssa.

Undine's chiseled from white marble, yet the woman's curves are impeccable and soft. The fabric drapes her body, rippling and wet as she rises from the water. She reaches toward the heavens, the skylight haloing her.

Nyssa tilts her head, studying every minute detail.

"Isn't she beautiful?" she asks. "It's my favorite."

"Yes," I answer. "It's breathtaking. One of a kind."

"It took Chauncey Ives two years to sculpt."

"So I've read."

"The marble's so delicately chiseled that light can shine through the portions that are supposed to be fabric," she explains, an excited beat about her. She glances at me, then grabs my hand to take me around the back and show me.

Warm sparks shoot up my arm. Through the rest of me.

Her touch so soft, yet so confident.

I'm enthralled as she leads me and points out the intricacy in the construction.

But I'm more distracted by her. The passion that blooms across her face as she goes into great detail about the famed work of art. Many details I've already learned but appreciate hearing from her sweet lips. She runs herself breathless talking, telling me about Undine and Chauncey and the difficulty in constructing such a piece.

She flushes, the subtlest glow touching her bronze complexion.

"What?" she asks finally.

"How long did you know I was following you, Miss Oliver?"

The corner of her lip quirks. "Aren't you going to tell me why you were following me first?"

I edge closer, looming over her. My tone deepens with a hint of authority. "Tell me how long you knew."

"The museum's empty. I saw your reflection in the glass."

"Yet you kept going."

We've inched even closer, her face tilting slightly up toward mine.

Mine angling down toward hers.

"You were leading me," I whisper, so close I can almost taste her lips. "You wanted to show me your favorite piece."

"You wanted to see… didn't you?"

My hands come up to cup her face as a crooked grin slants across my lips. "I find you absolutely fucking irresistible. Did you know that?"

"I had a feeling."

"And how do you feel? What do *you* want?"

"I feel like this is a mistake," she says candidly, her breath on my lips.

I've drawn her face closer to mine like I'm about to kiss her. I'm one impulsive second away from doing so.

Yet she hasn't pulled away. If anything, she's melted into me, letting me hold her like I am.

"A mistake," I repeat. "Why, Miss Oliver?"

"Because… because we're not supposed to be together."

"Says who?"

"Everyone."

"Should we care?"

"Yes," she breathes. "I do."

"Why?"

"Because you're a distraction," she confesses. "You're dangerous."

My pulse thrums harder, grin widening. I graze my lips against hers in a tantalizing tease. "But isn't that what draws you to me? Be honest, Miss Oliver. You like the danger. The forbidden. A curious mind like yours. You crave it as much as I do."

I don't bother waiting for an answer. Why should I when I already know the truth deep down?

My mouth claims hers, coming together in a kiss bursting with passion. Every ounce of desire that I have for her.

She immediately goes still in my arms, thrown by my brazenness.

That I'm kissing her like I am, hard and demanding. That, technically, even in an empty museum, someone could walk by and find us.

But I'm done playing cat and mouse. I'm done pretending as if the attraction between us isn't real. I'm a moth and she's the flame I can't resist.

Her sweet taste is one I simply won't give up.

Nyssa loses her breath. She gasps as I kiss her soft mouth. Yet she parts her lips for more. She lets me inside. Her wet tongue and mine mingle in a dance.

I clench her within my grip and feel the arousal surging through me. It's so potent, I could burst out of my skin. My pulse pounds in my ear and blood rushes to my cock. Arousal makes my normally sharp mind grow hazy.

All I can think about is Nyssa Oliver and the feel of soft, slick pussy.

I can practically feel it clenched around me.

"Professor," she sputters, finally finding an ounce of restraint. She turns her head away from mine.

But I merely kiss her cheek and jaw. I travel down to a spot on the side of her throat that makes her shudder in my arms.

"We can't," she goes on breathlessly.

"We will."

"Professor—"

I silence her with another kiss to the lips. I savor the taste of her, chocolate and peppermint from her earlier treat at a local bakery, and swallow down any more protests.

Gradually, we step back. We kiss as we walk toward the wall. My hands explore the curves that have been ruling my mind for days while hers wind up clinging to the front of my shirt. I bring her up against the wall with every intention of devouring the rest of her.

The lights go out before I can.

It's enough to finally break us apart. Glancing around at the sudden darkness, a second goes by before we realize what's happened.

The museum staff has left for the evening. They must've forgotten we were still here. Raindrops tap against the glass skylight above and reveal the downpour's only grown worse. The sky's darkened, signifying how late in the evening it's become.

Nyssa shoves at my chest and escapes from her position against the wall.

"This is crazy," she says, rushing out of the room. "We have to stop."

I'm quick after her. My scowl's returned. "That's not possible."

"Of course it is! And now we've been left inside here," she snaps. "I have to go home."

"Slow down."

"You know what, Professor?" On the move, she throws a furious look at me from over her shoulder. "Fuck off!"

"Get back here!"

"I'm leaving!"

The moment descends into another game of cat and mouse. A foot chase as she trots down the tunneled corridor and I dart after her. She doesn't make it far before I'm overtaking her, grabbing her arms, clenching her within my grip.

"You fight the inevitable," I growl. "Don't tell me you don't feel it. Don't pretend it's not real. If I shoved my fucking hand in your panties, don't think it won't be slick with your juices."

She shakes her head, eyes wide, though I can see the honest glimmer in them.

She can't bring herself to utter a word because she's well aware it's the truth.

I let go of her, a bitter twist of lust thickening inside me. Regarding her with the same kind of severity I had the first day she ran into me in the hall, I gesture at her sweater and denim jeans. "Take off your clothes, Miss Oliver."

Her features crease in protest. "You're joking. I refuse to—"

"Take them off," I say slower, each word emphasized. "Take them off... or as your teacher, I *will* punish you."

The threat hangs in the air for a moment that seems like an eternity.

She's been stunned into silence, gaping at me like I've lost my mind. Her breathing's hard, nostrils flaring, lips plump and parted.

The moment could go either way—she could knee me in the groin and run for it. She could scream bloody murder and pray someone's still in the area.

Or she could obey.

Nyssa Oliver chooses the latter, yet she does so in a way only she could.

Confident and defiant.

Searing me with a harsh glare, she rips her sweater over her head and lets it tumble to the ground. Her fingers go to the button on her jeans. We maintain eye contact as she strips the pair off, sliding them down her hips, then thighs.

My greed is what finally breaks our stare. I spend an aroused second drinking in the sight of her in her bra and panties. Though I've seen her nude, it was in secret.

It was as I watched her without her knowledge.

It was nothing like this, witnessing the lush curves in person.

Just for me.

My blood's hot. My pulse pounds in my ears. I'm composed, yet a ticking time bomb on the inside as I swallow hard.

"Take off your bra," I order.

Her eyes narrow. Her arms reach behind her back to do as she's told. The bra flops away as her breasts spring free, pert and soft, begging for my mouth.

I decide to grant their wish.

Nyssa gasps as I stride forward, knot my fist in her curls to yank her head back, and suck a peak into my mouth. Her puffy nipple thickens the harder I suckle. The more I nibble on the bead, grazing it with my teeth, making her claw at me.

It's all too much for her. Her breasts heave as she draws deep breaths and endures all the different sensations.

My hands that grope, fondle, pinch. My mouth and tongue that suck and lick.

Teeth that bite to her screams. Just hard enough to hurt a little before I'm back to kissing and swirling my tongue.

The breast play alone has her close. Right on the edge.

I shove my free hand down the front of her panties and tell her what I want. I'm driven by a dark lust that's washed over me. That won't be sated until I've taken what I want and experienced her like I've fantasized about.

She'll be withering, leaking cum by the time I'm through with her.

"On the bench, Miss Oliver."

She's still panting for breath as she turns away and does as I say. She crawls onto the nearby wiry bench, on her hands and knees, affording me a clear view of her gorgeous round ass. I admire how her panties cling to her pussy, so thin I can make out the folds of her labia, and then I step toward her.

Slowly, indulging in the moment, I slide the pair off her. The slinky fabric rolls past her hips, thighs, legs. I grip her ankle as I tug it over the arch of her foot.

Then I'm the one without air.

My lungs run empty as soon as my eyes flick up to her pussy.

Even in the shadowy corridor of the museum, it *glistens*.

She's soaking wet and plump. Her natural scent fragrant in the air.

I'm so aroused, I'm dizzy. I blink out of it and decide it's time to lose all pretenses. Unbuttoning my shirt and shoving down my pants, my hand grips my erect cock.

"Do you know what happens next, Miss Oliver?" I ask, my throat tight.

"Professor..."

"I fuck you," I say, stepping forward. I run my cock along the wet seam of her pussy lips and then slot myself inside.

Immediately, I lose myself to intense pleasure.

It rushes me as I slide straight into pulsing warmth. On all sides, my cock's sheathed in wet heat. The rest of me buzzes from sensory overload.

Every muscle's tense. Every nerve's tingling. My skin's flushed and my brain's mush.

I groan sinking into the soft hole, then grope Nyssa's hips and thighs.

She's squeezed shut her eyes and hung her head, like she's deep in her own pleasure. She's adjusting to the thickness and girth of me.

Her slender shoulders quiver, the center of her spine arched so gracefully.

Erotically.

I draw back slowly, building anticipation, then I return to the warmth. I sink back into the pulsing heat and revel in the instant clench.

Her pussy kneading me. Her pussy fluttering around me.

It's forbidden. It's something I'm never supposed to do. I'm never supposed to touch a student, let alone have sex with one.

But as I begin stroking into Nyssa Oliver, I know there's no going back. Nor would I ever choose to.

This obsessive, twisted, forbidden union between us is worth the world. It's worth every fucking thing on this planet.

Nyssa moans as I pump into her. She arches her back and takes my cock. Her pussy gushes with wetness, so slippery that I'm covered in her juices every time I withdraw. The sight of my length slick with evidence of her arousal makes me harder.

If possible.

I grip her flesh and deepen my strokes. I hit the back of her pussy, bottoming out, to more of her screams. The bench sways under us as I do.

As we surrender to how good we make each other feel.

The moment blurs into skin slapping and shared moans. Nyssa spreads her thighs wide as my cock tunnels deep and we ride to the finish line on the same wave of pleasure. It slams into us in a burst of tingling heat.

Seizing up, I'm spilling inside her. I come until we've made a mess of each other. I'm coated with her juices and she's leaking mine.

But it's not the end of the night—we clean ourselves up as best as we can in the dark of the museum and wander toward what exit we can find.

We're silent yet aware of where we're headed. Nyssa slides into the passenger seat of my BMW and I drive us to her apartment. The building's quiet as we ride the elevator up to the fourth floor and she digs inside her bag for her keys.

The second the door's unlocked, we're stepping inside and then slamming it shut.

We're colliding all over again.

Clothes are stripped away. Kisses are exchanged in the dark.

We fumble through the cramped space, unable to keep our hands off each other.

I press her up against the cold glass of her living room window and slam into her from behind. My hand snakes up her throat, my mouth grazing the edge of her jaw, and I fuck her like I've fantasized about fucking her so many recent nights.

The second round of what becomes an on-and-off game through the night.

Nyssa gyrates with me, writhing and whimpering, taking every inch of cock I give her. And when I bury myself inside her to come and kiss her hard on the lips, I know she finally understands.

She knows she's mine. She knows that no matter how wrong this is, there's no escaping what's between us...

16

NYSSA

BAD INTENTIONS - NIYKEE HEATON FEATURING MIGOS AND OG PARKER

"You have a scar on the inside of your thigh," Professor Adler says, tracing his fingers along the mark. His dark eyes sweep up to meet mine. "It's shaped like a banana."

The sound that tumbles out of me is half laugh, half snort. "A what?!"

"You heard me. A banana. I'd say a lightning bolt... but that's cliché."

"A lightning bolt and a banana are *very* different in shape, Professor."

"Don't," he says, climbing up the length of my body. He drops a kiss flush on my lips, then peers down at me, his unruly hair hanging over his brow. "Don't call me professor when we're like this."

"Like what?"

It seems like I'm teasing, being difficult, but it's a relevant question. Given what happened last night—*all night long*—we're treading new water.

We've hardly had time to sleep let alone discuss what it is we're even doing.

"When we're in bed," he answers, kissing me again. More softly.

I hum, tipsy just from his lips on mine. "But you loved me moaning professor last night when you had me against the wall."

"In the heat of the moment—yes. In the aftermath—no."

"What happened to call me Professor Adler. Just Professor Adler." I mimic his stern voice from the first day of class only to erupt in giggles. He's run teasing fingers against the sides of my ribcage.

"That was in the classroom, *Miss* Oliver," he scolds, gripping my hip. "Pillow talk is different."

"Mmm... pillow talk. Tell me more, Professor."

Laughter tumbles out of me all over again as he returns to squeezing my side, exposing how ticklish I am. Seconds of torture ensue, where I'm trapped under him, tangled in my wrinkled bedsheets, subjected to his payback.

On a Saturday morning like today, slivers of light peeking through my bedroom curtains, there's not much else to do.

Once he's had his fill, he settles beside me, still stroking my bare skin. Any part of me he can, as if he's aware this could be his only chance.

"You know what pillow talk is," he says huskily. "Though it wouldn't surprise me if the guys your age skip that part altogether."

"I have to be honest. Samson didn't strike me as the type."

His fingers travel up my stomach, past the swell of my breasts, reaching my shoulders... and the scrape on my collarbone. He spends a second studying the purplish mark that's slowly begun to heal, and it's in this moment that I pick up on the same darkness from Halloween night.

The side of Professor Adler I hadn't anticipated.

"I didn't realize he'd left a mark," he mutters.

My hand covers his, forcing his gaze to mine. "It's okay. You came in time. And I handled the rest."

"The... rest...?"

"Let's just say, Samson won't be going to the police. He won't ever mention it again."

"What did you say to him?"

"It's not important," I say. "But he got the message."

"He knows you're done with him?"

A smirk quirks at my lips. "Jealous, Professor?"

"Professor?" He raises a brow.

"Theron. Happy?"

"I won't be happy 'til you tell me you're done with him," he insists, his fingers curling at the base of my throat. He peppers me with more quick kisses, sending a warm current through the rest of my body.

I get what he needs. He needs to hear me confirm it's over.

"Samson and I were never serious," I say. "He was a means to an end."

"How so?"

I pause a second, caught between my truth and the act I've put on. No one knows why I'm doing what I'm doing except for Mom. And Peaches.

As far as anyone else knows, I'm *really* friends with Heather and the others. I was *really* dating Samson Wicker. I'm really in Castlebury to climb the elite social ladder and curry their favor.

Theron has no clue that as he poses his question, my memory takes over, and I hear Mom's cries all over again.

"Gone!" she sobbed on the floor of our living room. "All because of them! They did this... he... he did this..."

I was on the floor too, playing with my Lego blocks and stuffed animals. But I didn't understand why she was crying. She gasped for air like she couldn't breathe and more tears poured from her. Sounds of grief I wouldn't make sense of 'til I was much older...

"Nyssa," Theron says, shaking me slightly. "Are you lost in thought or am I that boring of a conversationalist?"

"Oh, I was... the first one..."

"It does make me wonder," he thinks aloud, "why you were with him. Why you're friends with a twit like Driscoll."

Where I was considering vulnerability a split second ago, now I snap back to my role. "Because sometimes people click, Theron," I say. "Sometimes different people connect. If you're going to judge my relationships, then maybe this was a mistake."

"What you call judging, I call curiosity. *Honesty*." His palm slides up the side of my neck 'til it's framing my face and he's close enough for another kiss. "You know damn well what I mean. A girl like you—so witty, so bright, so interesting—and the likes of *them*. Opposite of everything you are."

My offense fades for a faint smile. "I didn't know you thought so highly of me."

"I've had many thoughts about you. Some pure. Some... not-so-pure."

I giggle. "Okay, honestly, that feels like an accomplishment. I've worked so hard for your approval."

"Have you?" He raises a thick brow and strokes his thumb along my cheek.

"Mhmmm. Do you think I answer first in every class I'm in? I wanted you to notice me."

"Well, you did a damn good job at that."

"Thank you, Professor."

The mood becomes playful again as he plants a deep kiss on my lips and my nails rake down his chest. The hairs speckled there tickle the pads of my fingers and turn me on—so does the solid, masculine feel of the rest of his body.

Theron's not some muscular gym rat bench pressing hundreds of pounds, but he's in impeccable shape in other ways. His muscle tone's modest but defined and his build is trim and lean. He's got a happy trail that travels from his navel down the center of his pelvis, straight to his penis.

I grip him and stroke him and listen to the throaty groans he releases as I do.

He makes me feel sexual.

Hungry.

My body pulses with desire in ways it never has for Samson. For almost any other guy I've dated.

We kiss with tongue, the heat dialing up. He hardens in my grasp, his dick so velvety and silken yet stiff and hot. I need no other invitation than his erection to throw my leg over his side and mount him.

His eyes darken, his jaw clenched as I sink down 'til he's buried deep inside.

We're already so familiar and comfortable with each other that we slip into motion at once. He drags me back down to his mouth and I bounce my hips.

Theron fills his hands with my flesh. He encourages every undulation as I work my body and ride him.

I sit up, my head angled toward the ceiling, my lungs empty.

His dick deep.

Hitting all the right spots. Setting off the thousands of little nerves inside my pussy.

I come like this, bouncing on his dick 'til I'm clamping down and unraveling. My orgasm jets through me like a spout of water erupting.

Then Theron's throwing me off him. He's pinning me down and slamming back into me. We're gyrating amid my breathless screams as he crushes his lips to mine and drills deeper. He fucks me hard and fast without regard, his hands everywhere at once.

I can only shudder and take every punishing thrust.

In a matter of minutes, we're spent all over again. We lay side by side, gazes on the ceiling, without a thought in our heads.

Peaches purrs from my bedside table, nosy little face turned toward us. She's never seen her mother so... frisky.

She's curious.

And concerned.

But Professor Adler—*Theron*—does something no other guy has ever thought to do. He sits up slightly and clicks his tongue, patting his hands on his thighs.

My sweet little ginger girl leaps from the bedside table straight into his lap. I sit up too, eyes widening at the sight before me.

Peaches nuzzles Theron, then settles into the crook of his arm.

"Am I in the Twilight Zone?" I ask. "She's... never done that with a guy before."

"We've come to an understanding."

He smirks, looking so damn sexy with his floppy dark hair and lean muscles on display, cuddling my cat.

Before I can decide if I'm more endeared than I am disturbed, the lock clacks in the front door. It opens no more than a second later, and Mom breezes through calling my name.

"Nys baby! Are you home?"

SHIT!

I scramble to get out of bed while Theron's brow creases in confusion.

"My mom," I hiss, rushing to throw on clothes.

"She has a key to your apartment?"

"No... yes... she doesn't usually come by. Make yourself invisible!"

I dive for the door once I'm in sweats and a T-shirt.

Mom's still hovering in the small space that's in between my kitchen and the living room. Her round eyes brighten at the sight of me. She smiles and holds up a tote bag full of Tupperware.

"I packed you some meals, Nys," she says. "Sorry to drop by on short notice. I happened to be in town for once, so I figured I'd make sure my baby girl was good and fed."

"Oh... wow... thanks. You didn't have to." I swallow down my shock, though my breathing's still irregular. My hair's a mess and I'm sure I drip with guilt.

Especially in the eyes of a mother.

Predictably, Mom stares me down head to toe. "You alright, Nys? You seem startled."

"Just surprised you came by so... so unannounced," I choke out. "Remember how you said you'd call first?"

"But I was just stopping by real quick to bring you food—"

"Mom," I snap, "I'm an adult. This is *my* apartment. I pay for it. Respect my space. You said you'd call first."

Her plump face dims. My heart almost breaks. She glances around like she's searching for an excuse, then she spots the men's tweed jacket hanging off my sofa.

"Who's that belong to?" she asks.

My blood runs cold. I open and close my mouth, fuzzy on words. "It's... my... um..."

"Thank you, Miss Oliver, for letting me use your bathroom," comes Theron's voice. He appears suddenly from the hall fully dressed and composed. He's radiating the authoritative, refined energy he usually does in class. The professor who scolds students with a withering look. "I appreciate the last minute accommodation. I'll be on my way."

Mom and I gape at him as he strides toward the tweed jacket and shrugs it on.

"Uh... who are you?" Mom asks.

Theron arches a brow, pausing slightly, then steps forward with his hand extended. "I suppose I could ask you the same. I'm Theron Adler, Professor of Criminal Law at Castlebury University. Your daughter, Nyssa Oliver, is a student of mine. One of the brightest."

"Hmmm," Mom hums in naked suspicion. She doesn't shake his hand. "And what are you doing in my daughter's *apartment*?"

Theron chuckles. "Didn't I already make it obvious? I needed to relieve myself. Thankfully, your daughter let me use her bathroom."

"And what were you doing here in the first place?" Mom's hands notch at her wide hips, her face sharp with accusation.

"Mom, seriously? Stop," I scold.

But Theron has it covered. He's relaxed and confident as he flattens a hand along his tweed jacket and then starts for the door. "Actually, it's my fault. You see, when I was grading papers, I accidentally gave your daughter the answer key. I was coming by to pick it up and I happened to drink too much coffee. Unfortunately, nature calls at the most inconvenient times. I'm grateful she let me use her bathroom so I didn't have to use the gas station around the block. Do you have any more questions, Ms...?"

"Oliver," Mom answers. "Brooklyn Oliver."

"Ah, I see. Well, you should know your daughter is top of my class," he says, briefly glancing at me. "She's quite impressive, in fact. You should be proud."

"Hmmm." Mom says nothing else, peering at Theron like he's the antichrist.

I clear my throat and interject myself. "Anyway," I say, "Professor Adler was on his way out. Thank you for clearing that mix up."

"Of course. See you in class, Miss Oliver."

Theron gives a polite nod to the both of us before he walks out. Mom waits 'til he's gone before she rounds on me.

"Professor Theron Adler?" she asks. "Do these mix ups happen often?"

My jaw falls open in offense. "Mom, stop right now!"

"Baby girl, I'm worried. I'm afraid you're letting these people in too deep. You don't know what you're dealing with."

"Can I point out you're not supposed to even *be* here?"

Mom releases the breath she's inhaled, then tugs her lips into a smile. Her hands come up to cup my face like when I was a kid. "I'm just worried about my baby girl is all. You're out here living on your own. You're trying to avenge me. But there's real danger out there, Nys. These people will protect their own. Now it seems the Valentine Killer is back..."

"I can handle it all. Trust me, okay?"

Mom brushes a stray curl away from my face before

something else in her periphery catches her eye. Her hands drop to her side and she breezes past me. I turn around to track her through my apartment.

The stack of old Castlebury newspapers.

She scoops up the edition sitting on the top. The paper's wrinkled and tinged yellow with age while the ink's begun to fade, but these things aren't what bother her most. She reads the headline aloud.

"Valentine Killer Claims Another Victim in Professor Anton Vise."

"Mom," I groan.

"Baby girl, why do you have this?"

My skin prickling with heat, I wrench the paper out of her grasp. "Because it's my right to! I've told you I'm doing research about the time period you and Dad went to school. Part of that research includes the Valentine Killer. But it's not your right to snoop in my apartment. *After* turning up unannounced!"

"If you want to know about your father and what the Valentine Killer did, I'll tell you myself. Not some newspaper—"

"Get out, Mom!" I boom, thrusting a finger at the door. "You've got to go."

Mom tries several times to bait me into a conversation about the old newspapers I've dug up from the library archives. I'm so heated, so irritated, that I don't let her. I nudge her past the threshold as she resorts to once again warning me about what I'm getting mixed up in.

"You don't know these people like I do," she says. "Any one of them could be Valentine. Baby girl—"

"Goodbye!"

I slam the door shut in her face, effectively cutting her off.

My face falls into my hands as a rumbly noise vibrates from my throat. To say I'm frustrated by what just happened would be an understatement. Not only did Mom turn up unannounced, she came by while *Theron* was here.

She proceeded to treat him rudely and then turned her nosy endeavor onto the old newspapers from twenty years ago. How could she think it was any of her business?!

There's a boundary issue between us.

There always has been. But I've cut her slack because of what she's suffered.

The way the community in Castlebury treated her sickens me to my stomach. It was beyond unjust. Some fucked up cocktail of racism, misogyny, and classism that culminated in her expulsion for daring to hide her pregnancy and my father's murder at the hands of the Valentine Killer.

That included years of painful harassment and mockery for the both of us.

Mom seems like she'd rather take the high road. She wants to put the past behind us.

I'm simply not so forgiving *or* forgetful.

I wouldn't be dedicating years to this cause if I didn't believe in my heart I needed to avenge my family.

I needed to make everyone who had a hand in our destruction pay. The Driscolls, the Wickers, the Rothenbergs.

The Valentine Killer.

"It'll be sweet," I whisper to myself, setting the old newspaper back on top of the stack. "It'll all be worth it."

I wish I could say I was sensible enough to leave my hookup with Professor Adler as a one-time-only thing.

My body shakes uncontrollably, my orgasm exploding within. He grips my curls tighter with one hand and palms my ass with the other. His dick's so deep, I'd swear he were about to split me in two until he's tumbling over the edge with me.

I face plant into my pillows while he half collapses on top of me.

We huff air into our lungs, breathing like we've run several miles. The intense sex we've had is close enough.

The more I experience him, the more I learn Professor Adler enjoys getting a little rough. I enjoy it just as much.

A week has passed since that evening in the museum and we've made a habit of meeting up after hours. Always my apartment. Always under the veil of secrecy.

Mom hasn't dared drop by again.

It wouldn't matter if she did; I replaced the lock in the door.

Each night he shows up at my place, my body's left tingling with satisfaction after it's all said and done. I'm left getting the best sleep I've had in months.

But this isn't just sex—lying in bed by the moonlight streaming into my dark bedroom, we have some of the best conversations I've ever had in my *life*.

Professor Adler—*Theron*—is so easy to talk to it's almost frightening.

We talk about school. His class. Specifics on cases he took as a working defense attorney. I pick his brilliant mind for his opinions and input on criminal law.

We talk art and philosophy and about our quirks.

I even bait him into a conversation about pop culture.

"C'mon," I laugh. "You expect me to believe you don't watch TV ever?"

"Other than the news and documentaries."

"Professor," I say, aware of how I'm inciting him by using the P word. "I don't believe you."

He growls, leaning over me and grabbing me by the throat for a hard kiss. "What did I tell you about using that word?"

"Not outside the classroom or the bedroom... which we're technically in, by the way."

"And you know what I mean when I say bedroom."

"Coitus!"

He eases back, still lying on his side, a lopsided grin on his normally brooding face. "Are we sure I'm the forty-two-year-old? I'm not sure even I would use the word *coitus*."

Another easy laugh tumbles out of me. "Don't change the subject. Tell me one show you watch."

He thinks on my demand, then begrudgingly says, "I suppose the Wire was good."

"The Wire?!"

"Are you surprised? I'm a criminal law professor. If I do have to engage with TV, it's usually a crime drama."

"Actually, it makes sense when you put it that way."

We're interrupted by the loud bleat of a horn outside. Some delivery truck has almost run into a pedestrian scrambling across the road. We tense up for the paranoid half second it takes us to realize it's a false alarm.

It's never lost on us how wrong things could go if we really *are* caught.

Theron thumbs my bottom lip. "We should meet at my house next time. It's farther out of town. Less chance we're seen."

"You mean more opportunity to hide me?"

"Have you forgotten you're my student?"

"I thought the forbiddenness is what turned you on," I tease, poking my tongue out. I swipe at the pad of his thumb, my dark eyes alight with mischief.

I can feel his body temperature rise. Practically see his pupils dilate. "Is that what turns *you* on?"

"It definitely makes things interesting."

"I won't pretend I haven't imagined fucking you over my desk. Or swatting you over the ass with one of my rulers."

"Female students talk," I say. "And plenty of them think you're sexy as hell. But I don't think any of them realize you're so kinky."

He nips at my lips while reaching below to fondle my pussy. "I'd prefer to keep it that way."

"Oh?"

"You're the only female student I've got my eye on, Miss Oliver."

"Mm, you're right. Let's keep it that way."

"On your stomach. Ass up. I want to eat that pussy... again."

I'm scrambling to obey. Mere moments after our last romp, I've got my face buried in the pillows and his buried in my pussy. I grind my hips back against his mouth 'til his tongue is wedged deep inside me and I'm sobbing my pleasure.

I could get used to this.

17
THERON
POWER TRIP - J. COLE FEATURING MIGUEL

"You look like steaming dog shit," Theo says when I open the door.

"Just once it'd be nice if you said good morning like a normal sister."

"Ew, why would I ever do that?" She pushes past me like she did when we were kids, clutching two large coffees from the local Java King, as requested.

Atticus is excited to see her. He circles her every step of the way, tail wagging as he nips at her ankles.

I follow them into the kitchen. "I think my dog likes you more than me."

"Why wouldn't he? Dogs sense demonic energy."

"*I'm* the demonic one? Really?" I raise a brow at her as she kneels to scratch the fluffy golden dog all over his neck and chest and his tail flops about in a fast blur. I pass them by to collect the coffee cup that's mine—the one marked peppermint mocha.

Theo laughs. "I'd say in Dad's eyes, we're both pretty demonic. I'm a lesbian and you're... you."

"Why does that feel like more of an insult than steaming dog shit?"

"You know what I mean." She pauses long enough to scratch extra attentively behind Atticus's droopy ears. "You've never gone along with the program. Though neither have I. It frustrates Dad."

"And I would care because?" I ask in between sips of warm peppermint and sweet mocha.

"Well, you are his only son. His legacy is yours to carry on."

"His legacy of what? His wife moved two thousand miles away from him."

"Mom's on a sabbatical."

"What a charmingly PC way to say they've separated, sister," I taunt darkly. My lips spread into a grin against my coffee cup as she casts me a scolding look. "You and I both know the truth about their marriage. Or lack thereof."

"Are you going to tell me what's up with the bags? If I didn't know any better, I'd guess you'd been up all night."

...that's because I have.

Enjoying every inch of Nyssa Oliver.

"Am I not allowed to stay up late?" I ask instead.

"You've never been a night owl. Even when we were teenagers. Remember prom? You fell asleep outside in the rose garden."

I grit my teeth. "It's not my fault the night went on too long. So much glitter and pop music. I was bored."

"Most kids were off fucking. Anyway, point is, you're not a night person. You've been different lately." She's finally tired of lavishing Atticus with adoration and rises to her feet to join me at the kitchen counter. Her tone shifts from humorous to serious that abruptly. "This isn't about the V Killer, is it?"

Tension cords through me, gripping me tight like a lasso. Eyes narrowed and jaw clenched, I hiss at her. "Really, Theo?"

"Kane Driscoll's murder is still unsolved. So is Holly Driscoll. And there's that attack on the college student from Halloween night. The evening news is saying it could be Valentine. I know how personal this is for you. What happened with Josalyn and all—"

"One moment you're heckling me about Veronica. Now it's Josalyn?"

"You feel things intensely, Theron. If you need someone to talk to—"

"I have plans," I interrupt sharply. "Papers to grade. Lessons to plan. Thanks for the coffee."

The dismissal is cold, perhaps cruel, but necessary in the moment.

I turn my back on her and walk toward my home office, snapping my fingers for Atticus to be obedient and follow.

Theo takes the hint and leaves only minutes later.

But the rest of the afternoon's hardly productive. The papers to grade and lessons to plan that I had mentioned turn out to be a false alibi. Instead, I spend the time locked in my home office trying to resist the urge to seek Nyssa out.

I breathe through the fervid temptation and force my mind elsewhere.

Current events. Recent legal studies. Projects around the house that are in progress.

Anything to take my mind off her.

The obsession's taken a life of its own. It's left me thick in an addiction I promised myself I'd never fall prey to again...

You feel things intensely, Theron. If you need someone to talk to...

My heart races in my chest as I slam shut my laptop and leap to my feet.

"This isn't that," I grind out, then I start pacing the room wall to wall. "That was years ago."

I go from denying the past to feeling the warm sunshine on my skin.

Josalyn's smile was like no other. It was a flower blooming before my eyes. It was in the way her entire face glowed along with the spread of her lips and flash of her pearly teeth.

I sank down beside her in the grass, feeling anemic against the spring rays of the sun that shone down on us and signaled winter was finally over.

I preferred the dark. The moody and rainy season where I could bask in my brooding.

But Josalyn made me feel alive. She made me feel eternally young...

I rumple fingers through my unruly hair and banish the past.

Theodora has no idea what the hell she's talking about. I'm a man of reason and logic and I'm in control of myself. The supposed reemergence of the Valentine Killer has no bearing on me or my life.

"It's not real. She's never coming back," I mutter under my breath. I snatch the textbook for Criminal Law One off my desk and pop it open to the last page of the required reading I'd given. "It's *impossible*."

"Any questions?" I ask the class Wednesday afternoon.

The two dozen empty-headed cows blink and gape back

at me like I've asked them the most complex mathematical equation imaginable. A scowl clenches onto my face as I incline my head toward the door.

"That is all," I say. "If you have nothing else, get out of my face."

Students scramble. They hustle to shove their books and laptops into their bags and crowd at the door in their eagerness to exit.

All except one.

Miss Oliver.

She sits obediently at her desk, shiny gaze stuck on me.

Jose Zardoya's last out, letting the door thud heavily behind him. The silence takes over from there, swelling with the unfettered passion that's grown between us in even just a few short hours.

From the last time we were together, experiencing each other.

I nudge my black-framed glasses further up the bridge of my nose. My right brow raises, my stance at my desk authoritative.

"Well?" I say into the loud silence. "What have I told you, Miss Oliver?"

Her head tilts to the side and her teeth graze her deliciously plump bottom lip. She hesitates only a second longer, then does as instructed—she sinks lower in her chair and spreads her legs obscenely wide.

Offering me an unobstructed view of her sopping wet cunt.

No panties.

Just as directed.

Her pleated skirt's ridden up her thighs and her pussy lips resemble the soft petals of a flower. The pink center so warm and inviting. Her pussy blooming before my eyes like an orchid.

I square my jaw, biting down on the rush of chemicals that flow through me. That shoot straight to my cock.

When I open my mouth to speak, my voice sounds hoarse. Borderline strained.

"Come here. Hands flat on my desk."

Nyssa, being Nyssa, makes a performance out of the demand. She rises to the occasion, slipping out from under the small L-shaped desk with a sultry sway of her hips and a pout of her lips. Then she's strutting toward me, step by step down the cascade of student desks.

Her shiny curls shimmy. Her pleated skirt flutters.

It teases skin.

So does the tight button-up blouse she wears that's seemingly fit to burst. Several of the male students had eye-fucked her as she took her seat when class began.

Justin Hendricks practically had his tongue flopping out of his mouth.

But Nyssa hardly paid him any mind. She only had eyes for me.

Like now.

I remain composed and distant as she struts toward me oozing sex. She's a temptress, a seductress about to make me lose my mind.

We both know it, though we hold on as long as we can.

Flattening her hands to my desk, she pushes her hips out and spreads her legs. Her eyes link with mine in brazen challenge and she says, "Anything you want, Professor."

I work the tension from my jaw and remind myself to breathe. "I've told you before, Miss Oliver, about misbehaving in my class."

"I'm sorry, Professor. I thought—"

"You thought wrong. Which means now I have to teach you a lesson. I want you to count along with me. Ready?"

Her shoulders rise with the breath she takes in and then straighten into perfect posture. She gives a nod.

I step behind her and flip her skirt up over her bare ass. I've grabbed hold of the wooden yardstick from my supply closet and beat it against the palm of my hand, building suspense by the second.

Her backside's round and supple. A delicious juicy peach I'd love to bite into.

Devour and feast on.

Worship.

But first things first.

Punishment.

I wind the wooden stick back, issuing the question on my mind. "What were you up to last night?"

"Homework."

"Wrong answer."

The wooden ruler slams into her ass on the first strike. She does a little hop in place, managing to keep her hands flat on the desk.

"Count along with me, Miss Oliver."

"One, Professor."

"Why are you lying? Homework? That's all?"

She releases a shaky breath. "I went to dinner."

"With who?"

"A friend."

Strike two.

The wooden ruler collides with the round, soft cheeks of her ass, forceful and sudden. It leaves behind the faintest strip of pink against brown.

The erotic sight elicits a buzz inside of me. My pulse

throbs so hard, I wonder if she can sense it. If she's aware my cock's twitching in my pants.

I'm both wild with need and composed from discipline.

"A friend?" I say, palming her pinkened ass. "Care to provide any names?"

Nyssa screams as I bring the ruler down a third time. Harder than the other two times.

"J-Justin!" she calls out before I can go in for a fourth. "He asked to borrow my notes. He said he would buy me dinner."

"Buy you dinner?" I repeat slowly. "So... a date?"

"Professor!" she cries.

But it's too late.

I've swung the ruler. The wooden stick whacks straight into the underside of her thighs, and she groans in what could be pleasure or pain.

Or both.

Either way, she hasn't uttered the agreed safe word.

She's trembling on the spot, but she's pushing back her hips, effectively shaking her ass in the air.

More, it says.

So I give it to her.

The ruler rains down on her gloriously round ass several more times. Each swat, she screams out the number.

"Seven!" she calls.

Then comes the eighth.

She shakes, her head angling toward the ceiling. The number warbles past her lips before the next smack collides and she's starting all over again.

Nine.

Ten. Eleven. Twelve.

Twenty.

I'm feverish, achingly hard, as I beat the ruler against her ass and she cries out along with me. The slender stick slips out of my hand and I admire my handiwork. The artful way the rosy pink blends with the golden brown. I groan and pull out my cock to stroke.

Coming up behind her, I let her feel how hard I am. The head of my cock runs along the seam of her cunt and she shudders in silent pleading.

"Is your ass sore, Miss Oliver?" I ask huskily.

She nods. Her hands haven't budged. She's a good girl, keeping them planted on the desk.

My left hand reaches under her.

She drips for me. Moans for me. Shudders for me as I fondle her greedy little wet pussy.

I kiss the spot behind her ear, then brush my lips against the gentle flesh. "It's too bad you're sore. But guess what?" I whisper. "Your pussy will be too once I'm through with you."

Without warning, I drive my cock all the way inside. Nyssa bucks against me in a wild scream. I grip her by the hair and yank her head back so I can kiss her throat.

She's tight warmth wrapped around me.

The sleekest silk encasing my cock.

"You feel so fucking good," I whisper against her skin. "My beautiful little whore that'll do anything for an A, is that right?"

She gasps, taken aback by the crass words.

I've begun moving, setting a hard pace from the first thrust. She digs her nails into the wood of my desk and rises up on the tips of her toes as I palm her ass and slide my cock in and out of her.

It wouldn't be the first time I was rough.

I've gradually broken her in. Tested the waters to see how far I can go. How much she can take.

Nyssa whimpers as she takes my cock and the brutal thrusts I give. But her body—*her squelching pussy*—betrays her. She clenches me tight, massaging me, kneading me as I dig deep inside her and then retreat to start over again.

Soon she's riding the wave along with me.

She's turning her head to meet my lips in a sloppy kiss, our flesh smacking together.

I fuck her and grope her and then wrap my hand around her throat to cut off her whimpers. I'm deep in her pussy as I lick at her jaw and tell her how she's my naughty little slut who will work for her A in this class. I squeeze her throat and bask in the dazed look that glazes over her beautiful face, like she's ascended the physical moment. She's floated into the realm of pleasure, where her orgasm rules.

Her pussy flutters.

I feel her come undone firsthand, her walls spasming. Her body seizes up. She's locked in my hold as I simply thrust harder, slamming into her soaking cunt and squeezing her slender throat. I give my all until I'm spilling inside her and tiny spots appear before my eyes.

We fold over my desk. We don't move for what's a very long time.

Minutes before we come to our senses and rise up as civilized beings again. I cup her face and kiss her lips tenderly, like I didn't just fuck her roughly like a whore.

But it's the language we speak. The routine we've developed.

Nyssa's as willing a participant as I am. She likes things wild and untamed. She enjoys the games we've begun to play.

"Are you okay?" I ask. My hands reach around to palm her ass. Massage her sore, reddened cheeks.

She nods. "Are you?"

I chuckle. "No," I answer, brushing her lips with mine. "You drive me insane."

"That's the goal."

She's smirking, meeting my eyes. A spark lives in them, like she's aware of a secret I'll never know. The same kind of confidence I've witnessed from the first day in class.

...this girl will truly make me lose my mind.

"How about you meet me on the east side of campus?" I ask. "I'll pick you up and we can have dinner. Outside of town."

"I should finish coursework from my other classes," she says after a beat. "Maybe next time?"

Just like that, she's fixing her clothes and gathering her things. I stand back, putting on a composed front, hands in my pockets.

She kisses me goodbye, though it does nothing for the tension cording through me.

The lasso's back, cinching tighter and tighter.

"Next time," I remind myself. "There's always next time..."

Friday rolls around, and Nyssa's absent from class. I'm distracted throughout the duration of it. So much so, other students take notice. Katelyn Wicker raises her hand to question if I'm in the middle of a heart attack. A few others in class laugh.

But I give a withering look that makes her shut up on the spot.

It's no heart attack that has me clenching and snarling. It's the absence of the person who has been on my mind almost every waking moment.

I send texts that go unanswered. Calls that go straight to voicemail.

She's avoiding me.

But why?!

Dean Rothenberg catches me once class lets out, falling into step beside me. "Theron, how about you join me and some of the other board of trustees for cigars tonight? Your father won't be making it, but you would be a fine stand-in. We'll be discussing how we'll approach the campus-wide paranoia about Valentine."

"No."

A single one word answer that's cold and succinct.

It's to the point enough that there's no room for objection. The dean watches me stride down the rest of the corridor as if he's too shocked to figure out what else to say.

I don't give a damn.

The only thing I give a damn about is Nyssa Oliver and where the fuck she is.

Why would she skip my class? All of her Friday classes, according to her AirTag. Is she sick? Hurt? Does she need me?

I stride straight toward my car, tossing my leather satchel into the passenger seat. I pull my phone from my pocket and log onto her cloud.

Her social media provides no updates. Neither do her emails.

Her texts are a different story.

> hey bby, still good for 8? Scarlet Room?

> Yes. 8 works. I'll be there.

A bell clangs inside me. It rings and rings until I feel my entire body vibrating with the sound. I clench my phone in my palm and glare at the screen.

"Who the fuck is this?" I growl.

I'm off in a tear.

My BMW veers into traffic with a squeal of rubber and protest honks from other cars nearby. For the first few miles, I'm not even sure where the hell I'm driving to. I'm driving just to drive. A maniac on the roads, I cut off others and flout common courtesy and traffic rules.

It wouldn't be the first time I've spiraled after the object of my affection's suddenly become distant.

"Who have you been with?" I snarled, blocking her path. "Why won't you tell me what's going on?"

"Move aside, Theron. I can't... I can't... okay?"

"Are you hurt? Is he hurting you? Josalyn—"

"Theron, move!"

She brushed past me before I could stop her. Before I could get to the bottom of what was going on...

It's not until I pull up outside Nyssa's apartment that I tune back into the present.

I'm pounding on her door in another second. Damn anyone who sees or overhears.

Even Theo, who manages the building.

"Nyssa!" I hiss outside her door. "Open up!"

But she never does. She's not home.

She's... somewhere. Preparing to meet someone.

Her AirTag is useless, telling me she's left her bookbag in her apartment.

I let myself into her apartment anyway, just to be sure. A thorough search of the place turns up little to no clues, except I uncover a Composition Notebook full of Nyssa's musings. A list of familiar names of well-known people around Castlebury and another page with lipstick smudges and *my* name doodled among the lines.

I snap shut the notebook and stuff it back under her mattress, where I found it.

My pulse beats wildly in my veins as I rush back to my car and attempt to regain some semblance of rational thought.

I comb through her digital footprint again, searching for meaning. How could I miss this? If she's meeting someone, then there must be other clues...

It's not until I reread the text message exchange for the fifth time that I realize what I've overlooked.

"Scarlet Room," I say. Then I google. The search results turn up what I've suspected.

Scarlet Room is a nightclub. Some kind of underground club with a reputation for drugs, alcohol, and *sex*.

Anonymous hookups are so casual and frequent there, people show up with that intention alone.

Now that I think about it, I've heard the stories in passing. Read the news articles in the paper, reporting the alleged sexual assaults and druggings.

Night is falling as I hit the roads again and drive toward the club. My mind, once so clear and sharp, is riddled with neurotic thoughts.

Is she cheating on me?

...or prostituting herself? Is she getting mixed up with the wrong crowd?

Does she need money? Why wouldn't she say anything to me?

My thoughts spiral into insane paranoia. I park outside the club, against the curb, ignoring the derisive snorts and curious stares I receive from people with a dozen tattoos and bright neon-colored hair.

I'm here with one purpose and one purpose only.

Find Nyssa and figure out what the hell is going on.

It's true that we haven't discussed exclusivity, but I thought it was implied that we weren't seeing other people.

We've had sex *unprotected*.

Fury pulses through me by the time I'm descending the steps into the dark, dank, dungeon-like underground club. The music's so loud, it drowns out all thought.

Monotonous techno beats that feel like they might bust an eardrum.

I submerge myself among the sweaty, writhing clubgoers, my eyes peeled for her.

I stick out like a sore thumb. An older male with glasses and a button-up shirt, I'm hardly subtle as I search the club.

Is she not pleased with the sex we're having? Have I been too soft? Too rough?

Am I too old? Not interesting or exciting enough for her youthful mind?

These questions and more plague me as I explore every inch of the club. I come across the dance floor, where dozens of people gyrate to the edgy, dark techno music, and then I wander into another area of the club where it seems the hookups happen.

I witness things like a woman disappearing out an emergency exit with two men in tow and another couple snorting white lines off each other.

None of them Nyssa.

I'm left in the dark. I'm wading uncharted water without a clue where I'm going.

Just like before.

"You have no business here," Professor Vise snarled.

Josalyn hugged her books to her chest. "But we need to talk about what happened..."

"Nothing happened. How many times do I have to tell you?"

I hovered outside his office door, my heartbeat frantic. I was a second away from rushing inside and interrupting.

"How could you?" she sniffled. "I won't let you get away with it."

He grinned. "You're delusional, Miss Webber. Get out of my sight."

I was outside as the door flung the rest of the way open and Josalyn ran out in tears. I started to follow.

"Josalyn, Josalyn... what's wrong?"

"Mr. Adler," came Professor Vise's baritone. "Never mind what you think you heard. If you're here to interview for the TA position, we can begin..."

I shake my head and realize two hours have gone by. I'm entrenched in the pulsing beats and humid air of the club, hoping Nyssa happens by.

But it's vain hope.

Clearly, wires have been crossed, and I've misunderstood.

I sigh deeply, then start for the exit. Coming up on the outside, the night's turned into a chilly, drizzly mess.

My car is half a block down.

I begin my trek with hands deep in my pockets, only to stop after a few footsteps.

Nyssa's up the street, her usually springy curls sleek

and straight. The tight curls aren't the only thing that's gone—her preppy, sometimes vintage manner of dress has been traded in for thigh-high leather boots, hot pants, and a semi-sheer top.

She almost doesn't look like herself. If I hadn't been searching out every face on the street, I certainly wouldn't have recognized her.

She stands back as a bald, penguin-shaped older man opens a rear car door for her. From where I am, I can't see his face, but I *can* see the appreciative smile on hers. She slides into the backseat before he joins her, drawing the door shut.

The windows are dark, obscuring whatever it is going on inside.

I'm quick on my feet. My mind's lost to the feverish, obsessive virus that takes over. I rush toward the car like a madman with no care in the world.

Except to find out what the fuck's going on.

I'm closing in when the sleek black car finally pulls away from the curb and starts down the street.

Within seconds, it's slipping out of view.

Nyssa's slipping through my fingers.

18

THERON

LOVE CRIME - SIOUXSIE

"Follow that black car!" I yell, wrenching open the door to the first taxicab I see.

The driver's only response is to tap the sign dangling among the pine air fresheners on his rearview mirror.

CASH ONLY

Cash isn't something I usually carry around with me. I pry open my well-used leather wallet to dig out the few twenties I've got on me. "Here," I say, shoving the cash up front at the driver. "I know it's short notice, but you've got to follow that damn car!"

The crumpled twenty dollar bills spill onto the seat next to him. He throws me a glance over his shoulder, the baseball cap he wears low on his brow, the profile of his nose large. He's a middle-aged man not much older than I am, with touches of gray threaded through his ear-length hair.

"Address?" he asks.

"I've got no address," I grit out. "I just need you to follow that car—there! The license plate is CUY7131."

"Okay, okay," he says in an accent I can't place but that sounds vaguely Eastern European. "Calm down, my friend. We'll follow."

We enter traffic with six cars between us and them. We're hitting the downtown district, which means traffic becomes congested on a *good* evening. On a Friday night, with drizzle sprinkling down and the roads slick and shiny, the pace slows to glacial.

I sit on the edge of the middle seat, my arms propped up on the back of both front seats, peering out the windshield. The best vantage point for keeping up with the traffic up ahead… and keeping my eye on Nyssa and the mystery man.

"So what's your name?" the driver asks, seeking eye contact in the rearview mirror.

"None of your concern."

"Mine is Casimir. Where're you headed?"

"Casimir, I appreciate your attempt at small talk. However—and there's no polite way to say this—shut the fuck up and focus on following that car!"

He chuckles as if I've told a joke. "Okay, okay. This must be serious business. I'll pull out all the stops."

I'd be amused if my heart wasn't jackhammering in my chest. If I didn't have a sick, twisted feeling pitted in my stomach that whatever it is that's happening can't be good.

Why the hell would Nyssa be meeting older men at sex clubs on Friday nights? Why would she be getting in some man's car? *Where* is he taking her?!

…and to do what?

Traffic thins out once we're past the popular streets

with the boutiques, restaurants, theaters, and other establishments on them. The six cars in between us dwindles to three and then two.

Casimir seems to sense it's best to hover this far back. It's enough of a buffer to remain dubious and unseen while still following them.

"The car is turning left onto Vineland Avenue," he observes aloud, switching on his turn signal too. "A nice car like that. They are headed for the castle tower. Don't you think?"

Though my answer comes in a silent, stiff nod to Casimir's question, I'm working on the same theory.

The Castlebury Tower is the tallest building in town, second only to the clock tower on the university campus. The building's comprised of private offices and luxury apartments that run anywhere from one million to ten the higher the floor.

Dad owns an apartment in this building. At the time of purchase, he claimed it would make the perfect man cave getaway from Mom. This was before they'd given up on pretending their marriage was healthy and intact.

I'd gone with him the afternoon he previewed the property. He'd boasted about the other men in his circle who owned offices and apartments in the same building, telling me about how the likes of Rothenberg and Cummings brought their mistresses here in their spare time.

It didn't take long before Dad was joining in on that tradition...

As the car Nyssa's in turns down the tunneled path that leads to an underground garage, I'm typing quickly on my phone. I'm researching just who else owns property in this building and if my hunch is correct.

"Stop here," I say halfway down the street. "I'll make it the rest of the way on foot."

I start to slide out from the backseat, then pause to unlatch the stainless steel Rolex from my wrist. "Take this," I say, "as extra payment for getting me here. It's used, but it should still be worth about ten grand."

Casimir nods gratefully and wishes me luck on my mysterious endeavor.

By the time he's driving away, I've wrenched off the tweed jacket I'm wearing. My fingers furiously unbutton my crisp button-up shirt. I toss both in the nearest receptacle but not before pocketing my eyeglasses.

Now for my face...

I head toward the corner store half a block down that's lit up on an otherwise wet, shadowy street. In hopes of finding some kind of disposable face mask to don, I find something even more useful inside the tiny store.

Toward the back is the Halloween clearance section, where several masks dangle from the hooks of the rotating display stand. My fingers curl around the skeleton one that resembles a ski mask in design, and I snatch it off the hook.

The cashier checks me out up front, the transaction totaling four dollars and twenty-seven cents.

I return to the scene outside the Castlebury Tower in full disguise.

I'm in nothing more than a plain dark shirt and the skeletal mask. Perhaps not totally foolproof, but the best I can do on such short notice. It's damn sure better than Clark Kent when he changes into Superman.

I cross the rain-slick side street and come up on the back of the tall building. If memory serves me correct, there was a massive courtyard on the ground floor which offered an alternate entrance. On a wet, frigid night like tonight, something tells me few people will be lounging outdoors.

I'm proven right as I gently open the glass door and slip inside the far end of the lobby. A bellboy happens to be fifteen feet off, standing by the elevators as he converses with a miffed-looking older woman in pearls.

Ducking out of sight, I take refuge behind a collection of leafy bamboo plants.

The moment becomes surreal in the way all seemingly impossible scenarios do.

Suddenly, my life has become a video game, where I'm to evade detection and make it upstairs.

The top floor penthouse *if* my instincts are correct.

Nyssa and her older companion haven't passed through the lobby yet. I block out the disturbing mental imagery that they could be sitting in the backseat of his car talking... or doing other things.

Just when I'm pondering if I'm trapped forever behind these bamboo plants, a man in a maintenance uniform strolls by, pushing a cart. He whistles as he stops at the elevator, scanning his access card against the panel that grants him use of it.

My adrenaline drums inside me. My gaze swings from the bellboy still engaged with the woman in pearls to the maintenance man waiting for the elevator.

It's now or never.

As the elevator doors roll open and the maintenance man steps inside with his cart, I rush toward the entrance to join him. I've ripped off my skeletal mask, clutching it nondescriptly in my hands.

Ironically, the situation works in my favor without the mask—the man nods at me as if he recognizes me.

And won't question what I'm doing on this elevator.

We ride up several floors in silence, and then I take yet another risk.

"I believe I've seen you before. But we haven't been properly introduced."

"You have? Well, been working here for a decade. Guess that makes sense. Thought I recognized you too."

"Thurman Adler. I own property in this building. Fifteenth floor."

"That so? No wonder you look so familiar."

No... that would be my father...

"Well, it's a good one to have a stake in. Round-the-clock amenities. Even maintenance. Why d'you think I'm here so late?" He gives a gruff laugh. "Got a dishwasher I've got to repair on the eleventh floor. Actually, this is me. You need anything, you let me know."

"Enjoy the rest of your night," I say once we've reached his floor and he's stepped off.

He gives me a polite nod and picks up his whistle as he starts down the hall.

I smash my finger on the close button, then select the top floor. The maintenance man didn't notice—the tag pinned to his chest said his name was Walter—but as he talked, I swiped his access card.

Snuck it right off his cart.

Yet another insane risk I've taken in such a short amount of time.

...you have no idea the lengths I'm willing to go through for you, Miss Oliver.

But I will make sure you atone for making me do this...

I arrive on the top floor with my skeletal mask back over my face. While there's usually cameras in the elevators of buildings like this, I hope I've kept myself angled enough that I didn't appear too clearly.

I take the same care slinking down the hall of the top floor.

The entire floor is dedicated to the penthouse, the entrance straight ahead. The same type of black panel that had been outside the elevator in the lobby is mounted to the left of the penthouse door. I stop in front of it, inhale a deep breath, and scan the card I've swiped.

The little light blinks green and the lock clicks.

I'm not even sure what I plan to do now that I've gained entry.

Nyssa and her gentleman caller will be up any moment. I'll be faced with the immediate decision of whether to lurk and spy or sate my impulsiveness and confront them.

Both seem like possibilities.

Both halves of myself I'll have to choose between.

"It isn't what you think it is, Theron," Professor Vise chuckled. "The girl has so many crazy ideas. I regret ever trying to take her under my wing."

He approached with a kettle emitting curls of steam and poured hot water into our mugs. Soon the tea bag's turned the water a pale amber shade.

"What kind of ideas?" I asked, trying to keep a hold on my temper. I was running as hot as the boiling water in my mug.

A tall man with copper skin and broad shoulders, Vise reclaimed his seat across from me and brought his mug up to his mouth to blow on his tea. "You know, all kinds of things. She can't seem to leave well enough alone."

"Like what, Professor?" I pressed.

His dark eyes gleamed as he put down the mug again. His chuckle returned, weaved in between each word of his response. "Well, for starters, she's gone around making very damaging accusations. Specifically about who's behind Valentine."

"Such as?"

"Me," he answered, then his laugh deepened. "She thinks I'm *Valentine*. Isn't that absolutely ridiculous? Of all people... me?!"

My eyes darken staring at the penthouse door, waiting for it to open.

I haven't even bothered to claim a hiding spot. I'm standing defiantly out in the open of the massive forty square foot living room area among the bright pendant lights and bland beige furnishings.

A crazed, irrational part of me wants to see the look of surprise on their faces when they walk in.

I want to witness the way Nyssa's features round with sheer shock and watch as she struggles to stitch together an explanation.

An even darker part of me aches to reach for one of the knives in the immaculate kitchen and lodge it straight into his throat. The barbaric urges are far beneath me on any other occasion, except situations such as *this*.

Sometimes, in situations such as this, it's justified.

Voices sound from outside the door.

They're home.

The door sweeps open and Jackson Wicker ushers Nyssa through in the middle of telling her about his last yacht trip in the Maldives.

She's as poised and complimentary as expected, giving a soft hum of interest. His hand falls to the small of her back to guide her deeper into the spacious floor plan of the penthouse.

I've chosen to hide out of view after all.

Curiosity overtook rage, at least for the moment. At least until I understand what the hell's going on.

"Didn't I tell you no one would see us, darling? The

private entry is very discreet. It's for us VIP residents. Allows us to have very secret, very naughty visitors over."

Nyssa merely casts him a polite smile, her gaze borderline vacant as if to give nothing away.

"How about I pour us some drinks, darling, while you freshen up?" he asks. "Don't forget what we agreed. You know what I expect."

The corner of Nyssa's mouth twitches, almost disrupting her pasted-on smile. "How could I forget? I've been waiting for you."

It's then that I notice she has a small overnight bag with her. Jackson guides her toward the hall—again, with his damn stubby-fingered hand at the small of her bare back—and he directs her to where the bathroom is.

"In the bedroom, darling," he says. "Use the ensuite. I can't wait to see you all dolled up."

Nyssa humors him with a small giggle, then disappears down the hall.

Jackson Wicker starts toward the minibar that's set up against the large floor-to-ceiling window overlooking the city.

While his back is turned fixing drinks, I slip the skeletal mask back over my face and step out from behind the sectional sofa.

I stalk by the kitchen and pluck the largest knife from the wooden block perched on the counter. Jackson turns half around, speaking to himself aloud.

"Where did I put that corkscrew? Ah, yes. Here it is."

The oaf, who's as slow-witted as his jock son, turns all the way back around again. He adds ice to both glasses and then digs in his blazer pocket for a little baggy of baby blue powder. I recognize it at once as Euphoria, the same substance I'd planted on his son only a couple weeks ago.

The contents of the baggy are emptied into the drink on the left.

Nyssa's drink.

"For some added fun," he guffaws.

The same oafish guffaw as his son.

My grip tightens on the large kitchen knife I've grabbed.

For another unpredictable second, I almost rush him from behind. I'd love nothing more than to ram the blade into his back. Then his skull. Then any other part of him as he collapsed and looked up at me, dying.

But too many questions remain unanswered.

Questions like what the hell is Nyssa doing here in the first place? What is about to transpire between her and Mr. Wicker? Has she been sleeping with her ex-boyfriend's father all along, or is this some new development? Some kind of revenge ploy?

I creep from the kitchen, sight unseen. Mr. Wicker's now mixing the cocktails he's made in his stainless steel shaker. Nyssa's presumably still in the bathroom 'dolling' herself up. I enter the master bedroom that's about as large as the living room area. A king-sized bed sits in the middle, along with a reading nook by the window and balcony.

Turning left toward the bathroom, I realize Nyssa's left the door open. She's done changing, donning some kind of girlish costume.

She's put her hair up in hasty pigtails and slipped on a pastel pink babydoll dress that barely covers her backside.

Thigh high socks and black Mary-Janes complete the strange, childish yet sexual look.

Is this what Mr. Wicker requested? He's having her dress up like a *little girl?*

She spends a second longer hiking the socks further up her thighs, hardly paying attention to her surroundings. If she did, she'd see my reflection in the mirror as I flit by behind her.

I'm back to retreating, sliding open the mirrored closet door and stepping inside. It glides back into place just as she's wandering past.

Now that she's dressed, she leaves the bathroom to set the scene in the bedroom.

I crack open the closet's sliding mirrored door and watch as she places a stuffed teddy bear at the pillows and pulls out a wooden paddling brush.

...what the fuck is going on!?

Nyssa misses me as I make my next move. I slip out of the closet and dart toward the nearby armchair. I crouch down in time to be out of sight when Mr. Wicker finally enters clutching their drinks. His pudgy face brightens at the scene he finds.

"Excellent, darling. You're such a good little girl. I made you a drink."

Don't fucking drink that, Nyssa!

I clench my teeth and grip the knife, ready to pounce at any second.

When Mr. Wicker tries to hand the beverage to her, she folds her arms behind her back and shakes her head side to side like a child would.

"My mommy says not to accept drinks from strangers."

He chuckles, endeared by the role-play. "But, darling, I'm not a stranger."

"Will you read me a story?" she asks instead, then she pats the bed. "On here."

The oaf has the same doucheface syndrome his son suffers from—at Nyssa's suggestion, his grin stretches ear to ear and his ruddy skin gleams as if he's been out in the hot sun. He laughs some more and then says, "Of course, darling. But I'd prefer if you drink up first."

"Story first!"

"Nyssa, are you going to be a good little girl or am I going to have to take you over my knee and paddle you?" he scolds.

I shift to launch myself from where I've hidden behind the armchair, then I stop.

Something else I haven't noticed until now has caught my eye. Along with the wooden paddle, storybook, and teddy bear Nyssa's set out, is a card that's been placed on the bedside table.

A black, heart-shaped card with white lettering spelling out Jackson Wicker.

Valentine.

It can't be what I think it is. Nyssa can't be...

That would make no sense. It would be impossible. *More* than impossible.

My head hurts trying to make sense of this development. The past aches inside me like an old battle wound that hasn't healed while the present seems determined to rip it the rest of the way open...

"I said drink up," Mr. Wicker growls, grabbing Nyssa by the chin to force the beverage down. "Bad little girls disobey. Bad little girls get punished! Do you want to get punished? DRINK IT!"

"I SAID NO!"

Nyssa jabs a defensive knee into his gut before he can make her.

I've emerged at the same time, appearing in the skeletal mask, holding up the large knife from the kitchen. As Nyssa knees him a second time, her gaze lifts to spot me coming toward them, and she screams.

She vaults over the wide bed to put space between us.

But she has the wrong idea—she's not who I'm after.

Mr. Wicker staggers, groaning with a hand to his gut. "You little bitch," he spits. "What did you do?"

Nyssa's eyes widen as she peers beyond his shoulder and finally realizes what's about to happen.

I tap Jackson Wicker on the shoulder and wait for him to turn around. Before he can even properly react, the blade comes down and stabs him in the chest.

Right in the heart.

His meaty hands fumble at the knife handle sticking out of him, his mouth opening and closing in sweaty, blanching shock.

Then he collapses backward onto the bed and his eyes go blank.

Dead.

Nyssa hasn't moved an inch, except for the shake her body gives at the mysterious intruder.

Me.

I rip off the skeleton mask, aware how I must look. Questionable sanity—or lack thereof altogether—has begun to feel alarmingly normal.

"Hello, Miss Oliver," I say in my authoritative tone. "Care to tell me what the fuck you're doing?"

19
NYSSA
BITTERSUITE - BILLIE EILISH

Theron is dead silent as we meticulously stage Jackson Wicker's murder scene. We scrub the bedroom for all potential evidence leading back to us and then set up everything perfectly for when the police show up.

He's not found until the next morning, having bled out on his bed, stripped naked, lying right next to his personal laptop with the heart-shaped Valentine card directing authorities to check the files saved on the device. His thousands of files of sickening child content are easily discoverable once they do.

The news spreads like wildfire within minutes.

Theron and I are lying in bed at my apartment as we parse through the many stories pouring in from the media. He's still angry with me on some level, his tone clipped, though that didn't keep him from pulling me close lying in bed.

"It looks like it's gone as we hoped," he says, scrolling through the articles on his phone.

I'm seated beside him, my legs folded under me, as I browse on my laptop. "It seems the major headline is the fact that he was a pedophile. Which is exactly what it should be. If Valentine were still around, Mr. Wicker would deserve to be his victim."

Theron raises a brow at me. "If he was?"

"Twenty years later," I clarify. "Whoever Valentine was... if he's still alive..."

"That brings us to a topic of discussion we'll have to go over. Just why you're seeking to imitate the Valentine Killer in the first place."

"I never intended for Mr. Wicker to wind up dead. That was sort of... you."

"For good reason. That still doesn't explain why you were imitating Valentine."

I shrug. "I have my reasons."

"Which are?"

"It didn't involve you until you followed me. Are we going to talk about that?"

"No," he answers succinctly. "Because I saved your life."

"I had it under control."

He grabs my face to turn it toward his and then kisses me on the mouth. "You didn't have it under control," he says, our faces almost touching. "Jackson Wicker was going to drug you and do as he wished. You couldn't have fought him off. We will discuss this in more detail soon. And you will be punished for this stunt."

"More like you're looking for an excuse to use the yardstick again."

"I don't need the yardstick. I now have the lovely wooden paddle Wicker thought he'd get to use on you."

My cheeks warm as I turn away from him, scooting off the bed. Theron eventually follows, working in tandem with me as we make the bed and then get ready for the morning. He has to go check on Atticus while I have some art projects to work on.

We kiss goodbye as we walk from the bedroom to the rest of the apartment. It's as I stand back to let Theron step toward the door that I notice something off that I'd missed late last night when we'd come home.

"My sculpture," I mutter. "It's been knocked off the shelf."

Theron stops at the door to glance over. I've rushed toward the far corner where my little makeshift art studio is and knelt down to collect the cracked pieces.

"*Touch of a Lover*. It's broken..."

"How would that have happened?" he asks.

"I don't know. I must not've noticed last night. It was too dark, and we didn't turn on the living room light. Was this you, Peaches?"

My ginger girl purrs from where she's perched on my sofa. I know that haughty sound—she's telling me she knows better than to ever nudge one of my sculptures off the shelves.

Theron walks over to drop a kiss on top of my head. "I'm sorry it's shattered. It was a beautiful piece. Will you recreate it?"

"I'm not sure," I mumble. "I guess I have no choice."

We say goodbye for real this time, with Theron reminding me we still have a lot to settle about last night.

I spend the rest of the morning cleaning up around my apartment and working on my next art project. Occasionally, I check for updates about Jackson Wicker's murder, but I'm more distracted by the fact that one of the sculptures I worked so hard on has shattered out of nowhere. Did Peaches really do it, or was it someone else?

Someone with access to my apartment...

I'm still distracted midafternoon when knocks at the door interrupt. Peaches meows and trots toward the door as if about to go investigate.

"Chill, Sherlock Whiskers. I got it."

Along the way to my door, I stop to wipe my hands on a towel and check my reflection in the gilded wall mirror. I check the peep hole to find two unexpected faces on my doorstep.

"Remember that whole call ahead thing?" I ask, wrenching the door open.

Heather and Macey file inside clutching various gifts. Everything from bottles of wine to freshly made macaroons from a local bakery to a new purple passion plant to add to my collection.

I laugh at the offerings. "What's all this?"

"Courtesy of Heather. I'm just the help," Macey says. She sets down the white box of rainbow macaroons and shakes back her fringed hair from her face. "She insisted on making a million stops to pick you up some things."

I fold my arms and watch in amusement as the duo each set down the gifts on the table I call my dining room table, but what I've more often than not used for art and schoolwork.

"That true, Heather?" I ask.

The strawberry blonde seems kind of shy for once in her life, almost blushing. "You've been here for us, Nyssie. I figured we'd repay you."

...you're going to have to do way better than macaroons and a house plant to repay me, Driscoll.

"I'm impressed you remembered I liked the macaroons at Cake Couture."

"Heather ordered two dozen for you."

"You know, you should probably be with Katie right now. The news about her father..."

Heather scoffs. "Please, the last thing Katie needs are more snacks. We all know how she eats her feelings. Besides, Nyssie, you're my real friend. Not Katie."

I can barely keep from laughing at the fact that these girls are falling over themselves to impress me. It's so opposite from how our relationship was years ago that it's a form of sweet revenge in itself—years ago, they'd relished the chance to bully me.

Today, they've basically become my minions.

I've become Switzerland. The neutral party—wronged party in the Samson and Heather situation—who has the high ground.

Macey shakes her head and pins Heather with a scolding stare.

"Can't you be nice to Katie for once?"

"Why should I? She's annoying."

"And you're a bitch," Macey snaps.

"I've heard worse. Then again, Macey, so have you. Jocks talk."

Macey's face scrunches in disgust as she storms out of the apartment.

We remain in silence for the first few seconds that follow. I'm still amused, taking a bite out of my macaroon in between sips of rosé.

"She's insufferable just like Katie," Heather mutters finally. "Anyway, Nyssie, thank you for recommending that lawyer. I'm sure to get my inheritance."

"Let's hope. So, have you heard what the news is saying about Katie and Samson's father?"

She shudders out a sigh. "Valentine really is back. Luckily, it seems he's after these old people. Maybe he's finishing business from the first time."

Something like that.

"It's no wonder neither one wants to show their face in public," Heather goes on. "I heard Samson's even dropped out of this semester. That reminds me. What's going on between you and Professor Adler?"

For once, Heather catches me by surprise. I swallow my next bite of macaroon, battling the sudden dryness in my throat. "There's nothing going on."

"You always stay late," she says, smirking. "Reminds me of me and Professor York junior year of undergrad. That man and his hands…"

"I wish I could relate. But I can't."

"Hmm. Well, who knows? He could be a viable rebound. After, you know, Samson."

The blonde moves on as though she hasn't just stumbled upon my secret.

Professor Adler and I aren't simply *hooking up*. The nature of our relationship has evolved past anything I ever conceived.

He's come to terrify me at the same time as excite me.

Last night most of all, and how far he was willing to go the second he thought I was in danger…

There's still so much to sort out, including the matter of my punishment because of last night. Any amusement I felt from Heather and Macey fighting among themselves fades. Gooseflesh dances across my skin as I think about what's waiting for me in his classroom come Monday…

Professor Adler requests that I show up an entire hour early to his class Monday morning. He gives me instructions on the outfit he expects me to wear—the same rosy cashmere blouse, plaid skirt, and platform loafers I'd worn the day I bumped into him outside orientation.

He promised punishment was to come after what happened with Mr. Wicker. It seems that day has arrived.

Butterfly-like nerves quake in my belly as I raise my fist to his office door and then knock.

"Come in."

His tone's cool and effortless. Naturally chiding and authoritative.

My pussy clenches in response. I take a second just to gather myself, breathing in and out.

Keep calm, Nys. You got this.

From the first step inside his office, the atmosphere feels adversarial. The room's as warm and dimly lit as it had been that night weeks ago on Halloween when he'd first brought me here and we'd... given into temptation.

My eyes scan the dozens of legal books crammed on the bookshelves and the world globe perched along a filing cabinet against the wall. Flames crackle in the gated fireplace off to my left and raindrops speckle the leaded glass window.

Professor Adler sits behind his desk, his expression pinched. His glasses have slid halfway down his nose as he's angled his head downward and scribbles away furiously at some sort of document. My eyes can't help tracking his movements.

The sleeves of his button-up shirt have been unceremoniously rolled to the elbow, allowing his forearms to be on display. I can't remember ever seeing a pair that were as sophisticated yet solid and masculine as his.

Every indentation, every muscle and defined vein makes breath hitch in my chest. Sparse dark hairs pepper the length, like many other parts of his body. I almost close my eyes remembering how it feels to run my fingers along his arms.

Sink my nails into them as he grips me and fucks me...

I'm flushed and hot by the time I reach his hands.

His hands.

They're positioned so tightly around the pen he holds, his knuckles large and prominent. His nails clean and trimmed. Fingers long, thick, and deft.

Suddenly, I'm recalling how they feel on me. Wide, warm palms canvassing my bare skin, squeezing and groping. I can practically feel his fingers sliding inside my pussy, usually while he teases his tongue to mine and kisses me.

I'm damn near on the verge of orgasming by the time Professor Adler acknowledges my presence.

His gaze snaps up to my face. The pen drops from his grasp. A scowl edges his features, making them harsher, even more masculine.

"You're late."

"By a few minutes," I say, fussing with the strap of my leather bookbag. "I wasn't sure if you meant your office or the lecture hall."

"Don't move."

Simple instruction that should be easy to follow, but as he shoots up to his feet and comes around his desk, I wonder if he can hear my heartbeat. If the little butterflies in my stomach count as movement...

As a result, I hold my breath.

He approaches with an appraising stare. From behind the lens of his glasses, his dark eyes travel the entire length of me, making sure I've dressed as told. When he slips behind me, completely out of sight, I bite down on my lip and ignore how I can *feel* him.

His closeness. His heat.

He steps toward me and his woody, spiced scent fills my nose too.

Familiar notes of fine paper and clove.

Professor Adler must know what he does to me, because his hand falls to my hip and he comes up so close, I'm braced against his chest. His lips tickle the hot shell of my ear.

"I know you haven't forgotten about Friday night, Miss Oliver," he drawls in his thick, authoritative tone. "Today, you're going to regret ever misleading me. You're going to come clean about what you've been up to, and then you'll hopefully learn your lesson never to do it again."

"Yes, Professor."

"Hands flat on the desk," he orders. "Legs shoulder width apart. Now."

I rush to get into position, my breathing already labored. Palms pressed against the smooth oak wood, I spread my legs 'til it almost feels crass.

Professor Adler's stepped back to observe. "Did you wear no panties like you were told to do so?"

"Yes."

"Yes, *what*?" he snaps.

"Professor Adler."

"Professor Adler, *what*?"

"Yes, Professor Adler," I blurt out quickly.

"It seems in just a few short days, you've forgotten your manners, Miss Oliver. Don't worry, we'll fix that today."

He walks back to the front of his desk to retrieve an item from a drawer. I'm expecting the familiar slim, hard yardstick to make its appearance, but discover I'm wrong in the next second. He's pulled out the same wooden paddle from Friday night in Jackson Wicker's penthouse.

I hadn't ever meant for Mr. Wicker to get the chance to use it.

The entire situation was a trap. I'd set him up intentionally knowing he'd fall for it hook, line, and sinker. His sick proclivities for underage girls meant he couldn't resist the opportunity. He first messaged me on a site some rich men use to find women called NSFW. He'd recognized me at Kane Driscoll's funeral and suggested we meet up at the Scarlet Room for a potential role play scenario.

He thought he'd fulfill his sick fetish Friday night while I intended on making him the next Valentine victim.

So many years ago, he'd been on the board that voted to expel my mother from school.

More than deserved considering the evil he'd done in his life.

I'd never expected Professor Adler to show up. Or for the wooden paddle to make an appearance today.

"Look familiar?" he taunts. "I believe you know the drill, Miss Oliver. Spanking does seem to be your thing, doesn't it?"

Though he's giving me hell, he's still right.

Professor Adler's helped me discover that almost nothing gets me off as quickly as being spanked. I can come from that alone.

The hard swats against my ass make me wet. The breathless anticipation waiting for the next blow excites me.

There's the element of repetition as I sink into the contrasting sensations.

Pleasure... but also pain.

A swatting pain that actually feels good.

So good.

Professor Adler's massaging hands after the fact are the cherry on top.

He moves back behind me and flips my skirt over to expose my backside. "I expect total honesty from you. For every dishonest or dissatisfactory response, you get a blow. We'll be here all day if we must. If it takes you that long to come fucking clean."

Anger edges into his tone. Resentment I'm sure has grown over the past few days.

I give a nod. "Yes, Professor."

"Why were you texting Jackson Wicker?"

"We exchanged numbers. It was weeks ago."

"For what reason?"

Ugh. Here we go.

"He made a pass at me," I say. "I... I knew I could bait him into meeting up."

I squeeze my eyes shut a millisecond before the first blow. The wooden paddle connects with my ass, eliciting an instant scream out of me. The hot sting sears across my flesh.

For being the first hit, he's gone harder than usual.

"Why would you ever want to bait him, Miss Oliver?" he asks through clenched teeth.

"B-because... I've been... he escaped Valentine the first time."

And he deserves it.

"Why would you care about Valentine?"

I don't respond. I'm caught between the truth and the role I've been playing. No one else but Mom knows about what I'm doing at Castlebury. Nobody's even suspected that I'm infiltrating their circle in order to destroy them in the worst ways.

All out of revenge for my family.

"I found out Jackson Wicker was a pedophile. He told me about it on a meet up site called NSFW. We agreed to meet at the Scarlet Room. He made the proposition and I accepted," I recite half the truth. "He deserved to be taken out by Valentine."

"I thought you said you never intended for him to die."

Professor Adler deals the second blow. It comes crashing down on my ass as hard and brutal as the first. I keen in pain, arching my back despite the fact that I force my hands to remain on the desk.

My ass already feels like it's on fire. I'm sure it's turning red. Will I even be able to sit down in class?

Professor Adler gives me a second to recover before his interrogation continues.

"Are you aware how dangerous what you did is, Miss Oliver? Do you know what could have gone wrong if you did not handle Mr. Wicker properly?"

"Yes," I answer. "But... I did have it under control—*argh*!"

Professor Adler deals a double blow. Two quick smacks of the paddle in immediate succession.

The air in my lungs runs short. My ass burns and aches while my pussy's started throbbing.

"Tell me the truth," he says. "Have you been behind the Valentine murders?"

"I'm too young, Professor. I wasn't alive when—*ARGH*!"

The paddle slams into my ass with such force, I press against the desk for leverage. The wooden anchor slides forward from the impact.

I'm openly panting now, my legs shaking. Yet my pussy's wet. I can *feel* how slick I am.

"Do you need to stop?" he asks me. "You stop, it's over. We're done here. For good."

"No," I choke out. "Keep... keep going."

His rage pulses off him, circling around me in a wave. "Then tell me. Tell me the truth!"

"Yes!" I cry out as the paddle comes down again. And again. "Yes, it was me! I've... I've been doing it, Professor!"

"Why!?"

"Because they deserved it!"

"WHY?!"

The paddle knocks what little air remains out of me. I slump over the front of the desk, panting and shaking and aching as my mask finally slips.

It falls away, and next thing I know, I'm spilling my secret.

Hot, unshed tears brim my eyes and I'm telling Professor Adler about my father who was murdered decades ago. My mother who was ostracized. My childhood which began with the likes of Heather Driscoll, Samson Wicker, and their posse tormenting me.

The paddle slips from Professor Adler's hand and thuds onto the floor. He gathers me up in his arms, lifting me from where I've collapsed against the desk and tilting my head to the side for a look at him.

"Why have you never told me this before?"

"I don't normally go around telling every person I meet my trauma—or that I'm mimicking the crimes of some serial killer in a plot for revenge."

His thumb strokes my cheek. "The authorities won't trace Wicker back to you. We left the scene clean enough. No evidence or anything else traceable. The Valentine card will keep police occupied. Your alibi for that night is that you were studying late at the campus library. The computer system will show you checked out a book. I have known the librarian Ms. Chlebek for twenty years. She will corroborate this. Understand?"

"Yes... but... why?"

"Jackson Wicker *was* a terrible person. I have no sympathy for him."

I nod. "Thank you."

"But understand," he goes on, peering intensely into my eyes, "if you do something like this again, today will be a cake walk. I will *not* be happy with you."

"Yes, Professor. I understand."

"I don't think you do, Miss Oliver. The punishment's not over. Hands on the desk."

Words escape me as his warmth fades and his arms disappear from my sides. He steps back as if waiting for me to get in position. A whine almost starts up in my chest. Pain still stings my ass cheeks from the wooden paddle.

I'm not sure I can take many more. Even as wet and turned on as I am.

I flatten my hands on the desk and spread my legs.

Professor Adler reaches into the drawer to withdraw two items I can't make out before he's disappearing behind me again. The back of my skirt's tossed up over me so that I'm exposed and at his mercy.

Nerves flutter away. I focus on my breathing, waiting for the reveal.

I hear the click of a cap and then crinkle of a plastic bottle. "Have you ever been fucked up your ass, Miss Oliver?"

My eyes go big. "What?! No! Never."

"Never?"

"No, Professor. Not once."

"Well, today will be a first. We'll begin by easing you

into it. Lucky for you, Miss Oliver, I brought the smallest plug today."

A stunned breath sputters out of me. Once again, words elude me.

"Not so lucky for you, Miss Oliver," he goes on, "you'll have to wear it quite a while. That plump ass of yours should adjust nicely in due time."

Slick, cool liquid slips over my flesh.

Lube.

His fingers gather the liquid, circling my puckered, untouched hole. I squeak when he penetrates me with a single digit, sliding in then out to begin preparation.

"Very, very tight," he says. "I can't wait to see this hole swallow the plug right up."

His words are spoken so matter-of-factly yet carry an arousing element that makes my pussy spasm. I'm struggling to breathe as Professor Adler fingers my rear hole. He goes slow and gentle for a few minutes, then pushes me harder.

He squirts more lube and forces in a second finger to an even shriller squeal from me.

"Are you aware, Miss Oliver, that your tight little asshole sucks at me? It tries to draw me right in. I think you were made for this."

A moan falls freely from my lips as he slides two fingers into my ass and he kisses the side of my neck.

My body responds in ways beyond my mind's control.

My hips begin rocking with the pumping motion of his fingers. Arousal coats my pussy lips and heat burns me from the inside. I've lost all thought and can barely breathe as a kernel of pleasure is born.

It grows, swelling like a balloon that will soon pop.

Erupt with pleasure.

Professor Adler's patient, settling me into the penetration of his fingers. He grips my hip and drops a few more kisses on my throat as he tells me how filthy I am.

I've been so bad.

"Haven't you?" he growls. "You deserve to be punished. Don't you, Miss Oliver?"

"Yes," I pant, quivering. "I do. Please, do it."

"That's what I want to hear. You're ready."

He liberally applies more lube, including to the small spade-shaped steel plug, then begins carefully pushing it against my puckered hole.

My mouth falls open as I stand still with hands on the desk and legs spread. The plug breeches me slowly, opening me up more than I've ever imagined. The ring of muscle expands to make room for the shiny, slippery toy.

Tremors rock through my body. The room begins to feel like it's spinning.

Professor Adler kisses the spot behind my ear and slicks another inch inside. "If only you could see this, Miss Oliver. Your ass is swallowing it right up. It'll be buried deep in no time. You'll be sitting through my class with it inside you. Only you and I will know."

The sound I make in response might as well be a babble. I'm flushed and throbbing, braced against the wooden desk or else I'd sink to the ground.

"But," Professor Adler drawls into my ear, "what would everyone think if they knew? If they found out you were a filthy girl who let your professor insert an anal plug into you minutes before class? What if they found out you're my filthy little whore?"

"OH!" I scream out as he gives a surprise jerk of the plug.

The stretch sensation has me reeling. My pussy throbs

harder, one flick of my clit away from coming. I almost go for it. Take my hands off the desk to pleasure myself.

But I know better.

Professor Adler would love to punish me for it.

Finally, the last of the plug slips inside. The handle rests like a crown between my round ass cheeks.

Professor Adler squeezes my hip to mentally draw me back to him. "Is this too much for you, Miss Oliver? Say the word and I'll take it out. But you'll fail. You don't like to fail, do you?"

No... no... never...

I'm panting as I give a fervent shake of my head to the side.

Mom didn't raise a failure. I've never failed at anything in my life. While being able to take a butt plug wasn't an achievement I've ever imagined I'd pride myself at succeeding in, I refuse to give up now.

"Tell me, Miss Oliver. Yes or no?"

"Yes," I whisper. "Yes, I can take it."

"Good girl."

He reaches under me and his fingers glide along my folds to collect my juices. Next, his fingers find my clit to rub circles.

It only takes a few before I'm coming undone.

I cry out as my orgasm ripples through me and the heaviness from the plug applies a new level of pressure.

"Yes," Professor Adler drawls, feeling me shudder against him. He sinks two fingers into me and my back arches. "Fingers in your pussy. A plug in your ass. Miss Oliver, you are so fucking filthy, so fucking gorgeous like this."

My one orgasm multiplies into two as he pumps his fingers inside me and then twists the plug in my rear hole.

Heat licks its way through my body and I break apart in another deep quake.

"Too much?" he whispers, nibbling at my ear, fingers knuckle deep in my pussy. "I can't wait to fuck your pussy with my cock. Feel that little plug buried in your ass."

"P-Professor... oh my... god!"

It's all I can say right now as I slump in his arms, my head propped up against the hard line of his shoulder.

"Later, Miss Oliver. That'll come later."

All at once, his fingers are gone from my pussy and my skirt's righted.

He steps back in appraisal as I stand, wobbling.

He grins, the devilish glint in his eyes shining through his glasses. "Now, time for class."

20

NYSSA

DIRTY LITTLE SECRET - NESSA BARRETT

Heather frowns when she takes her seat beside me in class. "Nyssie, why are you sitting like that? Cramps? Such a bitch, right?"

I swallow against the thick feeling in my throat and give a stiff nod. "Yep."

"I've probably got some Midol. You should've ditched like I do. Who cares about mens rea or whatever?"

Heather's words go in one ear and out the other. My focus is on getting through the next hour and a half.

The plug's so deeply entrenched in my ass that no matter how I sit in my desk, I can feel it. But my skirt's so short and I'm without panties, so I'm preoccupied on multiple fronts. I clear my throat and grip the edges of the table, my posture straight as a board.

The rest of the class has finished sliding into their seats. Professor Adler enters no less than a second later, commanding the attention of the room.

The breathlessness I've been feeling only intensifies at the sight of him.

And the secret that hangs between us.

It's a wicked little secret that just might be our undoing.

In a room of twenty-four people, we're the only two who know about the plug inside me. We're aware of just what we were up to minutes ago in his office.

He tosses down the two textbooks he's carrying with him. The heavy books produce a loud thud hitting the hard wooden surface. Several students like Hannah Fochte in the front row flinch. The bespectacled, green-haired girl stares at him as if she's about to flee the room.

His energy transforms the entire vibe in the room. His frustration becomes its own feeling that surfs the air and prompts a few people to exchange glances.

But what no one knows is that his frustration is my frustration—as Professor Adler straightens his glasses and peers at the room with a clenched jaw, *I'm* clenching too. I'm clutching the small L-shaped surface of my desk and squirming as subtly as possible in my seat.

My pussy, still so slick and wet, throbs away. The soreness in my backside refuses to be forgotten while the dull ache the plug creates feels like cruel torture.

Professor Adler's dark, brooding gaze meets mine for the briefest second, a telepathic connection existing between only us, before he looks away and finally starts his class introduction.

A little sigh puffs out of me. Both frustrated and aroused, I flip to the page in the textbook we'll be covering today.

Every minute turns into its own eternity.

Where I'd usually be thoroughly engaged and following every word, my head's polluted with thoughts of Professor Adler. I'm recalling what it felt like to have his thick fingers knuckle deep in my pussy and how he'd slammed the wooden paddle into my ass as he made me answer his questions.

My imagination blooms into thoughts about what could possibly come after this class.

I lick my lips and notice how I immediately draw his attention. He goes from lecturing the class, practicing steady eye contact around the room, to his gaze snapping straight to mine the instant my tongue makes a brief appearance.

A subtle little moment that, again, no one else notices, but it means everything to me.

It's the awareness of the power I hold.

He may have punished me—the plug buried deep in my ass is proof of that—but I can punish him too.

I wield a unique power over him that no one else does.

The room retreats into studious silence as Professor Adler issues a reading and essay assignment. He returns to his desk to recollect himself, the muscles in his jaw pulled tight. He's barely composed enough to make it through this class.

Something tells me he's giving his all to stave off an erection. He's doing his damnedest to keep himself together.

I decide to make it that much harder.

I cross my legs and arch my back, sitting up like a sultry siren at my desk. At the first hint of movement, his attention's snapping back to me again. He noticed in his periphery and immediately shifts his gaze to me from across the room.

My lips form a pouty line while I hold him hostage with my sultry, low-lidded stare.

Any thoughts about what others will think—or say if they notice—go out the window.

My fingers drum against the top of my desk 'til I slide them underneath. Professor Adler's gaze dips right along with me. I let my hand rest on the inside of my thigh, *dangerously* close to the hem of my skirt...

His jaw squares from how hard he's biting down. His hands ball into fists and his already brooding glare darkens to new levels.

My pussy quivers at the thought of how angry and aroused he is.

He won't even step out from behind his desk now...

I smirk at him in challenge, uncrossing my legs to spread out. My fingers gently trail up my bare thigh 'til they're disappearing under my skirt.

Heat splotches his neck and reddens his ears. He slams both hands down on his desk, making students jump in alarm.

"Class is ending early today," he announces in a booming voice. "Gather your things, finish the reading and essay assignment on your own, and be prepared to speak to it next class."

When no one moves, shock pinging through everyone in the room at the abrupt dismissal, Professor Adler thrusts a finger at the door.

"NOW!" he barks. "Get your things and go! Class is ending early today. Only today."

The room goes from completely stunned and still to a flurry of movement. Two dozen students quickly jam their books and laptops into their bookbags and practically run each other over making it to the door.

I've sat up straight again, removing my hand from down below, trying to pretend I'm as shocked as everyone else.

Heather nudges me. "Coming? Early dismissal? Let's go shopping."

"Can't," I say. "I have a thing with my art group. Sorry."

Heather seems vaguely disappointed until she notices Claude Wesley on his way out and she scurries after him.

In a matter of sixty seconds, the room has emptied. The silence becomes poignant and deafening. Professor Adler hasn't moved. He's said nothing, his glare telling enough.

A cool shiver courses down my spine. I've done it now...

"Come here," he says finally. "Now."

I slide out from under my desk and do as he says, starting toward him. My short skirt flits about my thighs, a distraction as he watches me approach. The instant I'm within reach, he's grabbing me by the throat to draw my face to his.

Wedged in between him and his desk, I have no choice but to meet his ire head on.

"You think you're so clever, don't you, Miss Oliver?" he hisses. "Did you really think it was smart trying to tease me in the middle of class? Answer me!"

I blink innocently at him. "I have no idea what you're talking about, Professor."

His grip tightens at the base of my throat while he shoves his other hand under my skirt to roughly grope my pussy. "You know exactly what I'm talking about, Miss Oliver. I see going easy on you with the small plug was a mistake!"

My heart beats faster in excitement, but before I can respond, the door's tugged open. I'm shoved under the desk and Professor Adler desperately reaches for some papers to pretend he's shuffling them.

"Theron!" calls Dean Rothenberg obliviously. He starts down the steps that lead toward the front of the lecture hall. "I hoped I'd catch you. But I saw your students out in the halls. Have they been released early?"

Professor Adler takes his seat. I scoot further back underneath his desk and realize why once he does—he's sporting a *huge* bulge in the front of his pants. I clap a hand over my mouth to keep from releasing the petty giggle bubbling up inside me.

If that's not the definition of holding power over a man as composed and put-together as he is...

Clearing his throat, Professor Adler says, "Yes, I released them a few minutes early. I have an engagement to go to."

"I see. Already ahead of the course material, eh? You've always been one of Castlebury's brightest. Even when you were a student here."

"Yes, well, I aim to educate."

As the mundane conversation carries on above me and the butt plug aches no less inside me, I prop myself up on my knees and decide to finish my provocation. After what I've been put through, it's deserved as far as I'm concerned.

I reach for Professor Adler's zipper and tug it down. His hand shoots to mine to stop me, but he can't do much more than grip my hand if he doesn't want to rouse suspicion from Dean Rothenberg, who's prattling on and on about the school. His hard erection springs free and I quickly come in close to swipe my tongue against its veiny, velvety length.

Professor Adler hisses, then coughs to cover up the sound.

My lips curl into a little smile before I'm wrapping them around his thick head. I run my tongue across the top, tasting the light salt in his glistening precum.

Above me, Dean Rothenberg's moved onto talking about Professor Adler's father. "Thurman was an excellent legal scholar. As much of an asset as Vise was. It's no wonder he's had as much success as he has. Shame he retired early..."

My tongue twines around his thick girth before I take him in my mouth. He tenses up in his chair, his voice strained when he answers Dean Rothenberg's next question.

I stroke him and suck away, making it extra slick and wet, doing my best to push him to his limits.

It's a strange sense of power I have on my knees torturing him with my mouth, almost making him lose control. I bring him right to the edge, where his dick's throbbing and twitching inside my mouth and he's one flick of my tongue from coming...

"I'm guessing you can't meet with me and some of the other faculty and board members this afternoon. We really need to get a hold on this Valentine business. I'm sure you remember from last time how it damaged the school's reputation."

"If this is about Jackson Wicker, it does seem he was targeted for a reason. The news report stated they found him stripped naked with a teddy bear and his personal laptop open to the hundreds of children's photographs he had saved over the years."

"Well, we have no control over the personal lives of our board members."

"I think you and I both know, Dean, there are certainly ways to clean house," Professor Adler grits out, barely holding on.

His fingers dig deep into my curls 'til my scalp's prickling from sharp pain, and then he shoves my head all the way down against his groin. His dick slides straight toward the back of my throat and I almost choke.

The simple act of breathing becomes complicated as I struggle to breathe through my nose.

"I suppose," answers Dean Rothenberg. "Well, we'll have to figure something out. We can't afford any more scandal."

"Perhaps. But if you have nothing else to add, then I believe we're done here. As I said, I have an engagement to get to."

"Right, Theron. I'll come by some other time. I'm serious when I say we can't afford any more trouble with Valentine. *You* know that more than anyone."

I'm thrashing under the desk, my hands on Professor Adler's thighs to push myself up. He doesn't let me, forcing my head back down every time I try. I grow lightheaded, thinking about how I never imagined I'd pass out with a butt plug in my ass and my professor's dick in my mouth...

The door closes behind Dean Rothenberg. Professor Adler scoots his chair back and yanks my head back by his fist in my curls. Saliva drips from my swollen lips and my eyes are bleary peering up at him.

His dick gleams with my saliva, standing tall and fully erect.

He surprises me with a crude grin. "You never fail to impress me, Miss Oliver. Are you aware?"

"No, Professor..." I breathe.

He thumbs my wet bottom lip. "I can't even be mad with you when you're so damn brilliant. But this is still not over. There will be consequences for your disobedience. We'll start with you finishing me off. Right now."

I gasp for one more breath as he forces my head back down on his stiff, engorged dick...

It's nightfall by the time we're so sore and spent, we're rolling over in a daze on my bed. The afternoon blurred into a mad dash to my apartment where we proceeded to wrench each other's clothes off and make the most of our private time.

Professor Adler delivered like he said he would, ensuring I was sufficiently punished for acting out. He happened to have the medium plug in his satchel, which he proceeded to insert into my tiny, aching hole and forced screams of pleasure from me as he jerked it deep.

We fucked on the floor of my living room, then on the sofa, his hips bucking aggressively as I buried my face into a throw pillow.

Now, as the clock inches toward nine, we have nothing else to give.

I can barely bring myself to move, laying back against the pillows. He's the same, on his back with an arm folded under his head. The other grips my thigh like he still can't help himself, even in exhaustion. His hair's as wild as mine, rumpled and hanging over his brow.

"So..." I murmur, tilting my head to the side for a look at him. "Dinner?"

His fingers drum up my thigh, then across my stomach. "I wish we could have a real dinner."

"Is takeout not real dinner?"

"You know what I mean, Nyssa," he says, circling my navel. "At a sit down restaurant. A *nice* one. Out in public."

"You mean you want to take me on a date, Professor?"

He glowers which makes me laugh and then straighten up my act. He's being serious right now while I'm determined to keep things light and playful. I give a clear of my throat and then try again.

"Theron, I get it. We can't exactly walk the downtown streets together."

"But we should be able to. In a just world."

"What about outside of Castlebury? We could go to Madison—"

"Too risky. Anyone from Castlebury could be in the area."

"You sure you're not hiding me? You don't have a wife and kids, do you?"

"Hide you?" Offense thickens in his tone. "Why in the world would I ever *want* to hide you? Do you hear yourself? Do you realize how special you are? How privileged I am?"

The breath I release has a note of humor. "Theron—"

"I'm serious," he interrupts sharply. "I don't think you grasp how... you don't understand your worth, Nyssa."

"I'm a human being. Just like anybody else."

"Not to me." He grips my chin and plants his lips on mine in a kiss that's so abruptly passionate, my head reels. I find myself seeping into the kiss, seeking out more despite the fact that my body aches from our previous sessions. He kisses me 'til he's satisfied, then draws back to peer much too deeply into my eyes. "If you were just fifteen or twenty years older, you'd..."

I laugh at the frustrated sigh he lets out. "I'd... what? Be perfect for you? Theron, I think it's safe to say that ship has sailed. We've established our ages don't matter. But what does matter is what our hearts and minds want."

His thumb glides along my cheek. "I love that you included mind. The fact that you did proves what I said. You're brilliant. More brilliant than you realize or give yourself credit for."

"If you keep going, you'll give me a big head. Then I'll be like Heather Driscoll, and that won't be good for anyone."

"Heather Driscoll is the equivalent of swine next to you. You understand that, correct?"

"You say that, but she's rich, blonde, and has the right family name. Societal rules say she wins."

"Who gives a damn what society says? You're worth a thousand of her."

"I needed you when I was a kid. Hearing that would've helped."

"Tell me about what they did," he says, propping himself up on his elbow. He links his fingers with mine and stares down at me like I'm the most fascinating subject in the world. "You said you were seeking revenge for your family?"

Aware this is the pillow talk he's referenced in the past, I take my time answering. I've never been the sharing type, and I have to tread lightly. Nothing comes before my mission and Theron seems determined to chip away at my resolve.

The problem is, things have become more complicated.

Real feelings have started to form.

It's made me more conflicted about what I'm doing. How can I carry on when I've developed genuine affection for this man?

"I grew up in Castlebury," I say with a tense, unnatural shrug of my shoulders. "At least for the first few years of my life. We eventually moved. Before that... kids at school made my life hell."

"Heather Driscoll?"

"And her minions," I finish. "Her stepmother was friends with my mother. Their whole posse turned on her when she got pregnant freshman year of college. It wasn't a good look to be a teen mom. Especially back then. *Especially* as a young Black woman in an affluent circle."

His brows crease. "Your mother went to Castlebury U?"

"Both of my parents did. My mother was ostracized. My father was a victim of Valentine."

"He... was?" Theron says, the healthy color in his complexion fading slightly.

"Yes," I answer. "But once my mom was expelled and my father was murdered, I no longer belonged either. The kids at school made sure I understood. Heather taunted me about my 'broke mommy and dead daddy' as she called it. I was shoved into the ground and laughed at. I spent a lot of time getting knocked down back then. Some of the scars you've noticed... guess how they got there?"

I gesture to my thigh where the small, banana-shaped scar has served as a lifelong reminder of the bullying I endured. Theron's eyes follow, tracking my naked skin 'til he winds up where my hand rests on my thigh, pointing out the mark.

I *feel* his anger. His offense on my behalf.

As silly as it sounds, it's validating. Someone else gets it too. He sees how fucked up it was.

"Anyway," I sigh, "I've worked my whole life to make these people pay, Theron. I'm not about to stop now when I'm so close."

"And that's why you've been mimicking Valentine?" he asks.

Hesitantly, I nod. "I want them—him—to know they didn't get away with it. The real Valentine most of all."

A stretch of silence goes by where I'm certain a number of things could happen. Theron could get up and get dressed and insist we're done here. He could express offense that I've admitted to targeting the community he's known his entire life or threaten to turn me in.

Or he could do the thing I'd dread most—he could understand.

My stomach sinks as he chooses the latter.

"I'll help you," he says. "Get your payback. I'll do what I can. It's only fair."

"No," I say quickly. "This is my own thing. Not yours."

"I'm already involved. The night in Jackson Wicker's penthouse saw to that."

Shaking my head, I laugh at how absurd it is. "You can't help me."

"Too late. How about we order Thai and you can tell me all about your plans for Heather Driscoll?"

He hardly waits for my answer before he's getting out of bed. Peaches leaps onto his shoulder, where she remains affectionately perched and meowing. I sit up in shock watching Theron Adler walk out of my bedroom in his boxers to refill her bowls and then order us some takeout.

I'm even more stunned thirty minutes later when the paper bags are delivered on my doorstep and we settle down in the kitchen to eat over discussions of revenge.

I'm not sure whether to laugh or cry. No one has ever been so supportive, so open to backing me up, that it terrifies me. Vaguely, in the back of my mind, I'm reminded how this will only complicate things.

This could backfire on me.

And how, as I seek revenge for the past, no one else poses a threat like Professor Theron Adler. He very well could be my demise...

21

THERON

THIS LOVE - CRAIG ARMSTRONG AND ELIZABETH FRASER

Nyssa stands alone among a sea of people. They crisscross about the crowded sidewalk with places to be. The Christmas Market has finally started in Castlebury, which means every night is a festive, brightly lit celebratory occasion.

As people rush off to check out the snowmen display or grab a hot beverage from a street vendor, Nyssa's much more patient. She wanders at a calmed, almost subdued pace. Beanie and scarf keeping her warm in the early December frost, she's in no rush.

Neither am I.

I track every step at a distance. I pause and admire her as she converses with a vendor selling Christmas tree trinkets. The two exchange cash and warmth invades my chest.

Something tells me it was a small gift for her mother. Some kind of spontaneous purchase for someone she loves.

Nyssa maneuvers the rest of the crowds with ease, slipping in and out between them. I follow the mustard-yellow knitted cap that's been shoved over springy curls that still poke out. The crowds of the Christmas Market soon dissipate as the cobblestone street winds into another.

The gas lamps do their best to light up the space, though shadows persist, long and heavy. At the end of the curving road is the Castlebury Observatory, a large domed structure built of glass and limestone earlier last century.

You'd think, on a night so dark out, it would be as full as the markets. You'd be wrong.

I enter several paces behind Nyssa, swallowed up by the dark interior.

Every so often, a straggler passes us by. Usually on their way out while we're headed deeper inside.

My pulse thrums in obsessive anticipation. The intensity of it sets my teeth on edge.

This can't be normal. It can't be like anything anyone else has felt. No one would understand as I follow Nyssa Oliver deeper into the dark, domed building and the heart inside my chest feels like it's beating *for* her.

How can I make her understand how I feel?

In a short few weeks, I've fallen in a way I vowed I never would. I promised I wouldn't allow it after…

Nyssa finally comes to a halt in front of a telescope, her dark silhouette backlit by the blue tint in the domed room. I wander toward her until I'm coming up at her side in front of a different telescope.

Two strangers who are not-so-strangers hovering virtually in the dark by each other's side. Her head keeps straight as she bows it for a glance into the telescope.

"I hoped you were behind me."

"Always."

"I didn't see anyone we know."

"Me neither."

"I heard Cassiopeia will be visible tonight."

"So will Andromeda."

She presses her eye tighter against the round eyepiece. "I think I see her."

I smirk as I step forward to do the same. "I'm surprised you've never been here before."

"I haven't had the time."

"You mean between Driscoll's pool parties and girls' nights?" I taunt.

"No," she answers smartly, "I mean between making sons of bitches pay. You see Cepheus? I didn't expect to..."

A short chuckle leaves me. "Fitting considering their story."

"And what about *our* story?"

I pause long enough to drink in the starry splendor I'm viewing through the telescope and then stand up straight. Nyssa's still immersed in hers, eye pressed into the telescope so she can observe the vastness of time and space.

My fingers slip under her chin and ease her face away from the telescope.

We're too steeped in shadows to truly see each other, yet I can feel her dark, deep-set eyes on me. I have her undivided attention, standing so close, her soft lips so parted...

"I've made my feelings clear," I say huskily.

...*arguably*.

Nyssa still doesn't understand the extent of them. They would frighten her. Make her retreat and grow distant. Such intensity scares women.

While I am all in, she's confounded. She's hesitant and fickle. So wild and young, I can't blame her. Yet as the intensity of what I feel for her courses through me, it's hard to slow my pace.

It's hard to play nonchalant and pretend I can take her

or leave her when I would give the very heart beating inside my chest if need be...

"You have," she admits seconds later. She leans up into me, seeking the warm comfort of my kiss. "It means so much to me."

Our lips meet in this secret pocket we've carved out for ourselves. We kiss among the dark shadows of the Castlebury Observatory, relieved no one else has to know. Her lips melt against mine like butter, so supple that I almost groan and kiss her even harder.

Half an hour later, we leave the domed building several feet apart. You'd think we were strangers the way she practically goes one way and I go mine.

"Theron."

I stop short at the familiar voice.

Veronica appears among the others milling about. Some headed toward the Christmas Market. Others headed away. She appears in a wave of thick chestnut hair and imploring hazel eyes, the tip of her nose pink from the frigid temperatures.

In the past—only months ago—I would've seen it as my duty to keep her warm.

Now, instead, an indifferent coldness blows through my lungs. I give a polite nod. "Veronica."

"You never come to the Christmas Market. Why now?"

None of your damn business.

Nyssa suddenly appears at my side. "Want to grab some mulled wine? Oh... am I interrupting?"

An uncertain second ticks by, carrying an equally uncertain and peculiar air with it. The three of us exist in a brief stalemate until Veronica cracks a bitter smile.

"Oh. I see. You've replaced me for a younger one." She holds out her hand to shake Nyssa's. "Veronica Fairchild.

Theron's fiancée... ex-fiancée, I guess. Before he got cold feet and ditched me."

I grit my teeth. "That's not what happened, Veronica, and you know it."

"One day we were engaged. The next day we weren't, Theron."

"One day my BMW was fine. The next day it was keyed."

She lets out a dry laugh. "After all my time you wasted—"

"I didn't mean to interrupt," says Nyssa, glancing between us. "It's nice to meet you, Veronica. But Theron and I have to get going."

Veronica's brows tic up as she looks at me in disbelief. "Seriously? She looks like she's barely legal to drink, Theron. This is a new low for you."

"Nyssa's right. We've got to get going."

I grab her gloved hand and press onward, brushing past a shocked Veronica. It's a bold move given she knows my family.

But what other choice do I have?

Nyssa and I trek the rest of the way down the next few blocks until we reach my car. There's no sense in pretending anymore, at least for the night, when we've already been spotted.

I open the passenger door for her and look up to spot Veronica watching from the end of the block.

She shakes her head of chestnut waves and then launches herself into the surrounding crowd, effectively disappearing out of view.

We drive to Nyssa's apartment, where we break open a bottle of wine and let passion run its course. We wind up on the floor next to her art supplies in the middle of laughter as Peaches trots over and tries to join in.

"My sweet girl," Nyssa says, scratching the cat behind the ears. "She feels needy."

"I would too if some strange man started coming over and made my mother scream the way she has been."

She laughs and reaches over to slap my thigh. "It's not the mother's fault if the strange man refuses to keep his hands to himself."

"Debatable."

Nyssa simply rolls her eyes. "If anything, the two of you have become besties. I'm still shocked she's taken so well to you. She usually doesn't like men."

"I'm not most men."

"Is that your humble way of saying you're better?" She smirks as she rises to her feet and Peaches darts along with her toward the kitchen. I stay back, observing the surroundings of her apartment.

It's a space I've been in many times, both consensually... and not so consensually before Nyssa and I started seeing each other. Her easel and art supplies are still set up by the large bay window in the living room. Perfect for sunlight opportunities when they arise during the day.

On the small table she uses for sculpting rests her work-in-progress. Currently, it resembles nothing more than a clay fist. Though, once she's done, I'm sure the vision will become clearer.

"What are you working on?" I ask. "Another festival project?"

"Something like that." The dry kibble chinks against the ceramic bowl as she pours Peaches more food and then adds in some wet salmon.

"Something like that," I repeat, reaching out to gently

touch the unfinished female torso sculpture of hers. The one with the torn open chest and gaping hole where a heart should go. "Otherwise code for mind your damn business."

"No," she says with a hint of defensiveness. "I just don't like to talk about works-in-progress."

"I'm sensing a theme."

"How so?"

"You *were* a little reluctant to let me know about your revenge scheme."

"That's because no one knows. It's hard to trust people in this community."

I understand more than she realizes, though I change the subject. "Do you plan on finishing this one? The female form with the gaping hole?"

"Maybe. I've lost inspiration for it."

"The design is excellent. Very sensual in the same way Undine is."

She fights off a small smile. "That means a lot coming from you."

"What made you want to pursue law when you're so good at art? You could probably make a decent career out of it."

She sets the food bowl down for Peaches to feast on, then straightens up to think about my question. Because it was only moments ago that we were fooling around, she hasn't bothered to put pants on. She stands before me in nothing more than the kimono robe she shrugged on.

I'm no more dressed—I slid on boxers and haven't bothered with anything else.

"It runs in the family, I guess. It was always my mom's dream, but it never happened for her," she answers, plopping down on her quilted sofa. "Plus, it seemed important that I understand how the legal system works. What about you? What made you pursue law?"

"Isn't it obvious? I'm an asshole, so, naturally, litigation suits me."

"Very funny. A serious answer would be nice."

"Not smart enough for medicine. Not good looking enough for sales. Not talented enough for art. Does that make sense now?"

She cants her head to the side as if in consideration. "Some would argue against those points."

"Which ones?"

"All three. You're the professor most female students fantasize about," she lists on the spot. "You're obviously smarter than most people. And... talented... well, you're *very* good with your hands."

I chuckle at the naughty glint in her gaze. "You provide the ego boost I didn't know I needed."

"Any time. You did make me come three times in a row." She stretches out on the sofa, peering up at me with those beautiful sultry eyes of hers.

Restraint disappears for a few seconds as I bend over and kiss her. "What's next for revenge? Any other late-night meet ups with billionaire patriarchs to expose their sordid secrets?"

"Next up..." she trails off thoughtfully. "I finish the job."

"I didn't realize you were so far along."

"It's all set up," she says. Then she tips her head up to kiss me this time. "There's no going back."

Our kisses change as our position does. I sit down on the sofa and pull her into my lap, sliding my hand up the side of her neck to cup her face and revel in her plush lips against mine.

Nyssa still seems to believe this mission against those

who wronged her is something she has to do alone, but she doesn't realize there's no such thing.

I've fallen too deep and hard to let her carry this out on her own.

There really is no going back. Even if she doesn't yet grasp the truth, we're in this together.

The university library closes every evening by eight p.m. The head librarian, Ms. Chlebek, is usually the one to peruse the huge hall in search of anything amiss before lights out and lock up. The bespectacled woman with her silvery hair in a tight updo goes aisle to aisle to make sure there are no stragglers left behind before she flicks off the lights at the entrance.

Nyssa and I listen for the click in the main doors before we step out from the secluded section where we've hidden. I'm carrying a lantern with us that's dimly lit for discretion but bright enough when navigating the dark bowels of a library as huge as this one.

"We really need to stop," Nyssa giggles. "One of these days we're going to get caught."

"I thought that was what excited you, Miss Oliver."

"The blowjob in your classroom with the dean five feet away was exciting enough."

I step toward her and palm her ass through the sweater dress and tights she's wearing. "That's what you thought until tonight. You know the rules. You're to behave yourself and take this cock or else there will be consequences."

She backs up into the bookcase behind her wearing a smart-alecky smile on her face. "Sometimes I like the consequences."

"Take off your tights," I order, my tone losing any human inflection. I hold up the lantern to shine a light on her so I can watch. "Hurry up. I want to see how wet that delicious cunt of yours is..."

She shivers in excitement as her fingers hurry to bunch up the sweater dress and shove down her opaque navy-blue tights. Her bare pussy's visible as her pouty lips smirk and she lets her fingers slip between her thighs.

I watch, entranced, as she begins pleasuring herself for me. Her fingers dip in and out of her pussy, eyes closed and mouth open. Naturally, her body writhes and hips rock. She's close within only a minute which tells me she's been aroused the entire evening.

We had class earlier and then snuck away for an afternoon date, where I drove us two hours out of town so we could spend some public alone time together. We had dinner and browsed a local art gallery before we settled on our latest risky sex game.

Nyssa wanted me to take her in the school library.

If the moody, disgruntled man I was even a few months ago could see me tonight, he'd claim I'd gone insane. I'm acting entirely off emotion and impulse, two practices I've been against most of my life. But I can't resist how Nyssa makes me feel.

It's as if I'm young again. I'm adventurous and insatiable as I witness her masturbate to near orgasm.

Then I'm dropping the lantern and stepping forward to grab her wrist.

"*I'm* the only one who makes you come," I growl in her face. I kiss her hard while my hands undo the belt buckle of my pants. My cock flips out from inside, rock hard and ready to go.

She jumps with me as I lift her up and she curls her legs

around my back. I slot myself inside her a few times, slicking myself in her creamy juices, to her moans.

"Don't make a sound," I scold.

Clapping a hand over her mouth, I slam into her. She bows her spine at the harsh impact, trapped between me and the bookcase of books on legal morality.

But I'm already too far gone, swimming in the pleasure that's her tight heat.

I set a furious pace, fucking into her until she's scratching up my arms and her cunt's dripping.

The intensity between us reaches new heights. Neither of us can keep our hands off each other. We pant along as our bodies rock and our orgasms feel so close, yet so far.

The bookcase behind us seemingly sways to our fast movements. Two books slide off the shelves.

I only drive into her harder. She cries out, eyes clenched shut.

My hands stroke any patch of her naked skin I can while she writhes in answer. We break together, knocked into pieces by a wave of pleasure. I plant myself deep inside her fluttering pussy and bite her throat, feeling so hot and out of control it's almost like I'm not myself.

I've become some other kind of feral beast, incapable of rational thought.

It explains why I'm so lost and foggy-brained when the library lights suddenly flick on.

Nyssa and I are still panting and entwined against the bookcase when we look up at the approaching figure and the boastful smirk they wear.

"I knew it," Heather Driscoll says, stopping in front of us. "I knew you were fucking him, Nyssie. Looks like your secret's not such a secret anymore, is it?"

22

NYSSA

STREETS - DOJA CAT

"Nyssie, there's no need to worry. Your secret's safe with me. I was only teasing."

We're seated outside the local Java King among the crowded downtown sidewalk with our sugary lattes and obligatory baked goods. I'm doing my best to be casual while I convince Heather what she saw last night was nothing big.

It was just a casual encounter. Something Heather should understand more than anyone.

Theron was in a fit of rage and frustration when she caught us. It took me two hours just to calm him down enough to convince him I would handle it.

I would ensure Heather kept her mouth shut.

"I'm glad you get it," I say, sipping from my hazelnut latte. "The thing between me and Adler… it's casual. Very casual."

"A rebound after Samson?" Heather's perfectly penciled brow tics up. "I know I teased you about it… but you've never struck me as the casual type."

"I'm more low key than anyone."

She hums in consideration. "I guess that's true. We've known each other for almost three years and I've never even met your family."

...you're so mistaken, Driscoll, and you don't even realize it.

"You should bring them for the Fairchild's winter solstice dinner party!"

"I've told you my family lives several hours away," I fib. "They won't be in town this Christmas."

"Shame. Will you at least come?"

I tell Heather what she wants to hear to make her happy in the moment, then remind her one last time that what she witnessed between me and Theron isn't something she needs to ever mention again.

She winks at me. "Don't worry, Nyssie. Your secret's safe with me. Maybe I need to find myself another hot older man to fuck. It's been a couple weeks and I'm getting that itch."

"I'm glad we're on the same page. Just don't forget, friends don't betray friends. Friends help friends, like how I'm helping you fight for part of your father's fortune. Help you *need*, right?"

Heather's expression falters before she reluctantly nods. I smile in response, then bid her farewell.

It's still up in the air whether Heather will be stupid enough to make more problems for herself. Should she try to reveal what's going on between Theron and I, she'll regret it. I'll destroy her life in the matter of a few minutes.

I'm *already* going to destroy her life—it'll just be so much worse if she tries to fuck with me and Theron first.

For the rest of the afternoon, I lock myself in my apartment and work on my art. The latest sculpture I'm making has started to take shape. My hands focus on sculpting the more intricate detailing while my mind mulls over the final phase of my plan.

Hours go by before I notice they do.

The small Christmas tree I've put up twinkles in the corner as afternoon fades to dusk and the living room grows dark.

Peaches dozes peacefully on the armrest of my sofa, a fuzzy little orange ball.

I wipe my hands off on a rag to check my phone. Mom's calling.

To say things have been tense between us these past few weeks would be putting it lightly.

"Baby girl, Merry Christmas."

I smile. "Thanks, Mom. But it's not Christmas for another six days."

"The school's about to be on winter break, isn't it?" she asks. "Will you still be visiting?"

"I leave Saturday morning. I'll get there right before Christmas."

"I wish you'd come for longer," she says. "You get two weeks off, Nys."

"There's a lot going on here. Things are finally taking shape. You know I can't slow down now."

She sighs over the phone. "A part of me is regretting ever encouraging you to do this."

I've wandered into my kitchen, flicking on the light to draw open my fridge and pantry and sort out what I'm having for dinner. The phone rests in the palm of my hand as I listen on speaker and detect the note of regret in her voice.

"Mom, what's changed? Why are you so against me doing this? You've spent my entire life demonizing these people."

"I may hate them... but I love you more. You just need to be careful."

"So you've told me. But that still doesn't explain why I can't find any articles about Edward Oliver being a victim of the Valentine Killer."

"Baby girl, do you hear yourself? You *want* to read about how your father was brutally slain?" she snaps. "For your information, it happened during the summer. Weeks after school had already let out. There wouldn't be a school article about it."

We hang up after I've assuaged her fears yet again. But while I'm helping calm her about how dangerous what I'm doing is, the stack of old newspapers catches my eye again. The top newspaper has a headline I've memorized by now.

Valentine Killer Claims a Final Victim in Law Student Josalyn Webber

I walk over to pick up the wrinkled, faded newspaper, zeroing in on the date.

"June 2005," I read aloud. "This was before the end of the semester."

Once spoken out loud, my brows knit together, and I find myself repeating the words, trying to make sense of them.

"June 2005..."

"You look like you've got something heavy on your mind."

I look up to find Theron approaching with my glass of red wine as promised. I thank him with a smile, curling fingers along the glass bowl.

"Just relieved it's finally winter break."

"I am too. It means I could possibly see you more." He slips behind me, sipping from his own wine glass before he sets that down to grip my hips. His first kiss lands on the side of my neck. Others follow in slow, sensuous fashion as he peppers them up and down my neck in every spot he knows makes me wet.

My eyes close to savor the warm, gentle feeling. "It's nice to be at your place for a change."

"I agree. You should be here more."

He squeezes my hips as his kisses grow more passionate. He kisses the tip of my shoulder, then sweeps up my throat to place one on the edge of my jaw. The way he moves makes me feel like I'm irresistible.

He can't possibly restrain himself.

I sip from my wine glass, fully aware I'm no better. I have as much willpower as he does.

Put the two of us together in a room and we're going to give into the forbidden temptation that rules us.

"Are you ready to feel good, Miss Oliver?" he asks as if sensing my thoughts.

I nod, turning in his hold.

It's been another long week, making me grateful it's finally nearing the end of the week. Tomorrow I might have the dreaded winter solstice dinner party I agreed to go to, but for tonight, I can unwind a little. Let Theron lead in the pleasure we're about to experience.

"Excellent. Set down your wine glass. I have to leave the room for a moment. When I return, I want you stripped bare. In front of the bed."

His smooth, authoritative voice makes me shiver at the first words of his command.

I give another nod and listen to the pad of his footsteps as he leaves the room.

We're in his bedroom, which is unsurprisingly *Theron*—neutral walls with practical furniture for function's sake and tasteful décor—if a little bland. The bed is neatly made and the gray oak flooring beneath my feet is clean and spotless.

He's dimmed the lights and lit the fireplace on the far wall. The crackle of the flames soon becomes the only noise filling the room as I begin to strip.

My blouse is pulled over my head and I shimmy out of my pair of jeans. Folding up every article of clothing I've taken off, I walk it over to the armchair in the corner and set it down on the cushion. I glance over to realize Theron's already returned.

He stands in the doorway admiring me.

Theron left the room, and his alter ego returned in his place.

He's Professor Adler now. All dark, sexy energy and brooding, studious glares from behind the black frames of his glasses. His jaw's clenched as he leans against the doorframe and slowly tracks me from head to toe, his sleeves rolled up to his elbows and his hands plunged into his pockets.

My pussy throbs at the same time my belly flutters with nerves.

It's not lost on me how imbalanced we are in this moment—he's my professor and I'm his student. He's much older and experienced while I'm half his age. I'm completely nude in his bedroom as he lingers in the doorway fully clothed, enjoying the view.

I stand up straighter and decide to tease him like only I can. Pushing my chest out and placing a hand to my hip, I say, "I've been waiting on you, Professor. You're late."

He abandons the doorway and starts toward me feeling like a dark, ominous storm cloud moving in. In a few short strides he's eclipsed me, cupping my chin and forcing my gaze to flick up toward his.

"Let's get one thing straight, Miss Oliver," he says calmly, in complete command. "I set the rules. You will wait as long as I want you to. You will beg and cry for me to give you what you need. You will be a quivering little mess by the time I'm through with you. Is that understood?"

I lick my lips, already breathless. "Yes..."

He grips my hip in a rough clench and wrenches me toward him. "Yes, *what*?"

"Yes, Professor Adler."

"Good. Behave yourself and you might get a reward." He brings his knuckles up, gliding them along my cheek so tenderly, you'd think he wasn't cold and commanding a few seconds before. He withdraws a leather mask from his pocket.

It's delicate and feminine and reminds me of something you'd wear to a masquerade.

...except it has no holes to see.

"You'll be wearing this tonight."

"A blindfold? Great way to increase nerves for what's about to happen," I say sarcastically.

"I like the idea of you not knowing what's next."

"Hence the nerves."

"Blindfolds let you tap into the physical sensations much more... acutely." He turns me around and kisses the spot behind my ear, hugging me to him by the hips. "If you absolutely hate it," he whispers into my ear, "I will remove it. But beware, there will be a penalty."

"Penalty for backtalk. Penalty for removing the blindfold. If I didn't know better, Professor, I'd say you're looking for a reason to spank me."

He kisses his way from behind my ear to the nape of my neck. His hands roam over my naked body, his touch warm and shudder inducing. "You'd be a filthy little liar if you said you didn't want me to."

The palm of his hand collides with my ass in a playful spank that makes me yelp in surprise. He slides the blindfold over my eyes and everything goes black.

"Do you remember the safe word?"

I smirk, blindfold and all. "Law."

"Excellent, Miss Oliver. On the bed. Hands and knees."

Theron helps me, taking my hand and guiding me over to the bed for me to crawl on. Immediately, I discover what he meant about tapping into other sensations.

Once my sight's gone, everything sounds louder. From the soft pad of his footsteps to the slow thud of a cabinet being opened then shut. I take in a deep breath and pick up on the faint smoky scent from the fireplace much more acutely than I had without the blindfold.

My heart beats faster in my chest, counting down the seconds.

It's amazing how our time together has only just begun, yet he's already managed to take my mind off everything that's been plaguing me. Any thoughts about my revenge plan, keeping Heather quiet, tomorrow's dinner party, and the tension between me and Mom disappear.

I'm much more interested in what's about to happen in this bedroom.

If I had to guess what's coming, I'd bet it's some form of spanking. Professor Adler's aware how well I get off to it, and how can he resist when I'm blindfolded on my hands and knees? My ass is right out in the open for him to streak red.

How could he pass up the chance?

I'm bracing for impact when instead I feel the wet heat of his mouth. I flinch at the sensation being so different and abrupt than expected, then relax once I realize he's kissing his way up the back of my thighs.

He fills his palms with my ass cheeks, his grip firm and powerful.

A sharp shiver shoots up my spine at the thought of what he's capable of with those hands.

His mouth and tongue.

His huge, thick cock.

Professor Adler kisses and nibbles at my thighs, coming up to my ass that's on display. He releases a groan as he squeezes my flesh and spreads kisses along the round, curvy shape of my cheek.

I try to take in a breath but find myself short.

The anticipation's killing me. Every slow, warm kiss of his feels like worship. It feels like the build up to what will soon have me begging him, like he promised.

I shuffle in place on my hands and knees, doing my best to taper how my body reacts to him. My pussy refuses to listen, throbbing away, making me aware how empty I am, and how desperately I want to be filled...

His teeth sink into my ass cheek in a teasing bite that elicits a squeal out of me. He bites into the soft flesh of my ass like he can't resist. Then follows up with more kisses and flicks of his tongue. His hands squeeze my cheeks harder as he goes, making it clear he's nowhere near done with me yet.

The alternating wet kisses, firm bites, and rough gropes become too much.

It's so many different sensations at once that I can hardly take it.

I hang my head and moan along as his tongue returns. He runs the flat side of it along the cleft of my backside, then dips in between.

He licks and flicks at the sensitive space 'til he's at my puckered hole doing the same.

"Oh... Theron!" I whimper before I can choose my words wisely.

He stops immediately. "Who?" he growls.

"Pro-professor!" I gasp. "Professor!"

But it's already too late. His palm slams against my ass and my body jerks forward on my hands and knees. His fingers grip my flesh so hard, it's enough to bruise as I feel him at my rear hole again.

Not his tongue but his fingers.

"OH!" I cry out as I feel his saliva wet me and then he slides a finger inside. My arms quake at the intrusion that still feels like a lot to take, even after the experiments we've done with the plugs. I bite my lips and tune into how it feels to have him inside me in a whole new way.

He pumps his digit, then returns with his mouth and tongue.

It becomes impossible to predict.

He eats my ass like he's eaten my pussy—with a level of eagerness that has his tongue and mouth making my entire body shake.

The ticklish sensation at my rear hole warms into hot

pleasure as a flush breaks out on my brown skin. He opens me up using his finger before returning with his tongue and then *two* fingers.

I find myself grinding back against him in a plea for more.

More of his wet tongue and nibbling bites. More of his fingers slipping deep.

I'm close, my pussy tingling and dripping with arousal. If he just uses a little more tongue...

Right when I'm about to fall apart and come, he stops. I feel him shift behind me on the bed and then I hear the drawer sliding open again. The crinkle of plastic tells me what he's grabbed and where this is headed next.

Though, I'm blindfolded, I glance over my shoulder. When I speak, I sound winded. "Professor..."

"Hush, Miss Oliver. Speak when spoken to," he scolds from behind me. He slaps my ass for added affect. "First the plug. Then me. Trust me when I say, taking me in your ass will be no easy feat."

"Your dick?" I mutter.

"Yes, every inch," he says. He bends forward to press a kiss on the center of my dewy spine. "You will be so full, you won't know what to do with yourself. It'll be quite the accomplishment. You'll definitely be earning passing marks in my class after this."

I tug my bottom lip between my teeth as, once again, anticipation builds.

The lube spreads along my ass, slicks between the cheeks, gathers at my puckered hole. He takes his time massaging me, teasing me with his thumb poking inside and his other fingers lightly fondling my swollen, neglected pussy.

I'm expecting the plug to push inside when instead a buzz starts up.

Professor Adler reaches around me, grabbing my hand and placing a smooth, buzzing, phallic-shaped device in my hand.

A vibrator.

He guides me between my spread legs until it's against my clit, biting my shoulder for good measure.

"Keep this here," he commands. "If you take it away, you will be penalized."

"Y-yes, Professor."

Thank god.

I try to play it cool as I really want to sigh in relief. The vibrator feels so damn good against my clit after being ignored for so long. I stay propped up on my hand and knees, thankful I'm finally able to *almost* get off again.

"Oh, and Miss Oliver?"

"Yes, Professor?"

"If it wasn't already obvious, no coming. If you come, you will be penalized."

Ugh. Of course!

"Yes, Professor," I warble out, trying to mask my disappointment.

But then I concentrate on how good the vibrator feels buzzing against my achy clit and I'm sinking into pleasure again.

With no sight to distract me, it becomes all I know. The tingling sensation the toy draws out of me.

Professor Adler's behind me, still lubing me up and preparing me for...

I shudder along with the vibrator at the thought.

"Stay still," he commands. "Breathe. The easier you make this going in, the better it will be for you."

I do as he says, breathing and focusing on the tingling sensation in my clit. The plug prods against my other hole, slathered in lube.

Despite some initial resistance, it slips past the ring of muscle, my hole stretching to allow the thick toy inside. I bite down on my bottom lip and find myself shuddering again, even though Professor Adler warned against it.

"Miss Oliver, what did I say?" he asks, gripping my hip. He works the plug in deeper with the other hand.

"No m-moving... oh! It's... big."

"It's the medium plug again," he says. "But, yes, it's a lot for you. You'll adjust in time."

I groan as it roots itself inside me, heavy and intrusive. Suddenly, the vibrator isn't enough against how achy and full the plug makes me feel. I urge myself to remain calm and breathe through the sensation, but it becomes everything I feel.

My lungs refuse to let me draw another breath. Heat flushes my body, and the entire room turns into a furnace.

I can only remain in position as, slowly, Professor Theron begins moving it in and out of me. The plug slips deeper inside my snug channel before it retreats like it's about to be pulled out. Then it's returning, deep and weighty, spreading and stretching me all over again.

"You're doing so well, Miss Oliver," he praises as I moan. "Is your greedy little pussy jealous?"

The blindfold's thrown off my spatial orientation while too many sensations envelop my body. I can barely figure out how to nod my head *yes*.

He laughs as I do and almost drop the vibrator.

"Keep the vibrator against your clit. It feels good, doesn't it?"

"Yes!" I pant. "So good."

"And the plug?"

I groan in answer and he laughs, giving it another thrust deeper.

"Do you want my cock instead?" he asks.

"I want to come."

He swats at my ass. "What have I said, Miss Oliver? In due time. You have to earn it first."

He twists it in and out of me in rough, circular motions that have me thrashing. I can barely remember to keep the vibrator against my pussy as the aching stretch in my ass holds my attention.

The intrusion that's been a pain in the ass—*literally*—has begun to awaken a pulse of pleasure deep inside me.

As Professor Adler screws the plug in and out of my tight rear channel, I find myself moaning for more. My thrashes of protest become thrashes of pleasure as my elbow gives out and I crash down on the bed. I lay on my stomach, my arm under me so I can position the vibrator right where I want it, and I hike my hips up to offer him myself.

My ass hanging in the air as my throaty whines beg him to continue.

He plays with me some more, twisting the plug and then reaching under me to push two fingers into my pussy.

Stars shoot before my closed eyes and I erupt without even thinking. My first orgasm of the night blows through me so violently, I'm left panting and spasming.

It takes me several seconds to come down and realize Professor Adler's carefully pulling the plug out of me.

"Suck," he says.

I part my lips to taste the bulbous toy that was entrenched in my ass seconds ago. Pineapple flavor explodes on my tongue, revealing the flavored lube that's been used.

"Do you taste good?"

"Mhmmm."

"Are you ready for my cock?" he asks, fondling my dripping pussy lips.

"I need it... I want it... put it in!" I moan.

"Your pussy... or your ass?" he asks, and I can practically hear the triumph in his voice.

"My ass!" I call out. "Put it in my ass, Professor Adler! Please!"

"Spread."

The direct manner in which he speaks never fails to make me shudder.

Now is one of those times as I hurriedly spread myself wider. My juices slide from my pussy, down the inside of my thighs.

Rustling noises behind me reveal Professor Adler's stripping down himself. The bed shifts with his added weight again.

He groans at the sight that meets him.

Me with my face pressed into the bed and my ass high in the air, completely spread for him.

"Keep the vibrator going, Miss Oliver," he says, his voice suddenly huskier. He's stroking himself. I can *hear* his restraint slipping with each word. "You're going to need the distraction as you take my cock in that tiny little hole."

I practically draw blood from my lip biting down as hard as I do.

He's at my rear entrance, easing himself inside. He pushes past the resistance. Thick and long, he stretches me in a whole new way. I whimper at the intrusion and focus on my pussy.

"Oh... that's fucking good," he groans. He grips my ass and holds still. His breathing's gone ragged as he fights to keep himself in check. "You've swallowed me right up. You're bearing down on me so tightly. You are so fucking..." he pauses for another groan that makes my pussy clench. "So fucking exquisite."

It's such a Professor Adler thing to say that it feels like a reward.

I buck against him to show I'm ready for more. For him to continue and fuck my ass.

Thighs propped as wide as they'll go and vibrator to my clit, he draws back and then slams into me from behind.

We both fill the room with sound. His throaty groans and my needy whimpers.

It's only the beginning.

The moment descends into filthy, sweaty, rough passion as Professor Adler fucks my ass and I take every deep stroke. My body quivers all over, so stimulated that every sensation has merged into one.

Heat floods me and my skin burns up. I'm breathless and hot as Professor Adler's hips whip back and forth. He drives into me hard and fast. My ass gives way for his cock every time, swallowing him right up.

I clench my eyes shut behind the blindfold and watch the stars dot the black sea that's become my vision.

I haven't stopped holding the vibrator to my clit. The tortuous device has made my little nub go numb, though as I slide it between my swollen labia, it feels just as good on such soft flesh.

Professor Adler pushes his cock all the way inside and comes in close, his body pinning mine down to the bed. He drills into me with relentless abandon 'til I can't stand another second.

I break apart in an orgasm that tears through me. It starts in my pussy and then explodes. Pressing my cheek into the comforter, the vibrator buzzes away almost forgotten, as I feel like I'm floating.

The needy little whine I release doesn't even sound like me. But it doesn't matter as he reaches under me and uses his fingers to tease me some more. I keen as he fucks my ass and rubs my swollen, soaked pussy and tells me how I'll never need another dick again.

"My cock is the only cock that will ever be inside you," he growls.

I convulse, incoherent and dizzy. "Yes, Professor!"

He switches up the angle of his stroke, hitting even deeper, rougher. "This tight little ass belongs to me. That delicious fucking pussy. Mine."

"Oh, yes! Yes, Professor!"

I roll straight into yet another orgasm.

I come quaking against the vibrator as he follows me, coming buried deep in my ass. My hips buck wildly, mashing my clit against the vibrating toy to the point of madness.

...'til I'm crying out and coming so hard, my voice tears and goes out halfway through my scream.

He's hot and pulsing shooting ropes of cum inside me. He pumps every last drop he has to give before he's pulling out, and I moan at the wet mess he's left behind.

He rears back and admires me. Though still blindfolded, his gaze is visceral. His breathing's rough and labored.

Seconds pass before he's calmed down enough to do anything but pant and peer at me collapsed on the bed. He reaches for me, rolling me onto my back and taking away the vibrator that's buzzing faithfully away. The blindfold's removed and he greets me with a deep kiss on the lips.

"Are you alright?" he asks.

I nod, numb and spent.

"Clean up. Bath or shower?"

"Bath."

The corner of his mouth twitches in a near grin. "Come. I'll run you one."

23

NYSSA

SOBER II (MELODRAMA) - LORDE

"That feels so good," I sigh, soaking in the warmth of his bathtub.

Theron twirls his fingers in the soapy water, crouched beside where I'm sitting. He's spent the last few minutes ensuring the bath was everything I preferred—the right temperature, the right amount of suds and soap. He's brought my wine glass for me to sip on and has taken to gently stroking me here and there.

As I sink deeper into the water, he reaches over and brushes my cheek. "Are you sore anywhere?"

"The warm water's helping. So is your touch."

His hand falls to my kneecap. "I like having you here. In my home. In my space."

"Is that your way of asking if I'll spend the night?"

"You know exactly what I mean, Nyssa." His wide shoulders lift as he releases a deep, vexed sigh. "I don't know if I can wait so long."

I frown. "Wait so long for… what?"

"I'll be your professor for the next year and a half."

Oh.

Oh no.

Dread immediately thickens inside me at the realization he wants to talk about our future. Of course it would be on his mind at forty-two. We've been seeing each other for weeks now, but never with any label... or promise of anything more than the present.

It's been implied he's expected more. He thinks of me as his girlfriend.

We're exclusive.

His jealous rage over Samson and his father demonstrated that.

But I've always kept the idea of a real, defined relationship at arm's length. It's been what I've had to do in order to move forward with my plan. I can't plot and scheme for revenge if I'm emotionally invested in my crim law professor.

I can't do what I'll need to do if I'm leading with my heart, *not* my head...

When my silence answers him, he runs fingers through his rumpled hair and then lets out a dark laugh.

"Of course. I forgot to consider the very obvious fact you're twenty-two. You're just starting your life and probably want no real attachments. Certainly not to some man twice your age. The same man who happens to be your professor," he says matter-of-factly. "This is some kind of... fling for you. A rebound for Wicker—"

"You're not my rebound," I blurt out against my better judgment.

But he needs to know that much.

What I had with Samson was never real. Kissing him felt like kissing a slimy toad.

Every moment was torture.

Whereas every moment with Theron has been... my body trembles while my heart flutters inside my chest.

"This isn't some casual fling for me," I go on. "Trust me, I don't... do this often. I don't just go around and sleep with older guys. Or any guys for that matter. You've been my first in a while. I was, um, a little embarrassed by it in my circle. Heather stays with different guys and so do Katie and Macey."

"Is that why you started dating Wicker? For appearances?"

I sit back against the porcelain tub. "Something like that. Was Veronica your last?"

"Unfortunately."

I smirk. "That makes me feel very special."

"You should." He leans forward to kiss my cheek. "Hungry?"

"After that intense workout? Starving. But you don't have to—Theron!"

He disappears from the bathroom before I can finish protesting. I have no choice but to soak in the warmth and await his return.

In his absence I use one of the loofahs he's given me and begin working it over different parts of my body. It's true that I'm a little sore after our session in his bedroom, but the residual aftereffects outweigh any aching.

I'm still so sensitive in the best way, my pussy swollen and tingly. I'm already certain I'll have a good night of sleep.

No one has even come close to pleasuring me like Theron has.

Hell, most of the college guys at Castlebury barely know where to find a woman's clit, let alone give us orgasms.

Theron is unmatched.

"In every way," I mutter under my breath. I slump deeper among the frothy bubbles 'til they're coming up to my chin and the curls on my nape are wet. Lost in thought, I don't really notice.

Theron feels that I'm unmatched.

Some special woman that he can't stay away from.

There might be a huge age difference, but we connect mentally and physically.

...emotionally.

I squash that last thought with a sharp shake of my head.

Emotions don't matter. I promised myself when I transferred to Castlebury and started this long, tenuous road for revenge, I wouldn't be emotionally compromised. Everyone at Castlebury is a pawn or a perpetrator I'll make pay.

Nothing more.

Easier said than done when Theron returns a few minutes later holding a charcuterie board. My eyes round at the delicious offering as he walks it over to the edge of the tub and sets it down for me to dig in.

"Not the fanciest meal... but I remember you once mentioned you like them."

"Are you kidding? My mouth is watering."

"Enjoy."

I don't even know where to pick from first. He's set it up as meticulously as only he could—the large tray features deli meats and cheeses, pretzels and carrot sticks, toasted crackers, and several spreads.

Chocolate.

I scoop up a few slices of salami and cheese. "Eat with me. I can't finish this all by myself."

He obliges my request, selecting some carrot sticks. We

spend several minutes grazing on the board of finger foods as I go against my vow and press him about the future.

"You think a year and a half is too long to wait..."

"It would be longer than that, Nyssa," he says. "You might not be my student anymore after you graduate law school, but we'd still have to exercise caution. If we were to be together right after you graduate..."

"Then people will put two and two together and realize we were messing around before that."

He picks some crackers to add cheese spread on. "Precisely. *Your* reputation wouldn't recover."

"Mine?" I ask, my brows rising. I finish the apple slices I've been nibbling on and follow his lead, going for the crackers and cheese spread.

"Yes," he answers. "If we're being realistic about the situation. I've seen this song and dance before."

"Care to elaborate?"

He sighs, his brows pinched, his expression best described as tormented. "In this kind of society... in this community, I could maybe recover. My family name is enough. My standing is solid enough. But you..."

I laugh as I understand what he means. "You mean I'm a newcomer? Some young Black girl without the fancy family name to protect me?"

"I know these people. How these situations play out," he says, caressing his hand along my head. "It doesn't matter that I'm older. That *I* should get the blame. That I abused my power as a professor and took advantage of a student—"

"No," I interrupt, "you've never taken advantage of me. I've made choices to be with you. I've wanted everything we've done. If anything, I made a move on you—"

"Nyssa," he cuts me off right back. His tone's hardened,

grown more disciplinary. "Listen to me very carefully. If a situation does occur where we are caught—really caught—you will not tell them it was your choice. You will tell them I took advantage of you. I pressured you and used you. It was all me."

I blink at him. "You want me to throw you under the bus?"

"Yes. If there's even a chance we can save your reputation and career prospects. I'll be fine."

A feeling I can't describe washes over me and almost makes me want to tear up. An alarming enough turn of events considering I almost *never* cry.

Yet here I am, listening to Theron telling me he'll take the blame, and my eyes are suddenly itchy.

I look away, fighting against the intrusive thought about why I'm feeling this way...

Stay strong.

"Are you ready to come out?" he asks. He rises from the side of the tub and grabs one of his giant bath towels. "How about we get you changed into one of my hoodies and then head downstairs to watch one of these TV shows or movies you're always bringing up? Atticus also needs some attention. He's been whining in his bed."

A small laugh tumbles out of me as I give a nod and stand up in the middle of the bathtub. Water sluices down my naked body, cold air rushing me. Theron's wrapping me up in the warm, cozy towel not a split second later. He grabs my hand and carefully helps me out. I let him lead me out of the room into his closet with the same intense feeling trapped inside me.

No matter how many times I push back, it returns stronger than before.

They don't mean anything. None of them do.

Theron does...

"It seems Atty is as enamored with you as Peaches is with me," Theron says in amusement. We're huddled close on his sofa, the TV playing the movie we've selected for the evening. As soon as Theron put his arm around me and pulled me against his side, his golden retriever stood on his hind legs and dropped his head in my lap.

A soft giggle leaves me as he licks at my hand and peers up adoringly at me like I'm his new stepmom.

I indulge him with plenty of scratches and strokes. "You are such a happy boy, aren't you, Atticus? Your owner could learn a thing or two from you."

Theron glares. "Perhaps make sure I'm out of the room before you trash talk me to my dog."

"Don't worry," I whisper to Atticus. "I'll sneak you an extra snack when he's not looking."

"That's one way to win him over. He'd let burglars rob the entire house if they brought him a milk bone."

"Very smart. He might as well get something out of it." I lean back against Theron's side, watching as Atticus trots back over to fetch a toy from his bed. "I've been meaning to ask you. Did you name him Atticus for the reason I think you did?"

"If you're asking about Atticus Finch from *To Kill a Mockingbird*, then yes. You'd be correct."

I laugh despite myself. "Of course, you'd name your dog after a fictional lawyer."

"And one of the greatest literary works to ever exist."

"That's so... *you*."

His arm tightens around me and he nuzzles his face

against mine. "You enjoy these little brainiac details about me. Mainly because you're a brainiac yourself."

I hum in thought. "I *was* valedictorian."

"High school or college?"

"Both. You?"

"Same. Though I graduated high school a year early."

"Nerd," I snort. The word barely leaves me before Theron's making me pay for my teasing. He tugs me down 'til I'm laying head first in his lap and then drops several warm kisses all over my face and throat. Including the spots where I'm ticklish. I squirm amid his attack, trying to get up only to be held down in his lap.

The movie we've put on is long forgotten about.

So is the discovery I made only moments ago before I even came downstairs.

Theron had told me to pick something out of his closet to wear; something that's comfy and warm for the movie we'd watch. As he left the room, I padded into his closet and reached for one of the hoodies hanging on the rack.

The last thing I meant to do was knock over a shoebox that contained private documents inside. The contents spilled out of the box at my feet. I'd glanced up to make sure I was alone before I knelt to collect everything.

It was impossible not to notice what some of the papers were. There was a manila folder that had Theron's name scribbled onto the label. I peeked inside to find a police file about an arrest that had been made in June 2005.

A mugshot of a twenty-something Theron stared up at me. The same man, only two decades younger, with his unruly dark hair and glasses.

But that wasn't the only notable thing I'd found.

The other was a letter. Some kind of break up letter written to him by a woman named Josalyn Webber.

. . .

Theron,

I had to write this instead of telling you to your face. I knew you'd talk me out of it. You'd make me feel bad for walking away from you like this. But I've told you we can never be together. I've made my choices and you need to accept them. Your friendship has meant so much. It'll always be special, but please let it go. Please let me go.

Love, Josalyn

Theron had called my name from downstairs and startled me. I had jumped and then rushed to cram everything back into the shoebox and return it to its place in the closet. Half a minute later, he'd come up to look for me.

I'd put a smile on my face and pretended like I hadn't been snooping.

An hour later, as we cuddle on his sofa, I can't help keeping what I'd read on the back of my mind. I'm not sure what to make of it, except to note that Josalyn Webber had been one of the victims of the Valentine Killer.

Theron had been a law student at the time...

"What's on your mind?" he asks, interrupting my thoughts. He stares adoringly at me, stroking my cheek. "Hungry? Cold? Want to watch a different movie?"

"It's not even halfway over."

"I think we all know what's in the box. Though Kevin Spacey plays a convincing villain."

"Maybe it's a little true to life," I murmur, then I yawn. "I'm just tired."

"Tonight you'll sleep in my bed. Where you belong."

The fondness I already have for him expands inside my chest, fighting off the curiosity I'd had earlier in his closet. I'm still lying in his lap when I smile up at him and then nod. "Okay, Professor. You know what's best."

He returns my smile but punctuates it with a soft kiss to my lips. "How about we head on up?"

I let him lead me as we get up off the sofa, turn off the movie, and head toward the stairs, Atticus on our heels.

What I saw could mean something or it could be insignificant.

For now, I'm willing to pretend it's the latter.

Half an hour into the Fairchild's winter solstice dinner party, I'm itching to go home. Diamond-like Christmas lights gleam from every direction as I stand among the rich and fabulous. The hall the party's being hosted in is bathed in white and gold, from the tasteful but enormous Christmas trees lining the room to the golden wreaths and ribbons hung as decor.

I'm dressed in a shimmery emerald dress and heels with my curls cascading around my face. I've come solo despite the fact that almost every other woman my age dragged along a date.

Heather breaks apart from Claude Wesley and cuts a path straight toward me between mingling party guests. She's golden from head to toe, her long blonde hair blending a little too perfectly with the metallic gold dress and bangles she wears.

"Nyssie, you came! And you're stag. So bold." She gives me a quick hug I don't return. Before she pulls back, she whispers with a giggle, "But I'm sure *he* would've loved to be your date if he could."

"Samson?" I ask loudly.

Several people nearby glance over curiously.

"No," I continue, "remember, we broke up because you slept with hi—"

"I was kidding, Nyssie!" she hisses. She smiles politely at the people staring, as if she hopes they haven't figured out what I was about to say. "I didn't realize Adler's such a touchy topic for you."

"I didn't realize you were going to bring it up every time I see you. What happened to the secret's safe?"

"It's safe," she says poutily. "But, speaking of secrets, have you heard about Macey and Paul Templeton? Now *that's* a scandal."

I'm only half listening as Heather launches into the latest gossip about Macey sleeping with pimply-faced, overweight Paul Templeton.

Others in the room have caught my attention more.

Ms. Wicker seems to be in good spirits considering she lost her husband only weeks ago. It seems she's able to schmooze with the Cummings over champagne and luxury vacations.

My gaze swings from her to Dean Rothenberg in the middle of a deep discussion with Pamela Williamson, the faculty head at school. Lucas and some of his fellow rugby pals are loitering at the refreshments table.

Without Samson.

After being kicked off the rugby team and recently losing his father, he must've skipped tonight's event altogether. Katie isn't here tonight either.

I move on to other familiar faces, even spotting none other than Theron's ex-fiancée. Veronica Fairchild lets out a poised laugh as she chats up one of the board members for the school.

If only Theron were here to mock how insufferable they all are with me...

He's texted me a few times tonight to see if I'm okay. Texts I've left on read. I had decided I couldn't mix any more of my feelings into these situations where I have to be on my best game.

But as I stand in the middle of this party, I can't deny where I *really* want to be.

"Nyssie," Heather says, waving a hand in front of my face. "Did you hear what I said? I was asking about the attorney you've referred me to. They won't answer my calls—"

"I'm exhausted," I say. "I think I'll leave now."

"What? But the party just started."

I push my flute of champagne into her hand. "At least I showed up. Say hello to the others for me."

Heather calls after me several more times to no success.

I stride from the hall to a few more stares and some muttered gossip, but I don't give a damn. Any social damage, I'll worry about later.

I order a rideshare home and slide into the backseat firing off a text to Theron.

> Hey, just left the party. Are you home?

Part of me wants to give the driver his address and show up by surprise, though I decide against it and let him drive me home.

We pull up twenty minutes later with my feet aching to take off my heels and rain pouring from the sky. I ride the elevator up to the fourth floor, grateful that I'll at least spend the rest of the night cuddling with Peaches. I approach my front door as I always do, fiddling for my keys.

A premonition I can't explain washes over me the closer I make it. I stop and stare for a second, looking up and down the otherwise silent hallway.

No one's around. My neighbors are silent.

It's minutes after nine o' clock.

The creeping feeling goes nowhere as I step forward and unlock my door.

Right away, Peaches meows and darts toward me. I kneel to meet her. "What is it, my sweet girl? What's wrong?"

My spooked ginger cat doesn't need to meow or quake any more in order to point me to what's off about the moment.

I discover it for myself when my gaze lifts and I spot what's splattered on the floor.

A single droplet of blood...

At that exact moment, my phone pings with a text message from an unknown number.

> If you want the truth, find out for yourself.
>
> 21.8975° N, 52.0465° W

24
THERON
WHERE IS MY MIND? - SAFARI RIOT AND GRAYSON SANDERS

"You just might be perfect," Josalyn giggled. She peered up at me as she lay in the tall grass, the spring sunshine warm on our skin.

I was sitting up, a book propped open in my lap. We were in the clearing deep into the campus's pine forest, enjoying what we could of the rest of our afternoon.

It was one of the rare chances we'd had in recent months to spend time together. Soon I'd be graduating and taking the bar exam. Josalyn had been preoccupied with her own personal matters...

I grinned down at her, some locks of hair falling into my face. "If I were so perfect, you'd be with me, Jos."

"You know that's not possible. You're better off without me."

"Says who?"

"The world," she answered. "Everyone."

"Not me. Not you. So not everyone."

"Close enough." She sat up and brushed the loose lock of hair from my brow. "You need a haircut, Theron."

I caught her hand in mine. "You need to stop avoiding the situation."

"Not this again."

"I'm worried about you. If you get caught..."

She rolled her eyes and then started gathering her books. "I don't have time for this. I've told you it's my choice. I'll see you later. If you'll stop ruining our time together."

I watched on as Josalyn slung her bookbag over her shoulder and strode off until she disappeared among the thick pine trees...

The same pine trees whose branches sway in the afternoon's wind. I watch from my office window, a mug of Earl Grey in my hand.

Students still wander off into the forest, often late at night for bonfires and hookups, but I'll always remember the forest for other reasons.

Knuckles tap against my half ajar door. I look over my shoulder, expecting one of the students who received a failing grade on their papers, or the department head, Pamela, seeking me out with a tasking.

In a surprise twist of events, it's neither of these. Theo enters with her usual caffeinated offering.

Strange, but not entirely unheard of. She's an apartment manager over one of the town buildings that often houses students from campus. A few times a year, she's at the university housing office for meetings and other events.

"I didn't know you were going to be on campus today."

"I didn't either until a few hours ago. You available?"

"You wouldn't be asking unless you hoped I was. Sit."

We approach my desk from opposite ends. I take my seat behind the desk while Theo claims the visitor chair on the other side. She sets down the white paper bag of baked goods and slides my peppermint mocha from the student union toward me.

"We need to talk, Theron."

My head cants to the side at her severe expression and tone. I choose biting humor to counterbalance her. "Don't we do that about every day, sister? It was just yesterday you were calling me about how you got drunk at the Midnight Ale and went home with... what was her name? Emma? Or was it Chloe this time?"

"Shut up, assface. This is about you, not me." She grabs her coffee cup—presumably her favorite, a cinnamon dolce latte—and takes a sip. "You need to tell me what's going on."

I sigh. "If this is about what happened with Dad on my birthday, I'm aware he's still pissed—"

"It's about what you're doing."

"You're going to have to be more specific."

Though she's hated it her entire life, Theo has always resembled our mother—large, open, amber eyes and bushy hair that pairs with an oval face and slim nose. Right now as I give an answer she doesn't want to hear, her features sharpen. Her face morphs into our mother's.

No amount of fringy haircuts and nose rings can change the phenotypic similarities.

"If you're not going to come clean, then we'll do it the hard way. What's this?"

She smacks her palm onto the smooth wooden surface of my desk. I'm half a breath away from making another wisecrack when my gaze drops to a set of polaroids that are trapped under her hand. She slides them across the desk toward me.

I take the top one between my fingers for a closer look.

It's a candid photograph of Nyssa and myself, seated in the front row of my BMW. The photo was snapped during conversation as we sit parked against the curb of her apartment building.

I recognize the night immediately—the very first time I'd given her a ride.

Nyssa had been stranded outside Wicker's place and I'd *happened* by.

My right brow arches. I pin Theo with an unimpressed stare. "This is nothing more than me giving a stranded student a ride home. Is there a problem with that? Was I supposed to let her walk home late at night?"

Theo yanks the photo out of my grasp, then replaces it with another. "And this? What the *fuck* is this?"

The second photograph, unsurprisingly, features me in a baseball cap and shades... as I head into Nyssa's apartment building.

The same building Theo manages.

A cold sweat breaks out onto my skin. I stare at the photo, trying to maintain my poker face while simultaneously thinking up an excuse.

"Or *this*," Theo says when seconds go by. She brandishes yet another photograph.

This one is most damning of all.

It's of me outside Nyssa's apartment, the door drawn open as Nyssa smiles up at me, right about to step aside and let me in.

The icy beads of sweat trickling over me disappear for a hotter, more venomous heat. My face fixes into a deep scowl as I spit, "Have you been spying on me, Theo?"

"Don't you dare get self-righteous with me! Tell me what the fuck this is, Theron."

I have several options.

I can throw together some clumsy excuse like I did the day Nyssa's mother showed up at her apartment. I can pretend the photos aren't me or are misleading (particularly the ones where I am disguised in a hat and dark glasses).

Or I can come clean.

Sighing, I toss the photos back toward Theo. "Alright, if you must know, I am seeing her. She is a student of mine... but she's also a consenting adul—"

"Fuck, Theron! Do you know what could happen if you two get caught? It's against university policy."

"I'm aware."

"Then why the hell would you ever..." she cuts herself off, her nostrils expanding in frustration. She lowers her voice as if we're not alone. "Is it happening again, Theron? I need to fucking know."

A new current of hot anger rushes me. I snap, "You know nothing. You knew nothing then. And you know nothing now."

"I know enough. Everything that's been going on around here lately? Valentine being back?"

"We're done talking. See yourself out."

"What is it this time? What is it about this girl? Nyssa Oliver? Who is she?" Theo stands her ground like she usually does, scrambling to dig around in her purse some more.

I sit back, still scowling, a pulse throbbing in my neck. I'm half a second away from forcibly removing her. My best friend, my *sister*, or not.

This kind of interrogation won't stand.

"I was sent those photos, you know," she says. She holds up a few more, then throws those at me. "And these. They're from *inside* her apartment, Theron. Please... please tell me you didn't... you're not..."

Anger fades in a flash. The icy cold sensation returns as

I shift in my seat, my gaze on the various photos of Nyssa's private space.

Her bedroom.

Her bathroom.

The little corner in her living room she reserves for her artwork and sculptures.

Peaches dozing on the windowsill.

The last photo is of Nyssa at home, unaware of the fact that she's curled up in a baggy T-shirt and nothing else on her sofa, yet she's being filmed.

"What the fuck is this?!" I growl, popping to my feet. "Who took these?!"

Theo blinks up at me, her brow knitted. "You don't know? I thought—"

"Leave," I snap. "You have to leave right now, Theo."

"No way. You're clearly involved in some shit again and I refuse—"

"LEAVE!" I roar so loud, she almost slips out of her chair.

I've never raised my voice like this before.

Not at her.

She's rightfully startled.

And though, as my sister, I'd never hurt her, she sees the side of me she rarely has before—the darker, impassioned, intense man that I am beneath my cold mask of composure.

"Oh god," she sighs, splotches of color on her face and neck. "I wish you'd let me help you."

"You need to go. This is none of your concern."

She goes to collect the photos, but I slam my hand down on the desk.

"Leave them."

Theo tosses several hurt looks over her shoulder on her

way out. The second she's gone, I rush toward the door and twist the lock.

What the hell is going on?! Who has been watching us? Who's been... inside Nyssa's apartment to snap such intimate photos of her and her space?

Other than me.

"It wasn't me," I whisper to myself. "I didn't... but... but who?"

I race home, going thirty over the speed limit. My first instinct was to head straight to Nyssa's apartment—she had no classes this afternoon—but then I stopped myself. If someone's been watching us, then that's exactly what they'd expect me to do.

Instead, I head home, firing off several texts to her. She had some kind of social engagement tonight with the likes of the Fairchilds and other well-to-do families in Castlebury. I could certainly show up myself as an Adler, citing I've come in my father's absence.

But I'm much more preoccupied with her apartment and what the hell's going on.

Atticus whines as he chases up the stairs after me. Normally, when I come home early on Fridays, I take him to the park and we play fetch.

"Not today, Atty," I snap. "I'll make it up to you this weekend."

The sunny golden retriever lays down on the floor and lowers his head between his paws, his tail flopping morosely side to side.

I rip off my put-together professor clothing—the crisp

button-up shirt and well-fitted pants. The tweed blazer gets tossed onto my bed. I stride straight into the dark mouth that's my closet and emerge only once I'm in my disguise.

A hoodie with jeans and the skeleton mask I'd used the night I followed Nyssa and Jackson Wicker.

Checking my phone, I'm unsurprised to see Nyssa hasn't responded to me.

A bad habit of hers she takes on from time to time. That I'll have to address next time we're in the bedroom...

For now, I try to keep my messages even keeled and nondescript.

> I read an article about Chauncey Ives and his artwork. Couldn't help thinking about you...

The sun has set and drizzle's started up by the time I leave the house. My first order of business is figuring out what the hell's going on inside Nyssa's apartment. Who else would've had access to film her in that way?

I might've set up my own means of watching her, but that was because I was looking out for her. I was making sure she wasn't entertaining Wicker and that she wasn't in harm's way. My surveillance might have been intrusive and a violation of trust, but it was warranted.

For Nyssa's own good.

These rationalizations and more play out in my head on the drive over.

Her apartment windows are dark. She's nowhere in

sight. I check her iCloud and verify she's en route to the Fairchild's dinner party.

The rest of the five-story apartment building feels quiet and unpopulated.

Slipping my mask on, I use the side entrance instead of the front. Then the stairwell instead of the elevator. I come up on her door with the spare key I've swiped from Theo's office—and she apparently hasn't noticed is missing—and let myself inside.

When Nyssa's gone, she only leaves the dim light above the stove on and a few other strategically placed plug-in lights for Peaches's convenience. I flick on the hallway light to survey the space and then scope out the rest of the apartment.

Peaches's soft little meow comes out of nowhere as the ginger cat makes her first appearance. She stops in front of me with her eyes innocent and bright. I kneel and give her an affectionate scratch under her chin.

Though I have my mask on, she still seems to sense it's me.

"Hey, Peaches. Don't be alarmed. I'm here to find out who's spying on your mom."

She meows in answer, then trots at my side as we explore the apartment together.

I'm fast canvasing each room, picking up photo frames and books in search of any tiny spy cameras. In several of the photos Theo showed me, it seemed like a camera had been positioned directly in front of her sofa.

Retracing the area from the same angle, I gently check around the shelves nailed to the wall, coming up empty.

I move on to the bedroom with my new ginger sidekick, where I do the same. Any time I move an item, I'm careful to place it back in the exact same way. I'm considerate of her space, forgoing the urges to take my time and indulge in smelling her pillowcase or admiring her artwork.

That can wait for a less pressing time.

Right now, it's imperative I find out who has been watching her.

Us.

I finally resort to checking things like the air vents and outlets. I swipe my hand across the blade of the ceiling fan and even remove the thermostat's cover on the wall. The stupid thing refuses to slide back on as easily.

My teeth clench, and I try to muscle the cover back on.

Peaches meows from where she's stationed at my ankles.

"Not now, Peaches," I say. "This damn thing is…"

I go still.

In the loud silence of Nyssa's apartment, there's a clack in the front door. The sound of the metal gears turning from the inside as someone sticks a key in the lock.

Someone's about to come inside Nyssa's apartment.

Someone who's *not* Nyssa.

"Damn it," I breathe under my breath. I abandon the thermostat, leaving it without the cover, and scan her bedroom for a quick hiding spot.

I'm diving inside her closet and drawing the door closed in the same moment the front door's creaking open.

Heavy footsteps clatter on the wooden floor tiles.

The person's hardly trying to be subtle. Whoever they are, they've explored this space before.

My adrenaline has spun into overdrive. Senses on high alert, my body tenses up and I strain my ears to pick up every sound, gauging where the person is in her apartment.

They move through the living room, then predictably come into the bedroom.

I step further back, trying to disguise myself among the racks of clothes.

The person opens and closes the drawers in her dresser. They sit down on her bed and rummage through her nightstand.

I grit my teeth, barely containing my temper. The sudden, pulsing dark urges demanding I act.

Stay calm. Stay hidden. Stay... shit!

The bed squeaks as the person stands up and lumbers over toward the closet. They grapple with the handle, then jerk it open.

The shadows conceal me enough that I go unseen.

But the intruder isn't so lucky.

Samson Wicker peers into Nyssa's closet like the meaty oaf he is before he gives a grunt and then slams it shut. His heavy footsteps begin to fade.

"What are you doing here, Wicker?" I whisper to myself, my knuckles white and clenched into a fist. "And just why have you been watching us?"

25
THERON
THE WHISPER OF FOREST - SURAN

"Theron, the last thing you need is some girl ruining your future," Theo sighed. "When are you going to wake up?"

"Wake up to what, Theo? Just because you don't like her—"

"It's not about liking her or not," she interrupted. She dogged my every footstep around my apartment, arms folded.

It was unlike her to care about my personal affairs these days. Struggling in several of her undergrad classes at Castlebury, she had her own issues going on. But she'd made the time this morning to show up and pester me.

I shoved a property law book onto my bookshelf and grabbed a different one.

"I'm trying to get work done."

Theo frowned at me. "I can't believe you're going to ruin your entire life over this. She's not worth it!"

"You have no idea what you're talking about."

...she's worth everything.

The memory fades in the dark, returning me to the deep shadows of Nyssa's closet. I'm biding my time, waiting for Wicker to leave, urging myself to stay still.

Remain rational.

The brawny oaf's halfway out of her bedroom when he suddenly stops. He turns his head to the left and stares.

He stares in the direction of where the thermostat's on the wall.

Peaches, who has watched him closely from where she's perched on the windowsill, hisses at him. His attention's drawn away from the thermostat I've left in a half put-together state to the hissing cat.

Good girl, Peaches. I knew we were friends.

"Oh," Wicker says, his tone flat. "It's just you. Stupid cat. Scram."

He swipes his arm at the windowsill. Peaches is too fast for him. The ginger cat leaps from her perch and lands gracefully on her feet.

"I said get away!" The oaf starts chasing after her, his face reddening in irritation.

Don't you touch her. If you touch her...

I'm fuming as I watch through the crack in the closet door, barely holding myself back. I've never been the type to solve problems with my fists—no, I've always much preferred clever words and sharp wit—but I'm no pacifist either.

Witnessing Wicker chase Nyssa's cat out of the room like the brute he is makes my blood boil.

It takes my mind back to Halloween night, where he'd knocked Nyssa down into the dirt and almost forced himself on her...

"Dumb cat!" he yells, drawing his foot back and then launching it forward. He delivers a crushing kick to Peaches's side.

The little orange tabby flops halfway down the hall with a feeble cry. Wicker gives a crude laugh.

The thin rope of restraint keeping me inside that closet

vanishes. The closet door flies open as I charge forward. Wicker's barely sensed a figure shooting toward him by the time he's turning his head to glance over.

My fist sails through the air. It lands on the apple of Wicker's cheek. Knuckles against his cheekbone, forcing a grunt out of him. He stumbles back several heavy-footed steps. His large form knocks into some painted artwork on the wall. The frames flip off their hooks and to the ground.

Shit. Sorry, Nyssa! I'll fix that later.

Peaches shrieks and jumps out of the way, fleeing to a safe space under the sofa.

I rush forward for a second blow. My fist meets his gut and steals the breath in his lungs. Wicker curls an arm around his stomach as if on the verge of collapse.

It's a fake out.

The large oaf releases an angry howl worthy of a beast and then plows into me. We're airborne for a brief second. Two bodies flying across Nyssa's apartment. Whereas we start in the hall, we wind up scattered on the floor of her living room.

We clamber to our knees, then feet, at the same time.

It's clear Wicker outweighs me. He's taller, broader, generally *bigger*.

But he's also slow and stupid, two things I can use to my advantage.

I admit, I'm not the most capable fighter.

But I improvise. I think on my feet. I'm about winning, not flexing muscles and brawn or showing off.

As Wicker launches at me, I wait until the last possible second and swerve to the side. His meaty fist collides with nothing more than air. I grab a book off Nyssa's shelf and slam it over his head. The same spot where I'd beat him with a rock mere weeks ago.

Wicker howls again. This time out of pain.

The stitches are likely still fresh. A fact that gives me a twinge of petty satisfaction as I bring the book down a second and third time.

Wicker's crouched over, an arm thrust up to try to block me.

When that fails, he swipes at my legs. His arms lock around them and he's yanking with full brute strength. I'm ripped off my feet like a rug has been pulled out from under me. I crash down on my back, pain radiating up my spine.

The whole world feels like it's been flipped upside down.

That's because, as I look up, Wicker's hovering over me. His hand reaches out to wrench off the skeleton mask.

No... no... DON'T!

A nasty grin curls onto his lips once he sees my face. "Professor," he says. "Thought so. It was you that night too, eh? So they were right?"

He grabs the front of my hoodie and lifts me up. Before I can gain my footing or grapple him off me, he tosses me forward so that I land several feet away on my stomach. He closes in at once and wrenches me over, drawing his fist back and slamming it into my face.

His fist is like colliding with a brick.

Pain explodes across my face as he pulls it back for another hit.

Do something, Theron. Right now. You're losing!

My hand searches desperate and blind at my side for something, anything, to grab onto. My fingers wrap around a metal chisel that's resting on the coffee table. One of Nyssa's sculpting supplies that she uses to smooth down her sculptures.

The point's sharp like a blade.

As Wicker slams his fist into my face yet again, I jam the chisel into his side.

Once, twice, again and again until the metal point slicing into his flesh and organs produces a squelch noise. He freezes up, giving his loudest howl yet.

Blood leaks from both of us. My lip's split open. His side's torn open.

Yet, suddenly, I'm in the better position. I roll out from under him as he drops to his knees in agony. The same bruised-knuckled, meaty hand he's been using to clobber my face clutches at his bleeding side.

I'm not through with him yet.

I raise the pointed metal chisel and drive it into his jugular.

Satisfaction blasts through me, so euphoric and powerful, it's almost orgasmic.

Blood seeps from the slit, dribbling down Wicker's hands as he wraps them around his own throat. His eyes are on me in shock, his face paling.

I glare back at him, heaving for air, slicked with sweat and blood.

It's several minutes before Samson Wicker bleeds out on the floor of Nyssa's apartment.

He's an inch away from death as I'm quick to start cleanup. Nyssa has a decent enough selection of cleaning supplies under her kitchen sink that allow me to do a full wipe down of her furniture and the floors.

I hang back up the artwork Wicker had knocked down and straighten the other knickknacks that had been pushed over.

In the bathroom, I do my best to patch up my face. Wicker's fists did enough damage that I'm sporting a busted lip and swollen cheek and jaw. I scrub the blood from my fingers, then thoroughly clean her bathroom to cover my tracks.

Peaches has finally emerged from her hiding spot under the sofa. She meows as I dig inside Nyssa's hall closet for the large trunk where she keeps her backup art supplies.

"I know, Peaches... I shouldn't..." I pant, heaving it from the back of the closet. I take out most of the art supplies and place them back inside the closet. "But desperate times. I've got to dispose of him. I'll buy her a new one. Filled with plenty of art supplies, alright?"

The ginger cat blinks and then meows again.

"I'll bring you more salmon."

That seems to do the trick as Peaches purrs affectionately and I haul the huge trunk into the living room.

Cramming Samson Wicker's bulky, oafish body into the trunk is no easy feat. It feels like a morbid game of Tetris cramming him inside the piece of luggage. I'm sweating bullets all over again as I survey Nyssa's apartment, taking inventory for any evidence left behind.

Besides the fact that her trunk will be missing.

I'm hoping she won't notice at least for a day or two.

The riskiest moment is still to come. I'm on edge as I drag the trunk down the fourth floor apartment hall and step into the elevator. Thankfully, it's empty.

I ride it all the way down to the first floor, where I proceed to tow the two-hundred-and-thirty-plus-pound piece of luggage to my BMW.

In the back of my mind, I'm fully aware I could be seen. I'm aware this moment could come to bite me in the ass should someone happen by or spot a suspicious man carrying a giant trunk to his car late at night.

But I have to keep going. There's no turning back now.

I'll worry about the rest later.

For a meticulous and careful person like me, it's extremely difficult to disregard these things. It feels reckless and insane that I've done what I've done.

I've killed a man... again.

Once again, it was in Nyssa's honor.

It was to protect her and ensure no harm comes her way. Though I'm fully justified, it doesn't change the obvious fact that I could be ruining my life.

I could be found out.

"How could you keep this from me?" I demanded in a rumble.

Josalyn shook her head, on the brink of tears. "Theron, I warned you to stay away. This was none of your concern."

"None of my concern!?" I shout. "You're my concern!"

"Leave me alone! I don't need you!"

She rushed past me on her way to the door. I clenched shut my eyes and urged my fists to stop shaking, urged the rage inside me to go away.

But I couldn't let this go. I couldn't look the other way like I had in the past.

How could she?!

I black out once I hit the roads. They're empty and dark, my windshield wipers whizzing across the front window to keep the raindrops at bay. I drive for miles, far across Castlebury, in search of the location I know will be safe.

The place where I can dispose of Samson Wicker and then forget this night ever happened.

It wouldn't be the first time...

Half an hour later, I pull up thick in the forest that surrounds the university. I heave Wicker's body from the trunk along with the snow shovel I keep in my car. I'm lost in a daze, digging up a hole deep enough to bury him in.

His pale, lifeless body flops into the hole and I cover him

shovel by shovel. Soon he disappears, embedded deep under the wet earth.

I'm drenched once it's all said and done, soaked by sweat and the rainfall. I leave the burial site behind, scrubbing a hand over my face as I head back toward my car. Darkness surrounds me. Only the smell of sodden earth and *tap-tap-tap* of rain fills my ears and nose.

...until out of the stillness comes the soft pad of footsteps. The bright white light from a cell phone. I squint in the direction it's coming from.

Nyssa steps out of the blanket of darkness looking unlike I have ever seen her. Accusation lives in her expression, her face lacking its usual warmth.

I blink in the rain and vaguely wonder if I'm hallucinating.

"Nyssa... how did you...?"

"You... killed Samson?" she says slowly, her eyes widening.

Shit. Shit!

I shake my rumpled wet hair away from my brow, aware how crazed I must look soaked through with a shovel in my hand so late at night, in the middle of nowhere. "It's a very long story. But allow me to explain."

"So it's true," she says. "It was you."

"What's me? You think I... that I'm...? Nyssa!"

But as I stagger toward her, she retreats back into the wooded shadows. Bright light falls directly on me as three police cars emerge from the other end. They've turned off road into the forest as if given the exact coordinates to look for. Their high beams burn my retinas and I have no choice but to lift up my arm to block the light.

The police cars roll to a stop over the rocks and dirt. A stern voice issues a command over a megaphone.

"Stay where you are."

My stomach bottoms out as the gravity of the moment weighs on me.

This is bad. Very bad. The worst possible thing that could happen...

The police car doors spring open and out step four officers starting toward me.

I glance over at the trees Nyssa had been standing between.

She's gone, having vanished into the darkness.

26

NYSSA
LOSE MYSELF - REYKO

My favorite holiday is Christmas.

We never had much growing up, but on Christmas, it was like we had everything. Mom did her best to make sure there was always a small collection of presents under the tree. She made hot cocoa and snowflake-shaped pancakes and took me around the neighborhood to see the Christmas lights.

It was often just the two of us, but I hadn't needed anything else.

Even as I returned to school and was forced to listen to the extravagant holidays the likes of Heather Driscoll and Macey Eurwen had had.

When I arrive two hours away in Roseburg, the first snowflakes of the holiday are falling. Mom's waiting at the train station to pick me up and drive me home. I step into the entrance hall of her modest townhouse and smile at the strung up lights and little Christmas tree she's set up.

"Sorry it's not bigger, Nys," she says. "I know you love seeing all the lights on the tree."

"Mom, this is great. Thank you."

And I mean it.

But as I shrug off my puffer coat and unwind the scarf from my neck, the vibe feels off in more ways than one.

I've been unable to eat more than a bite or two of food since the Fairchild's winter solstice party. My appetite's nonexistent since I left the party and made one of the grimmest discoveries of my life.

As I sit down on Mom's sofa and she happily boasts about the hot cocoa she's making, I can't help feeling like my visit evokes the same feeling out of me.

Some kind of bottomless feeling in my stomach, like I'm in a permanent state of free fall. She brings me steaming hot cocoa in my favorite cracked mug—the one with the tiny cartoon Rudolph the Red Nose Reindeers imprinted on the sides—and I force another smile to my face.

"What's the matter, baby girl? You're too quiet."

"Am I? I guess I'm just..."

Tired is the word I mean to use but find that it wouldn't be the whole truth. There are other emotions welled up inside me that refuse to be ignored. Emotions that would probably trouble Mom as much as they're troubling me.

Confusion.

Guilt.

Dread.

The lack of triumph I thought I'd have this deep into my mission.

No more than twenty-four hours ago, I watched the man I've been seeing be hauled off by the police. I could've stopped it from happening; I could've warned him, yet I'd retreated into the darkness and let the police lights flood him.

In the moment, I was defiant. I was certain it was the right move to make.

All the signs were there. All the clues.

The anonymous text told me where to go to find what I was looking for. A second text told me that the police would be on the way.

I had been drawing the Valentine Killer out for months, hoping I would incite him enough to reveal his identity.

Theron had been on my radar from the beginning.

He was on the short list of suspects, but if I was going to carry out the rest of my plan, I had to be sure. I had to get close to him.

I was pretending until I wasn't.

...until our engaging conversation, heated passion, and achingly real moments began to feel like I wasn't acting anymore. It made me want to be wrong.

Maybe I was mistaken.

Valentine was someone else.

Then I discovered the police file and crumpled break up letter that were hidden inside his closet. I read the date on the file and thought back to what Theron had told me about his time as a student at Castlebury. Though he was the son of highly regarded Thurman Adler, he was largely an outcast.

He *resented* many in his social circle.

Valentine's revenge matched his sentiments about the very same people.

But what would drive him to kill my father? How could a student like Edward Oliver incur his wrath like the others? Why would he choose to take his life when Mom said my father was a good man?

He was a law student just getting his start. He wasn't a crook or rapist like some of the others. He wasn't some vile child abuser.

He took Edward Oliver's life out of bloodlust. The same thirst for violence that drove him to kill Samson last night.

I should've known he was Valentine after how easily he killed Jackson Wicker. But I had rationalized that he was acting out of self-defense. He was protecting me. That didn't make him Valentine. The same man who left behind heart-shaped cards and went on a mass killing spree so many years ago, eventually turning his wrath on my father.

"I'm sorry," I sigh. I set down the cracked mug of hot cocoa. "My head's pounding. I think I need to go to bed early."

Mom's face dims, but she nods in understanding. "Hope you feel better, Nys. I put fresh linens and towels up in your room."

I head toward the staircase, feeling Mom's gaze on me every step of the way. At the bottom stair, I pause and glance over to find she's still watching. She smiles, though it doesn't reach her eyes. Unlike earlier, I find I can't fake one in return.

I pad the rest of the way up the stairs until I'm locked inside the bedroom that used to be mine. Not much has changed about it in the few years I've been gone. Standing among the old mood boards hung up on the wall and the sequined lavender bedspread almost eases the bottomless feeling inside me.

So many memories in one place.

I wander over to my old desk to pick up one of the first sculpture's I'd ever made—a tiny kitten paw that was supposed to be Peaches.

Except it's what's lying underneath the kitty paw that holds my attention.

A photo album that I had used years ago during a class project that required us to put together a collage of our family. I slide it out from under the clay molding of Peaches's paw and prop it open, hoping the trip down memory lane will finally get me into the festive spirit.

It works at first. I flip through old photos of Mom when she was younger, laughing at the '90s hairstyles and clothes. In many of the photos, she's with other family. Her parents who have passed away. My uncle who lives on the other side of the country and who I've only met twice. Another girl that looks vaguely like her, only a few years younger.

I pull a photo out from a graduation. Mom's in a tank top and jeans, a huge smile on her face as she wraps an arm around the shoulders of the other girl, who's swallowed up in burgundy and gold Castlebury U graduation robes. Her cap sits askew atop her head of long braids.

In one hand she clutches her undergrad diploma. In the other, she's holding up a tiny girl against her chest who can't be older than two. The small girl's smile is bright, curly little afro puffs at either side of her head.

She's me.

Goosebumps spread across my skin as I flip the photo over. The penmanship I've seen before. It's the same handwriting from the crumpled letter in Theron's closet. Handwriting that's not far off from my own...

Brooklyn and Josalyn w/ baby girl,
May 2004

"What..." I trail off. My pulse soars so fast, a drumbeat starting up in my ears, the room feels like it's about to spin. I rush toward the door with the photo as I rack my brain for possible explanations.

The letter Theron had in his closet was addressed to Josalyn.

The same Josalyn Webber who died in 2005. Another victim of Valentine.

I leap down the stairs until I'm on the ground floor breathing erratically, seeking Mom out. She's gone from her place in the living room where I'd last seen her.

The townhome I once called home suddenly feels like some kind of distorted maze as I rush through the dark halls with only the twinkling red-and-green Christmas bulbs to guide me.

Mom's in the kitchen when I finally find her, seated at the dinner table as she nurses a now cold mug of hot cocoa. From my first stumble into the room, I can tell she's aware what's on my mind. Her expression is flat and dull, her stare borderline vacant.

"Who's this?" I ask, tossing the photo at her. "Brooklyn and Josalyn?"

The photo floats in the air 'til it touches down in front of her.

"You know who that is. That's my sister, Nyssa."

"Josalyn?"

Her mouth puckers like she's bit into a lemon. "That's right. Why are you asking? Why now?"

"Because I want to know why you've never told me my aunt was killed by Valentine?" I ask. "Why have you never told me she graduated from Castlebury too? And... and if you graduated undergrad this year like you've always said, where are *your* robes?"

"Nyssa..."

"Mom, if I look up Castlebury's year one law students for 2004-2005, would I find your name?" I snap. "Or would I find this... Josalyn Webber?"

"Enough. Fix your tone." She half rises out of her chair, doing her best to be the stern motherly figure she has been so many times in the past.

The difference is, this time it falls flat. I press on.

"None of what you said checks out, Mom. Everything you've told me suddenly seems like it makes no sense," I say. "The only Edward Oliver I could find is some White guy who majored in economics and who graduated before Valentine was even a thing. You said my father was killed the summer after school let out. But how is that possible when all news reports say Josalyn was the final victim and that was in June 2005?"

She closes her eyes. "Nyssa, you're speaking on things you don't understand!"

"Then tell me! Tell me why you lied about when my father was killed by Valentine! Why is Josalyn Webber holding me in this photo and not you? Why is Josalyn Webber in the graduation robes and not you? Why does her writing..."

...match the writing in the letter Theron had?

I stop myself at the last second, the cotton in my throat too drying. I'm fuming, shaking on the spot, as hot tears mist my eyes.

Mom sighs as if it pains her. She finally looks me in the face, the heaviness on hers telling me all I need to know.

"Because," she says, "I'm not your mother."

27
THERON
BROKEN MAN - ST. VINCENT

"Well, Adler? What do you have to say for yourself?"

Officer Brewster rests his folded arms on his pot belly that he's grown after years of a diet of beer and chicken wings. He sits opposite me in the sparsely lit dungeon the Castlebury Police Department call an interrogation room.

I'm not in handcuffs. I'm not even *technically* under arrest.

Once the police pulled up on me late at night in the pouring rain, they informed me they had received an anonymous tip. Someone claimed to have seen me fighting with Samson Wicker and then spotted me hauling a large piece of luggage to my car moments later.

This so-called *anonymous* tipster told the police I was driving deep into the forest.

Brewster and his colleagues damn near blinded me shining their flashlights in my face, sweeping it up and down my soaked, mucked up clothes. They hovered on the muddy shovel in my grasp and then asked me what I was doing out in the middle of nowhere.

"Why don't you come with us?" asked the officer with a

thick mustache that was silver in the moonlight. "Make things easier on yourself."

I had cooperated, but not without one last glance at the wall of pine trees nearby. My eyes had long ago adjusted to the darkness. They sought out the different shapes, looking for her.

Nyssa.

She'd shown up seemingly out of nowhere only to disappear just as seamlessly.

What in the hell did she think she was doing? How had she followed me? Did she really believe I was some murderous psycho? *I'm* Valentine?!

You did just kill a man in cold blood.

Again.

Her ex-boyfriend...

I grit my teeth at the dark, raspy inner voice that contradicts me. I might have let myself get a little carried away... but it was justified.

I was protecting Nyssa. I was fucking protecting *Peaches*. Would she rather I let the oaf harm her precious ginger girl?

As I peered into the darkness and realized Nyssa was far out of sight, I conceded the moment. It was a small victory in what's a longer war. I could have pressed the matter, insisted the police search the area, but I let her have the win.

For now.

It was in my best interest to simply acquiesce their request. At their suggestion, I accompanied them to the local police station.

Sitting in the interrogation room, my boots still have dried mud on the steel toes. My hair hangs around my face, disheveled and dripping wet. Dirt cakes my fingernails from spending so long digging a grave.

"Well?" Brewster prompts when I've said nothing.

"Well what?" I spit.

"Why don't you tell me about your evening?"

"Which part, Officer?" I ask in a tone that strikes a balance between calm and condescension. "Would you like to know what I had for dinner? I confess I'm not much of a chef, but I seared a wonderful ribeye with a garlic-rosemary-infused butter that turned out better than most steakhouses. Very nice and juicy. It was delicious. I paired it with crisp asparagus and—"

"Damn it, Adler. Stop being a smartass and tell me what the fuck you were doing in the middle of the woods! Why did some anonymous asshole think you were up to no good?"

"I'm afraid I'm not qualified to assess why an unknown source would tell you I was, what did you say, up to no good? Being that I am neither a psychologist nor a mind reader, perhaps it's best you go to the source and ask them about their delusion."

"Keep sassing. That won't help you," he grunts, looking the part of a disgruntled bear in a chair far too small. "And the woods? Why the hell were you there?"

I cock my right brow, then click my tongue in admonishment. "Officer, you know better than to think I'd be so foolish as to answer that question. I'm not required to tell you about my whereabouts without probable cause."

"Who's to say we don't got it?" he asks. "You're here for questioning. We made that clear. You think Daly and Tran stayed behind for shits and giggles? They were going to search the area. Check out the anonymous tipster's claims you were doing something in that forest. If you were smart, you'd have already requested a lawyer."

I smirk darkly at him. "No need. I'm already here."

He bares gritted, coffee-stained teeth at me. "You think you're so smart, eh? You better hope we don't find anything on you. Then you'll be sorry."

"Officer, that sounds like a threat. Are you harassing me?"

"I'm telling you you're in for a world of trouble if you're up to something! You got lucky the first time. We couldn't find anything solid, but we all knew it was you."

"I had nothing to hide then. I have nothing to hide now."

"Then mind explaining why Samson Wicker hasn't been seen in over twelve hours?"

"I don't know, but it's also not my responsibility to do your job for you. Why don't you figure that out for yourself?" I lean closer, pinning him with a hard, unblinking stare. "Now, if I'm not under arrest and you have no further questions, how about I see myself out?"

Officer Murphy Brewster glowers as I stride out the front doors of the Castlebury Police Station.

The time inches toward two a.m. The rain's hardly lightened up.

I slide behind the wheel of my BMW and flick on my headlights.

The truth is, I could be on borrowed time. If Brewster was serious that his colleagues Daly and Tran stayed behind to investigate the area, then they very well could come across the body I buried.

And the others.

But until then, I'm a free man.

A confused man. An enraged man. A man on the cusp of sinking into a deep, dark black hole I'd long ago promised myself I'd never return to again...

"Why can't you just leave me alone?" sobbed Josalyn, the distress in her voice. "Why can't you just accept my decision?"

"What decision, Josalyn?" I asked on a beat of desperation. I grabbed her by the elbow to whip her around and peer into her deep-set eyes. "Don't you see what I'm doing? Don't you get I'm trying to protect you? Even if it's from yourself? For your own good?"

She wrenched her arm free of me. "You have no idea what's good for me."

"You're still in love with him," I said, my voice dropping a decibel. My tone darkened. It turned deadly. "That's why you're doing this."

"You have no idea what you're talking about! It's over, Theron! Leave!"

Josalyn's voice still plays in my head. I blink out of my deep stupor, driving fast down a long, slick road with only my headlights to guide me.

My phone's ringing. I answer on speaker.

"You've got to be fucking kidding me!" Theo screams. "This has got to be some elaborate joke of yours. Some April Fool's shit!"

I scowl at the Bluetooth screen on my dashboard. "If you're going to scream like a banshee, I *will* hang up on you."

"And I'll smack you upside the head for pulling what you are!"

"How about you tell me your grievance first, sister? That seems like a logical place to start, does it not?"

The anger only blooms in her voice. "You know exactly what my grievance is, Theron! Why were you arrested?!"

"I was not arrested."

"Emma works as a secretary at the station, numbnuts!" she screeches. "She's on night shift this week, which means she saw you come in! She said they had you in an interrogation room—"

"I was asked to come in for questions. I was *not* arrested."

"You're spiraling again. You're losing it. You're out of control. I have to... Theron, we need to call Dad."

"Don't you call him!" I hiss at her. More heavy raindrops splash onto my windshield in answer, as if spurned by my temper.

"You're leaving me no choice. I refuse to stand by as this goes down."

"Nothing is going down. But you need to calm down. Right now."

"Where are you?"

"None of your business."

"I'm coming to get you. Tell me your address."

"You're annoying me. Goodbye, sister."

I hang up on her without further warning. When she tries to call back a few seconds later, I send her straight to voice mail.

You'd think I'd be smart and drive straight home. I'd take a hot shower, clear my head, and get some sleep.

All things I'm in desperate need of.

But I do none of these things.

Driving past the on-ramp that will take me to the suburb where I live, I drive deeper toward the heart of Castlebury.

I park several blocks down from the apartment building where Nyssa Oliver lives. The street's asleep. The building's dead. Everything's silent and still except for the monotonous *pitter-patter* from the downpour.

"Come out, come out wherever you are, Miss Oliver," I whisper under my breath.

The lock clacks as I let myself into her apartment, indifferent to the possibility she could be home. She could be gone.

It doesn't matter anymore.

I'm no longer a man driven by rationale and logic. I'm a man operating off dark impulses that would concern me in the light of day.

I stalk her shadowy apartment without bothering with any lights. My boots thud on the flooring, a heavy and threatening sound in the middle of the night.

Her bedroom's empty. Peaches dozes peacefully on her pillow. I sit down on the edge and reach out a hand to affectionately stroke along her spine. The little tabby shudders out a soft breath as she continues sleeping.

Nyssa Oliver has no idea what she's done by betraying me tonight. She has no idea what will be waiting for her when she returns home.

I rise up and wander the rest of her most private space. I pull open drawers and check shoeboxes in her closet. Books are overturned and old suitcases dug into.

Soon I lose myself in my frantic search for it.

The notebook I'd come across before where I'd seen a list of names written down. My own was on a separate page with lipstick smudges.

Little did I know then, the rest of the book detailed her great master plan.

A grunt of triumph leaves me as I check under her mattress and my fingers feel the paper-thin notebook pages.

I wrench the book out from under and then flick on her bedside lamp, poring over what she's neatly written inside.

Handwriting I've admired from the first day of class.

Handwriting that looks more and more familiar as I read through each line...

Finally, the last page emerges with my name scribbled down and a myriad of bullet points that serve as evidence she's gathered. Reasons she's pieced together to figure out that I'm who she thinks I am.

Valentine.

I smirk as I'm doing the same for her. The epiphany hits me like a freight train collision, and suddenly I see Josalyn clear as day.

The truth has been right in front of me all along.

"Tsk, tsk, Miss Oliver... you put in the effort, but it's a failing mark. You might not understand who I am. But I know exactly who you are."

28

NYSSA

ME AND MY HUSBAND - MITSKI

Professor Adler is waiting at the front of the classroom come Monday morning after winter break. My heart stops as my feet do. I hover in the doorway to the lecture hall, clutching my bookbag over my shoulder, my skin running cold.

Heather's right behind me and makes a sound of annoyance. "Nyssie, hello? Move out of the way so the rest of us can walk in."

"Oh... sorry..." I step aside, then my gaze snaps back toward the front.

My eyes meet his.

His dark, mysterious pools that are already on me. His face more stoic than I've ever seen it.

A shiver courses my spine. I blink and look away, stumbling toward my desk next to Heather.

What in the hell is he doing here? I thought after that night...

Actually, I'm not sure *what* I thought would happen.

I just know that I didn't expect to return from my trip to

Roseburg and find Professor Adler waiting to resume criminal law as scheduled.

"Silence," Professor Adler demands the instant the clock strikes ten.

The soft murmurs around the room die off and he peers at his captive audience with a distinctly unimpressed air.

For everyone else in the room, it's the same Professor Adler he's always been. For me, after everything we've been through, it feels like I've walked into some alternate universe.

Our relationship never happened.

The past three months have been nothing more than a figment of my imagination.

...until a news alert pops up on my phone with the headline:

Where is Samson Wicker? Where Has the Son of Recently Deceased Billionaire Jackson Wicker Gone?

My head's bowed, my attention on my phone screen and nothing else.

"Miss Oliver," comes the smooth, commanding voice from the front of the room. "How about you put your phone away during classroom hours so that you might actually learn something?"

Professor Adler's reprimand feels like a slap across the face. My cheeks warm as other students shoot me amused looks like I haven't outperformed every single one of them in this class.

"Sorry, Professor," I mutter.

But I'm ignored.

Professor Adler presses on like I haven't uttered a word. He instructs us to open the case study folders we've been given and then proceeds to quiz us on various legal elements involved in the case.

Jose Zardoya raises his hand from the front of the room to answer his question about double jeopardy. My hand is up in the air too, as it's often been during class, eager to show Professor Adler what I know.

Zardoya's called on. He answers, and Professor Adler gives an impressed nod of his head.

The class rolls on. Some students, like Heather, begin to lose steam. As the topic shifts to the jury deliberation for the case, Heather's admiring the glossy finish on her gel nails.

When the next question comes, my arm's shooting up to answer first.

Professor Adler skips right over me and selects Macey instead.

The hollowness I'd felt over winter break returns. It's a bottomless sensation that tricks my mind into thinking my body's in free fall.

Really, it's my heart. The manifestation that represents the feelings I've developed.

Try as I might, I can't pretend it wasn't real.

The relationship Professor Adler—*Theron*—and I had wasn't as pretend as I'd originally intended. Though I might've betrayed him the night he murdered Samson, it doesn't mean it was an easy decision to make.

It was the hardest move I've made yet, not warning him about the police on the way. Letting him find out firsthand as they showed up.

In this revenge plot I've been carrying out, it was like betraying the one person who hadn't hurt me in some capacity.

...but he has *hurt you.*

He's Valentine. He murdered your mother. Your real mother.

The whisper is like a hiss in my ear. An icy, slithery reminder that I'm devoted to my mission until the very end.

...but what if he didn't? What if it's all a lie?

The counter question sounds as a much stronger, clearer voice that's closer to my own. I squeeze shut my eyes and bow my head as if it's too heavy to hold up when it's the conflicting thoughts doing me in.

What if it really is all a lie?

Winter break in Roseburg with Mom hadn't exactly been a joyous occasion. It was so bad, I left early. I scraped together some savings and stayed in a local bed and breakfast to bide my time away not only from Theron and Castlebury, but now Mom as well.

I'm not your mother.

Four words that have been so earth shattering, I haven't finished processing them yet. I could barely speak trying to wrap my head around what she was saying. Her mood shifted from indignant and chiding to resigned and regretful.

Macey's still answering Professor Adler's question when the moment plays back to me in the middle of class...

"I guess it's true what they say. Secrets born in the dark will always die in the light. There's no escaping it," Mom sighed.

I said nothing, letting the loud silence speak for me.

"Nys," Mom said when my silence became unbearable. *"Please answer me."*

I sat borderline catatonic in the same chair I'd eaten breakfast in for years as a clueless teen girl. I'd done my homework in this chair. We'd decorated gingerbread cookies at this table. I cried here the night of my first date when Trey Smith stood me up...

Mom slid back into her seat and reached for my hand. "Baby girl—"

"Don't call me that," I snapped, wrenching my hand away. I eyed her like I never had before, like she was one of them. One of the people who had ruined our lives.

Maybe she was.

Everything I ever thought was true seemed not to be...

She sighed. "You've got to understand, Nyssa. Decisions had to be made."

"Decisions?" I choked out. "What was I? Some stray you found and didn't know if you wanted?"

"I'm your aunt," she said. "I was Josalyn's older sister. She was only nineteen when she got pregnant. Far too young to be. It would've ruined her life if anyone at Castlebury found out."

I jolt like I've been pricked by a needle.

There's movement all around me. The other students are gathering their things and making their way over to the door.

Class has ended.

Heather smirks at me. "You're really out of it today, Nyssie. Should I be concerned?"

It's a question posed as a joke.

It's facetious, bordering on ridicule. Heather flips her strawberry blonde locks over her shoulder and slides out of her desk with hardly any concern at all. Collecting my things, I'm aware this is her subtle way of getting back at me.

Yet another moment for the frenemy memory banks.

But I'm much more concerned about the man at the front of the room.

Hugging my books to my chest, I approach his desk craving... something.

Anything.

A crumb, a morsel, a sliver of his attention.

His validation.

The way he used to make me feel like I was worth the world. I was special and he was in awe of me.

I stop in front of his desk and wait for him to acknowledge my presence. Pin me with an intense stare through the lens of his black-framed glasses or utter my name in that cool, harsh voice of his that is like fine leather...

Instead, he jots away in some type of ledger as he ignores my presence.

We're back to square one.

I clear my throat. "Professor Adler—"

"Class is over," he says. "Please see yourself out."

Hannah Fochte is making it to the door as I glance over my shoulder to make sure we're alone. The door snicks shut once she's out of the cavernous room, granting me permission to drop my polite act.

"Theron," I say, "we need to talk—"

"You are to address me as Professor Adler," he scolds immediately. "I believe I made that quite clear on the first day of class, did I not, Miss Oliver?"

My heart races as his gaze snaps up to my face for the first time since I've approached his desk. Heat rises from the inside, almost making me dizzy. His burning stare alone is enough to remind me how I'd fallen so deep down the rabbit hole.

How I let things get as far, as real, as they did...

"Professor Adler," I correct. "Can we talk?"

"There is nothing to discuss. Please show yourself out."

My brows knit. "But I want to explain why I did what I did."

"Even if I had any clue what you were talking about, Miss Oliver, I wouldn't care."

"Us," I say, stepping even closer to his desk. My arms tighten around my books. "Me and you. Everything that's happened between us—"

"Let's get one thing straight. There is no *us*. There is nothing between you and me. You are just one student of many in my class. You are mistaken."

"There is an us!" I argue. "We've slept together… many times. You've slept in my bed. I've bathed in your bathtub. We talked about a future—"

"You. Are. Mistaken." He pops to his feet on a dangerous pulse of anger that feels like it could quickly spiral out of control. He thrusts a finger in the direction of the exit. "See yourself out. I believe I've asked three times now. There won't be a fourth. Campus security will simply be called."

So thrown by his blatant denial of our history together, I find myself without a real defense. I blink at him in shock and offense, as if it'll make any difference.

It doesn't.

He sits back down, picks up his pen, and begins furiously scribbling in his ledger all over again. His face sharpens in concentration. His glasses sit perched on his strong, straight nose while a lock of his unruly dark hair brushes his brow.

He's ignoring me. Pretending like I don't exist.

We never existed.

It's worse than outright condemnation.

I'd almost rather he bend me over the desk and take the yardstick to my ass…

When several seconds go by and nothing changes, I finally take the hint.

I show myself out, feeling lost and hollow.

For the rest of the afternoon, I'm a wanderer. I roam the campus, going from the darkest corners of the library to the farthest patches of land neighboring the pine forest. The same forest that holds so many secrets.

Professor Adler had driven to the northern edges just to dispose of Samson. Had he disposed of bodies there before?

I don't know what to think as I sit down on a stone bench and drop my face into my hands.

"I don't understand why you've lied," I said, my throat aching with every word.

"Would it have made it any better to know the truth?" Mom asked.

"You mean that you're my aunt and not my mother? You mean that my entire life has been a lie!?"

"No," Mom snapped immediately. Aunt Brook *snapped as she grew indignant again. "You think we had any other choice? Your mother couldn't be in those circles as a young, pregnant teen girl... a Black girl. She would've been outcast. Banished."*

"Isn't that what happened anyway, or was that all a lie too?"

"The mistreatment Jos suffered was not a lie."

"So she was found out? And what about Edward Oliver? That a lie too?!"

Aunt Brook shut down after that. With a somber shake of her head, she left the room and refused to answer...

Peaches gives a squeaky little meow when I walk through the apartment door. She's waiting for me perched on the armrest of my sofa, her bright eyes shining with affection.

I walk over to scratch behind her pointy ears. "You're my only companion, my sweet girl. Everything else... everyone else..."

...it's all a lie.

She leaps into my lap as I plop down on the sofa and stare blankly at my latest sculpture. Where do I go from here? Should I carry on with my revenge? How can I when it seems so many secrets and lies have been exposed and I can no longer tell what's real anymore?

A week goes by where I'm trapped in a sullen stupor. Concentrating on any task feels near impossible. My course work piles up by the hour. Any art projects are indefinitely on hold. Outside of class, only quick runs to the local market, no one sees me.

I lock myself into my apartment and drive myself to the brink of insanity.

The worst part is Professor Adler's denial.

Every time I show up in his class with eyes only for him, he has eyes for everyone else.

He's icing me out. He's pushing me away, treating me like I'm nothing.

Less than nothing.

And though it might be deserved for what I did, it makes my chest hurt. I find it difficult to breathe as the hour stretches on and he calls on Heather Driscoll with her broad, boastful smile. She shoots me a sidelong glance once she gives him the wrong answer and he offers an amusing quip versus the condescending retort he'd utter in the past.

It's the academic version of torture—your favorite professor that you admire, ignoring your existence for the blonde twit who can barely read.

The envy blooms inside me like a toxin that's poisonous yet incurable. Rationale tells me to let it go. Clearly, things between us are over.

Professor Adler is moving on. He wants nothing to do with me.

I should take it as a sign to either proceed with the rest of my plan or figure out a new path forward.

That would be the sane, rational thing to do.

Yet as Friday morning rolls around and I meet up with Macey in the student union, she informs me Heather won't be joining us for coffee.

Macey shrugs, her attention fixed on the menu up ahead. "Heather will meet us in class. Something about Professor Adler asking her to come by his office an hour before class starts."

An arctic chill washes over me. I go still at once, like I've been delivered the worst news of my life.

"What is it?" Macey asks, barely noticing. "Don't tell me you're mad about the flavors they're offering again—"

"I have to go."

Macey asks me where, but I'm already half out the glass door of the student union. People grumble and rush to step aside as I shoulder my way through the crowds in the long, tunneled hallways.

I pivot at the next intersection and then dash up a cascade of stone steps. My bookbag slaps against my back as I trot across campus in record time.

He wouldn't... he wouldn't...

The two words are all I can manage of the incomplete thought, practically gasping for air. I round the corner in time to spot Heather's golden head bobbing among the other students clogging up the corridor. She's headed straight for the hall that leads to Professor Adler's office.

No! NO!

The scream is deafening inside my head. The panic that grips me is sweeping. I rush down the rest of the hall, heartbroken and desperate to intervene.

He can't replace me with her. He can't see in her what he saw in me.

He wouldn't... he wouldn't... HE WOULDN'T.

I fling open his office door and barge inside without knocking.

I make it three steps past the threshold before I realize Heather's not in here. She must've gone through a different door.

"Wha...?"

"Hello, Miss Oliver," comes a familiar smooth, authoritative voice from behind me. "I had a feeling you'd show up."

The door swings shut with a resounding thud. He steps up behind me as the air empties from my lungs. Yet I find I can't turn around. I can't bring myself to, vaguely aware that it would mean trouble.

It would only confirm what I've walked into.

"Professor," I mutter breathlessly, "I thought... I followed..."

"Yes, I know. Because I know everything there is to know about you. I told Miss Eurwen about Driscoll meeting me. I knew she'd tell you. And I knew you couldn't resist," he says, gripping me by the waist. His other hand comes up toward the side of my neck and I feel the sharp prick of a needle piercing my skin.

My legs give out almost instantly, no longer able to hold myself up. I slip backward into his arms, left peering upside down at him and the twisted smirk spreading across his face. The edges of my vision have begun to blacken, consciousness fading away.

"Believe me when I say, Miss Oliver... we're about to get to know each other exceptionally well."

29
NYSSA
SUGAR - GARBAGE

It feels like being born again the next time I open my eyes. I fight through the deep sleep that's held me captive for who knows how long and push my eyelids open. Both feel like they weigh a ton.

So does my body, aching and throbbing as I find myself immobile.

I'm passed out on some kind of bed, a thermal blanket thrown over me.

The room I'm in is foreign, one I've never been in before. The walls are made of limestone, like most of the campus at Castlebury, though there's a hollowness to the space. It's almost as if it isn't supposed to exist; it's been carved out of another, deeper space, and then set aside.

A draft lingers in the air that seems permanent.

As permanent as the heavy silence seems to be, the walls likely soundproof.

The blanket that covers me slides down my body as I push myself up on the bed. Bleariness fades for restored eyesight. I use the moment to scan the area.

It might as well be a bedroom.

I'm lying in one corner where the bed's been placed, and there's a desk and chair pushed up against the wall to my left. On the far wall in front of me there's a row of bookcases. Other than the books crammed on the shelves, there're items like a world globe, scales of justice, and a glass case of what looks like a anatomically correct human heart.

Where the hell am I?

My head pounds as I search my mind for the last traces of memory.

I was following Heather. She was headed to see Professor Adler and then...

A choked gasp pours out of me. I stare wide-eyed at the limestone walls, recalling how Professor Adler had grabbed me from behind and whispered into my ear.

"I know everything there is to know about you," he told me, gripping my waist. "I told Miss Eurwen about Driscoll meeting me. I knew she'd tell you. And I knew you couldn't resist."

My legs gave out at the sharp prick of something lodged into my neck. A needle of some kind?

Almost immediately, things started to fade.

"Believe me when I say, Miss Oliver... we're about to get to know each other exceptionally well."

I cover my face with both hands and let the gravity of my situation sink in.

Professor Adler has taken me captive.

This must be one of the secret rooms he had once mentioned existed on campus.

"Castlebury was built centuries ago," he said with a wondrous glance at the chain-link chandelier that hung from the ceiling. "Back when it was fashionable to have bookcases that led to other rooms and hidden dwellings underground. Many still exist today..."

I leap off the bed, arrowing straight toward the single, solitary door that's next to the row of bookcases. I step right into a glass divider that is invisible up until I collide with it. Staggering back a couple steps, I blink at the structure that's blocked my path.

A glass wall that divides the half of the room I'm trapped in with the other half of the room where the bookcases and door are.

Standing up close, I can see how the light reflects off the see-through wall. But from my bed, it was undetectable. Glass so fine and thin it's basically invisible unless you're close enough to touch it.

My hand extends toward it, fingertips tracing over its delicate surface.

There appears to be no opening. No way in or out.

How did Professor Adler put me inside here?

"Help!" I start to scream. I pound a fist against the glass. "Anyone there? Can anyone hear me? HELP!"

Frustration boils up inside me fast. I go from a pound at the glass to slamming my fists against it one after another. Pain radiates through my knuckles and up the rest of my arm. Yet I beat the other fist against the glass in hopes it'll finally be the hit that cracks the surface.

For as thin and fragile as it appears, it's nothing of the sort once I'm smashing into it. I'm making no headway whatsoever.

Not even the slightest crack.

Breath sputters out of me as fatigue sets in and I take an exhausted step back. My eyes scan the length of the glass that stretches floor-to-ceiling, then I let out a frustrated cry.

Why would he ever put me in here? Is he planning on returning? Will he kill me like he's done so many others?

I bang my head into the glass, resting my forehead against its smooth surface.

I've worked for years at my plan. Strategized and studied every minute detail. Devised backup plans to the backup plans and alternatives in case things ever went sideways.

And yet never once did I ever plan for *this*.

For Theron Adler to trap me in some secret room behind a glass wall.

Is this how Mom met her end?

Had Professor Adler trapped her in here before he murdered her?

The letter I'd found in Professor Adler's closet pieced everything together.

I'd always known my mother was ruined by Castlebury.

But family secrets still hid the extent to which she had been ruined; she hadn't simply had her reputation tarnished like I'd been led to believe.

She'd been murdered.

Her death was then covered up like many of the others.

Professor Adler was the only person who made sense.

He was Valentine, a bitter man who hated the community and acted out to make them suffer; he sought *my mother* out to make her suffer.

He was bitter and jealous and angry.

The same man he'd been when he'd taken out Mr. Wicker and then Samson. The same man who will probably take me out next...

The door near the bookcases sweeps open. In steps none other than Professor Adler. He's as I remember him—his charcoal-gray sweater vest juxtaposes the white dress shirt he wears underneath, the sleeves rolled up to his elbows and the collar creased and neat. The watch on his wrist glints under the room's lighting, his large hand wrapped around the doorknob.

His glasses sit perched on his nose, the black frames and clear lenses offering a window to his soul. His eyes that are dark and intense as they fall on me and he snaps the door shut behind him.

My insides ripple in uncertainty. I'd be a liar if I said he doesn't look good, his hair as rumpled as ever, with the signature lock still hanging over his brow.

But with that attraction comes an unmistakable and visceral disgust. He sickens me to my stomach. It must reflect on my face, because as he starts toward the glass, his brows crease out of curiosity.

"Miss Oliver, I see you're awake," he says. "How are your accommodations treating you?"

I scoff at him from through the glass. "Accommodations? Is that what you call this?"

"I took great care to ensure you were comfortable. The bed isn't the absolute best, but if you'll notice, I brought you a thermal blanket and pillow. I've ensured you had food should you become hungry." He juts his chin at a point past my shoulder.

At the desk, where there's a domed tray on top. I hadn't even gone to look at what was inside. I was much more focused on finding an exit.

"Let me out of here, Theron."

The corner of his mouth quirks slightly. "Theron? So *now* I'm Theron. I can't help but think of all the times you called me professor when I told you not to."

"Let me out of here. This isn't funny. This isn't a game."

"Oh, but to the contrary, Miss Oliver—*Nyssa*—isn't that what you've been playing all along?" he asks in rebuttal. The quirk at his lips turns into a full grin. It shouldn't make him more handsome, yet it does. Enough to draw me in. "You've been making moves like this is some game board the entire time. I admit, I was charmed by it. Impressed by you. Until you turned those moves against me."

I lift my chin in open defiance. "That's where you're confused, *Professor*. The moves were against you the entire time."

"Ah, there she is. The spark of brilliance I expect out of you. But you're right. You have been making moves against me, haven't you?" he asks, scratching his stubbled jaw. "I was simply too… pussy whipped to notice."

He chuckles at his own admission, the sound sexy and dangerous all at once.

My skin heats up, air thinning out inside my lungs. I watch him through the glass barrier like I'm fascinated by him. Really, I'm studying him, trying to figure out what's to come.

He rubs his jaw and pins me with an amused look. "I spent so long watching you, Miss Oliver. Hours and hours. Not once did I catch on."

"Sounds like I was doing my job."

"But I admit, I did pick up on your need for validation. Your thirst for approval. You sought me out almost as much as I sought you out. In more subtle ways, sure, but hardly any different. You wanted me," he says, leaning closer to the glass. So close, I can make out the follicles of hair on his jaw and see myself in the reflection of his eyes. He drops his voice as if we're surrounded by others and he wants this kept between just the two of us. "You wanted me just as much as I wanted you. You wouldn't have entertained me as long as you did otherwise."

"I had a goal in mind. You were nothing more than a means to an end."

He tuts his tongue and leans even closer until I'm sure he's about to reach straight through the glass for me. "We both know, Miss Oliver, that's a lie. I bet that delicious little cunt of yours is nice and wet thinking about us together. I bet it would love nothing more than to be wrapped around my cock right about now."

Stubbornness won't allow me to admit the truth in his accusation. I resort to silently glaring at him, practically shaking on the spot from the anger coursing through me.

...and the arousal pooling in my panties.

I'll never admit it aloud.

Ever.

"I can practically smell you," he goes on in a whisper that racks a shiver down my spine. He licks at his lips, meeting my dark eyes with even darker orbs of his own. "I can still taste you."

Shaking my head fervently side to side, I take a wide step back. I'm in need of a buffer. Some space between us to keep a clear head.

In order to do so, I voice aloud the beliefs I must have. The truth I can't lose sight of.

"I don't want you," I mutter, eyes shutting. "I don't want you because I *hate* you."

"Look at me, Miss Oliver."

"You ruined my life. You ruined her life!"

"Miss Oliver. Open your eyes."

"I HATE YOU!" I scream, conviction blooming in my voice. My eyes snap open to sear him with a glare that's twenty years in the making. Air puffs in and out of me erratically, my chest heaving. "You're a murderer! You killed my mother!"

He gives no reaction either way, though his inflection

changes. The taunting humor vanishes. His monotone returns. "Is that what you think?"

"I don't think—I know! You're Valentine, right? It was all you!"

"You don't know what you're talking about."

"Josalyn Webber, my mother," I spit at him, taking several angry steps back toward the glass. "You killed her in cold blood. You killed her because she wouldn't have you. She wanted nothing to do with you!"

His jaw clenches. "That's not true."

"It is true!" I yell. "IT IS TRUE!"

"You are a lost girl," he snipes, stuffing his hands in his pockets as if in restraint. "You are more foolish than I ever thought you could be."

"Josalyn didn't want you. Isn't that true?" I ask, eager to goad him. I crack a smirk at him. "Just like I don't want you, Theron. I've never really wanted you. Josalyn wrote you to tell you to leave her alone. I read the letter. I saw it in your closet. Why couldn't you just leave her alone?"

"NO!" he booms suddenly. Rage flashes in his dark eyes. "You have no clue what the fuck you're talking about!"

"Are you angry, Professor? Why would that be? Because someone's finally calling you out? Are you really surprised I'm here? That I did what I've been doing? Guess what? *You* created me."

His nostrils flare as he glares at me through the glass wall.

I'm putting on a show, acting defiant and petulant. But the smirk on my face is nothing more than a disguise for the turmoil raging inside me. I'd quiver on the spot if I hadn't thrown myself into the role I have. I'd be a mess on the floor if I didn't cling to strategy.

What I want out of riling him up, I'm not sure.

Maybe if I stall long enough, some kind of opening might come...

Professor Adler lets my accusations fester in the heavy silence. He seems to be deep in his own mental calculations, drinking every part of me in.

Then he steps toward the left, walking over to the wall.

I watch in shock as he undoes a latch that's attached to the limestone. It's what connects the glass barrier. He unlocks it with a key, then nudges it aside.

It glides out of the way like a glass sliding door.

He's coming in.

I take several steps back as a precaution.

The glass door slides back into place. The enclosure suddenly feels a lot tighter.

"Ready to finish me off?" I ask, trying to sound braver than I feel.

Professor Adler remains where he is, his expression controlled. "I'm ready to make you understand how wrong you've been."

"Save it. There's nothing you can say to explain what I've discovered. Are you saying you weren't obsessed with my mother? With Josalyn Webber?"

No answer.

He inhales a deep breath, his Adam's apple bobbing in his throat. "Sit down."

"I don't take orders from you. Let's start there. Unless you're about to let me go and turn yourself in, I have no interest in anything you have to say."

"You would if you were interested in the truth."

"I know the truth! You're Valentine. Did my mother catch you in the act? Or did you kill Josalyn because she wouldn't love you?"

His temper returns in the glare that narrows his eyes

from behind his glasses. He takes several steps toward me until he's within reach, though his arms remain at his sides. "I've already told you, I would never hurt her."

"But you did. You killed her. And now history's about to repeat itself, right? I'm next?"

"I would never hurt you either, Miss Oliver. Punish you? Yes. But truly hurt a hair on that beautiful head of yours? Never."

"LIAR!" I scream in his face. "You killed my mother!"

"I did not kill her..." he snarls through clenched teeth. "Stop talking about things you don't understand."

"You killed Josalyn and buried her somewhere in that forest! And if I ever get out of here, I'm going to the police. I'm going to tell them all about how Valentine's been under their noses this entire time!"

Professor Adler cuts me off with a hand to my throat. My eyes widen as he wrenches me toward him 'til my body's flush against his and he's giving me a threatening squeeze. Peering into his face, madness stares back at me.

It's in his bared teeth. His curled lip. The muscle ticking in his jaw.

His dark eyes unsettlingly stuck on me and my every move.

"I. Did. Not. Kill. Her." Anger punctuates each word, his hold on restraint fading by the second. "I would have never harmed her. I protected her. I... I *loved* her."

A disbelieving laugh bubbles out of me the same time tears spring to my eyes. "You expect me to believe that? You expect me to believe a word you say after everything I know, Professor?"

"It's the truth—"

"It's a lie!"

"No... it's not a lie. It's the tru—"

"A LIE!" I yell over him, despite how I'm subdued in his hold. "IT'S A LIE! YOU KILLED HER!"

"SILENCE!"

He slaps a hand over my mouth to shut me up, his other still cinched around my throat. His dark eyes bore into mine as he stares at me so intensely, yet another cool shiver trickles my spine. "You insist on doing things the hard way, Miss Oliver. It seems to be the only way you'll learn. Very well. I'll show you the monster you think I am."

30
NYSSA
MAKE YOU MINE- MADISON BEER

"I'm not afraid of you."

I challenge Professor Adler with a brave glare. He's let go of me, backing up a couple steps to slide fingers through his hair and catch his breath. He's never looked more out of control. More deranged and insane.

He's lost all composure. All restraint.

Every principle he lives his life by has seemingly disappeared.

He's operating off impulse and adrenaline.

The rough breaths he husks out tell me he's right on the edge of truly snapping. I've driven him to the brink.

...and, as shameful as it is to admit, there's something darkly sexy about him like this. There's something strangely empowering in the most fucked up way. I've pushed a man known for his intellect and cool—if not icy—demeanor to such a point that he's transforming into some kind of crazed monster before me.

It's just more confusion at a time where I don't know what to think. I don't know what to believe.

I could be locked inside this glass cell with a man who

murdered my mother. The same woman I've been avenging all along, even if initially I wasn't aware who truly was my mother.

Or he could be telling the truth—he didn't murder my mother, but he *did* love her.

Trying to get a read on the situation feels impossible.

After the web of lies I've found myself tangled in, what's real and what's not has become relative.

Seconds stretch into a full minute as heavy silence hangs between us. Professor Adler works to catch his breath while I search for any clues.

I swallow against imaginary cotton that's materialized in my throat and force myself to remain calm anyway. I'll deal with the trauma of everything I've been through later.

Right now, it's more important I stay sharp and focused. Professor Adler's smart and quick-witted, but so am I.

I just have to come up with an exit plan.

"Professor?" I say cautiously, softening my tone. "What are you—"

"Silence!" he snaps, then he starts pacing back and forth. "You don't believe a word I've said. You think I took her life? Do you realize what that does to me? No. But you will. You know what to expect by now, Miss Oliver. Punishment's on the menu."

"But what if..." I gulp down some air, taking a step toward him. "What if... maybe I do... maybe I could believe you?"

He stops short, looking over at me, a stray hair curled against his brow. "You believe me?"

"Of course I do," I say gently. "The more I think about it, the more it makes sense. You've been nothing but protective of me. I'm sure you were the same way over my mother."

"I tried to be. But she was hardheaded. It seems she and her daughter have that in common."

He starts toward me, his energy so ambiguous, I'm not sure what to expect. I flinch as he smooths his palm along my cheek and slides his other arm around my hips. "I know you're afraid of me. I even know you don't truly believe me."

"No, I meant it when I—"

"You really think I don't know when you're lying, Nyssa?" He gives a laugh, his dark eyes gleaming as they peer into mine. "But it's okay. Because I care so deeply for you, I'll get you to see things my way. I'll prove it to you. I have to leave for a couple hours. You'll remain here until I can return."

"Please don't leave me in here—"

"But first," he goes on, "as some insurance, I can't have you getting loose."

He's slipped something from his pocket that he slaps onto my wrist before I can even object. It's a leather cuff attached to a chain.

"Why don't you get some rest while I'm gone?"

"Professor, don't... Professor!"

He escorts me back toward the bed, where he connects the other end of the chain to one of the iron bars. The chain's so short that I can't even fully stand up from the bed without being pulled back down.

"There. That should be fine." He leans in and kisses me softly on the lips like he's a husband bidding his wife goodbye before leaving for work. "I promise I'll be back soon. And I'll show you the truth. I'll prove to you everything I've said is true."

"I believe you!" I cry out. I start tugging on the chain to free myself. "Please, Professor... please just... come back! I BELIEVE YOU!"

My voice goes out from the sheer desperation tearing from my throat.

Professor Adler carefully slides the glass wall back into place and then presses a hand to the transparent surface as if he's missing me already. As if this situation and why I'm trapped behind here isn't his own doing.

Dread pits in my stomach watching him go.

The door snaps shut and silence commences around the hidden room. I'm left all alone between thick walls of limestone, stuck inside some kind of glass cage.

"Great..." I mutter under my breath.

Apparently, I'm not as good of an actress as I hoped I was. Professor Adler hadn't bought my ploy for a second. I've managed to fool everyone else in Castlebury, taking on the persona I have and befriending people like Heather Driscoll, but he knows me too well to fall for any pretending.

That's what happens when you open up too much to a person.

I lay down on the bed with no other option at the moment. I have to trust that Theron will keep his word and he'll return sometime soon. What could he possibly retrieve that could make me change my mind?

I'm pondering that thought when I nod off.

Sleep comes suddenly, dragging me into a dreamless void where minutes or even hours go by, and I'm none the wiser.

The snick of the door wakes me. I flinch from where I'm lying on the bed, my right wrist tethered closely to the iron frame.

It takes me a few bleary-eyed blinks to realize the person who's walked through isn't Theron. I blink several more times, sitting up, disoriented and foggy-brained.

My heart stutters inside my ribcage. I'm so thrown by what I'm seeing, I'm vaguely wondering if I'm still dreaming...

Theron's ex, Veronica Fairchild, has shown up. The chocolatey-haired brunette smiles at the sight of me. She's wearing a ruby-red lipstick that clashes horribly with her pale complexion, though something tells me she's put it on for one person only.

"Miss Oliver," she says brightly. "I thought I'd find you here."

I temper my reaction, peering at her with suspicion. "What are you doing?"

"Theron left, didn't he? I figured we could, I don't know, have a little chat. Just us girls." She waltzes over like she's come across me in the park and not a glass cage. Stopping in front of the transparent wall, her smile widens. "I see he's still putting people in here."

"He's... put people in here before?"

"I've known Theron for most of my life. You wouldn't understand." She pulls up a chair from the other side of the room and sits down, crossing her legs in poised, ladylike fashion. "Has he told you about how we got engaged?"

"What does that have to do with me? Are you going to open the door?"

"*I* proposed," she simpers. "My father didn't appreciate that very much, but what else was I supposed to do? I've been waiting for him for *decades*. I wasn't going to stand by and let him wallow in some stupid grief over a woman who had been dead for years. I'm a Fairchild, and my biological clock was ticking."

"You might want to take that up with Theron. He says it's been over."

"*Professor* to you." A quick glower comes to her face before it passes, and then she lets out another little giggly laugh as if playing off her irritation. "But I suppose that's just it, isn't it? You've been crossing lines for a while now. The both of you have been very, very inappropriate. I should've known he'd leave me for someone like you."

I arch a brow, still tethered to the bed frame as I sit by and watch her bitterness unfold. "Theron didn't leave me for you. You were already broken up."

"We've been on and off for years. Ever since our college days. He always comes back. I always find a way to make him. Then *you* came along. You were an unplanned inconvenience."

"I'm sure Theron would view that differently too."

"You have no idea how hard I've worked," she says, resting her chin on her fist, her arm propped up on her crossed leg. She peers at me through the glass cage like I'm some repulsive creature at the zoo. "It's taken a lot keeping track of you two. I've had to figure out ways to pull you apart. It hasn't been easy."

The shock that washes over me does so like a wave breaking at a shoreline. I half rise off the bed before the chain reels me back down. But it doesn't even matter, because I'm gaping at Veronica Fairchild as though *she's* the repulsive creature.

And she is.

"It was you," I say slowly. "You broke into my apartment. You smashed my sculpture. You knocked over my potted plant. You sent me the anonymous text and tipped off the cops that night."

She wiggles her brows, smirking proudly. "I've done a lot more than that."

"You've been watching me. Following me. Sometimes I've sensed it. I've assumed it was Theron. Even Samson. But it was *you*."

"I had to sabotage you whenever possible," she quips. "I also tipped Heather Driscoll off to the two of you in the library. I sent Theodora photographs of you and Theron together. I even sent some to Samson Wicker knowing he would head to your apartment and Theron would confront him, and guess what? I was right."

"And now what? What's the big plan from here? Theron still doesn't want you."

"Oh, but he will. Once you're gone." She rises from the chair and withdraws what looks like a Bowie knife from the pocket of her peacoat. "You see, you'll be dead and gone. I'll be there to comfort him as he grieves. It'll be poetic in a way. History repeating itself..."

Cold sweat rushes me as I shake my head and realize how screwed I am. I'm tethered to the bed while Veronica has a knife and free movement.

How can I even begin to defend myself when she can simply start stabbing away?

"Don't do this. You don't want to ruin your life over this."

She smirks as she approaches the corner of the glass wall where the latch is. "How much clearer can I get, Nyssa? Nothing and no one's going to take Theron from me. Most of all you. If I have to eliminate you myself, then so be it."

31
THERON
ALWAYS BEEN YOU - CHRIS GREY

For the sake of my sanity, I have to remove myself from the room. I need a moment to cool down and regain composure. Because I'm not confident Nyssa won't try to escape, I have to restrain her to the bed. It'll only be for a short period.

A few hours at most.

I'm in the middle of locking my office door when Dean Rothenberg appears, dripping every bit of his usual arrogance. "Theron, I was just talking about you with Veronica. She was on campus to discuss her father's latest donations."

"Why would I care?" I shove my ring of keys into my pants pocket and start down the opposite way of the corridor.

Unfortunately, Rothenberg follows like an attention-starved little puppy I can't shake.

"Well, you know," he says. "Your history, of course. Shame you two couldn't work it out."

"Yeah, real shame."

"Theron, listen, between the two of us, there have been

some rumors circulating." The dean lowers his voice with a glance to our left and right as we walk the corridor.

The halls have begun thinning out so late in the afternoon. The last batch of classes are in the process of wrapping up and most students are eager to escape campus and begin their weekends. I pretend I'm more preoccupied with starting mine in the same vein while the dean blathers on.

"Are you going to tell me what sort of rumors, or do you expect me to guess?"

"I'm sure you can imagine. Castlebury's no stranger to scandal. This whole Valentine Killer ordeal has everyone extra sensitive to anything amiss. I've heard some rumblings about you."

"If this is about the questioning with the police—"

"The police are investigating Samson Wicker's disappearance," he interjects, holding up both hands. "I understand that. They've interviewed me and several other professors. Students as well."

That's not the only reason they were interviewing me, but go on...

"I'm talking about the rumors about student-teacher relations. I've had someone anonymously reach out and mention there is inappropriate conduct between you and Miss Nyssa Oliver."

I cut him a sideways glance, the severity in my glare making him stutter.

"W-Well, it's none of my concern what consenting adults do. Lord knows there have been a few college-aged cuties I've had my fun with. But discretion is the key, Theron," he says hastily, cracking me a toothy smile. "You never bring it to campus. You never bring it to any professional setting. Particularly with your history and the weirdness of what happened before. Josalyn Webber and Professor Vise—"

"I have places to be, Dean. Is there anything of actual importance you wanted to discuss?"

We've reached the end of the corridor, which opens up into the faculty parking lot. We've turned to face each other with the dean deciding to fumble with his pocket watch to check the time.

"I hope you know it's not malicious, Theron. I stopped you to warn you. Not dredge up the past."

"Yet that's exactly what you did. Good evening, Dean." I turn away to head off and then stop when a thought strikes me. It's not my blue BMW XI that pushes the thought into my head, but instead, it's the familiar little ruby-red convertible parked across the lot. "Veronica... where is she?"

Dean Rothenberg frowns. "I'm not sure. She was only here to visit me. She must've made another stop afterward if she's still on campus."

She's making another stop, alright.

The exact place she shouldn't be.

Tension lances through my jaw as I clench my keys in my fist and rush past the imbecilic dean.

I'm on a race against the clock, cutting down the same corridors I just walked moments ago. I leap down a short stack of stone steps and shove aside two jocks guffawing about some 'rager' later tonight.

Veronica is more or less harmless... *until* she believes something poses a threat to our relationship.

Once, when I broke up with her, she broke the living room window in my house and then claimed it must've been a burglary. On another occasion in between a failed round of our relationship, she called me to rescue her from a kitchen fire.

But, to my knowledge, she's never hurt anyone.

"She wouldn't," I pant under my breath as I sprint down the corridor toward my office.

And yet as I come up on the unlocked door, I'm not so sure.

My footsteps slow up and quiet down the closer I make it to the door leading to the hidden room.

It's cracked open.

Just enough for me to press my eye against the crevice and see for myself what's going on.

Veronica has slid aside the glass wall and started toward Nyssa on the bed. But that's not the most alarming part of what's about to happen—clenched in one hand is a knife that she's raised into the air.

"How much clearer can I get, Nyssa? Nothing and no one's going to take Theron from me. Most of all you. If I have to eliminate you myself, then so be it."

"Come near me and I'm going to smack the shit out of you!" Nyssa yells defiantly, though I see the hesitancy in her eyes.

She's aware she's at a disadvantage due to the chain.

Veronica ignores her and advances anyway.

"Silly girl getting in the middle of things she doesn't understand. Your fault you'll have to pay the price now—ahhh!"

I've abandoned the doorway to stop Veronica myself.

The knife's snatched out of her hands and as she spins around in shock. I grab hold of her by the throat. Her eyes bulge at the sight of me, and she sputters out protesting words that go ignored. I grit my teeth at her and bring her up against the limestone wall, tightening my grip around her throat until she's clawing at my hands.

"Theron!" she chokes out. "Theron!"

But I only squeeze harder.

"What do you think you were about to do, Veronica?" I snarl in her face, savoring the desperate gasps for air she gives. The way she squirms and drags her nails into my flesh. "Did you think you were going to hurt Nyssa? How dare you!"

The harder she tries to fight, the tighter I clench her throat. The more her lungs give out, losing air.

I can't bring myself to let go. I've fallen prey to the dark impulse that drives me to continue, to eliminate a problem that's only grown more threatening over time. If Veronica lives, she won't stop. She won't give up on our failed relationship.

She'll try again.

She always has.

This is not just for myself. This is for *Nyssa*.

Like everything I do has begun to be for her.

Veronica's fight fades as the seconds go on and she depletes what's left of her energy. Soon she's merely squirming, and then her eyelids are growing heavy. She loses consciousness for what may be the last time.

I let go and step back, allowing her to slump to the floor.

It's then that the present moment returns. That I'm suddenly aware of the fact that I'm not alone in the room.

Nyssa's still on the bed, chained to the iron frame, gaping like she's never seen me before. But the look on her face reads more ambiguous than anything. As if, once again, she's conflicted over how to feel.

She's at war with herself.

"I had no idea she'd show up," I say, half breathless from the physical force I've used. I gesture to Veronica's unconscious body. "She must've been following me or keeping tabs."

Nyssa blinks and opens and closes her mouth a few more times. "She... she told me she's been sabotaging us. She's the one who broke my sculpture and the potted plant outside my door. She took photos of us together. She told Heather about the library. It was her who called the police the night you and Samson fought."

"That... that fills a lot of holes left. I suppose she's the one who's spread rumors to the dean."

"Is she... dead?"

"Just about." I kneel beside her and check her weak pulse. Then I glance up at Nyssa. "You understand why I've done what I have, don't you? She was about to hurt you. She wouldn't have gone away. She'd try again."

"What are you going to do?"

I pause for another second. "I have to get rid of her. There's no choice now."

"Theron," she whispers with a shake of her head. "Please let me go."

"Soon. Very soon. But now this has come up. I'll return once it's handled."

Grabbing Veronica by the ankles, I drag her toward the other end of the room. Luckily, I still have the large trunk I'd borrowed from Nyssa the night I dumped Samson Wicker's body. If it fit an oaf of his size, it'll easily fit Veronica.

I sigh as I head out to my car to grab the trunk. "The things I do for love. Perhaps I am insane."

It's late into the night before I'm done in the forest surrounding the school grounds. I toss the shovel in the back of my BMW and run a hand through my already slick hair. Veronica's joined the collection of others buried in the forest and won't be posing any issues in the future. I'll have to work at making up a story for her sudden disappearance.

Perhaps she ran off to Europe with some boy-toy type.

It's on my mind during my entire drive home, where I shower and dress in what's become a uniform of mine over the years—a white button down shirt and dark gray slacks.

Nyssa's been alone for hours and I intend on making up for it. Besides, there's still several matters we need to address and get to the bottom of.

I still owe her so many truths. So many things I have to tell her to convince her I'm not the man she thinks I am.

Sure, it seems incriminating from her point of view. No less than a couple hours ago, I strangled someone before her eyes. I've kept her captive. I'm sure from her perspective, I seem insane and dangerous.

She deserves to learn the truth. But she also must pay for some of the little antics she pulled. Including trying to manipulate me earlier.

"Miss Oliver, how have you been resting?" I ask upon returning.

I find her lying despondently on the bed, curled up with her gaze on the limestone wall to her right. I'd assume she were asleep if not for the blink of her eye that I catch.

She doesn't bother giving me an answer.

"We can do things the hard way or the easy way. But either way, you'll be punished. You simply decide the extent. Will you behave yourself?"

No response.

I set down the satchel I've brought with me on the desk. "Very well. Tonight is as good as any to continue our play."

Nyssa's stare is rapt and unblinking, watching every

move of mine almost as if we're adversaries. I unsnap the leather flap on the front and begin pulling out the items I've brought with me. The first I set down is the familiar bottle of silicone-based lube.

Then the blindfold.

And then the paddle.

Other items join the first few, like the vibrator she's become acquainted with, three different sized butt plugs, a pair of nipple clamps, and lastly, a ball gag.

All items I may or may not use tonight, depending on the moment and where it takes us.

"On your belly, Miss Oliver. You know what to do."

Nyssa disobeys me. She remains as she is, glaring harshly at me like we're enemies.

She's angry and frustrated. Perhaps still convinced I'm Valentine.

Fair enough.

I haven't done my due diligence to convince her. Yet as I strangled Veronica before her eyes, she hardly uttered a peep. Not a single protest as I came to her rescue and eliminated another person posing a threat to her.

Pretend as she might that I'm an abhorrent monster, some part of her can't help being drawn to me. Deep down, she knows the truth. She feels the same about me as I do her.

On some level, Nyssa *wants* to be mine.

She wouldn't have worked for my approval if she didn't. At the first sign of my intense infatuation, she would've run scared and never looked back.

But she's stayed.

She's sought me out herself.

This is just another obstacle of our relationship. A bump

in the road we'll get through together, coming out the other side triumphant and closer than ever.

I'm sure of this as I approach the bed with measured footsteps and an unyielding gaze. Though she's the one chained to the bed, I'm the one caught in her trance. I'm just as much of a prisoner as she is, unable to do the right thing and let go of her.

I couldn't walk away any sooner than I could stop breathing and survive.

Both are intrinsically one and the same.

I kneel before Nyssa and caress her cheek, bringing her face close to mine. Our lips brush in a slow tease, my tongue slipping out to trace a quick outline of her mouth. My fingers travel to her curls, and I bask in how we're so close and the room's so quiet.

I can hear her breathing. The soft, stilted little breaths she's drawing in then pushing out.

There's an intimacy about it. Something erotic about listening to the sound of her breathing, a second away from making her mine all over again.

But she denies me.

As I go to swipe at her mouth a second time with my tongue, she turns her head away.

My fingers clench in her curls, and I snap it right back.

Roughly. Dominantly.

An immediate reminder I'm in control and she's yet to be punished.

I crush my lips to hers, the kiss harsh and forceful. My tongue plunges into her mouth to pillage and plunder, taking what I want from her. I'm savoring the sweet taste of her and the addictive supple feel of her lips.

Nyssa grips my shoulder with her free hand as if hoping to push me back.

But she doesn't. Her fingers clench into the fabric of my shirt and she parts her lips *wider*. She releases a throaty moan that awakens a possessive instinct inside me and makes me grip her tighter. I kiss her even deeper, establishing that she's mine and mine only.

My hands undo the buttons on her blouse. My mouth explores the slender column that's her throat. I push down the straps of her bra and roughly grope her breasts once they're free. She throws her head back at the sharp tweak I give her nipples.

I play with her breasts just enough to make her tremble against me.

Just enough to have her panting for more, nipples puffy and erect.

"I believe you heard me the first time," I say, drawing back for a warning glare. "Get on your fucking belly, Miss Oliver. Now."

The cold, severe tone snaps her into action. She lifts her legs onto the bed and shifts her body until she's on her hands and knees. Her right arm remains beholden to the leather cuff chained to the bed post.

It takes a little more maneuvering before she's able to lower herself flat on her stomach, propped up by her elbows.

I let the stillness settle in the air, seconds going by. My gaze roves over her slowly and appreciatively, adding my hand to glide down her bare back. Her skin is smooth and luminescent, inexplicably erotic as my palm charts a path to the little dip at the base of her spine.

Nyssa's closed her eyes. Her lips remain slightly parted, like she's secretly enjoying this as much as I am.

If I know my favorite student like I think I do, she is.

"This goes how you want it to go, Miss Oliver," I say

sternly, taking on the same authoritative tone I use in the classroom. I rise up onto my feet and reach over her. My hands slip under her to unbutton the front of her skirt, and then I tug it down her hips and thighs. Her panties meet the same fate, discarded somewhere in the distance once I've pulled them off her.

Nyssa Oliver lays before me beautifully naked.

My mouth waters at how perfect and round her bare ass is. I'm tempted to sink my teeth into the curvy flesh and go to town.

Eat her out like she's never been eaten out before.

'Til she's withering and coming, and I'm throbbing from a painfully hard dick.

But I tamp down on the urges and focus on what must come first.

"I must say, Miss Oliver, you look so erotic like this. It's a very big turn on. First things first." I roll up my sleeves to the elbow and turn toward the desk. It's as I do that I sense her sneaking a glance. She's curious what I'm going for. My hands enclose on the medium butt plug and the bottle of lube.

When I turn back toward the bed, I can sense her wariness. She's done well any time we've done anal play, though I know it's not her favorite.

Tonight isn't about pleasuring Nyssa. Tonight is about getting her to see reason. Making her understand the truth and the inescapable reality that she's mine.

We belong together.

"You must really think I'm a monster, don't you?" I ask, uncapping the lube bottle with a snick. I squirt the lube into the palm of my hand and then begin working it all over. It becomes an impromptu sensuous massage as I spread it along the tiny puckered hole, between her ass cheeks and pussy.

She's slick and sopping wet by the time I'm through.

Though not all of it is lube.

My fingers graze her pussy, and I find some moisture there that's entirely self-lubrication.

Nyssa's already turned on. She bites down on her bottom lip when I let my thumb rub against her clit. I travel back up toward her puckered hole, slipping my thumb inside there instead. She turns her head to the other side as if to mask her reaction.

But it doesn't matter—I feel her body shudder even at the merest intrusion.

"You might like this more than you let on, Miss Oliver. You've had the medium before. Let's see how you do having it in you during more intense play. Remember the safe word. You speak it, it stops. But at what costs? Are you willing to lose?"

"I... I don't... I never lose," she huffs out stubbornly.

"Good girl." I lean forward to press my lips to the back of her bare shoulder. "But don't forget to breathe. This will still be a lot to take."

Holding the silicone butt plug in hand, I begin pressing it against her tight little entrance. It's tapered in shape, with a special feature that I haven't yet used, though I will tonight.

Nyssa groans at the feel of it. Her body tenses up and she bites into the pillow she's propped up on. I hold her still, one hand on her lower back, the other easing the plug into her rear puckered hole.

The tight ring of muscle widens to allow the tip in. I pour some more lube and slick another inch in. The muscle gives way to let it in, swallowing up the silicone toy 'til it's deeply embedded inside her.

Arousal courses through me. My cock twitches in my pants.

Just the erotic sight of watching it disappear into her is enough to make me hard. Admiring how the handle of the plug sticks out between her ass cheeks is enough to make me come.

I'm practicing discipline, keeping composure. Instead, I squeeze an ass cheek and bow my head to kiss the other.

"How does that feel, Miss Oliver? Too much?"

"Would it matter?" she asks breathily. "I'm not quitting, and you're not stopping. So what does it matter if it is?"

"Very mouthy of you. Are you angry with me?" I ask in mocking.

Her expression tightens, eyes opening for a glare. "You can play these games all you like. I still want nothing to do with you after this. If you think I'll forgive you for being Valentine, you're mistaken."

Anger shoots through me as quickly as arousal had. I clench my jaw and grip the bottle of lube so hard in my hand it would shatter if made of glass. Nyssa's pushing my buttons; she's intentionally trying to rile me up.

Almost as if she wants me to unleash myself on her. She craves it.

"Up on your hands and knees," I command, pivoting toward the desk. "Now. No talking."

Nyssa obeys with the petulance of a child. Again, a strategy of hers where she makes it known she's pissed off and hates me.

It doesn't really matter. I'm more than happy to dole out some punishment.

Two more items are retrieved from the desk. Before

Nyssa can glance to see what they are, I'm covering her eyes with one of them.

The leather mask that takes away her sight. She flinches as I pull it over her, clearly startled by yet another disadvantage working against her.

The other item is the paddle that she brought to Jackson Wicker's that night.

I beat it against the palm of my hand as I pace back and forth in front of the bed.

"There's so much you don't know, Miss Oliver," I say in deep thought. "Where to even begin?"

"It doesn't matter. Nothing you can say changes anything!"

SMACK!

I swat the wooden paddle hard against the curve of her ass in warning. She jerks in place, surprised by the sudden reprimand.

"Didn't I tell you no talking?" I ask, pacing some more. I stop to go for a second blow, swatting the paddle into her backside. She releases a shaky breath in answer. "This isn't the time for you to speak. This is the time for you to *listen*.

"I should've known from the first time I ever saw you—the day of the year one orientation—that there was something different about you. I suppose I did know in a way. There was a reason I couldn't throw away that damn note. Some reason I stayed to chat when I saw you at the art festival. But that was nothing compared to what came after. I followed you home."

I give her another harsh spank with the wooden paddle, enjoying how she sways in place. How the plug entrenched in her ass remains firmly planted inside.

"I had to," I say. "Samson Wicker was trouble, and you didn't seem to grasp how much. Do you know what kind of rumors follow him and his friends? Are you aware I overheard him speaking about you? I couldn't let him be anywhere near you."

"It wasn't your place!" she snaps.

SMACK!

I slam the paddle into her ass once more, then double and triple back for extra emphasis. She deserves all the discomfort that's coming to her if she can't obey simple rules. The wooden paddle is hard and punishing as it collides against her supple brown flesh and streaks it faintly red.

Yet her pussy lips glisten. Her thighs quake. She's biting down on her bottom lip to keep from blurting anything else out. But also to keep from moaning.

I can practically feel the sound of pleasure bottled up inside her.

I step forward and fondle her pussy as yet another means of torture.

"But I have to be honest, Miss Oliver," I say composedly, despite how hard I am. My pulse pounds away in my ears and blood has engorged my cock. A weaker man would've come already. "Once I started keeping an eye on you, I realized a few things. I realized that you were an exquisite young woman and I couldn't stay away from you. It was wrong in every sense of the word. Yet I was invading your life more and more.

"I snuck into your apartment when you were gone. I monitored your online activities. Read your text messages and put a tracker on you so I knew where you were. Nights I turned up suddenly—when I gave you a ride home and bludgeoned Wicker—were intentional. They were no accidents. But don't you understand why I was doing what I was doing?"

"You're Valentine," she mutters under her breath.

I respond with another swat of the paddle. My palm falls to the curve of her ass. The same spot I've just struck a blow and left streaked red. "If I were Valentine, I would've gotten rid of you a long time ago. You know it deep down. Tell me you do."

She shakes her head side to side.

I forget about the paddle, letting it clunk on the floor. My hand returns to her pussy, rubbing her little clit and then pushing two fingers deep inside her.

Her jaw drops open and she shudders out a breath.

"Tell me, Miss Oliver," I whisper, bending over her. I nip at the side of her face and work my fingers inside her just the way she likes. Her pussy walls are soft and slick, pulsing against my touch as I go slow and torture her. "Tell me you know what I do. You can't stay away from me any more than I can stay away from you."

"No…" she pants. "No…"

"Yes," I say, my tone dark and authoritative. "Yes, Miss Oliver. It's true, isn't it? You sought me out because your heart called to mine. You set up each and every victim to be slain. You wanted me to do it."

"NO!"

"YES!" I bark, tilting her face toward me for a rough kiss on the lips. "Face it. If I'm Valentine, so are you."

Nyssa shudders as I begin twisting the plug inside her. I stuff my slick fingers into her mouth and make her taste herself. She moans around them, licking and suckling away. Her body's a quivering, dewy instrument of pleasure as I tease and torture her beyond what she's ever conceived.

I reach into my pocket and press the button on the remote to the plug. A vibration starts from deep inside her rear tunnel, drawing yet another visceral reaction out of her. Her spine bows as the tremors rock through her in intense fashion.

"Does that feel good?" I whisper, biting her jaw. I kiss her mouth and then return my fingers to her soaked cunt.

I can feel the vibration.

"Fuck," I groan. "It must feel very good, doesn't it? You want me to turn it up?"

Nyssa whimpers in answer, clenching around my fingers like it's my cock. She's right on the edge of coming. She's reached the point where she can no longer intelligibly respond, so I decide for her—I dial up the vibrating sensation to the second highest setting and watch it rack through her beautifully naked body.

My fingers toy with her pussy. Arousal coats them as I pump them deep, curling them until I'm pressing on the little ridged button inside. Her G-spot being stimulated is the final straw for her. Nyssa comes undone as soon as it's touched, her pussy rippling in a warm wet wave.

I pull my fingers to find them more drenched than ever.

She didn't just come. She *squirted*.

A new level of primal, possessive need is awakened. It unleashes itself, consuming me whole. Suddenly, all discipline washes away. My cock jerks against the constraints of my pants, desperate to be inside Nyssa.

I undo my pants in a flurry and hike Nyssa's hips back toward me.

The handle of the plug stares up at me, vibrating like the rest of the toy wedged inside her.

"Fuck... yes..." I growl, giving it another tug to her whimper. My grip's bruising on her hips as I coat myself in her juices and warn her of what's to come. "Breathe, Miss Oliver. You're about to be fuller than you've ever been in your life. The question is, can you take it?"

With no further warning or preparation, I slide deep into her soaking wet cunt. The clench of her and vibration of the plug hits me all at once. I half topple over her, so thrown by the intensity of sensations slamming into me that it takes me a moment to adjust.

Planting a hand on the bed beside her, my eyes snap shut and blood pulses and throbs in my veins.

I'm buried in her pussy as it draws me in deeper. All while I feel a vibration against the thin wall separating her pussy from her ass.

"This is..." I pant, dizzy from how good it feels. "This is so fucking good. You feel so fucking incredible."

Somehow, I find the strength to recenter myself. I hold off the orgasm already welling up inside me.

I raise up and draw back my hips enough for my cock to slide out, then I slam forward. Nyssa collapses at the brutal thrust, falling face first into the pillow. Her hips rise to meet me. I grope them and slap her ass.

I watch transfixed as my cock disappears into her glistening wet pussy and the handle of the butt plug quakes from the vibration. Her flesh jiggles too, after I slam a hand into her ass a few more times and piston my hips forward.

Quickly, I'm picking up a pace that's rough and merciless. My thrusts come one after another, sinking deep into the wet heat of her pussy. Then retreating until I'm at the head, about to drive back in, then bottoming out.

Nyssa muffles her screams into the pillow.

Her cunt flutters tightly around me. My cock rubs against the vibrating plug with every deep stroke. Every pulse shoots straight through my cock and then the rest of my body. I grit my teeth and fuck her harder, fighting through the orgasm that inches ever closer.

Anger and frustration fuse with lust and possession.

I'm furious with her. Enraged she'd ever think I was Valentine. That I could hurt not only Josalyn but hurt *her*.

All dark emotions that are purged with every punishing stroke I give her. The smacks of my palm and rough twists of her nipples.

I tangle my fingers in her curls and use my grip to force her up against my chest. I'm panting as I grind into her and suck at her jaw.

Nyssa whimpers, shuddering in my hold. She reaches behind us to grip the hair on the nape of my neck and turns her head to meet me in a hot, passionate kiss.

We've become animals fucking with no other thought in our heads except the pleasure that drives us.

Her pussy clamps down on my cock. Another orgasm overtakes her.

I hold her through the deep quakes that pass through her body. She practically goes slack in my arms, yet I don't slow down.

As she folds forward, half out of it, I pick up the pace and pound harder.

The vibrator buzzes away, torturing us both. My cock twitches in warning before I bury myself and unload deep inside her. We collapse together in a heap, sheened by sweat, pleasure spasming through us.

My vision becomes double everything. Easily the most intense orgasm of my life.

My whole body feels the aftereffects in the moments to come. I lift myself off Nyssa with aching limbs that feel as if they've been through a war. Considering everything we've done tonight, it's a fair assessment.

But even through the haze of my orgasm, I remember to focus on her.

I gently roll her over and carefully remove the vibrating

plug and leather blindfold. She's dripping with evidence from our encounter. Sweat and cum, yet she's never looked more beautiful to me. Caressing her cheek, I place a kiss on her brow.

"Would you like me to clean you up?"

Nyssa peers into my eyes with a yearning that I've recognized many times. Sincere longing for me that's real no matter what she says.

Then she snuffs it out. She blinks again and then turns her head away from me.

"Don't touch me," she says coldly. "Don't you ever touch me again."

"Nyssa—"

"I told you it wouldn't change anything. You're Valentine. You killed my mother and I'll *never* forgive you."

The tenderness I'd shown her disappears for my equally cold mask. I rise from the bed and begin dressing.

She'll never believe me... unless she knows the whole truth.

As ugly, hideous, morbid as it is.

"Alright," I say. "Suit yourself. It's your choice to refute the truth. I've told you I was never the Valentine Killer. But if you must know, I'll tell you who was. You look just like her."

32
NYSSA
JUST YOU - JAMES WARBURTON AND JADE PYBUS

Theron's words render me speechless.

Five words that unload on me like an avalanche, striking me dumb, making the room spin. I sputter out a breath, then shake my head. My lips spread halfway into a disbelieving smile until I shake my head again as if I've just heard the most preposterous news imaginable.

I've just been told pigs fly. Fish can walk. Dogs can talk. And every other outlandish impossibility that can never be real.

Yet as Theron stands before me, solemn and patient, the real horror reveals itself.

The invisible inkling creeps up on me and whispers in my ear.

It's true.

"That... can't be true," I whisper finally, gathering the sheet to cover myself. I divert my gaze away from his, choosing to stare at the limestone wall instead of him. "You're lying."

"We both know it's the truth, Nyssa. You have tears in your eyes."

"That's because... because you're fucked in the head!" I snap, anger returning to my voice. I draw my knees to my chest, the bedsheet like a shield that separates me from him. "You're so twisted you think you can manipulate me. You can make me... you can make me feel things and make me come and then what? I'm under your control? FUCK YOU!"

Theron gives no reaction. He barely blinks.

Somehow, his non-reaction is ten times worse. It feels patronizing and insulting.

As if my heart being shredded in half means nothing.

It's of no consequence to him in this fucked up game of secrets and revenge.

When I can't bear to let him look at me any longer, I cover my face with my hands. I hide behind them as tears ache for release. Could I be any more pathetic right now? About to cry my eyes out to my crim law professor that's told me a bigger truth than my own family has?

Aunt Brooklyn never bothered; she was content letting me believe she was my mother and I was seeking revenge in her name.

"If it's any consolation," Theron says after a stretch of awkward silence, "I didn't know about you. I never met you."

I sniffle, my face still covered. "That's real convenient for you. A real guilt eraser for fucking me."

He sighs, the sound tinged with something I can't place. Regret? Remorse?

"It wasn't until I was taken in for questioning that I realized what was going on," he says. "That you were her daughter. But of course you were—I was drawn to you from the moment I saw you. How could I not see it before?"

"Stop. Just stop." I wipe at my puffy eyes, still fighting back tears. "I don't want to hear about how in love and obsessed with my mother you were. In case you haven't figured it out, it's fucking disgusting. You disgust me."

"Your sweet little cunt didn't think so a few minutes ago."

"Stop. Stop. Stop!" I chant over and over again. My hands clap over my ears in hopes of tuning him out.

Yet when he speaks, I can still hear him. His calm, measured voice is inescapable. He himself is inescapable.

"It hurts now, Nyssa," he says. "But I can make sense of it all for you. If you'll listen. I can tell you everything. Every sordid, twisted, morbid detail."

The tears won't go away. My eyes sting blinking them back. My lungs struggle keeping up with my intakes of air. Rarely an emotional person, it's like years' worth of curiosity, confusion, and trauma have rushed me all at once.

I've grown up believing the lies Aunt Brooklyn told me.

She was my mother. Edward Oliver was my father.

We were ostracized by the Castlebury community in the wake of the Valentine Killer slayings.

I was ruthlessly bullied.

That wasn't fake. That was real. I lived it myself.

I have the childhood memories seared inside my head. The scars on my knees. The emotional hang ups from being taunted about my broke mommy and dead daddy.

But how could my memories be real when everything else wasn't?

My entire reality—my whole backstory—has been nothing but fiction told to me for ulterior motives.

What if what Theron says are more lies? How can I trust it's the truth?

Fat tears roll free, slipping down my cheeks. I dare myself to glance in Theron's direction. He hasn't budged an inch. He hasn't taken his eyes off me, like he's so enamored by me even now.

Even like this.

When I'm a sweaty, teary-eyed mess full of cum, clutching a fucking bedsheet.

I swallow against another rising tide of emotion and whisper hoarsely, "Tell me."

He slides fingers through his unruly dark hair, tousling it further. "I'm guessing you know about your mother—Josalyn Webber—becoming pregnant her freshman year at Castlebury."

"My aunt told me. She took a year to study abroad, but really it was to have the baby. No one had to know, and it was passed off as her older sister's."

"Brooklyn. Her older sister. I'd never met her... or even known her name. She'd only mentioned her sister in passing," he confirms with a nod. "I didn't meet Josalyn until several years later. She was a 1L and I was a 2L. She caught my eye as soon as I saw her crossing a courtyard. I'm sure it's no surprise to learn that I was a loner... even back then. I was quite fine being on my own. But that was only until she walked into the picture.

"She was... striking. In the same way you are. The kind of beauty and grace that stands out in a room. The kind of wit and cleverness that's addictive. I knew as soon as I saw her—certainly once I spoke to her—that I wanted her. More than wanted her. She became a compulsion I couldn't let go of. I was obsessed."

I'm not sure how to respond other than to blink at him.

So many questions are trapped in my throat. Questions about my mother, Josalyn Webber. Questions about me and the extent of this obsession he's admitting to.

"But Josalyn had her own issues. You see, despite the fact that she had covered her pregnancy and hid it from the upper crust of Castlebury, there were other problems. Your mother was at the university on a scholarship. Something that already put her at a disadvantage in the eyes of many. And then there were... racial biases at play."

A scoff tears from my throat. I shake my head. "Why am I not surprised? So Aunt Brooklyn *was* correct."

"To an extent. But she didn't tell you the whole story. She told you the version that I'm sure she believed protected you... and her and her sister's lies. See, despite her disadvantages, Josalyn still flourished at Castlebury. At least initially. She made friends in Holly Bunton—now Holly Driscoll—and several other followers of hers. She believed she was finally gaining access to spaces that were long denied to her.

"Until rumors began. Rumors about where Josalyn Webber was sneaking off to at night. Unsavory rumors that sullied her reputation in the eyes of many," he says. "It was around this time that I became friends with her. She was being ostracized, and I sought to ease the pain. I wanted to make her feel special. Make her see everyone else was an imbecile for how they were treating her."

"Rumors?" I mutter, my brows drawing close. "What rumors?"

"Josalyn was in love," he says, almost begrudgingly. His eyes darken, face twisting in contempt. "But not with me. She was in love with her professor. A man by the name of Anton Vise. My mentor and someone Josalyn greatly admired herself."

"Professor Anton Vise," I repeat in a whisper. "He was a criminal law professor here, wasn't he? I remember seeing his name in several of the newspapers I pulled from the school archives."

"Yes, he was brilliant. So brilliant, he charmed her. And many of the female students. But she was the only student he had eyes for."

"Wait..." I can't finish my sentence as my brain lurches to a halt and no new thoughts form. The little hairs on the back of my neck rise one by one. I meet Theron's gaze and I *know*. I understand where this is going...

"They had a relationship. Or as close to a relationship as you can call a nineteen-year-old freshman sleeping with her forty-nine-year-old professor."

"No," I say.

Theron's mouth shifts into a tight line of sympathy, his jaw clenched. "Yes, Nyssa, he got her pregnant."

My face falls back into my hands. I can't bring myself to give any other kind of response.

The revelation's enough to make me want to run away and never face any of this again. How could Brooklyn keep this from me?

"As soon as he found out she was pregnant, he demanded she abort it. She refused. That's when she went away to have the baby."

"Me?"

He sighs. "Yes. But that wasn't the end of their affair. They continued seeing each other on and off through the years. When I found out, I demanded she leave him. I told him if he ever touched her again..." he pauses, the tension in his jaw visible. "Professor Vise got worried he would be exposed. So what did he do? He exposed Josalyn first. He made it look like *she* was coming onto *him*.

"Back then, in those times, young women were rarely believed. They were often blamed. Even when the man involved was old enough to be their father. The rumors spread like wildfire. Josalyn was shunned and put up for expulsion by Dean Rothenberg Sr. Holly Bunton and the rest of their clique targeted her and made her life a living hell."

"And where were *you*?" I ask accusatorially. "Why didn't you help her!?"

"I tried. I pleaded with my father to intervene with the board of trustees," Theron snaps, taking several steps toward me. "I threatened Vise. There were times I almost... I almost hurt him very badly. But then I discovered what Josalyn was doing. A spate of murders had started to rock the local community. All individuals linked to the university in some manner."

"Valentine."

"Valentine," he repeats. "No one knew who it was. Not even me. It sure as hell put the fear of god in everyone around campus. It seemed finally some retribution was coming their way, and they were shaking in their little designer boots. Josalyn and I laughed about it, though when I began to notice she was disappearing, I kept a close eye on her."

"You mean you stalked her."

He grits his teeth. "If that's what you want to call it. She had no idea I followed her. I kept such close tabs. One night, she drove into the forest, and I realized what she was doing —she was burying a body."

"No, she couldn't have been. There's no way she would. It was you! You were responsible! You're Valentine!"

I leap up out of the bed, still clinging to the sheet, and begin pacing. Manic energy has suddenly shot through me and made me jittery and scatterbrained. I can't process what Theron's saying, because none of it makes sense.

My mother might be dead, but I know she wasn't a killer.

She couldn't have been.

There's no way...

Theron blocks my path and grips my shoulders. "Look at me," he commands, "your mother was Valentine. She was jilted over what happened with Vise and facing expulsion, so she began exacting revenge against the community. She left the heart-shaped valentines as her calling card to instill fear in others. In Vise himself."

My eyes round. "You mean she was..."

"He was on the list."

"No, my mother didn't kill my father," I sputter out. "He's not even my father. He's not—"

"Your name," he interrupts sharply. "Nyssa Oliver. What's your birth certificate say?"

A chill trickles down my spine. "I don't... I don't have a birth certificate. Not an official one. I was born out of the country, and Brooklyn said it wasn't registered. I was given a backdated letter of record instead—"

"I'll tell you what it says," he cuts me off with passion blooming in his voice. His hold on me clenches tighter, almost painfully. Our faces are so close, our noses almost touch. "I know what it says because I went to the Castlebury Hall of Records myself and looked it up days ago. After being questioned at the police station. Rosalyn Vise."

"What? That's not my—"

"Rosalyn Vise is your birth name, Nyssa. Your mother gave you his last name. She wanted you to have it as irrefutable proof. As a reminder to him the baby was his.

But when she died, your aunt decided to change it. Rearrange the letters in Rosalyn Vise and what do you get?"

I wrench myself from his grip and stumble a few steps back. The letters appear in my mind's eye, shifting back and forth to spell out the two names.

Rosalyn Vise.

...and Nyssa Oliver.

Then I think back to the newspaper articles I've read. Dozens of them from twenty years ago when Valentine was wreaking havoc on Castlebury, and I remember the headline for Anton Vise.

"Interview with Amelia Vise, Widow of Valentine Victim Anton Vise: How She and Their 3-year-old Daughter Rosalyn will Seek Justice," I whisper the newspaper article title aloud. "That was me?"

"His wife didn't fight Brooklyn Webber for custody or legally changing your name. She was relieved to have you out of her hair. Evidence of her husband's infidelity and philandering ways. Brooklyn won custody easily, changed your names, and assumed the title of your mother."

I scrub at my face, dizzy by these revelations. "I'm the daughter of Anton Vise? My real name's Rosalyn Vise? That can't be true, Theron!"

"But it is true! Don't you see? It is all true!"

I ease back to put more space between us, but Theron advances. He cuts the distance I've sought and grabs me by the wrists to draw me back toward him.

His rumpled hair's messy and his eyes are crazed behind his glasses.

He holds onto me like he's desperate for me to understand.

It's then that I realize he hasn't told me everything.

There's more.

There's another revelation that's possibly more disturbing than the rest.

A shaky breath tumbles out of me. My throat aches enough that I can only speak in a whisper. "Theron," I say slowly, "what happened to my mother? If she was Valentine, then what happened to her? What did you do to her!?"

The passion fades from his face for a darker, more unsettling vacant look. "I tried to warn her. I tried to tell her."

"Theron... Theron... tell me you didn't! Tell me you didn't really do it!"

I tug and twist against him, trying to free myself. Panic rises, growing and expanding inside me the tighter he grips my wrists.

"LET GO!" I scream wildly. "LET ME GO!"

"I didn't," he says, dragging me closer. Bringing me right up against his chest, bedsheet and all. "Nyssa, you have to believe me when I say—"

"How could you?" I cry. "How could you do it?"

"I didn't... I would never!"

"You killed her!"

"I KILLED HIM!" he barks in my face, effectively silencing me. He gives me a hard shake. "Don't you fucking get it? I killed him *for* killing her! She went against my warnings and went after him, but he overpowered her. He stabbed her right in the fucking heart. My heart. I felt it. The knife running through. He watched her bleed out and die like it was nothing.

"And when I came across the scene, I... I lost it. I blacked out. I slaughtered him. Tore his chest open. Ripped out his innards. I made him suffer. I kept him alive as long as possible 'til he couldn't stand anymore and his body gave out. Right inside this glass cage, his old office and hidden study. But she was still gone. He had taken her from me. Because I failed to act sooner. I let my heart die."

He lets go of me. His fingers wrapped around my wrists are gone. He turns his back on me as if too pained to stand the conversation another second.

"The heart in the glass dome," he says, "is her heart. I preserved it all this time. As a reminder of what happens when I fall in love. It's best you stay away from me. You get the hell away while you have the chance. Leave."

I watch in stunned silence as he slides open the glass door.

He's letting me go.

33
THERON
THIS MESS WE'RE IN - THOM YORKE AND PJ HARVEY

I leave the glass sliding door open for Nyssa to escape. I walk out of the hidden room altogether. And then my office.

Castlebury's campus slips behind me in the rearview mirror as I drive far away. For once, my mind's vacant the entire drive home. I'm operating on autopilot until I pull into the driveway of my home and blink out of my stupor.

Atticus pounces on me the moment I step through the door.

My golden companion spins in circles, dying for quality time. It's no wonder when I've been gone since early in the morning. I haven't been home as often as I usually would be the past few days.

Weeks.

Since Nyssa Oliver entered my life.

Then again, in a morbid sort of way, we've always been involved in each other's lives. Though neither of us were aware of the extent.

I'm still struggling to process the very truth I revealed

to her today. Everything she's ever believed about her existence was a lie. Right down to her birth name.

Twenty years ago, I fell madly in love with Josalyn Webber.

Twenty years later, I've fallen madly in love with Rosalyn Vise, her daughter.

It sounds unfathomable thinking about it, even in the plainest of terms.

Yet as my heart aches, the truth rings louder. I have loved and have lost Josalyn Webber, and now I've found love again... in her daughter.

I open the kitchen back door and let Atticus run wild. The happy-go-lucky canine is in a mood for zoomies as he speeds out the door and runs circles around the yard.

My gaze is on him, though I'm actually blind to what's in front of me.

Instead, I'm witnessing the past and future converging. Two Theron Adler's confront each other, old and new, young and matured, hopelessly in love with the same woman only different. It feels wrong in every sense of the word.

More wrong than Nyssa and I already were, given our age gap. Given my position as her professor and her status as my student.

As if things couldn't become any more twisted and taboo.

It's life's latest cruel joke to deny me the love I desperately sought so many years ago. The home I bought in hopes of a bright, perhaps cliched, future, where the woman I adored married me and I gave her a picturesque life in the suburbs.

The result was a dead paramour who I've spent twenty years mourning.

The reality of today is that I've now fallen, even deeper, for a woman I never should've gone near. The daughter of my dead paramour, without even realizing that was who she was to begin with.

A montage of our time together plays in my head. All the moments I basked in Nyssa's presence or lurked in the shadows, enjoying every trivial detail about her. She was so special, so unique that it took my breath away.

It made me feel alive. My dead heart beat for the first time in decades.

Atticus barks as he halts in the middle of the grass. It's begun to drizzle but he wants to play fetch. He's signaling for me to pick up the tennis ball a few feet away and chuck it so he can chase after it.

I sigh, stepping out from under the patio covering. "You are perhaps the only dog who likes water, Atty."

I grant his wish, tossing the ball toward the other end of the yard. He races across the wet blades of grass in his desperation to catch the little neon ball. I'd laugh if it didn't feel like the heart beating inside my chest was being ripped to pieces.

Rationally, I'm aware of what I need to do. I know there's only one way forward.

The only way I can exist in a world where she does when I can't have her. The only way I can show the depth of how I've come to feel.

Make her understand, as dark and morbid as it may be.

"Someday," I whisper under my breath. "You'll get it."

A cautious pad of footsteps sounds from behind me. I tear my gaze from Atticus fetching the tennis ball and look over my shoulder at the ajar kitchen door.

Nyssa has appeared, still in her wrinkled sweater and pleated skirt, dampened by the evening drizzle. Hair that was once springy and voluminous has started to flatten thanks to the downpour, though she doesn't seem to notice or care. She's breathless, lips parted, chest heaving, like she's rushed to be here.

It takes me a moment to process the fact that she's standing in the doorway. She abandons her spot, crossing the patio to meet me halfway on the grass.

"Make me understand."

"Nyssa—"

"Theron," she interrupts sharply. She sucks in some air, her chin quivering. Her eyes glisten, the look in them a silent plea. "Make me understand."

I rake fingers through my wet hair and peer at her through water-speckled lenses. "What else is there to make you understand? Except to say that I spent years wallowing in what ifs and would have beens. I grieved for twenty years a woman who I never got to have only to be blessed twenty years later with the woman her daughter had become. It's the cruel irony of my life. Always has been, always will be."

"I'm not her," she mutters, blinking against the thin sheet of rain.

"No," I admit with a bittersweet twist of my lips. "You're certainly not. Because what we have is real. What was before was not. It was... a delusion on my part. Unrequited and unanswered."

"I don't love you. I won't ever be able to."

"You don't need to. It doesn't change a thing, Nyssa. It doesn't change what we've shared. It doesn't erase my memories of you or the way you made me feel. It certainly doesn't erase how I feel about you. Nothing ever will."

"Theron..." She pauses to shudder out a sigh, her slender fingers bunching into loose fists at her sides. "It has to be over. We have to forget about each other."

I laugh. The sound's hollow and dark. "Nyssa, I don't get to forget you. I'm not allowed that luxury! So my option's a tortured existence without you, living in the memories in my head from what *was* once real. Because... well, I'll take any scrap of you that I can get. Anything... anything better than going back to life before I knew you existed."

"You're a monster," she says, though her tone lacks confidence. It lacks certainty, almost as if she's trying to convince herself. "You killed my father. You stalked my mother. You stalked *me*. Then... then you've killed again! Mr. Wicker. Samson. Veronica. I can't ever... I can't ever be with someone like you. I wanted revenge, not—"

"You wanted what I gave you!" I growl, abandoning any patience. I start toward her before stopping myself a few steps away. "Who are you kidding, Nyssa? Don't fool yourself! You dropped the gingerbread crumbs. You led me down their path. You wanted me to do exactly what I did. All for you!"

"No," she says, shaking her head profusely. "That's not what I wanted—"

"BUT IT IS! It's exactly what you wanted deep down!" I roar over her. I finish the last couple steps 'til she's backing away and I'm advancing, grabbing her by the arms. "I'm not a killer, Nyssa. But I will kill for you. I *have* killed for you. Because I am so deep in my feelings for you that I'll do anything—anything, don't you see—just to hold onto even a piece of you. Because what I feel is deeper than love. Love doesn't even begin to scratch the surface. Love doesn't do what I feel justice. But know that it's what I feel for you, and everything I do—every last fucking thing—is for you."

"You can't love me. You can't feel the way you say you do!"

"You'll see. I'll show you. I'll prove it to you."

"Theron, what does that mean? What are you going to do?" She squirms 'til she's slipping free of my grasp. "Please tell me you're not going to do anything dangerous or crazy. You're not going to hurt anyone—"

"I'm going to do exactly what you set out to do," I say with a quick quirk of my lips. "I'm going to get the revenge you so desperately thought you wanted. I'm going to give you that vindication. That release you've sought. It's up to you whether you want to finish what you've started or if you'd rather watch from the sidelines."

Her eyes widen meeting mine, so dark and shiny I can see my reflection in them. "You're... serious? You're going to finish my plan for revenge? While under investigation?"

"I've never been more serious."

She blinks, then looks away. Her conflicted feelings play out on her face, almost a spitting image of her mother the longer I stare and admire her. Right down to the fullness of her bottom lip as she gnaws on it.

"I... I..." she whispers. "I want to help."

34
THERON
SACRIFICE - LONDON AFTER MIDNIGHT

Miss Driscoll,
It would be a pleasure to have dinner with you, if you are free, this Friday night.
Sincerely,
August Rothenberg

Nyssa looks over my shoulder as I jot down the words and then lay down the pen. She's fresh out of the shower, clutching at the robe I've given her to wear.

Things between us are ambiguous at best, but in the midst of the uncertainty, we've settled on spending the night together. Nyssa was soaking wet after being in the rain, and I was still holding onto the chance my feelings weren't completely unrequited.

As I glance over my shoulder at her, she gives little away. Her features are relaxed, yet her expression vacant, like she hasn't made up her mind.

For all I know, she very well could leave any second. She could never speak to me again.

The truths that have been unloaded on her in the last forty-eight hours are enough to distort anyone's reality.

I turn in my chair and grab at her hands to draw her toward me. "Tell me what you're thinking."

"Theron... I..." she sighs then shakes her head. Her hair's been twisted into thick braids as it dries. I reach up and slide my fingers along the underside of her scalp, giving her a light and comforting massage. Her eyes naturally flutter closed.

"Tell me, Nyssa. Tell me every little thing on your mind. Sit."

I tug her until she tips over into my lap.

"I don't think..." she starts again. She bites down hard on her bottom lip. "I don't think I can leave you alone."

"Who says you have to? Look at me." I clip her chin between my thumb and forefinger for her attention. "You don't have to walk away from this... us. We can make our own rules."

Her carefully groomed brows knit together, her eyelids lowering as if tempted to slip into avoidance again. I stroke my thumb along the soft curve of her jaw to bring her back to me.

"Everything you said," she whispers. "It was true."

"Every last word."

"My father?"

I understand what she's asking. "Yes, unfortunately."

"And my mother?"

"Yes... also unfortunately."

"And you?" she asks. "You killed him? Because he killed her?"

Tension cords through my jaw, causing the muscle to contract. "That's right."

"But you're not Valentine?"

"Nyssa—"

"Tell me," she demands. "Tell me you're not Valentine."

"Your mother was. Though she had reason to be. As horrible as that is to say. None of the victims were good people."

"That doesn't make it any easier to process the fact that my mother was a serial killer and my father—who was more than twice her age *and* her professor—killed her."

"No, I don't imagine it would."

"Why are you still here?"

I raise a brow, still stroking her face. Only now my thumb's traveled up to her cheek. "This is my home."

"You know what I mean."

"I've already told you. Because I've meant every word I've said. That includes my confession about how I feel."

"You're... in love with me?"

"More than in love with you. Even if you don't feel the same. It doesn't change the fact that you are the nexus of my world."

"It doesn't feel deserving," she says. "After everything. My scheme for revenge made you *murder* people, Theron."

"I made choices that I don't regret. In each instance, I was protecting you. Something I will never apologize for."

She sits in my lap in thoughtful silence, taking even more time to sort through what she's learned.

"You're going to finish my plan. You're writing Heather to lure her?"

"I read your Composition Notebook. You were going to frame me by making it seem like I had taken out Heather.

Make it seem like there was something between us. Is that correct?"

"I'm not sure what I was going to do anymore," she mumbles. "I was wrong about everything."

"But you had the right people. Except for me. Everyone else has played a part."

Nyssa leans forward until her brow brushes against mine. "How are you so calm about this? How are you not angry I was going to ruin your life?"

"Because I understand you. You were reacting out of a place of hurt. Justifiably so." My palms slide along the side of her neck to bring us together in a slow kiss. "I've been thinking about an alternative to myself. There's one other person who deserves to go down for everything he's done."

She pulls back to gaze into my eyes with a spark in her own. "So that's why you signed his name."

Heather Driscoll shows up a few minutes after nine, as agreed. She's dressed up even more than usual in a low-cut, blood-red dress that hugs her body and black heels that accentuate how toned her legs are. Her strawberry blonde hair is loosely curled about her shoulders, offsetting the heavy makeup she's used to paint her face with.

She waits outside the Castlebury Tower with an impatient roll of her eyes. Every minute or so, she resorts to tapping furiously away at her phone. Likely texting someone to bitch about how late I am.

I'm watching from afar as her phone rings in her hand and she answers on the second ring after recognizing the number.

Mine.

Or the number she believes is mine.

"Why don't you head on up using the private entrance?" I ask in my smoothest tone. The code is 3698. Make yourself comfortable and help yourself to some pinot noir while you wait. I'll be there soon."

Heather hangs up with a satisfied curve to her mouth. She pockets her phone in the small clutch purse she has with her and then shakes back her locks of hair as if preparing to strut on a runway.

It takes her another five minutes before she's able to punch in the code and ride the elevator up to the eighteenth floor where Thurman Adler's penthouse is. The door opens when she tries it.

Heather takes my advice about making herself at home.

She kicks off her high heels and browses the large penthouse apartment with dollar signs gleaming in her eyes. In the wake of her money troubles following her father's death, it must be a comfort to see such nice furnishings.

It's a reminder that the ritzy life is the only one for her.

She helps herself to a glass of the pinot noir I'd mentioned before she sets off on an exploration of the rest of the penthouse.

"Wait 'til you see the older man I've caught, Nyssie," she sneers in between sips of wine. "University dean trumps a measly professor any day. I always come out on top."

She giggles at her own remark, stopping in the bathroom to freshen up. Her ivory skin tinges pink as she turns on the faucet and reaches for a towel to dab herself with.

"It's so warm in here," she mumbles. "Eww, why am I sweating?"

Eighteen stories below, Dean Rothenberg arrives via a private driver. He thanks his chauffeur and then heads for the same private entrance Heather used moments ago.

He's in the elevator by the time Heather's stumbling out of the bathroom on the verge of collapse. She makes it over to the unmade bed, where the sheets are wrinkled and a Composition Notebook rests on the night stand, open to a page full of lipstick kisses. She notices none of it as she coughs, then plops down on the edge, wheezing for air.

The front door opens to Dean Rothenberg surveying the furnishings with an impressed nod. His reaction mirrors Heather's in that way, as though he recognizes he's made the right choice in showing up tonight.

He hadn't needed much convincing.

He used NSFW, the same VIP site as Jackson Wicker had, often meeting up with women across the city at places like the Scarlet Room and other obscure clubs.

But tonight's proposal was so special, he couldn't turn it down.

The use of Thurman Adler's penthouse *and* a young woman propositioning him?

MzSexi99 was a flirtatious blonde looking for an older man to spoil her. Dean Rothenberg was more than willing to volunteer in exchange for some sexual gratification.

Nyssa was behind the account on NSFW. I was behind loaning him my father's penthouse for the evening.

I'd done so under the guise of feigned ignorance. Just an innocent offer I sensed Rothenberg couldn't refuse. Since Wicker's penthouse was off the table after his murder, the dean couldn't resist the next best thing for his indiscretions.

"Hello?" he calls into the silent penthouse. He takes a few steps toward the open layout, which leads into the living room area and the floor-to-ceiling windows overlooking Castlebury. "MzSexi99? Are you hiding from me?"

No one answers him.

His brow creases as he explores some more, wandering toward the other half of the penthouse. Mere footsteps outside the master bedroom, he finally picks up on the fact that he's not alone.

"MzSexi? Is that you?"

He nudges the door open all the way only to choke on air.

"Ms. Driscoll? What are you... why are you...?"

The dean can't bring himself to finish his thought as he peers at the passed out strawberry blonde on the bed.

He hesitates for half a second and then hurries over to check on her. His fingers press at the pulse point at her neck as he leans closer to see if she's breathing.

"Wake up," he says, shaking her by the shoulders. "Ms. Driscoll, open your eyes. Are you MzSexi? Why would you lie? Is this some kind of set up?"

He shakes her some more as her eyelids slowly lift open.

Heather goes from catatonic to shaken awake. A scream erupts from her throat, her arms flying up to slam into Rothenberg.

"Will you stay still?" he grunts, trying to dodge her hits. "I'm trying to help you!"

"GET OFF ME!" she screams.

"Not until you stop being stupid. Don't you hit me again!"

I sigh from where I'm hidden inside the closet, my skeletal mask on for identity protection. Heather wasn't supposed to wake up from the sedative in the wine, but apparently she hadn't drunk enough of it.

The plan was for Rothenberg to walk in on a passed out

Driscoll and then be knocked unconscious himself to set up the crime scene.

The Valentine Killer, caught at last.

All the evidence that Nyssa had been planning to use against me was already planted on Rothenberg—the pages in the Composition Notebook, the messages exchanged using the NSFW chat function, even Driscoll's own words to friends about seeking out an older man.

But the plan wasn't for her to wake prematurely and then fight the dean.

As she claws at his face, he retaliates with a sharp smack across her cheek. She releases another feral, catlike scream and struggles even harder against him.

It goes against the plan to intervene, but the longer they fight, the more uncontrolled the situation becomes. I ensure I have the syringe with the same sedative we fed Driscoll in her wine and then I emerge from the closet.

Rothenberg is too engrossed in trying to restrain the blonde to realize I'm coming up from behind.

I jam him in the neck first, then move onto Driscoll. Yet another wild scream leaves her as I pin her down and stick the needle in, injecting her with the sedative.

Within seconds, they're both nearly in a coma.

Nyssa appears at my side, having come out of her hiding spot. "Now what?"

"We continue to set the scene," I say. "Driscoll has to die. Rothenberg will be framed."

"Uh... Theron... I think he's suffocating?"

I glance down to see what Nyssa's talking about. August Rothenberg's face has begun to tinge blue as froth bubbles from his lips.

"He's having some kind of allergic reaction to the sedative."

"A lot of people are allergic to anesthetic drugs. He must be one of them."

It's not long before August Rothenberg's heart stops altogether. We're standing around the bed when it happens, left to think of a new story to spin.

If he's dead, we can't pin Valentine on him. We have no more use for Driscoll.

Nyssa bites her bottom lip, looking up at me. She seems to know exactly what I do.

The only option we have left if we're to finish crossing off the names on the list.

There's only one thing left to do.

※

It's nearing three a.m. when I stick the shovel in the dirt for the last time and cover the deep hole I've spent the past hour digging. Nyssa's at my side, helping with a shovel of her own. As I flick the last heap of dirt on the makeshift grave, a sigh of relief leaves me.

Done.

We're finally done.

Our original plan didn't work out like we hoped, so we improvised. We pivoted to a new solution that leaves two individuals six feet under and the public soon scandalized by the fact that the Dean of Castlebury ran off into the sunset with a student, never to be seen or heard from again.

Given the evidence we've gathered, it still fits.

Except now we'll have to make it look like they both left town.

Nyssa has a spare key to Heather's apartment, and I'm certain I can find a way to access Rothenberg's devices to make it seem as if he'd planned a getaway (I did make sure to keep his phone after all).

It'll likely be a couple days before either one is reported missing.

It buys us some time.

"That was... exhilarating," Nyssa laughs. Her eyes shine even in the dark as they meet mine. "Is burying bodies always like this?"

"Sometimes. Other times, like Wicker, not so much."

"You came here with my mother. You two... here in the forest?"

"When I initially found out what she was doing and helped her get rid of a body, yes. But then she refused to stop."

"And now you're here with me."

"I suppose life really does come full circle in the strangest ways."

"A couple who digs graves together, stays together."

"A murder quip right now? Really, Miss Oliver? Too soon."

We drift closer 'til we're distracted by each other's kiss, shovels still in our hands. Covered in dirt from our after hours' activity, we're both in need of a hot shower and some rest. The night's grown colder and wetter as time has gone on, which has only made our task more grueling.

I stroke Nyssa's cheek affectionately as our kiss ends. "Alright, time to get out of here. You're shivering."

The wet earth squelches beneath our boots. We shine a flashlight at the path ahead, where my BMW is parked in the clearing some feet away.

Then I hear it. I see it.

The whir and flash in the dark.

Coming closer. Growing louder.

The red and blue light emerges from the dark as police cars arrive on the scene.

My adrenaline surges to untold levels. I react at a moment's notice, doing the only thing that makes sense in my mind. For a man as deeply devoted to the woman at my side. I shove my skeletal mask in her hand and yell, "Run! Quickly! Get out of here!"

"What? Theron—"

"Go! You have to go now," I say, giving Nyssa a shove toward the trees. "Run as far away as possible. Head south. It'll lead you to campus. If they do find you, you remember what I told you to say if we were ever caught."

She shakes her head in confusion. "I'm not blaming you—"

"Get out of here!" I hiss at her.

The police cars invade the area, their headlights flooding the area with bright white light.

Nyssa fades into the dark at the last possible second. Her glassy eyes are the last part of her I see as she vanishes and I'm confronted by a familiar scene.

The doors flinging open on the three squad cars before the officers step out.

This time, with firearms drawn.

"Hands where we can see 'em, Adler," comes Officer Brewster over a megaphone. "We've finally caught you in the act."

"Caught me in the act? I have no idea what you're talking about."

"Cut the shit. We've been following you for days! We uncovered the bloody boulder in the bushes from Samson Wicker's campus attack and guess whose DNA was on it?"

I raise my hands as the officers point their weapons at

me, playing it cool. My tone's calm as I ask, "I'm sorry, officers. But what does that have to do with tonight?"

"You know exactly what it's got to do with tonight, Adler! You're going down!" he grunts, grinning. "You and your family think you're above the law. You and all your rich as dirt friends think you can do no wrong! But I've got you dead to rights this time. You're going down no matter what. Everything Valentine's ever done. I'll make sure of it."

35
NYSSA
CRAZY IN LOVE REMIX - BEYONCÉ

TWO YEARS LATER...

Peaches meows at the knock on the door.

I'm by the bay window, perched on my stool as I work on my pottery wheel. I'm not even sure what I'm working on yet, except it'll likely be similar to my last few projects—a sculpture dripping with heartache and misery.

It seems to be the running theme of my artwork these days.

My ginger girl meows a second time when I don't move fast enough to answer the door.

"Okay, okay, Peaches," I say, grabbing a towel to wipe my hands. "Chill, alright? I'm going to get it."

She blinks at me from where she's lounging on the armrest of my sofa. I move toward the door, rising on tiptoe to check the peephole.

I should've known.

There aren't many people in Castlebury interested in visiting me. Even fewer who I'd want to. I draw the door open to the happy pants of a golden retriever that circles my legs and paws at my thighs.

A light laugh leaves me. "Hi, Atty! Long time no see. No wonder Peaches was nagging me to get the door."

"He got excited as soon as he saw where we pulled up to," Theo says, inviting herself inside. She's clutching two large lattes and a white paper bag of pastries.

I help her with what she has as Atticus races over to greet Peaches. The dog and cat somehow get along, though he's a burst of energy while Peaches is more low key.

"Sorry I'm late," Theo says, shrugging off her jacket. "I didn't want to come by empty handed."

"You coming by at all is appreciated."

Theo's mouth dips into a frown. "We'll get it all figured out. He always comes up with something. He's a genius like that."

"Yeah... I know. It's just..." I blink to fight off the sudden onslaught of tears.

Theo picks up on it right away and puts her arms around me. "You sure you don't want to go in person? Maybe the moral support from you would really help."

"Can't," I croak, wiping my eyes. "It wouldn't be a good idea."

"Right, it could open up a can of worms." Theo sighs, hands on her hips as she glances from the coffee cups on the counter to the small TV mounted on the wall. "Well, I guess that's one good thing about it being televised. Never mind all the national coverage and sensationalized headlines. At least we can watch from the comfort of our homes."

We settle down on the sofa and flick on the TV in time to see Channel Nine's field reporter speaking in front of the courthouse.

"Hello, Rob and Jessie, and viewers at home," says the svelte blonde in an emerald wrap dress. "I just arrived to the Castlebury courthouse today for what's day five of the Valentine Killer trial, where Criminal Law Professor Theron Adler is being tried on five counts of murder. In a few short moments, we'll be heading inside for the opening statements from the defense.

"As a reminder for some of the viewers just tuning in at home, Mr. Adler has made the controversial decision to represent himself during this trial. Once a defense attorney, he rejected all other legal counsel and seemed to think it was in his best interest to argue his own case. Legal experts have expressed concern about this, citing past cases where this has turned out to the defendant's detriment."

"Oh god..." I mutter, brushing a hand over my face. "I hope he knows what he's doing."

"Theron is sharp in the courtroom," Theo says. "He's always been. Even Dad was impressed. You don't know our father—it's damn near impossible to impress him."

I aim a small, sad smile at Theron's sister. "Thanks for trying to keep me from breaking down."

"We're pretty much all each other has at this point."

Theo's speaking facts.

Over the last two years that Theron has been arrested for the Valentine murders, the scandal consumed Castlebury. Accusations were thrown. Suspicions were raised. Past allegiances were severed. Many people in the circles I ran with turned on each other.

There were rumors. Lots of them.

Some of them involved me.

I heard it all. From a theory I was Theron's accomplice (somewhat accurate) to I was almost one of Theron's victims before he took mercy and let me go (not so accurate). But one thing emerged crystal clear out of the chaos—I had to keep my distance.

For my sake, but especially for Theron's.

If I was linked to the case in the eyes of the authorities, then that opened a whole new can of worms—and potential problems—for Theron.

Some digging and poking around would be done. My background would be discovered. Professor Vise's murder would come up. So would Mom's.

It was best that I stayed distant. That I watched and fretted from afar as Theron was put on trial for the Valentine murders.

But I wasn't the only social pariah in Castlebury.

As Theron's sister, Theodora was suffering a similar fate. Many rumors swirled about her as well, like *she* was his accomplice all along, or an even crazier rumor that theorized Theodora was actually Valentine and Theron was protecting her.

The two of us realized we were all the other had, gradually becoming close.

It wasn't difficult, considering Theo was the manager of my apartment building and she was the kind of friend girls like Heather had never been.

Theo, who visited Theron every other week—and spoke to him on the phone even more often—said she believed he appreciated that we were keeping each other company during his absence.

The two closest people in his life were now close themselves.

But that hasn't made it any easier staying apart from him. I haven't been able to so much as write him a letter without rousing suspicion of our past relationship.

I miss his voice. His presence and his touch.

Every last thing about him.

Life without him feels muted and joyless.

Selfishly, watching the televised trial has been the most contact I've had with him since he was taken away...

While the outcome worries me, I'm also reminded how brilliant Theron Adler is. I remember just why I'd admired him in the first place. Legal experts might claim it's a mistake that he represents himself, but they don't know Theron like I do.

On day five, when it's the defense's turn to cross examine Officer Brewster about his team's investigation, Theron's brilliance is on full display.

He's dressed in a simple suit and tie, his dark hair rumpled in the perfectly imperfect manner only he can pull off. Stubble frames his handsome face while his glasses accentuate how intense his gaze can be.

He approaches the witness stand with an intimidating sense of calm, looking refined yet authoritative all at once.

"Officer Brewster, you were on the case for the 2005 investigation into the Valentine murders, were you not?"

The stout police officer peers around the large courtroom as if vexed to be on the stand at all. "That's right. I've been on the force for damn near thirty years."

"Thank you for your service," Theron says. "The 2005 investigation went on for months with little headway made. Can you remind the court what ended up happening with that case?"

He folds his arms and mumbles, "It was deemed unsolvable."

"What was that?"

"It was deemed unsolvable!" he snaps.

"You'll have to clarify for the court, Officer. What do you mean by unsolvable?"

Huffing out a breath, he says, "We had little to no leads and no prime suspects. It wasn't going anywhere, so we had to leave the case unsolved."

"Interesting," Theron says, pacing back and forth in front of the stand. He nudges his glasses further up his nose and strokes his chin in thought. "Would you say that damaged the credibility of Castlebury PD?"

"We have some of the lowest crime rates in the country!"

"I believed I asked you about credibility. Would you say the Valentine case going unsolved damaged the Castlebury PD's credibility?"

"Objection, your honor!" cries out the lead prosecutor, popping to her feet. "Relevance?"

Presiding Judge Mary Quarles raises her brows at Theron. "Mr. Adler, care to explain?"

"The Castlebury PD's history on the original Valentine case provides necessary context as it pertains to today's trial."

The judge thinks on it a second. "I'll allow it."

Theron turns back to the potbellied officer. "Please answer the question, Officer Brewster."

"We will never have a credibility problem... no matter what you say, Adler!"

"But would you say that with resurrecting this case a second time, there was a pressure to finally solve it?"

He grits his teeth. "I seek to solve all crime, Adler. Don't be so smart."

"Of course you do. Except... this case is quite high profile. You said so yourself. I would go down for it no matter what."

"Well... all I meant was... I'd work as hard as I needed to...."

"Would you say you have a bias against certain individuals in this town, officer? Individuals you perceive as part of the upper class?"

"What? I don't..."

"I would like to present some video recordings of the witness if I may, your honor. This footage has been obtained by request from the city police department themselves."

"Proceed."

Theron walks over to the defense table where he picks up a remote and presses play on the TV that's been wheeled into the courtroom.

The footage begins right away with Theron in handcuffs and Officer Brewster looking feverish.

"You know exactly what it's got to do with tonight, Adler! You're going down!" he grunts, grinning. "You and your family think you're above the law. You and all your rich as dirt friends think you can do no wrong! But I've got you dead to rights this time. You're going down no matter what. Everything Valentine's ever done. I'll make sure of it."

"From the body cam footage recorded by Castlebury PD yourselves, do you think it's fair to say you have an inherent bias, officer?"

"You son of a bitch!" Officer Brewster barks, going red in the face. He rises from his seat. "You really think you're going to weasel your way out of this? I told you I wouldn't let it happen!"

"Order, order in the court!" booms Judge Quarles, banging her gavel.

The prosecution's risen to try to control their witness, but Officer Brewster's temper can't be tamed. He proceeds to cuss Theron out 'til he's so bright red, he looks on the verge of passing out from his anger.

The bailiff eventually escorts him out.

Theron calmly watches him disappear through the double doors.

"As you can see, the Castlebury PD was very passionate about catching the Valentine Killer. Perhaps a little too passionate. I rest my case."

On day nine of the trial, Theron manages to trip up the medical examiner who did autopsies on Samson Wicker, among some of the other bodies found buried in the forest.

Theron exudes the same calm yet authoritative energy as he has every other day of the trial. He starts off simple, asking the medical examiner about his autopsy reports and what he believes each victim's cause of death was.

Theron rubs his jaw, walking back and forth at a casual pace. "Would you say the wound you noted on Samson Wicker's skull played a role in his demise?"

"Mr. Wicker suffered a severe concussion brought on by a heavy object I believe to be the boulder the police found in the bushes. The same boulder with your fingerprints on it."

"Right," he says, stopping in front of the witness stand. "But I'm afraid that doesn't answer my question. I asked you if the concussion Samson Wicker suffered played a role in his demise."

He purses his lips and narrows his eyes. "Samson Wicker's cause of death was a deep stab wound to his jugular. The concussion was several weeks prior and unlikely to have played a factor."

"Interesting. So the one piece of physical evidence with my DNA happens to not be the murder weapon. Would you say that assessment is true, ME?"

"It's not the murder weapon. However, Wicker's blood was on the boulder and so were your fingerprints."

"Circumstantial at best."

"Objection!" the lead prosecutor says, rising out of her chair. "He's attempting to lead the witness."

"Mr. Adler, get to the point."

Theron smirks. "Of course. Can you clarify one last thing—were any of the victims, including Samson Wicker—found to have DNA evidence of the person who killed them?"

"No. No DNA evidence whatsoever."

"Excellent. Thank you, ME."

I breathe a sigh of relief on day eleven when each side makes their closing arguments and Theron knocks his out of the park. He's managed to cast doubt on several witnesses, most of all Officer Brewster, while also proving the evidence against him is flimsy at best.

"No murder weapon, that's good, right?" Theo asks, seated beside me on the sofa. Peaches is curled up in her lap dozing away.

"It's very good. They have no direct evidence tying him to these murders. The boulder doesn't prove he murdered Samson; it just proves he got into a past altercation. He's cast enough reasonable doubt that I'm not sure the jury can convict."

"Unless they're biased like Brewster."

Jury deliberation arrives in the coming days.

I'm a nervous wreck for every hour they're in deliberation. It lasts for over a day, where I can't eat, sleep, or do anything but frantically check my phone for any updates. Finally, a breaking news banner scrolls across the screen early in the morning, announcing the jury has reached a verdict.

Theo races over to the apartment so we can watch together.

"And how does the jury find the defendant?"

The older woman, who's stood up to announce the results, takes in a deep breath and then says, "We have found the defendant not guilty on all five counts of murder in the first degree."

The courtroom erupts in an array of different reactions. Families of the victims break out in hysterics, crying and screaming about the grave injustice. The prosecution looks floored, conferring among themselves about the verdict that's been delivered. The media in the room snap into reporting mode at once, rushing to update their audience.

And then there's Theron, who sits coolly where he is, as if he hasn't been delivered the best news of his life.

My pulse races watching him, so impressed and relieved I can barely remember to breathe.

"He's not guilty," I whisper. Then I beam at Theo, who's jumped up and whooped the air. "He's not guilty! That means..."

"He'll be coming home. Charges cleared!"

I cover my face with shaky hands and release a delirious-sounding laugh.

Thank God.

Because if he was *found guilty, I'm not so sure I wouldn't resort to breaking him out of prison myself...*

36

THERON

TRUE LOVE WAITS - RADIOHEAD

"Alright, Adler, you're a free man."

There's a deep grimace on Officer Brewster's face that his silver walrus mustache almost hides. His discontent with the verdict drips off him as he stands in front of the iron bars of my jail cell and rests hands on his wide, rounded waist. His gut hangs over the front of his belt, barely contained by his starched uniform shirt.

He's one of many.

Just about the entire Castlebury Police Department is openly dissatisfied with the not guilty outcome.

My acquittal causes a real problem for them. The decades-old serial killer that has plagued the community either remains at large or they're allowing him to walk out the door a free man.

Pick your poison.

Choose which is worse.

Which is more humiliating for the Castlebury PD?

For a gruff, no-nonsense man like Brewster, it's the latter. The idea that he's facilitating the Valentine Killer's release is torture for him. A little hunch tells me he'd rather eat only salad every day for the rest of his life. A challenge for a man of his generous size.

But I've kept the faith. I've bided my time. I've never once wavered, even as others scoffed and mocked the idea of me providing my own legal defense.

Admittedly, it can often be a disaster regardless of the defendant's profession. There have been numerous arrogant lawyers who have attempted to represent themselves in a court trial that wound up sorely regretting their decision.

Still, I never second-guessed mine.

I knew from the moment I fulfilled Nyssa's revenge scheme that I would sacrifice myself. Once the case moved to trial, I would rely on no one but myself to earn my freedom back. If I failed, it would be with the knowledge that I had done what I promised I would.

I had given my life up for the woman I love.

After what happened to Josalyn and my failure to save her, I refused to make the same mistake twice.

Nyssa needed to know how much she meant to me. She was worth giving it all up for.

She was worth everything...

"Adler," Brewster grunts when I don't move from the twin-sized bed chained to the wall. "Hurry the piss up. I ain't got all day, and if you want to get out of here today, get a move on."

I snap out of my reverie with a subtle nod of my head.

There are little to no belongings to collect. Two years in jail, awaiting trial, standing trial, awaiting the verdict, and the only belongings I have are a handful of letters and my favorite book on criminal law theory that I was allowed to keep in my cell.

Officer Brewster glares at me as I cross the jail cell's

threshold and walk past him. The iron-barred door clangs shut and the keys attached to his hips rattle. He pushes past me without an *excuse me*, his shoulder knocking into mine.

"This way, Adler."

I follow, more amused than I have been in a while.

Except for maybe during the trial, where I got to humiliate the assistant district attorney and his entire prosecutorial team.

Brewster brings me to the processing desk. I stand before the Emma that Theo had made a huge deal about seeing again, though she refuses to meet my eyes as she processes my discharge from the jail.

I don't take it personally. Many people become uncomfortable around suspected serial killers.

Let alone real ones.

Emma may not know which I am, but the possibility is unnerving enough for a bland woman such as herself, who eats granola for breakfast and considers purple hair dye peak rebellion.

I step out of the police station breathing in the fresh, warm summer air. The sun's high in the sky and there isn't a cloud to be found.

Neither is Theo's Volkswagen Beetle.

Unfortunately, you're not allowed cars while in jail, so mine is presumably still parked in front of my house.

Theo was supposed to be here to pick me up.

Through my jail time and court trial, she's been just about the only support I've had. Dad long ago abandoned any association with me, choosing his reputation over the possibility that his son was the Valentine Killer. Mom's been in such emotional hysterics, she's decided to remain overseas for another few years (a convenient excuse, as far as I'm concerned).

But Theo showed up for every visitor weekend. She placed phone calls and wrote letters—the stack of letters I have are all exclusively from her. My sister proved she truly would stick by me if I ever needed help burying a body at three a.m.

Luckily, for her, after the past two and a half years of my life, I have no intention of ever going near a dead body again.

I'm not sure what will come of my future. My tenure at Castlebury University is obviously long over, though I'm not sure I'd return even if I could. I have a house and car that are paid off and a nice nest egg in my savings from the inheritance I received years ago.

Theo claims I have emails from publishing agents who want me to write a tell-all book about my ordeal and shop it around to all the major publishers.

I could always travel. Move overseas. Perhaps teach English in another country. Would parents care if an acquitted murder suspect taught their children their English ABCs?

I sit down at the bench in front of the police precinct and wait patiently for Theo to show up. Something I've become remarkably good at after sitting in a jail cell for twenty-three hours of every day. While I'm waiting, I sift through the stack of letters that I've read each of at least half a dozen times before.

...except for one.

The one that stands out from the rest, packaged in a neat vellum envelope and wax seal.

My brows crease together.

I've never seen this envelope a day in my life. It certainly wasn't a letter that was delivered to me inside the cell.

Emma must've slipped it in the pile as she out-processed me and I filled out the necessary paperwork.

I tear at the envelope as carefully as possible, making effort to preserve the fancy wax seal. Then I glance down at the letter inside and recognize the neat, loopy writing...

> *Professor Adler,*
>
> *A wise man once said you only get one chance at making a relationship work. That wise man never heard of bribing someone with their favorite caffeinated beverage. Would you like to grab coffee sometime?*
>
> *(please say yes)*
> *Miss Oliver*

I laugh out loud like a madman. My laugh is so abrupt and jarring that a couple of the birds hopping around on the sidewalk screech and take flight.

I hardly care, so amused by the notecard I've been written that I can't contain the grin that spreads onto my face.

To describe the level of joy that beats in my heart would be impossible. It's simply... limitless.

It's a second chance that I wasn't at all expecting.

"Yes, Miss Oliver," I whisper to no one. "I would very much love to grab coffee sometime."

37
NYSSA

SPRING IS COMING WITH A STRAWBERRY IN THE MOUTH - CAROLINE POLACHEK

I'VE NEVER BEEN MORE NERVOUS IN MY LIFE.

I'm seated at one of the small tables outside a local café, pretending I'm not searching the crowds for his face. Midafternoon on a Saturday, it feels like everyone in Castlebury's out and about, enjoying the breezy spring weather.

A stiff breath shakes out of me, my fingers wrapped around the cup of coffee I've been sipping on for the last twenty minutes.

He's late.

He's *never* late.

Professor Theron Thurman Adler prides himself on being punctual. He's a man of routine. A man of structure and stability.

...or at least he was until he spent the last two years of his life on trial for murder.

Murders I subtly pushed him to commit, even if I hadn't understood the full extent of what I was doing.

My eyes clench shut at the difficult memories. I had been wrong about so many things and hadn't known I was. My entire life had been a lie.

The woman who I believed to be my mother was really my aunt.

The man who I was told was my father was of no blood relation at all. He didn't even really exist.

My real father was a vile man who tried to destroy my mother—and succeeded once he'd tarnished her reputation and then ran her through with a knife.

Then the man I'm in love with ran *him* through with a knife.

The same man who was once in love with my mother many years ago...

I've tried to reconcile what it all means, and the only conclusion I've drawn is the same one I'd sensed from the beginning.

I can't stay away from Theron.

Every moment he's been away has felt like agonizing torture. It's felt like a piece of myself has been missing.

He has my heart.

And I have his.

Five minutes go by and then another ten.

My latte gets cold. The people seated at the tables around me eventually leave and new customers trickle in. Caffeine sets in and makes me jittery, my knee bouncing in place.

He's not coming.

I sigh, working through the devastating level of disappointment, and then I remind myself it's justified. He lost two years of his life have been because of me. Because he chose to take the fall for things I had taken part in. He was forced to defend himself in a court of law, and though he was found not guilty, his reputation was irrevocably ruined.

I never once wrote him. I never visited.

Instead, I obsessed over him from afar. His sister, Theo, became my avatar. The only means I had for contact.

He probably assumed I didn't share his feelings.

It must've looked as if I'd forgotten him and moved on.

If only he understood I kept my distance to protect him. I was staying away to avoid tarnishing his reputation any further in the eyes of the public. What would they think if they found out Theron Adler not only could be the Valentine Killer, but he had taken advantage of one of his female students?

I knew the truth. We both did.

But no one else would get it.

In the public's view, I would seem like a lost young woman. He would seem like a predatory older man, already accused of unthinkable crimes.

The best thing was to keep my distance. Protect his reputation the only way I could...

It doesn't matter now.

What's done is done. Theron has every right to feel betrayed. He has every right to never want to see me again.

My throat aches as I swallow against a tide of heartbreak and push my chair back to get up. I'm halfway out of the chair when the face in the crowd is finally the one I've been searching for.

Among the half a dozen other passersby coming and going on the sidewalk, Theron appears, looking just like I've memorized him in my mind.

He's as tall and lean as ever, the jeans and Henley shirt he wears clinging to him in all the right ways, hinting at the muscle tone underneath.

His hair's still ruffled and floppy, like he's recently run a hand through it, and the stubble that peppers his jawline only accentuates how angular it is.

His glasses sit obediently on his straight nose, hardly doing anything to disguise his dark and intense eyes, instead adding to his usual severe and authoritarian vibe.

I'm breathless watching him approach. My skin warms, all thoughts vanishing.

I'm back to being a nervous wreck like I'd been years ago when I'd first bumped into him in the corridor of Harper Hall.

He stops before me, his hands deep in his jean pockets. "Miss Oliver, what a coincidence. I was just coming by for some coffee. Is this seat taken?"

I smile without even thinking about it, then shake my head. "It's all yours."

"Excellent. A wise woman once said bribing people with caffeinated beverages is quite effective."

"Well, she tried it on her crim law professor after she spilled his coffee on him. Do you think it worked?"

His eyes gleam staring at me from across the small table. "I'd say it more than worked. I believe he became infatuated with her to the point of turning into a national headline on the news."

"I wish… I almost wish he hadn't," I say, my smile fading. "Because it wasn't what he deserved."

"You should know, he doesn't regret a thing." Theron leans closer, holding my gaze captive, a lock of his hair curling against his brow. His closeness immediately puts me under his spell, making it impossible to look away. "I regret nothing, Nyssa. Every last thing I did was for you, which will never make it wrong. I would happily do it all over again if it meant getting to be with you even for a minute."

The emotion I've been holding in finally rises up and breaks free. I find myself drawing in a shaky breath, overwhelmed by the man before me.

After everything he's been through, there's no bitterness to be found. No judgment or anger.

The only thing to be found is... fondness.

Genuine, sincere adoration that makes me feel unworthy and renders me speechless.

"You can have me for much longer than a minute," I choke out in a hoarse voice. "You can have me as long as you want me... which, I hope, is a very long time."

He reaches across the table, his thumb smoothing along the curve of my cheekbone. "Trust me when I say, Nyssa, I want you every day of the rest of my life."

We talk for hours.

We talk so long, the sun sets and the café closes. Neither of us wants our time to come to an end, so we get creative.

Any surroundings fade to the background as we walk the streets of Castlebury.

I update Theron on what he's missed since he's been away. I'm estranged from Aunt Brooklyn after all the lies and deceit she's put me through and I've graduated top of my class from Castlebury's law school. I'll be taking the bar soon and then the rest of my future's wide open.

Theron tells me what the last two years were like for him. He tells me how the police officers of the Castlebury PD treated him and how he grew to like the structure and routine of life behind bars. He explained how he'd received fan mail from all over the country—often from fanatical women who were closely following the nationally covered news story and found him dark and alluring.

"Some proposed marriage," he says with a scratch to the back of his neck. "One told me I was the third serial killer she had proposed to. She seemed to think the third time would be the charm."

"Theron, you have a fan club! Just what every sulky, loner law professor wants."

"Sulky? What do you mean *sulky?*"

"I'm sorry, does that hurt your feelings?" I laugh.

"I am *not* sulky. Brooding? Sure. A little short-tempered and condescending at times? Perhaps. But sulky? What am I, a fifteen-year-old girl menstruating?"

"See, there it is! You're being sulky right now!"

His face darkens as he stops us under the soft glow of a gas lamp and I find myself backed up against the limestone wall of a nearby shop. I'm biting down on the smirk threatening to take hold while he's glaring into my eyes.

He thumbs my cheek and leans closer, as if about to kiss me. He's already studying my mouth.

A frisson of excitement racks through me, making me shudder on the spot. It's little moments like these that I've missed. The few seconds leading up to our kiss. The smooth touches and quick banter that get my heart racing and pussy throbbing.

Theron draws my face toward his 'til our mouths align and I can feel his warm breath on my lips. "I see you want the first order of business tonight to be punishment, Miss Oliver. Please believe I will make you come to regret it."

"Just so long as you make me come, I don't care, Professor."

My naughty smirk blooms in the split second before he silences me with a hard kiss.

At the touch of his lips, the tiny sparks of excitement explode. Blood rushes my veins, creating a pulsing rhythm in my ears. Sheer adrenaline washes over me and leaves me dizzy and spinning.

It's like our first kiss all over again.

It *is* our first kiss all over again.

After two years without Theron, I'm a woman dying of thirst in the desert. Feeling his warm lips against mine for the first time in so long, it's water touching my tongue, quenching me in a way only he can.

I've spent every moment of the last two years waiting for him. I've gotten myself off dozens of times to the mere *thought* of him. Celibate for two years, I haven't so much as looked at another man since.

My mind, body, soul, all crave Theron Adler and only him.

My heart *belongs* to him.

As he pushes me back against the smooth limestone, I'm sliding my hands up his chest. I'm reaching for the back of his neck to pull him even closer, like I can't get enough of him. His firm, lean body traps mine in place, and his mouth elicits a moan out of me.

It doesn't matter that we're on a public street.

We're off in our own little world, kissing in the brisk night, celebrating our reunion.

His tongue strokes against mine in a sensuous dance. I play along, teasing him in return with soft flicks that only make him more aggressive.

He grips me tighter and wedges his knee between my legs as if half a second away from hoisting me off the ground.

Catching himself at the last possible second, his mouth travels to my jaw for more peppered kisses.

When he pulls back completely, the carnal hunger is visible on his face. His eyes are dark and cloudy while his nostrils flare. He licks at his lips like he's attempting to taste me still, then he squeezes my hips.

"Do you... want to take this somewhere?" he asks huskily.

I can't contain the smile that lights up my face. "Peaches has missed her bestie."

The night's a passion-fueled blur. We find our way back to my apartment, where we proceed to strip off our clothes and collapse in bed.

The sex between us is raw and animalistic.

Needy and desperate.

It's a homecoming long in the making.

My pussy clenches around Theron's cock as I come for the third time. My orgasm ripples through me and breaks me into a million little pieces of pleasure.

He's between my thighs, stroking away. His expertise feels even more poignant after so long apart, as he rolls his hips and his cock reaches parts of my pussy that make me see stars. I can only cry out as my body seizes up and I sink nails into his arms.

He slips deeper, so thick and engorged inside me that my walls spasm around him. He comes in close to capture my lips, still gyrating away. Still torturing me from the inside.

He bites my jaw and nuzzles my neck. His breaths husk

out of him, ragged and masculine, like he can't hold off much longer. He's right on the edge.

I wrap my arm around his shoulders and rock with him. My pussy massages his dick, knowing how crazy it drives him when I do.

He's only able to stroke into me a few more times before he finally gives in. He comes with a hoarse grunt, a fist in my curls to tilt my face and smash my lips to his. We melt into each other at the peak of our pleasure, so lost it takes us a moment to mentally return to the bed where we lay.

I meet Theron's eyes when they open and brush away the loose strand of hair that's fallen over his brow. "I've missed this so much. I've missed you…"

He bows his head to drop a tender kiss on my lips and then takes his spot beside me in bed. I'm brought with him, his arms slipping under me to drag me closer.

"I'm here now," he says. "It's safe to say everything we've been through has been leading to this. This moment where we can finally be together."

Excitement rings through me at the mere possibility. "I'm no longer your student."

"And I'm no longer a professor at Castlebury." He gives a gruff, sardonic laugh at that. Half a bitter sound and half genuine relief and amusement.

I place my hand on his chest and kiss where his heart lives underneath. His flesh is warm and soft, lightly peppered with hairs. I could touch and feel him all night long and still want more.

Just the fact that he's here in my bed, alive and well, feels surreal.

A part of me is so paranoid, I'm worried I'll close my eyes only to open them again to find the room empty. He was simply a figment of my imagination.

Theron runs his hands up and down my naked curves, as appreciative as ever. He's keeping me anchored to him as though similar thoughts occupy his mind. He'll let me go, and I'll disappear. He'll still be in his jail cell.

I rest my chin on his chest and peer curiously at him, studying the subtle signs of aging on his handsome face. Things like the crease of his brow and the sporadic silver hairs in his stubble that make him even sexier than he'd been just two years ago.

"You were brilliant in the courtroom," I say. "I watched every minute of the trial."

The corner of his mouth quirks, almost forming a grin. "I hoped you would."

"Professor, were you showing off for me?"

"Possibly," he admits. Then he lets out a short laugh. "It was surprisingly easy work dismantling the prosecution's argument."

"You were clever to discredit Officer Brewster and the others."

"He was an easy mark. Very impatient and hot-tempered. I learned that much from the night they brought me in for questioning."

"And the doubt you cast on the medical examiner's testimony... I got chills."

He runs a gentle hand over my curls, cupping the back of my head. "I prepared for the case as if I were teaching your class. As if it were just another case study we were reviewing."

"I hope I'm half as good as you if I ever have to defend a case like it."

"As a defense attorney," he says sternly. "*Not* the defendant."

"I always thought it was a possibility. Doing what I was doing. There was a chance I'd get caught..."

"And you wanted to understand the legal system," he says, repeating my words from two years ago. He pulls me further up 'til I'm hovering over him and he's a second away from bringing me down to kiss him. "Suddenly, it all makes sense why you chose law school over art. You're so fucking exquisite, Nyssa."

"I feel the same about you."

"There's a lot for us to figure out. I'm no longer a professor and my reputation's tarnished—not guilty verdict be damned. I have some offers from publishers for book deals and a sizable inheritance stashed away, but I'm aware I come with baggage. There are some in society who will always look at me as the Valentine Killer, and I'll probably never have a tenured position again at any university. I'm twice your age, and I'm a boring man of routine. I like books and staying in most nights.

"But we can do it. If you're up for the challenge. I can promise you I will always seek to make you happy. I will sacrifice it all for you like I've already done. I'll give you my heart and love you unconditionally until I'm old, feeble, and finally dead."

I kiss him softly, going at a slow pace. "Theron, I'm already yours. I've been yours. Maybe a lot longer than we realized. I know it's not reincarnation. It can't be. But I'm not sure this isn't some kind of... I don't know... divine intervention either."

"You mean by your mother?"

"Anything's possible, right?"

He pulls me in for another kiss. "I've come to realize that's truer than I ever imagined."

THE END

...Please please take a quick second to drop me a rating/review on Amazon! This greatly helps promote my book and gets Amazon's algorithm to push it!

WICKED LITTLE SECRET PLAYLIST

Listen to the playlist here on Spotify!

Prologue. The Perfect Girl - Mareux

1. Ghost in the Machine - SZA featuring Phoebe Bridgers

2. Too Sweet - Hozier

3. Dark Red - Steve Lacey

4. Demi God - Kimbra featuring Sahtyre

5. DISTRACTION - Montell Fish

6. New Person, Same Old Mistakes - Tame Impala

7. Teacher's Pet - Melanie Martinez

8. Who is She? - I Monster

9. Older - Isabel LaRosa

10. Devil's Advocate - The Neighbourhood

11. Fire of Love - Jesse Jo Stark

12. Cherry Waves - Deftones

13. Hush - the Marias

14. My Kink is Karma - Chappell Roan

15. Love me - Ex Habit

16. Bad Intentions - Niykee Heaton featuring Migos and OG Parker

17. Power Trip - J. Cole featuring Miguel

18. Love Crime - Siouxsie

19. Bittersuite - Billie Eilish

20. Dirty Little Secret - Nessa Barrett

21. This Love - Craig Armstrong and Elizabeth Fraser

22. Streets - Doja Cat

23. Sober II (Melodrama) - Lorde

24. Where is My Mind? - Safari Riot and Grayson Sanders

25. The Whisper of Forest - SURAN

26. Lose Myself - REYKO

27. Broken Man - St. Vincent

28. Me and My Husband - Mitski

29. Sugar - Garbage

30. Make You Mine- Madison Beer

31. ALWAYS BEEN YOU - Chris Grey

32. Just You - James Warburton and Jade Pybus

33. This Mess We're In - Thom Yorke and PJ Harvey

34. Sacrifice - London After Midnight

35. Crazy in Love Remix - Beyoncé

36. True Love Waits - Radiohead

37. Spring is Coming with a Strawberry in the Mouth - Caroline Polachek

Or listen by scanning the QR code below:

STAY CONNECTED

Subscribe to my newsletter and follow me on my socials below! 🤍

ALSO BY SIENNE VEGA

The Capo and the Ballerina

Book 1 - Vicious Impulses

Book 2 - Brutal Impulses

City of Sinners Series

Book 1 - King of Vegas

Book 2 - Queen of Hearts

Book 3 - Kingdom of Sin

Book 4 - Heart of Sin (Louis & Tasha Novella)

City of Sinners Special Edition Boxset

Gangsters & Roses Series

Book 0 - Forbidden Roses

Book 1 - Wicked Roses

Book 2 - Twisted Roses

Book 3 - Savage Roses

Book 4 - Devious Roses

Book 5 - Ruthless Roses

Gangsters & Roses Special Edition Boxset

The Steel Kings MC Series

Book 1 - Kings Have No Mercy

Book 2 - Kings Don't Break

Book 3 - Kings Fear No One

Book 4 - Kings Against the World

The Midnight Society

Book 1 - Cruel Delights

Book 2 - Cruel Pleasures

Book 3 - Cruel Cravings

Seattle Wolves

Book 1 - Break the Ice

Savage Bloodline

Caesar DeLuca

Lunchtime Chronicles

Brown Sugar

Stand Alones

Wicked Little Secret

Shared by the Capo

For A Price

Or scan the QR code below for a direct link to my books!

ABOUT THE AUTHOR

SIENNE VEGA
Romance so sexy, it's a sin.

Sienne has a thing for dark and brooding alphas and the women who love them. She enjoys writing stories where lines are blurred, and the romance is dark and delicious. In her spare time, she unwinds with a nice glass of wine and Netflix binge.

Printed in Great Britain
by Amazon